Child of Darkness

V.C. Andrews® Books

The Dollanganger Family Series
Flowers in the Attic
Petals on the Wind
If There Be Thorns
Seeds of Yesterday
Garden of Shadows

The Casteel Family Series
Heaven
Dark Angel
Fallen Hearts
Gates of Paradise
Web of Dreams

The Cutler Family Series
Dawn
Secrets of the Morning
Twilight's Child
Midnight Whispers
Darkest Hour

The Landry Family Series
Ruby
Pearl in the Mist
All That Glitters
Hidden Jewel
Tarnished Gold

The Logan Family Series
Melody
Heart Song
Unfinished Symphony
Music in the Night
Olivia

My Sweet Audrina
(does not belong to a series)

The Orphans Miniseries
Butterfly
Crystal
Brooke
Raven
Runaways (full-length novel)

The Wildflowers Miniseries
Misty
Star
Jade
Cat
Into the Garden (full-length novel)

The Hudson Family Series
Rain
Lightning Strikes
Eye of the Storm
The End of the Rainbow

The Shooting Stars Series
Cinnamon
Ice
Rose
Honey
Falling Stars

The De Beers Family Series
Willow
Wicked Forest
Twisted Roots
Into the Woods
Hidden Leaves

The Broken Wings Series
Broken Wings
Midnight Flight

The Gemini Series
Celeste
Black Cat
Child of Darkness

CHILD OF DARKNESS

POCKET **STAR** BOOKS

New York   London   Toronto   Sydney

Following the death of Virginia Andrews, the Andrews family worked with a carefully selected writer to organize and complete Virginia Andrews's stories and to create additional novels, of which this is one, inspired by her storytelling genius.

An *Original* Publication of POCKET BOOKS

 A Pocket Star Book published by
POCKET BOOKS, a division of Simon & Schuster, Inc.
1230 Avenue of the Americas, New York, NY 10020

ISBN: 0-7394-5132-4

First Pocket Books paperback printing March 2005

Cover design by Jim Lebbad; Cover illustration by Lisa Falkenstern

Manufactured in the United States of America

CHILD OF DARKNESS

Prologue

Doctor Feinberg's Report

♊

Doctor Clayton Feinberg
State Forensic Psychiatrist
Community General Hospital Psychiatric Unit

Notes on patient Celeste Atwell, Age seventeen and four months

<u>Background Information</u> (Provided by investigating officer Steven Gary, Sullivan County Sheriff's Department):

Celeste Atwell lived with her mother, Sarah Atwell, and an infant who is thought to be Celeste's mother's child, fathered by her second husband, Dave Fletcher, deceased. They lived on a farm on Allen Road just a mile or so southeast of the hamlet of Sandburg, New York. The infant is also named Celeste, but was distinguished in the home from the first Celeste by the family referring to her as Baby Celeste.

However, identical names for two siblings never became an issue because for some time immediately after the apparently accidental death of her twin brother, Noble, Celeste Atwell was brought up as her twin brother. She was made to assume a male persona and to deny all of her feminine characteristics. At the time of Noble's death, Sarah Atwell convinced the law enforcement authorities that her daughter, Celeste, was a kidnapped and missing child. The reasons for all this subterfuge remain obscure. There is an ongoing investigation as to the actual cause of Noble Atwell's death, Baby Celeste's lineage, and the events recently transpired that resulted in Betsy Fletcher's death.

Dave Fletcher's daughter, Betsy, moved into the residence recently with a male child born out of wedlock, one Panther Fletcher. Some altercation between Betsy Fletcher and Celeste Atwell resulting in the death of Betsy Fletcher occurred either right before or soon after the death of Sarah Atwell. The best information we have at this time is the death was caused by a fall on the stairway during a struggle that resulted in Betsy Fletcher breaking her neck. Celeste Atwell then buried Betsy's body in the family's herbal garden.

Coroner's inquest concludes Sarah Atwell died of heart failure. It has also been concluded that her remains remained in her bed for at least two to three days.

The county sheriff's department brought the patient to the psychiatric ward following the order of the Honorable Judge Levine, assigning her to my care, and to perform an analysis to determine whether or not she can be held accountable for her actions and whether or not she can be of any assistance toward the solution of these additional questions.

After a night during which she was sedated, she was brought to my office for her initial visit.

First Psychiatric Evaluation Session

The patient was remarkably comfortable and at ease despite the traumatic events that had brought her to the psychiatric ward to be placed under my care. She appeared to understand where she had been taken, and offered no resistence nor voiced any complaints. Her complacency led me to feel she had a fatalistic approach to her own affairs and destiny. After establishing the necessary trust between us for my session, I conducted a dialogue, the highlights of which I have so noted below.

Patient Interview

I see from the police report that you said you were trying to keep Betsy Fletcher from carrying a pot of boiling water up the stairs. You said she was threatening to throw it on your mother, who was not well and was in bed?
Celeste Atwell: Yes.

Why did she want to do that?
Celeste Atwell: She thought my mother was stealing the money her father left her and wouldn't give it to her.

And it was during the course of that struggle between you and Betsy to keep her from hurting your mother that she fell down the stairs and broke her neck?
Celeste Atwell: Yes.

If you killed Betsy Fletcher accidentally, Celeste, why didn't you call the police or call for an ambulance? Why did you bury Betsy Fletcher in the herbal garden?
Celeste Atwell: Baby Celeste told me to do that.

Why would you listen to a six-year-old? (The patient smiled at me as if I was ignorant.)
Celeste Atwell: Baby Celeste is not just a six-year-old. She has inherited the wisdom of our family. Our family spirits told her what to tell me.

How do you know they told her these things?
Celeste Atwell: I know. I can sense when they are with her and she is with them.

Why didn't they just tell you directly?
Celeste Atwell: Baby Celeste is special, very special.

Aren't you special to them, too? (The patient showed some agitation and did not respond.) Was there another reason, Celeste? Was there some reason that prevented them from speaking to you directly?
Celeste Atwell: Yes.

What was it?
Celeste Atwell: I had disappointed them. They were angry with me.

Who exactly was disappointed in you and angry with you?
Celeste Atwell: All of them. All of the spirits of my family, their souls.

How did you disappoint them?
Celeste Atwell: I . . .

What made them angry at you, Celeste? (Patient became more agitated. I gave her a glass of water and waited.) Can you tell me why you think you disappointed them, now, Celeste? I would really like to know.
Celeste Atwell: I let Noble die again.

How did you do that? Wasn't Noble already dead?

How can he die again if he's already dead? (At this point the patient would not respond to any question. She kept her eyes closed and her lips tight. Her body began to tremble. I determined I had gone as far as I could for the first session.)

Doctor's Feinberg's Conclusion

Celeste Atwell suffers severe intense guilt and pain over the death of her twin brother, Noble. We have not established the reason yet, but my best estimate is she will and should remain under psychiatric care and treatment for some time and should be remanded to the psychiatric hospital in Middletown. At the time of her actions and at this time, she was and remains incapable of understanding the consequences of her actions or the difference between an illegal act and a legal act.

Doctor Clayton Feinberg

From Baby Celeste's Diary

A long time ago when I was in pediatric therapy, my doctor asked me to write down everything I thought, everything I saw, and everything I believed happened and was happening to me. It was something I never stopped doing. It was truly as if I was afraid that all of it was a dream, and the only way to prove it wasn't was to write it down so I could read it later and tell myself, See, it did happen. All of it did happen!

1

"I'm With You Again"

♊

I wouldn't go until I had brushed my hair. Mama always spent so much time on my hair while Noble sat watching, as if he were jealous and wanted to be the one to brush it. Sometimes I let him, but he would never do it in front of Mama because of how angry it would make her. He would make these long, deliberate strokes, following the brush with his hand because he needed to feel my hair as much as see it. As I looked at myself in the mirror, I could almost feel his hand guiding the brush. It was hypnotizing then, and it was hypnotizing to remember it now.

"Mother Higgins said right now," Colleen Dorset whined and stamped her foot to snap me out of my reverie. She was eight years old and my roommate for nearly a year. Her mother had given birth to her in an alley and left her in a cardboard box to die, but a passerby heard her wailing and called the police. She lived for two years with a couple who had given her a name, but they divorced, and neither wanted to keep her.

Her eyes were too wide, and her nose too long. She was doomed to end up like me, I thought with my characteristic clairvoyant confidence, and in a flash I saw her whole life pour out before me, splashing on the floor in a pool of endless loneliness. She wasn't strong enough to survive. She was like a baby bird too weak to develop the ability to fly.

"Where that baby bird falls out of the nest," Mama told me, "is where she'll live and die."

Some nest this was, I thought.

"Celeste, you'd better hurry."

"It's all right, Colleen. If they don't wait, they don't matter," I said with such indifference, she nearly burst into tears. How she wished there was someone asking after her. She was like someone starving watching someone in a restaurant wasting food.

I took a deep breath and left the small, almost claustrophobic room I shared with her. There was barely enough space for the two beds and the dresser with the mirror above it. The walls were bare, and we had only one small window that looked out at another wall of the building. It didn't matter. The view I had was a view I owned in my memory, a view among others I gazed back at the way people peruse family albums.

The walk to the headmistress's office suddenly seemed longer than ever. With every step I took, the inadequately lit hallway stretched out another ten. It was as if I was moving through a long, dark tunnel, working my way back up to the light. Just like Sisyphus in the Greek myth we had just read in school, I was doomed never to reach the end of my long and difficult climb. Each time I approached the end, I fell back and had to begin again, as though I were someone caught in an eternal replay, someone tormented by wicked Fate.

Despite the act I put on for Colleen, as soon as I was told I was to meet with a married couple who might want to become my foster parents and perhaps adopt me, my heart started to thump with anticipation. The invitation to an interview came as a total surprise; it had been years since anyone had any interest in me, and I had just celebrated my seventeenth birthday. Most married couples coming to the orphanage look for much younger children, especially ones just born. Who would want to take in a teenager these days, especially me? I wondered. As one of my counselors, Dr. Sackett, once told me, "Celeste, you have to realize you come with a great deal more baggage than the average orphan child."

The baggage wasn't boxes of dresses and shoes either. He was referring to my past, the stigma I carried because of my unusual family and our history. Few potential foster parents look at you as your own person. It's not difficult to see the questions in their eyes. What bad habits did this one inherit? How has she been twisted and shaped by her past, and how are we going to handle it? Why should we take on any surprises?

None of this was truer for anyone than it was for me. I had been labeled "odd," "strange," "unusual," "difficult," and even "weird." I knew what rejection was like. I had been nearly adopted once before and returned like so much damaged goods. I could almost hear the Prescotts, the elderly couple who had taken me into their lives, return to the children's protection agency and, as if speaking to someone in a department store return and exchange department, complain, "She doesn't work for us. Please give us a refund."

Today, perhaps because of this new possibility, that

entire experience rushed over the walls of my memory, where it had been kept dammed up for so long. It pushed much of my past over with it as well, so that while I walked from my room to the office to meet with this new couple, the most dramatic events of my life began to replay. It was as if I had lived and died once before.

Truthfully, I have always felt like someone who had been born twice, but not in any religious sense. It wasn't that I had some new awakening after which I could see the world in a different light, see truth and all the miracles and wonders that others who were not reborn did not see. No, first I was born and lived in a place where miracles and wonders were taken for granted, where spirits moved along the breezes like smoke, and where whispers and soft laughter came out of the darkness daily. None of it surprised me, and none of it frightened me. I believed it was all there to protect me, to keep me wrapped comfortably in a spiritual cocoon my mother had spun on her magic loom.

We lived in upstate New York on a farm that had belonged to my family for decades and legally still belongs to me. I was a true anomaly because I was and remained an orphan with an inheritance, property held in trust and managed by my mother's attorney, Mr. Deward Lee Nokleby-Cook. I knew little more about it, but more than one headmistress or counselor had shaken her finger at me and reminded me I had far more than the other orphans.

The reminder wasn't made to make me feel better about myself. Oh no. It was meant to encourage me to behave and obey every rule and every command, and was usually held over my head like some sort of branding iron. After all, property, having anything of value, meant more responsibility, and more responsibility meant you had to be more mature. If they had it their way, I would have completely skipped my childhood—not that a childhood in an orphanage was anything to rave about, anyway. I wish I could forget it all forever, every moment, every hour, every day, and not have it all come up inside me like so much sour milk.

Despite the fact that I was a little more than six when I left the farm, I still remembered it quite vividly. Perhaps that is because my time there was so dramatic, so intense. For most of my infancy, I was kept under lock and key, hidden away from the public. Even though my mother thought my birth was a miraculous wonder, or perhaps because of that, my birth was guarded as the deepest, most treasured family secret. I was made to feel like someone very special. Consequently, the house itself for nearly my first five years was my only world. I knew every crack and cranny, where I could make the floor creak, where I could crawl and hide, and where there were scratches and nicks in the baseboard, each mark evidence of the mysterious inhabitants who had come before me and still hovered about behind curtains or even under my bed.

For most of my life at the farm, I was taken out after dark and saw the world outside in the daytime only through a window. I could sit for hours and hours and stare at the birds, the clouds, the trees and leaves swaying in the wind. I was mesmerized by all of it, the way other children my age were hypnotized by television.

I had only one real companion, my brother, Noble. My cousin Panther was just a baby then, and I often helped care for him, but I was also jealous of any attention he stole from my mother and brother, attention that would have been directed at me. Right from the beginning, I resented it when he and his mother, Betsy, came to live with us.

Betsy had lived with us before. She had moved in soon after her father married Mother. I was never quite sure if he was my real father as well, but immediately he wanted me to call him Daddy. He died before Betsy returned. She had run off with a boyfriend, and she didn't even know he had died. The whole time she was away, she had never called or even written a letter to tell her father where she was, but when she returned and learned of his death, she was very angry. I remember she blamed us for her father's death, but she was even angrier about the way her inheritance was to be distributed. The air in the house felt filled with static. Mother stopped smiling. There were ominous whispers in every shadow, and those shadows grew deeper, darker, and wider every passing day, until I thought we would be living in darkness and no one would be able to see me, even Noble.

Before Panther's mother, Betsy, had invaded our home and spoiled our lives, I had Noble completely to myself. He was the one who took me out, the one with whom I worked in the herbal garden and took walks about our farm when I was finally permitted to be out in the daytime. Often he read with me in the living room and carried me to my bedroom to put me asleep. He taught me the names of flowers and insects and birds. We were practically inseparable. I felt he loved me even more than my mother did. I was so sure that someday I was to understand why; someday, I would understand it all.

And then one day he disappeared. I can't think of it any other way or of him as anything but who he had been to me. It was truly as if some wicked witch had waved her wand over him and in an instant turned him into the young girl I had been told was my half sister, Celeste, after whom I had been named. I had seen pictures of her many times in our family albums and heard stories about her, describing how bright she was, how pretty. It would be years before I would understand it, and even then I would wonder if everyone else was mistaken and not me. However, I would learn that my mother believed it was Celeste who had died in a tragic fishing accident, and not Noble, her twin brother.

Eventually and painfully, however, I would discover that it really was Noble who had drowned. Mother refused to accept it. She forced Celeste to become her twin brother, and all I knew about Celeste now was that she was in a mental clinic not far from the farm. As I said, I would make many shocking discoveries about myself and my past, but it would take time. It would be a long, twisted journey that would eventually bring me back to my home, to the place where all this began and where it was meant to come to a finalization, when I would truly be reborn.

I have been told that when I was brought to the first orphanage, I was a strange, brooding child whose demeanor and piercing way of looking at people drove away any and all prospective adoptive or foster parents despite my remarkable beauty. Even though I was advised to smile and look innocent and sweet, I always wore a face that belonged on a girl much older. My eyes would get too dark and my lips too taut. I stood stiffly and looked as if I would just hate to be hugged and kissed.

Although I was polite when I answered questions, my own questions made the husbands and wives considering me for adoption feel very uncomfortable. I had the tone of an accuser. More than once I was told I behaved as if I knew their deepest secrets, fears, and weaknesses. My questions were like needles, but I couldn't help wondering why would they want me. Why didn't they have children of their own? Why did they want a child now, and why a little girl? Who wanted me more, the man or the woman? They might joke or laugh at my direct questions, but I wouldn't crack a smile.

This sort of behavior on my part, alongside my unusual past, would sink the possibility of any of them taking me into their home. Even before the interview ended, my prospective new parents would look at each other with NO written in their eyes and make a hasty retreat, fleeing me and the orphanage.

"See what you've done," I was often told. "You've driven them away."

It was always my fault. A child my age shouldn't ask such questions, shouldn't know such things. Why couldn't I just keep my mouth shut and be the pretty little doll people hoped I was? After all, I had auburn hair that gleamed in the sunlight, bright blue-green eyes, and a perfect complexion. The prospective parents were always drawn to me and then, unfortunately, repulsed by me.

At the first orphanage, where I remained until I was nearly ten years old, I quickly developed a reputation for clairvoyance. I always knew when one of the other girls would get a tummy ache or a cold, or when one would be adopted and leave. I could look at prospective parents and tell if they were really going to adopt someone or if they hadn't yet decided to take on such a serious commitment. There were many who were just window shoppers, making us all feel like animals in a pet shop. We were told to sit perfectly straight and say, "Yes, ma'am," and, "Yes, sir."

"Don't speak unless spoken to" wasn't only written over doorways; it was written on our brows, but I wasn't intimidated. There were too many voices inside me, voices that would not be still.

My first orphanage caregiver was a strict fifty-year-old woman who demanded we all call her Madam Annjill. As a joke, I think, her parents had named her Annjill, just so they could laugh and say, "She's no angel. She's Annjill." I didn't need to be told. She was never an angel to me, nor could she ever become one.

Madam Annjill didn't believe in hitting any of us, but she did like to shake us very hard, so hard all of us felt as if our eyes were rolling in our heads and our little bones were snapping. One girl, a tall, thin girl named Tillie Mae with brown habitually panic-stricken eyes the size of quarters, really had so much pain in her shoulder for so long afterward that Madam Annjill's husband, Homer Masterson, finally had to take her to the doctor, who diagnosed her with a dislocated shoulder. Tillie Mae was far too frightened to tell him how she had come to have such an ailment. She was in pain for quite a number of days. The sight and sound of her crying herself to sleep put the jitters into every other orphan girl at the home, every other girl but me, of course.

I was never as afraid of Madam Annjill as the others were. I knew she wouldn't ever shake me as hard. When she did shake me, I was able to hold my eyes on her the whole time without crying, and that made her more uncomfortable than the shaking made me. She would let go of me as if her hands were burning. She once told her husband that I had an unnaturally high body temperature. She was so positive about it that he had to take my temperature and show her I was as normal as anyone.

"Well, I still think she can make herself hotter at will," she muttered.

Perhaps I could. Perhaps there were some hot embers burning inside me, something I could flame up whenever I wanted to and, like a dragon, breathe fire at her.

I must say she worked hard at finding me a home, but it wasn't because she felt sorry for me. She simply wanted me out of her orphanage almost as soon as I had arrived. Sometimes I overheard her describing me to prospective foster parents, and I was amazed at the compliments she would give me. According to her I was the brightest, nicest, most responsible child there. She always managed to slip in the fact that I had an inheritance, acres of land, and a house kept in trust.

"Most of my little unfortunates come to you with nothing more than their hopes and dreams, but Celeste has something of real value. Why, it's as if her college education or her wedding dowry was built into any adoption," she told them, but it was never enough to overcome all the negative things they saw and learned.

"Where are her relatives?" they would inevitably ask.

"There aren't that many, and those that there are were never close. Besides, none of them want the responsibility of caring for her," was Madam Annjill's reluctant standard explanation. She knew what damaging questions her answers created immediately in the minds of the people who were considering me. Why didn't her relatives want her? If a child had something of value, surely some relative would want her. Who would want a child whose own relatives didn't want to see hide nor hair of her, land in trust or no land in trust?

I wondered how valuable the farm really was. Of

course, in my memory, the house and the property remained enormous. After all, it was once the whole universe to me. For years I believed that not only were the house and the land waiting for me, but all the spirits that dwelled there were waiting as well. It would be like returning to the womb, to a place where there was protection and warmth and all the love I had lost. How could anyone put a value on that? I wanted to grow up overnight so I could return. When I went to bed, I would close my eyes and wish and wish that when I woke in the morning, I would be a big girl. I would somehow be eighteen, and I could walk out of the home into a waiting limousine that would carry me off to the farm, where everything would be as it once was.

What would I really find there? I believed my mother was gone, buried, and my only living immediate relative was in a mental home. The attorney might hand me the door keys, but wouldn't I be just as lonely and lost as ever? Or would the spirits come out of the woods and out of the walls and dance around me? Wouldn't they all be there, my mother included? Wouldn't that be enough company? It used to be enough for me, Mama, and Noble.

Why weren't the spirits coming for me now? I would wonder. Why weren't they appearing in the orphanage at night to reassure me and tell me not to worry?

As mad as it might seem to the other girls, I was longing to hear whispering, see wisps of people float by, feel a hand in mine and turn to see no one there.

Eventually, I did. Noble was there with me.

"Hey," I remember him calling to me one night. I opened my eyes and saw him. "You didn't think I would accompany you to this place and then just leave you here and forget you, did you?"

I shook my head, even though I had believed that. Seeing him again was too wonderful. I couldn't speak.

"Well, I'll be around. All the time. Just look for me, especially if anything bothers you, okay?"

I nodded.

He came closer, fixed my blanket the way he always did, leaned over, and kissed me on the forehead. Then he walked into the darkness and disappeared.

But I knew that he was there, and that was the most important thing of all.

I saw him often after that.

"Whom are you talking to?" Madam Annjill would ask me if she caught me whispering. "Stop that right now," she would order, but then she would cross herself, shake her head, and mumble to herself about the devil having children as she quickly fled from the sight of me.

I knew she was watching me all the time. Noble would know it too and warn me.

"She's coming," he would say.

"Whom are you looking at so hard, and what are you smiling about?" Madam Annjill would demand at dinner if I stopped eating and stared into the corner where Noble was standing, his arms folded, leaning against the wall and smiling at me.

I didn't reply. I turned to her ever so slowly and looked at her, not a movement in my lips, not a blink of my eyes. She would huff and puff and shake her head and reprimand some other poor, homeless little soul who had washed ashore on her beach. No solace here, I thought. No one waiting with open arms. No welcome sign over this front door. No one to tuck you in and kiss your cheek and wish you a good night's sleep. No one to tickle you or smother you with kisses and embraces and flood your eyes with smiles.

No, here the sound of laughter was always thin and short, cut off quickly like the sound of something forbidden. Where else did children our age feel they had to choke back happiness and hide their tears? Where else did they pray so hard for a nice dream, a sweet thought, a loving caress?

"Oh, the burdens, the burdens," Madam Annjill would chant at visitors or to her husband, referring to us. "The discarded burdens, someone else's responsibilities, someone else's mistakes."

She would turn and look at us with pity dripping from her eyes, crocodile tears.

"That's what you all are, children. You've been cast away like so much worthless riffraff," she would moan with the back of her hand pressed to her forehead like some terrible soap opera actress. "I will try, but you have to help me. Clean up after yourselves. Never make a mess. Never break anything. Never disobey me. Never fight or steal, and never say anything nasty."

What about the nasty things she would say to us? I wondered. Why did she want to run an orphanage in the first place? Was it only for the money, or did she enjoy lording it over helpless young girls and seeing the fear and the gratitude in their eyes?

At night she walked past our bunks and inspected, just hoping to spot some violation, no matter how small. Everyone but me would have her head turned away, her eyes closed, holding her breath and praying Madam Annjill did not find anything wrong and assign some punishment or shake her. Only I would lie there with my eyes wide open, waiting for her. I wasn't afraid. Noble was standing beside me, waiting, too.

She would stop, even though I sensed she wanted to keep going and avoid me. After all, she had to hold on to her authority. She had to pause and snap at me.

"Why aren't you trying to sleep?" she would demand.

I didn't answer. I glanced at Noble, who shook his head at her and then smirked at me.

Dealing with my silence was far more troublesome and difficult for her than the whining others did, or the poor little attempts to escape blame. Silence had always been my ally, my sword, and my shield.

Madam Annjill would look at Noble, whom I knew she couldn't see, and then she would simply nod at me.

"You know you were hatched from an egg of madness, don't you? If you're not careful, it will grow inside you, and you'll end up like your mother and your sister."

I didn't say a word. I stared at her until she walked away, muttering to herself.

Only then did I turn to Noble and show my unhappiness.

"Can't we go home?" I whispered.

"No, not yet," he said. "You have to be patient, very patient, but I promise you, Celeste. Someday you will go home again."

"Take me home now. Please. Take me home," I begged. He brushed my hair and told me to be patient again, and then he walked into the darkness.

Actually, I had no idea where home was anymore, or even what it was. It was just a wonderful word, a word that rang with hope.

Home.

Surely Noble is right, I thought. I will return, and everyone who has loved me will be there waiting with open arms. Surely they've missed me as much as I've missed them.

After all, I could still hear their screams of pain and agony as the car and the social workers took me away that dreadful afternoon. Even now, nearly ten years later, the memories of how I was scooped up and taken away from the farm and the only life I had known were painful. I remembered those agonizing days in terms of colors, red being the most prominent. I was so full of anger then. Why had Noble gone after Celeste appeared? I'd wondered, wearing a scowl like a permanent mask. It was all Betsy's fault, I'd decided. Somehow, it was because of her that he was driven away. I'd been happy she was dead, and I wanted to see her buried and gone from sight.

If I tried really hard to recall specific moments about that last day, I felt my insides tightening up, as if all my organs were being woven into knots around my heart.

It was far worse immediately after I had been taken. Then I would actually have a hard time breathing, what the doctors diagnosed as an emotional seizure. In fact, during the first few months after I was separated from the only people I had known and loved and loved me, I would often fall into a sleep so deep and long, it resembled catatonia.

Sleep was, after all, a way of turning my face away from ugly reality, but even sleep wasn't a total escape. A stream of nightmares would flow through my head: Noble being pushed back into his grave, Betsy with a twisted smile, laughing at me after she died, Mama glassy-eyed and cold, her lips squirming like earthworms. I would eventually wake screaming, and no matter what anyone said or how lovingly they treated me, I never lost the sense of foreboding, a sense that something dreadful was following me, sometimes disguised as my own shadow. I still felt it now, even at seventeen. I had the habit of glancing into corners, looking back every once in a while when I walked. I knew it drew attention to me, but I couldn't help it. Something was there. Something was always there. I didn't care if people thought I was still a mental case.

There is no way to avoid revealing that I was brought to a children's mental clinic almost immediately after being taken from the farm. I do vividly remember a beautiful woman with light brown hair and soft green eyes. She was tall and stately with an air of authority about her that made me feel confident, as confident as a baby in her mother's arms.

She was, I would learn, a pediatric psychiatrist, although she never wanted me to call her Dr. anything, just Flora. There would be others. In the beginning Flora spent hours and hours with me trying to get me to speak, to tell her why I was so angry. She knew most of it by then, of course. She had learned how my mother had died in her sleep and had been left in her bed, how my sister had accidentally killed Panther's mother, Betsy, on the staircase and then buried her in the herbal garden. Soon after, Noble's grave was uncovered as well, and the whole story of our twisted turmoil spilled out into the community like untended milk boiling over the edges of a pot.

I would learn that people came from faraway places to look at the farm, to talk about all of us with local people. Newspaper articles turned into magazine articles, and someone even wrote a book about it. At the time there was even some talk about a movie being made. We were that infamous.

Ironically, the community that had once considered us pariahs had suddenly embraced us. Everyone was anxious to tell about an experience with us, and of course with every retelling the exaggerations grew, until the truth was as lost as youth and innocence.

Flora worked very hard with me, and eventually she

got me to talk and tell her the things she wanted and needed to know. She was always reassuring me. The truth was, I wanted to talk to someone badly. Noble hadn't come with me into that place. I was totally alone, so eventually telling Flora some of my secrets gave me relief. I could feel the weight slowly being lifted off my brow and the smiles beginning to return, first with a tiny movement at the corners of my mouth and then in my eyes. I so wanted to learn again, to read, to listen to music and stories. My appetite returned, and I didn't have to be forced or convinced to eat. I came out of the darkness as if I had been released from prison.

It was then that she brought me together with children my age, and over time the past became less and less oppressive. I celebrated a birthday at the clinic. They made me a nice party, and Flora bought me a beautiful pink dress with lace trimming about the sleeves and hem. My emotional seizures became far and few between and eventually disappeared entirely.

In a way I was sorry I had gotten well. My healing, my return to a normal life, meant I was ready to be discharged. I had come to live for Flora's visits and talks. Now the prospect that I would never see her again was a blow that almost drove me back to catatonia. I had gone from clinging to one skirt to clinging to another. Whom would I cling to now? Who would be there for me? The outside world was truly outer space to me. I would surely dangle or float aimlessly.

Flora knew my fears. "It's time you got on with your life, Celeste," she told me one morning in her office. "You have nothing to be afraid of anymore. You're a very, very bright little girl, and I'm sure you're going to be successful at whatever you want to do later."

"Am I going back to the farm?" I asked her.

"No, not yet. Not for a long time," she said.

She rose from her chair and looked out the window in silence for so long, I thought she was deciding whether or not to take me home with her. In my secret heart of hearts, where I dared treasure hopes and dreams, that was my most precious. If she had done so, how different my life would have been, I often now thought.

She turned and smiled at me, but I saw the disappointing answer in her eyes, in the film of sadness that had been drawn over them. This was the beginning of a good-bye that would last forever. Someday her face would drift back into my sea of memories, gradually sinking deeper and deeper until it would never again surface.

"First, you are going to a place where you will live with other little girls much like yourself," she explained. "It's a home managed by a nice couple, the Mastersons. You will finally go to a real school, too, and on a school bus.

"But you're too precious a child to be left there long, I'm sure," she continued, walking to me to brush strands of my hair off my forehead. "Some nice couple will quickly take you into their hearts and their home."

I was holding my breath. I really wanted to scream or close my eyes and never open them.

"I'll always inquire after you to be sure you're doing all right, Celeste," she said.

I looked up at her so sharply, she froze.

"No, you won't," I said.

"I will. I promise." She smiled at me, but she smiled at some of the other children the same way, and some of them were gone and forgotten.

I looked away, and I remember the color gray, the

color of steel suddenly raining down around me. Although I was too young then to put my feelings into proper words, I vowed never again to get too close to anyone, except my spirits, my precious, loving spirits.

The people who came to the clinic to take me to that first orphanage, a man and a woman with black hair streaked with gray, reminded me of those who had come to the farm that dreadful day. These people looked bored and annoyed that they had been given the task. Even before she introduced herself, the woman petulantly asked, "Did you go to the bathroom? We have a long drive ahead of us, and we don't have time to look for places to stop."

I nodded, and the man took my small suitcase. Flora wasn't there. I thought she wasn't even going to utter her good-bye and repeat her promises to me before I left, but when we reached the doorway of the clinic, I heard her shout, "Just a minute!" and then I heard the *tap, tap, tap* of her high-heeled shoes over the tiled floor. Dressed in her doctor's robe, which she rarely wore when she was with me, she hurried down a corridor toward us, the robe snapping under her swinging arms. One of her assistants, a young woman with curly blond hair and large blue eyes that made her look habitually surprised, was practically running to keep up.

"Do you have everything?" she asked the social worker, who had quickly introduced herself as Mrs. Stormfield. "The prescriptions are very important."

"Yes, yes. It's all here," the social worker said, showing her the briefcase she carried.

"Okay. Good luck to you, Celeste. I will inquire after you. I will," she stressed.

I looked down.

She squatted to look into my eyes and gently lift my chin so I would have to look into her face.

"You have to be strong," she said, almost in a whisper. "You have to get through it. You won't be alone, I'm sure."

That brought a smile to my face, but it wasn't a smile that made her comfortable. I could see that. My smile was too cold. It made my face years older.

"I know," I said. "I'll never be alone."

Suddenly she looked very worried. She looked as if she was considering keeping me.

Mrs. Stormfield cleared her throat and tapped her foot in impatience.

Flora looked up at her.

"We have a long ride," Mrs. Stormfield said. "It's best we get started immediately."

Flora blinked, thought, and then shook her head.

"Yes, of course," she said, standing up. She took a deep breath, glanced at her assistant, and in a quick decision that broke some rule she had imposed upon herself, knelt down again and kissed me on the cheek. Then she turned and started away, those heels clicking like a clock ticking toward some hour of reckoning, winding down into an explosion of dead silence. I put my fingers on my cheek, where she had kissed me. I so wished I could keep her lips there forever.

Mrs. Stormfield dropped her hand on my shoulder firmly to direct me out the door and to the automobile. Her fingers pressed so hard, I wanted to cry out, but I didn't utter a sound. Instead, I got into the car and sat as far away from her as I could. She followed and closed the door. Then she sighed deeply, as if it had all been such a terrible ordeal for her, far more than it had been for me. The driver put my suitcase into the trunk, got in, started the engine, and drove us away. I didn't even look back.

It was only then that I thought about my cousin Panther. How odd that I hadn't thought of him until now, I remember thinking. Was it that I simply didn't care about him, or had I truly forgotten he existed? Where had he been taken? Where would he end up? Was he at some clinic or at some orphanage, or already living with new people?

And then I thought about Noble. I hadn't thought about him for so long, but now I couldn't help it. In my memory he was there. He was still Noble. He hadn't changed. I heard his laughter, his voice as he repeated the vowel sounds or explained a picture in a book. I closed my eyes and once again felt his arms holding me, carrying me up the stairs to bed, pulling back the blanket and tucking me in with a soft goodnight. I remembered all the hours we spent together in the turret room, keeping as quiet as we could so the people below would not know I existed.

Most of all, I remembered working beside him in the garden for hours and hours after I was permitted to be out in the daytime, watching and learning how he cared for the herbal plants. He would recite their names for me, and talk about them as if they were his children. Every morning I was always so anxious and excited about getting out there to see how much they had grown, how healthy were their leaves, and how close they were to fulfilling the promise of their maturation and healing powers.

Back in the house Mother cooked and stirred, ground and mixed Noble's children into remedies she poured or spooned into bottles and plastic bags for people who made their pilgrimages up and down the country road to our farm. Mother described the spirits of our family standing along the driveway, nodding and smiling their approval and pride as the customers, or clients, as Mother liked to call them, came onto the property, their faces full of hope and faith.

Where were our family spirits this very moment? I wondered. Now that I had been released from the clinic, were they waiting for me, anticipating my return? Suddenly that thought sparked a panic in me. Yes, they were waiting for me, and they would be disappointed if I didn't return.

"I have to go home," I remember saying.

Mrs. Stormfield turned slowly and lowered her glasses down the bridge of her bony nose to peer across the seat at me with her steely gray eyes.

"What's that?"

"I have to go home right away," I said. "They're waiting for me."

"Who's waiting for you?"

"My family."

"Oh." She pushed her glasses back into position and turned to look forward.

"They are. They really are."

"Yes, well, why don't you just wait for them to call for you," she said.

The driver laughed.

"Yes," I said. "That's a good idea."

She looked at me again, this time surprise lifting her right eyebrow.

"Oh, you think so, do you?"

"Yes. I will wait. And they will call," I added, and I sat back in the seat. I remember I smiled. I was so confident that I radiated with it.

"This one's a corker," Mrs. Stormfield declared.

"Ain't they all," the driver said. "Ain't they all."

I didn't say another word to either of them. Long ago I had learned how to swim through the empty hours. I didn't need to be entertained or amused. I could simply rewind a book I had read and then turn the pages in my mind once more. I was vaguely aware

of Mrs. Stormfield's eyes on mine as they moved back
and forth. She slid a few more inches away from me,
the way someone might move away from a person who
might infect them with a disease.

I smiled.

She didn't know it, but I was very happy she had
moved away.

She was making room for Noble. Thinking so hard
about him again had brought him back to me.

He sat between us, took my hand into his, and said,
"Don't worry. I'm with you again."

"What are you smiling at?" Mrs. Stormfield asked
me. "I'm speaking to you, young lady," she said as
firmly as she could when I didn't respond.

I still didn't answer, and there was nothing she
could do about it.

I just turned away from her and stared ahead. Noble
was holding my hand. Just knowing he was there beside me gave me the strength and the courage to face
all the Mrs. Stormfields to come along with all the to-
morrows, no matter how cloudy or dark or filled with
static in the air they might be.

2

A So-Called Normal Young Woman

♊

Orphans don't know what to think about tomorrow. It's like we're afloat at sea in the dark and the sky is always overcast, so we don't know in what direction we're heading or if we're heading anywhere. We even wonder if we will ever have a Christmas or a birthday. Who really cares if we do? The state? The caregivers at the orphanage? Even though all these people might have good intentions, it is still not the same as being in a living room on Christmas Day or on birthdays, opening presents with people we love and who love us. We know about it, of course. We see it on television or in movies, and we read about it in books, and of course there are those who had families for a while, those like me.

In the deepest places of my memory, I hear a piano playing on Christmas Day. I smell the hot apple pie and I see snowflakes sticking to the windows, the light of our living room illuminating them so they twinkle as though their edges consist of tiny diamonds. No matter how cold it was, the world inside our home was warm. It would surely be the same for all of us, but to have all that, we had to have families.

Think about never celebrating a Mother's Day or Father's Day or anyone else's birthday in your family. Think about the word *family*, and imagine it not being in your vocabulary. Think about feeling as if you are a whole other species. That's how it was for us.

People always say, "Blood is thicker than water." For us it was truly as if we had only water in our veins. No wonder I clung so hard to the memory of my spiritual family, despite the efforts of my therapists and counselors. Who else did I have? It's a terrible thing to be dependent only on the kindness and charity of strangers. No matter how they help you and what they say when they do, you can't stop yourself from feeling obligated. I hate having to feel grateful constantly. No one says thank you more than we do. The words are practically pasted to our tongues.

It is so important to have family, to have someone who is part of you and whom you are part of as well. What you do for each other comes from a deeper place, a place you'll share forever. There is no obligation. There is only love. That was the way it still was for me and Noble. How could I ever give that up?

However, over time while I was at my first orphanage, attending a public school, making some friends, I began to see and hear Noble less and less. It wasn't that I no longer needed him. I would always need him. He was too much a part of whom and what I was. It was more that things that interested other girls my age began to interest me. I wanted to watch more television, read magazines, go to movies, and Noble never did any of that or talked about it. Although I had no boyfriends as such, I flirted with boys and fantasized like my girlfriends did.

Eventually, I overheard Mr. Masterson tell Madam Annjill that she was worried about me for no good reason, after all.

I had discovered years ago that if I put my ear to the vent between their kitchen and our bathroom, I could hear their conversations clearly. Somehow, I anticipated when they would be talking about me. Maybe it was because they often were.

"See," I heard Mr. Masterson say, "all little boys and girls have imaginary friends, Annjill, especially our little orphans. Celeste is no different, and now, as you say, she's doing it less and less."

"I still think there's something very wrong with that child. How could she be brought up in a world of such madness and not have anything permanently wrong with her?" Madam Annjill insisted. "Why are we having such a terrible time finding any couple willing to take her into their home? On the surface, she is attractive enough, and she is certainly a very intelligent child. I'll give her that. Look at her school grades."

"Someone will come along," Mr. Masterson insisted.

"No. No one will come along. She's had too many chances, too many lost opportunities. We'll have to go fish them in," Madam Annjill said.

I always suspected that was just what she finally went ahead and did, and that was how I found myself being taken into a couple's home for the first time. The Prescotts, the couple who came to see me soon after I overheard Madame Annjill and her husband talking about me, had already raised their family. They had grandchildren, in fact, but their rationale for seeking to become foster parents at this late stage was that their children and grandchildren all lived far away. They needed to fill their lives with something meaningful. I think that was more true of Mrs. Prescott than it was of Mr. Prescott.

As soon as she met me, Mrs. Prescott immediately asked me to call her Nana and her husband Papa, as if they could snap their fingers and *poof,* make me into their new granddaughter. She said I would have their daughter Michelle's old room, with my own television set and school desk. They sounded very generous, but I knew that they would be getting money from the state to use to pay for my necessities and clothes.

Unlike the other couples who had met with me, they weren't at all put off by my demeanor. Perhaps Madam Annjill had prepared and warned them about me ahead of time. Mrs. Prescott's face looked molded out of plastic. The smile sat there and never so much as twitched. Nothing I asked or said seemed to bother them, even when I asked Mrs. Prescott why her daughter or her son and their children wouldn't need the room I was to have when they visited. From the way she glanced at her husband, I did sense that they were not visited that often by their children and grandchildren, and that truly bothered both of them, perhaps Mrs. Prescott more.

Mr. Prescott was a tall, thin, balding gray-haired man with a pale complexion and watery dull brown eyes. Almost the entire time he was there, he tapped his long fingers on the arms of the chair as if he was keeping time to a marching band.

"And when they do come, we'll always find a way to accommodate everyone, dear," she told me. "Not to worry. Oh, how wonderful it will be to have a little person in our lives again! Why, I even had some clothes in the attic that would fit you, and I know I have lots of toys in the closet, lots of pretty little dolls, too," she declared.

She clapped her hands together and rubbed her palms as if she was washing them. She was stout, with a small bosom and wide hips. I imagined that long ago she had lost her waist, and the person she had once been had faded away like some very old photograph.

"Won't your grandchildren be upset about your taking me in and giving me so much of what belonged to them, especially dolls?" I asked.

Even at that young age, I could fix my eyes as a prosecutor fixed his on a witness in a courtroom. Madam Annjill always told me that was impolite, but I did it anyway. Most orphans wouldn't dare ask such a question for fear of bringing up a reason for their prospective parents to reject them.

But it was an important question for me. The last thing I wanted was to be taken somewhere else to be resented. I was already nine years old, and I knew about envy. Jealousy lived beside each orphan and could instantly turn any of our eyes green as soon as someone else had received a gift or had a prospect of being adopted. Surely it would be even worse when it came to my taking a part of the Prescott's grandchildren's world.

"Oh, no, no. No, no," she chanted.

During the whole interview, Mr. Prescott looked out the windows with an obvious longing to be out there instead of in here with me and all this adoption business. Later, I found out he lived for golf, and anything that interrupted his usual schedule was distasteful.

If Mrs. Prescott knew that, she ignored it or didn't care. She was in no rush. She talked incessantly, describing their house, which she said was a modest two-story Queen Anne with a wraparound front porch. She told me they had a pretty sizable backyard, with lots of room to exercise my little legs.

"Papa will fix the swing set in the back, too, won't you, Papa?" she asked him.

"What? Oh, absolutely," he said. "All it needs is a good paint job and some grease."

The fact that it had been left to degenerate told me how little time their grandchildren spent at their home.

"You can walk to the school, but we won't ever let you go by yourself, will we, Papa?"

"Oh, no, never," he said firmly.

They lived in a small village just outside of Kingston, New York. Mr. Prescott was a retired accountant. Mrs. Prescott had always been a housewife and had never been to college. They told me they had been high school sweethearts and had married as soon as Mr. Prescott had graduated from college and gotten his first job with a big accounting firm in Kingston.

"Eventually, Papa formed his own company. We're not wealthy people, but we've always been very comfortable," Mrs. Prescott explained. I think she wanted to share their personal history with me as quickly as possible so I would feel like part of their family as quickly as possible.

Afterward I heard Madame Annjill, who was practically salivating at the prospect of someone taking me off her hands, tell the Prescotts that I was the neatest ward in her orphanage, and I had the most promise for a good future.

"She's a very independent little girl. You'll be so pleased, and you'll be doing a wonderful thing by giving her a real home and showing her what life is like with a normal family," she added. "Besides, Arnold knows well how to handle the property held in trust for her when the time comes. Who better to guide this poor unfortunate child?"

I had no idea how much they knew about my background, but I had the sense that Madame Annjill had made it seem as if I had been too young to be harmed in any way by the events. I was simply a lost little girl unfairly left on her own. From the way they talked about me and themselves, I knew Madam Annjill had probably worked on them for some time. In the end they signed the papers and told me I would be coming to live with them. It all happened so fast, my head spun, but they hoped I would be happy and that it was something I wanted at least as much as they did.

When the other girls learned I was going to someone's home to become part of a family, they all looked at me as if I had won the lottery. No one said anything unpleasant. Some of them even said they would miss me, but all of them had that distant look in their faces, telling me they felt even more left behind than ever. After all, I was the little girl no one wanted. Each of them was supposed to find a family first.

The following day the Prescotts came to get me and my meager belongings. As it had started to rain before they came, there wasn't much time to linger in the orphanage's doorway. Madame Annjill had my things packed and ready the night before. She came for me right after breakfast and made me wait in the entryway, as if she wanted to be sure they didn't come, fail to see me, and leave again. I smiled to myself at how happy she was at finally getting me off her hands. She rattled on and on about how lucky I was to have such a nice loving couple take an interest in me.

"You should be thanking me, thanking me, thanking me," she said.

I turned to her slowly and glared at her so hard, she had to raise her eyebrows. I was sure I saw a dark shadow hovering about her shoulders. It looked like it was edging over them very slowly.

"What?" she demanded.

I stepped farther away from her because I didn't want the dark shadow to touch me. I could see the fear filling her face like blood in a glass.

"You better behave yourself," she warned, waving her right hand at me. "You just better. I'm not taking you back."

I smiled coolly at her.

"You won't be able to take anyone back," I said, and she looked like she had lost her breath.

When the Prescotts did arrive, Madam Annjill hurried me out with a simple, "Good luck with her."

I felt her hand on my back, literally pushing me out the door, her palm rolling along my wing bone for what I knew would be the last time.

Because it had begun to rain, Mr. Prescott held the umbrella over my head and guided me to the car. I looked back once and thought I saw Tillie Mae staring out a window, rubbing the shoulder that Madame Annjill had dislocated. It was something she always did when she was frightened or sad. In the window she looked as if her face was made of candle wax, with her sad, hot tears melting it away. A few moments later we turned into the driveway and were off, me supposedly to a brand-new hopeful life.

It began to rain harder and quickly became one of those early spring downpours that had decided a moment before it fell not to turn to snow and sleet. The raindrops were heavy, pounding the roof of the Prescotts' car so hard it sounded more like steel balls rolling back and forth above us. There was a clap of thunder, and a stitch of lightning made Mrs. Prescott squeal and jump in her seat.

I sat in the rear, my hands folded over my lap, and stared ahead. Because I was so silent, Mrs. Prescott was fidgety and nervous and couldn't stop talking. She asked me one question after another, and when I didn't answer one, she just went on to the next as if she had never asked the first.

"Give the child a chance," her husband kept telling her. I had yet to say a full sentence. All of my answers were monosyllabic. I was still thinking about how fast I had gone from what had been my home for so long to this new home.

All the time I had lived at that first orphanage under Madame Annjill's iron rule, I was never truly afraid. Her meanness made me stronger, her threats, more defiant. I was in a pond with the rest of the helpless fish, only I had my faith, my secrets, my brother, Noble, at my side when I really needed him. It all kept me well above the swirling waters of unhappiness and well out of danger.

Madame Annjill wasn't all wrong about the things she had told the Prescotts about me, however. She did not exaggerate everything. I was truly more independent than most of the other girls at the orphanage, and I was not a problem at school. I did do well, and I was very neat and organized.

But as I was being ripped out of this orphanage world almost as quickly and dramatically as I had been torn from my family years ago, I felt myself sinking back into the cocoon that had been woven around me at birth. Once again, silence became a warm, protective blanket to wrap around myself. That was why I didn't want to talk very much.

What frightened me the most was the idea that I

was not going home. I was being detoured, perhaps forever, and I would lose the only family I had ever known. Success here and in this world would push my past back further and further, until it would be as buried as my ancestors in the little old graveyard where Noble's body had rested.

Can families replace families? I wondered. Can Nana Prescott and Papa Prescott really become my grandparents? Would I inherit all of their ancestors, their stories, their likes and dislikes? Was it like a blood transfusion after all? Is it finally true that someday for me blood would once again be thicker than water?

And how would my spiritual family feel about all this? Wouldn't they feel betrayed? Wasn't I betraying them simply by being here and pretending I wanted to become part of the Prescott family?

"Please, dear," Mrs. Prescott said again and again, "call me Nana and call Mr. Prescott Papa."

It was almost like asking me to speak profanity. What about my real Nana and Papa? Would they sulk in the shadows, be forced to disappear? And then how would all my other real relatives feel? Surely they would think me ungrateful, deserting them, and they would take away my visions and my strength. I would never be able to go home again, inheritance or no inheritance. What was I to do?

"We're home!" Nana Prescott cried the moment we turned into the driveway, as if she had feared we'd never arrive.

Their home was much as she had described. It was a modest but very pretty house with Wedgwood blue shutters and a walkway bordered by waist-high bushes, a flower bed in front, and a small fountain with a pair of birds at the center. The water ran down their beaks as though they had just dipped them into the pond for a drink.

The two-car garage door went up, revealing a very organized and well-kept garage with cabinets and shelves. Even the garage floor looked like it was scrubbed clean daily. Their second car was an SUV, and I could see the golf clubs in the rear, the heads of which were looking out the window, impatiently waiting for Papa Prescott to make use of them. He carried my things into the house, and then Nana Prescott showed me about.

Everything looked untouched. It was like a model home, with magazines neatly in the racks, furniture polished and looking unused, not a thing out of place. They had a big-screen television set in their family room, as they called it. Somehow, I expected to see a piano. In my mind's eye, there was always a piano in a home. It couldn't be a home without one. I could often hear Mama playing it, the melodies trailing through my memory, weaving in and out of visions like so much musical thread.

Something's not right here, I thought. It wasn't just the neatness, either. What was it? I wondered, and then I realized, that this house was too quiet. There were no voices whispering, no footsteps to be heard, no doors opening and closing. Even the dust didn't move when it was caught in a ray of light. Stillness lay like cellophane over the doors, the walls, the windows and floors. Because of that, the Prescotts spoke very softly, and when they walked, they seemed to be tiptoeing over the carpets and flooring, as if there was someone sleeping upstairs who must not be woken.

"We'll get you settled in," Nana Prescott said. "Papa will be off to play golf with his buddies, but you and I can get to know each other better. You can help me in

the kitchen. Do you like roast pork? I thought we'd
have that as a special occasion dinner."

"I don't know," I said. I really didn't. I couldn't remember ever having it.

"Well, if you don't, I'll just make you something
else right away," Nana Prescott promised.

They took me up to see my room, hoping it would
be to my liking. My liking? How could I, an orphan
for so many years, not be happy to have my own
room?

Nana Prescott had gone out and bought brand-new
bedding for the queen-size bed and had Papa Prescott
hang new white and pink curtains. They had a maid
twice a week, and it was obvious she had spent a lot
of time getting everything looking brand-new. Spotless
windows gleamed. The mauve carpet was vacuumed
so that it looked recently laid, and all the furniture had
been polished until I could see my face reflected in the
wood. It was a pretty room, much prettier than anywhere I had slept since I had left the farm, of course.

"We want you to be as comfortable as a baby blue-
bird in her nest," Nana Prescott told me.

I mouthed my thank-you's, but I was still too nervous and afraid to really smile. The two of them
watched me look over the room, both standing in the
doorway, smiling like proud new grandparents should
smile. The happier and more excited about me they
were, the more nervous I grew, and the tighter and
tighter I drew that cocoon around me. I'm sure that,
among other things, was what eventually discouraged
them.

As soon as I had put away my things, I went with
Nana Prescott to the kitchen.

Once again she was the nervous one, babbling about
her childhood, her school days, her parents and grand-

parents, moving from one topic to another like a bored television viewer flipping channels. It was as though she was told she had to get everything about her past out and in my head before I went to sleep. I was polite and spoke a little more about myself, mainly because I was curious about her and Papa Prescott and their children and grandchildren. I looked at all the pictures and heard her descriptions of everyone.

"They're all going to love you," she predicted. "You'll see."

Was that possible? Could anyone just look at me and love me, or was that just another one of the lies that trailed adults like so many ribbons caught in the wind?

I helped her set the table, and then I went up to my room and looked at the books on the shelf, children's book and young adult books their daughter Michelle had read and kept. Some of them I had read, too, but others attracted my interest. Strangely, I felt guilty every time I saw something I liked or took pleasure in anything that would be mine.

At dinner, Nana Prescott bragged to Papa Prescott how much I had helped her. I had done very little, but I could see she thought exaggerating would make me feel good. I did enjoy the dinner she made. It was tastier than the food at the orphanage, and there was her homemade blueberry pie and ice cream for dessert. Papa Prescott talked about his golf game, even though it was pretty clear Nana Prescott had no interest and thought he should be talking about something that would interest me. It was as if he didn't see her, or me, for that matter. At times it was more like he was talking to himself aloud.

Is this what happens to people when they grow old together? I wondered. Do they begin to separate in lit-

tle ways until they wake up one morning and discover
they are all alone again? They didn't have what I had, I
thought. They didn't have the something wonderful
that held us all together, all of us tied together by whispers and shadows. Yes, that was what I missed the
most now. Just thinking about it made me sad.

"Are you all right, dear?" Nana Prescott asked me.
She saw the expression on my face, I guess.

I nodded.

"She's just tired," Papa Prescott said, smiling at me.
"It's been a big day for her."

Why didn't he say *you? It's been a big day for you?*
I wondered. He made me feel like we were all talking
about someone else, or like I was in a glass case and
they were observing me.

Finally, I went up to bed.

The first night I went to sleep in my new room, I
continued to have a battle with myself. One part of me
wished I was back in the orphanage, even under the
control and terror of Madame Annjill. Once again, I
was reminded about betraying my real family. Another
part of me didn't want to feel that way. It wasn't a rich
and ornate bedroom, but after spending the last six
years in a room with three other girls, each of us con-
fined to a small space for our possessions and schoolbooks, I was excited.

This was the first night I had slept anywhere but the
orphanage for nearly four years. I couldn't keep my
eyes closed, even though I was so tired. Every sound in
the house made my lids snap open. I would wait and
listen for the next tinkle, the next creak. Was that the
sound of the front door opening? A window? Were
those footsteps on the stairway? Was that my bedroom
door being opened?

At one point it was opened. Nana Prescott had come

to my room to look in on me and see if I was all right. I quickly closed my eyes and pretended to be asleep. She stood there for a few more moments and then quietly closed the door.

Immediately afterward, I heard Noble say, "Hey."

I turned and saw him standing there. He didn't look happy, even though I was overjoyed to see him.

"I was afraid you wouldn't know where I had gone," I said. "I haven't seen you for so long."

"That's not my fault. You stopped looking for me. You even stopped thinking about me."

"No, I didn't."

"It doesn't matter. I'll always know where you are," he told me. "And I'll always see you."

I watched him walk around the room, looking at everything.

"It's a nice room, isn't it?" I asked him.

"No," he said. "You have a nicer room waiting for you at home. This room smells like a laundry. Whoever cleans it uses too much soap and polish. It reminds me of a hospital room. And what are you looking out at here?" he continued after he went to the window. "Another house and a busy street. I've already checked their backyard. They don't have a garden; they've never had a garden, and that swing set is pathetic."

"Papa Prescott's going to fix it and make it look brand-new again," I said.

"Papa Prescott?" he said, grimacing with distaste.

"That's what they want me to call him."

"Please," Noble said.

He turned around and put his hands on his hips.

"They want me to be happy," I told him.

He shook his head.

"You won't be happy here, Celeste," he declared. "Don't ever think or imagine you will."

Then he turned and walked into the darkness of a corner and was gone.

"Noble," I called. "Noble!"

I must have been shouting because Nana Prescott came to my door quickly. She was in her nightgown, her blue-gray hair down to her shoulders. Silhouetted in the hall light, she looked like some deformed creature. Then I did scream.

Papa Prescott came quickly behind her, tying his robe as he approached.

"What is it?"

"I don't know. What's wrong, Celeste, dear?"

She flipped on the light. I was sitting up, staring at the corner in which Noble had disappeared. Tears were streaming down my cheeks.

"Was it a nightmare, dear?" Nana Prescott asked.

She approached me tentatively, hoping for some sign from me that I welcomed her comfort, but all I could do was stare at the corner and hope Noble would come back.

"What was it?" Nana asked now, stopping a foot from the bed. "Celeste?"

I didn't respond.

She turned to Papa Prescott and shrugged.

"What should I do?"

"Celeste," he said more firmly. "What seems to be bothering you? Did something frighten you?"

Finally I turned to them and wiped my cheeks, flipping the tears to the side.

"Noble was here, and I'm afraid he won't come back," I said.

"Who?" Nana Prescott asked. "Did you say someone was here? Celeste?"

I didn't answer. I dropped myself back, my head on the pillow, and stared up at the ceiling.

"She must be having a dream. I think she's still in it," Papa Prescott said.

"Yes, that's it. Poor child. The hard times she's gone through as an orphan are unimaginable," Nana Prescott said, and finally came to my bed and fixed my blanket around me. "There, there, dear. Papa and I are right nearby if you need us. Would you like me to leave the door open?" she asked.

I looked at her.

"Yes," I said. "Leave it open. Maybe he'll return."

"Maybe who will return?"

"Noble," I said. I loved saying his name, and it had been so long, so very long, since I had told it to anyone.

They looked at each other.

"She'll feel better in the morning," Nana Prescott forced herself to conclude.

"Yeah, we all will," Papa Prescott predicted, and they walked out, she pausing once to look back at me.

"Come back, Noble," I whispered. "I won't be happy here. I promise."

But he didn't appear again that first night. Nevertheless, I knew he was sulking somewhere in the shadows. I could feel him there. Afterward, I knew he was following me everywhere, too. He even followed me to the new school I was to attend, and after I had been assigned my desk and had been introduced to the class by my teacher, I spun around and caught him standing in the back of the classroom. He smirked, fell backward into the wall, and was gone.

Over the next few weeks, I never stopped looking for him. My teacher complained to me and then to the Prescotts that I wasn't paying attention, that I was very distracted. She told them she couldn't understand how I had been doing so well in school. My first grades on her tests were always failing, and whenever she called on me in class to answer a question, I would simply stare at her.

Nana Prescott continually asked me why I was doing so badly. She volunteered to read with me, but I knew that would make Noble even angrier, since it was what he always did with me. I told her I didn't need her to do that.

"Noble will help me," I said.

"Who is Noble?" she asked.

"My brother."

"Your brother, but where . . . when do you see him?"

"Whenever he wants me to," I said.

She shook her head and busied herself with some household chore. Later, she and Papa Prescott talked about me. I could hear them speaking softly in the living room after I had gone up to bed. Noble told me to tiptoe out to the top of the stairway to listen.

"I don't know," Papa said. "I don't like it. We might have bitten off more than we can chew, Julia."

"Oh, I'm sure she'll get better after a while. It takes time to get used to a new home, Arnold. Children often invent imaginary friends."

"This isn't an imaginary friend. It's her brother who died. Can't say it doesn't give me the creeps to hear her talk about him," he said. "And the way she stares at nothing, as if she sees someone. Frankly, it gives me the chills. Funny how Annjill didn't mention anything about this."

They were quiet.

I started back to my room. Noble was standing in the doorway.

"See what I mean? You don't belong here," he said, turned and went inside.

But he wasn't there when I entered. I went to bed and waited and listened for him. He didn't return, and I fell asleep.

The following day Mr. Fizer, the school counselor, asked to meet with me. He had curly blond hair and very friendly and warm blue eyes. I saw the picture of his wife and two children on his desk. He had a girl who looked to be about fifteen in the picture and a son, whom I had seen in the hallway, who was eight years old and two grades below me. I couldn't help wondering why there was such an age difference between his two children. In the family portrait, I thought his wife looked older than him.

"It's always hard to start a new school," he said almost as soon as I sat in the chair in front of his desk. "We all understand that, Celeste, but Miss Ritowski thinks you're having more serious problems. Is there anything bothering you that I can help you with, perhaps? I really would like to help you and to see you succeed."

I didn't answer. I stared at him, actually right through him.

"You're with very, very nice people. I've known the Prescotts for a long time. I went to school with their son, in fact," he said, smiling.

The windows of his office were behind his desk, which I thought was a bad idea. Anyone who was called to his office and sat in front of him could ignore him and gaze out the windows to see birds and even students who were having physical education classes on the ball field.

"Don't you like Miss Ritowski? All her students are very fond of her," he added before I could say otherwise.

I shrugged, which encouraged him.

"You shouldn't be finding the work too hard, not from the school history you have," he added, tapping on a folder opened on his desk. "So," he continued, leaning toward me, "why aren't you doing better, Celeste? I can't believe you're really trying. Are you really trying?"

I was about to answer him when I saw Noble walking up from the ball field. I was sure it was Noble, even though he was walking with his head down. I remembered too well that plodding gait of his and the way his head and shoulders would bob along with each carefully chosen step.

"Celeste? Are you listening to me?"

"My brother isn't happy about my being here," I said, my voice laden with anger.

"Pardon me?" He leaned back. "Your brother?" He thought a moment and then leaned forward again and quickly read some pages in my folder. "When have you spoken to your brother?"

"I saw him last night," I said.

Now Mr. Fizer was the one simply staring.

"Oh," he finally said. "Well, then, we'll have to find out why your brother is unhappy about your being here," he said, forcing a smile. "How do I get to speak to your brother?"

Noble turned abruptly to the right and disappeared from view.

"You can't talk to him," I said.

"Why not?"

"He doesn't talk to strangers," I said. "He never liked it when any came to our home. He would pretend they weren't there."

"Okay, if he won't talk to me, then maybe you can tell me why he is unhappy about your being here," Mr. Fizer said.

"He thinks I should go home," I said. "He's afraid I will forget."

"Forget? Forget what?" Mr. Fizer asked.

"My family," I said.

"Oh. Well, I don't think you will ever forget your family, but that doesn't mean you can't let other people help you and care for you and eventually love you the way your family loved you," he said.

"No one can love me like that," I told him, my eyes so narrow and fixed on his face, he actually raised his eyebrows and look flustered. "Don't ever say such a thing," I chastised, as if he was the child and I was the adult.

"Yes, well, I don't mean to upset you. I'm here for you if you need to talk. Any time, Celeste, any time at all," he said.

I pressed my lips together and turned away from him, slamming the door shut on everything else he said.

There were more conferences, but none with me. The talks were between the Prescotts and my teacher. Nothing they did or said changed anything, and the Prescotts grew more and more concerned. I overheard Papa Prescott tell Nana Prescott that it was even affecting his golf game. They began to argue more and more about me.

When I began to sleepwalk, as Nana Prescott described it, Papa Prescott grew even more concerned. She found me downstairs in the living room talking to Noble, and once she found me in the kitchen having a glass of milk while I talked to him. Each time, I told her what I was doing, and each time she had me go back to sleep.

I knew they were having endless conversations about me with their children, too. None had come yet to see me, but Nana Prescott spoke to someone, perhaps Madam Annjill, who advised her to do more family-type things with me.

They tried taking me on what they called fun rides. They bought me some new clothes, and Nana bought me a new doll, even though there really were dozens of old ones in one of the closets. I couldn't play with them anyway, because they had the fingers of the Prescotts' grandchildren still on them. I felt like my hand was over another every time I touched one or picked one up.

They took me to parks and amusement parks, and they tried to get other girls my age from my class to come to their home to be with me, but I hadn't really made any friends at school. Most of the other girls kept their distance. I often saw them whispering about me.

My schoolwork didn't improve. I began to sleep a lot and eat poorly, too. Finally, Papa Prescott told Nana Prescott that they should "throw in the towel." I heard her cry about it, and I did feel sorry for her.

"She is a nice lady," I told Noble that night.

"The world is full of nice ladies. You need to be with family," he insisted. He wouldn't compromise.

In the end the Prescotts did give up on me, but they discovered they couldn't bring me back to the orphanage run by Madam Annjill and her husband, Homer. That orphanage was closed. Madam Annjill had suffered a massive stroke and died. All of the children living there had been transferred to other orphanages. This disturbed Nana Prescott even more.

"We're going to turn her over to a strange new place," she moaned. "How dreadful for the child."

"It's not going to be any more dreadful for her than things are for her here," Papa Prescott insisted.

"Maybe we're just too old for this sort of thing. She needs a younger pair of parents, and maybe a home with a child already there, too."

"How sad. How sad," Nana Prescott moaned.

They conferred with the children's protection agency, and a little more than a week later, they gave me the news.

"I'm sorry," Nana Prescott said. "I think we're just too old to raise a little girl like you. You need more energetic, younger people. It's not fair for us to keep you," she added to make herself feel better.

I said nothing.

I didn't shed a tear, which I knew bothered her more. It made Papa Prescott feel better about it all, however. He felt justified in his decision to give me up. I saw it in his eyes. I was far too big of a problem for them.

A new orphanage was found for me, but when the Prescotts returned me to the children's protection agency, they told them all about my conversations with Noble, and arrangements were made for me to visit with another child psychiatrist who donated his time to the needy.

His name was Dr. Sackett, and I grew to like him very much. He was very understanding about Noble.

"It's not unusual to cling so hard to someone who loved you so much," he told me. "But you have to let go, just the way any little person lets go of his or her imaginary friends. As you get stronger and more self-confident, you will," he assured me. "After all, Noble comes to you only when you're afraid or insecure, or even feeling guilty about something, right?" he gently prodded.

In time I thought he was right, and as I grew older

and stronger, I did see and hear Noble less and less at this new orphanage, until he was virtually gone.

That was where I had been up until the very day, nearly six years, in fact, when I was called quite unexpectedly to meet a young man and woman apparently looking for a foster daughter my age. It was really the woman who was looking for me, who needed me even more than I needed her. The reasons for that would not be clear for a while, and when they were, I found myself in the most frightening situation in which I had ever been.

I should have paid more attention to the shadows thickening around me, perhaps, but I had promised myself I would try hard, very hard, to put all that aside and be as close to a so-called normal young woman as I possibly could be. Dr. Sackett had convinced me that the voices and visions were all coming from inside me, from my own insecurity. If I was ever to be a truly successful and independent person, I would have to shut the doors on all that.

The question was, would I be right or wrong to do so? The answer wasn't long in coming.

3

A Curtain Dropping on My Past

♊

"**H**i. I'm Ami," a very pretty young woman said, rising quickly to greet me when I entered the office. She didn't look much older than me. We were about the same height. I was five feet five by now. Our figures were similar, too. I thought we even had the same shoe size, but what truly amazed me was how close to the color of my hair hers was.

She held out her hand, which had long, polished fingernails, a hand that obviously never performed any hard work. I took it and shook, glancing simultaneously at the slim man in a charcoal gray pin-striped suit and black tie seated beside her. He swung his soft hazel eyes to her and twisted his thin lips up at the right corner.

Ami held on to my hand and turned to him.

"Isn't she just perfect, Wade?" she asked him, keeping her eyes on me. Then she stepped beside me to face him. She bumped her hip against mine. "Look at us. She could be my sister."

He raised his light brown eyebrows and widened his eyes. With his fingers held out stiffly, he pressed his right palm over his thin, closely trimmed dark brown hair as if he sensed a strand had fallen out of place, and then he grunted what sounded like agreement.

"You are perfect. You are," Ami insisted. "I want to know all about you. Every little thing. Nothing is unimportant. We're going to be great friends."

I turned to Mother Higgins, the headmistress of the orphanage. I saw she was amused by the young woman's outburst, but instead of smiling, she raised her eyes slightly toward the ceiling, just as she did when she was about to begin a prayer of thanks at our dining table. Then she looked at me with her most officious headmistress's face.

"Celeste," she began, "this is Mr. and Mrs. Emerson."

"Oh, please don't call us Mr. and Mrs. Emerson. I'm Ami, and this is Wade," Ami insisted. She was still holding my hand. I didn't know whether to pull it out of her grip or just turn my fingers into limp noodles to get the message across.

"Why don't you take your seat, Ami," Wade suggested in a monotone.

She turned back to him sharply.

"So that we can get on with it," he explained with a little more feeling. "There's a lot to do."

"Oh, yes. Yes, of course," Ami said, and released me. She sat and folded her hands over each other on her lap, primping and smiling like an impatient little girl whose daddy had just told her to behave or she wouldn't get any ice cream.

"Please take a seat, Celeste," Mother Higgins told me, nodding at the chair across from the small sofa where both Mr. and Mrs. Emerson now sat, staring at me. Something wasn't right about them, I thought. Something wasn't quite right, but I wouldn't permit that feeling to frighten me. Instead, I let it make me more curious about them.

Wade Emerson had his legs crossed, but his back was so straight, it looked like a steel rod had been shoved alongside his spine down to his waist. He pursed his lips, which further tightened the skin around his narrow, almost square jaw. The eyebrows he raised for emphasis were long and full, but his hands were not much longer or bigger than Ami's, and just as soft looking.

I was still wearing the school uniform that the orphanage provided all the girls, a navy blue top and skirt with thick-heeled dark blue lace-up shoes and white knee-high socks. The navy blue top had a big, masculine-looking collar with large black buttons and tight cuffs. It was loose-fitting, and I'm sure appeared a size or so too large. However, I had long ago stopped being self-conscious about my clothes or my looks. As Mother Higgins often told us, "It's not how you appear on the outside that matters; it's how you are on the inside." I don't think any of the other girls ever really believed that, especially when they contrasted themselves with other girls who weren't orphans, but sometimes it helped us get through the day and kept the sadness from taking control of our eyes and lips.

Just on first glance, I could tell that I didn't have to be any sort of clairvoyant to easily conclude Ami Emerson wasn't someone who would ever believe in Mother Higgins's adage about what was and was not important. Everything about her outer appearance was too perfect, too well planned.

"The Emersons," Mother Higgins began, "are very interested in providing a healthy home environment for a young woman just your age. Mrs. Emerson—"

Ami turned to her quickly and gave her a pained look.

"I mean, Ami," Mother Higgins corrected. Ami smiled. "—and her husband Wade are relatively newlyweds, having been married only four years."

"Four years and five months," Wade gently added. He looked at his wife. "Not that I'm counting the days or anything."

"I hope not. Only people in prison count the days," Ami said, and laughed. Mother Higgins nodded and smiled, too.

"Well then, Celeste," she continued, "as Ami has explained to me, she and Wade have decided to begin their own family in about two years, but in the meantime, they would like to offer their home, their family life, to a young lady such as yourself."

As if she could no longer hold it all in, Ami Emerson burst out with her own version of the explanation.

"I know the hardest years of my life emotionally were the teen years. You're a woman, but everyone still wants to treat you as if you were a little girl. You're not sure of what's right and what's wrong. It's a dangerous time!" she declared, nodding in agreement with herself. "You are capable of making some very serious errors if you are not given the proper guidance and advice.

"I'm sure this is a wonderful place," she said, smiling at Mother Higgins, "but you can't possibly get all the personal attention you need at this climactic time in your life. And there are experiences that are just not . . . well, in the experience of your guardians," she continued. "Not that I'm saying there is anything wrong with that," she added quickly. "It's just not in their lifestyle."

Wade's eyes widened, and Ami caught it.

"I don't mean to sound critical of you or anyone else here, Mother Higgins."

"Of course you don't, dear," Mother Higgins said generously, a slight smile at the corner of her lips that only I could discern.

"Anyway," Ami continued, turning back to me, "it just came to me the other day that a girl in your circumstances would be the perfect foster daughter for us at this time, right, Wade?"

He nodded, now looking at her as if he was truly amazed by her himself.

"I said to Wade, Wade, why don't we do something wonderful and generous with our money and our time? Why don't we take in a young woman and provide her with foster care?

"I'm sure you understand why I don't want to start with a much younger girl. It's much harder, much more difficult, to care for a little person, and when my own baby is born, well, she or he would get all the attention. I would just hate to end it for the little girl we had taken in to live with us, or to have her think she isn't loved as much as my own child will be loved," she said, scrunching her face as though she were about to cry for this imaginary little girl.

Wade grunted again.

"That's why you are so perfect," Ami continued. "By the time I give birth, you'll be out there on your own or in college. Why, we understand you have property, too. Of course, you'll always have a place in our home and our hearts, but that's quite different from being a year-round resident for the rest of your life or until you got married or something.

"What do you think?" she asked me, but before I could respond, she continued. "We have a very large house. It's a mansion, in fact."

"It's not a mansion, Ami. Please don't exaggerate," Wade chided.

"Well, how big is it, Wade? Go on, describe that," she ordered, folding her arms and nodding her head once as though she was throwing down a challenge.

He turned, and after a deep sigh, said, "It's eight thousand square feet on twenty acres."

"Eight thousand square feet. There you are. How big is the orphanage, Mother Higgins? Well, how big?"

"Well, I don't know exactly, but I think it's about that, if not a bit smaller."

"Yes, precisely." She turned back to me. "You live in a building the size of our house or a bit smaller, with a dozen or so other young women. I'm sure you're crowded. And how many acres do you have here, Mother Higgins?"

"Please," Wade pleaded.

"How many?" Ami insisted.

"Five, I believe."

"Five. Exactly my point. We have twenty."

She turned back to me and nodded her head firmly.

"So you see, I wasn't exaggerating. Our house will certainly seem like a mansion to you. Why, I bet your room in our house is as big as the living room here."

"Ami, you're making us sound like snobs," Wade gently complained.

"I am not. I've never been a snob. I hate snobs. My mother made me into a debutante, but I hated every minute of it, and you know I did."

"All right, Ami. All right. Let's get on with it, is all I'm saying."

She turned back to me.

"Wade is always embarrassed by our good fortune. I don't think of it all the same way. If you have it, if you've been blessed with it, be proud of it, but most of all," she said, beaming at me, "be generous and charitable." She turned to Mother Higgins. "It was like a surge of goodness came into my head. It was like an electric shock. I thought, Why not go out and help someone in need? I'm sure you understand why I feel it was like a holy moment."

"Yes, yes, I do," Mother Higgins said, holding on to her tight, amused smile. She raised her dark eyebrows. "The Good Lord acts in mysterious ways."

If she could have, she would have winked at me.

"Amen," Wade said dryly. He kept his gaze on the floor. Ami scowled at him and then turned back to me.

"I'll enroll you immediately in the nearby private school, Celeste," she continued, barely taking a breath. Her hands fluttered about as she spoke, the large diamond ring on her left hand catching the sunlight that poured through the window and then sending beams of reflected light over the walls, Mother Higgins's face, and me. "The timing is perfect. You've just begun your senior year, so transferring won't be so damaging. I'm sure you'll catch up quickly, Celeste.

"By the way," she said, lowering her voice, "I absolutely adore your name. Celeste. Your mother was so imaginative. My name is like a nickname," she said, grimacing. "Ami. Mon Ami, my father used to say. That means 'my friend' in French. Who expects to be called my friend by her father? My friend?"

"Could we please get on with it, Ami?" Wade pleaded in a tired voice.

"Yes. Back to what I was saying, Celeste. Wade and I have already discussed it and decided the private school would be the best place for you. The teachers will give you the personal attention you might need to make the transition from the school you are now attending. And don't worry," she quickly added, "they don't make you wear those stupid, ugly uniforms at this private school. The girls and their mothers wouldn't stand for it," she said, and laughed.

Wade didn't crack a smile. He stared ahead like someone counting to himself. Mother Higgins looked a little upset now, but kept her face as stoic as she could manage. I stopped smiling. I didn't like to see her irritated. She had always been very nice to me. I didn't want to bring it up, but it wasn't the school that had us wear this uniform; it was the orphanage. It was Mother Higgins's way of keeping us from being upset about our wardrobe. There was no way we could compete, and wearing the uniform made that irrelevant. At least, that was Mother Higgins's hope. In truth, although the uniforms solved our immediate concern, they served to identify us all as orphans. I couldn't keep track of how many times and how often other students, especially the girls, asked us why we had to wear "those stupid outfits" all the time. Memories of how I felt and how the other girls felt when that happened rushed back over me.

"Oh," Ami said, "I see you're upset about what I said. You're worrying about your own meager wardrobe, I'm sure," Ami continued, before I could even think of that problem.

In fact, I don't think I managed a breath in between her excited speeches.

"Well, don't worry at all. The first thing I'm going

to do with you is take you shopping to my personal boutiques. Wade and I have already agreed about that, too, haven't we, Wade?"

"Yes, Ami," he said with even more fatigue in his voice.

"Money, despite Wade's modesty, is not an issue for us. Wade is an important businessman. He manages his family's very large plumbing supply company, although he doesn't really know anything about plumbing, do you, Wade?"

"I do too," he protested, his face finally taking on some color. "I worked with Dad for—"

"Oh, Wade." She waved at him. "Does he look like he worked with wrenches and pipes all his life? His mother wouldn't let him work that hard."

She laughed.

Wade's blush rippled down his neck. He smirked and shook his head. Then he forced a smile at Mother Higgins.

"My mother always told me you could lift more with your brains than with your muscles," he said in his own defense.

Mother Higgins nodded.

"I quite agree with your mother."

A look of satisfaction sat on his face. He turned triumphantly to Ami.

"Whatever," Ami said, already bored with the topic. "How soon can she come to live with us?"

"Well," Mother Higgins said, eyeing me. "Before we get into any of that, I suppose Celeste should tell us what she thinks. We do let the girls think for themselves, especially when they reach Celeste's age. In a year, she will be on her own—not that we would ever desert her," Mother Higgins added, smiling my way.

"Oh, yes, of course. I'm sorry. I just thought . . ."
Ami paused, glanced at Wade, who shook his head,
and then sat back and folded her arms under her
breasts. "Go on. Tell us what you think."

They were all looking at me now. Even Wade's face
suddenly was full of interest. Something was swirling
about them, something I had never sensed. What had
brought these people to me now? I had always har-
bored the deep belief that nothing happened to me
without a reason, that my destiny was clearly and
plainly laid out in a map of events solely designed for
me. These people didn't simply find me. It was meant
to happen. But why?

Ami looked absolutely terrified that I would reject
their offer.

"I don't know. It's true that since the academic year
has just begun, it wouldn't be a terrible burden to
change schools. I suppose I'm fine with it all," I said.
"As soon as whatever has to be done is done," I added,
looking at Mother Higgins.

She smiled at me.

"Oh, how wonderful!" Ami cried, nearly leaping out
of her seat. "How long will it all take? Do we need an
attorney? We have dozens of attorneys, don't we,
Wade? What do we need?" she said, grimacing as
though she expected a dreadfully long laundry list of
preparations.

"You don't need an attorney," Wade said slowly.
"Why don't you and Celeste take a walk and get to
know each other while Mother Higgins and I go
through the paperwork?" he suggested.

Ami brightened again, and her skin, which was so
soft looking and so smooth it looked smeared over her
body with a butter knife, took on a rosy blush at the
crests of her high cheekbones.

"What a wonderful idea. Thank you, Wade. Celeste, shall we?" she asked, rising.

I glanced at Mother Higgins. She wasn't smiling now. Her eyes met mine as they had often. She had a way of reaching inside me to find out what I really thought and felt. I liked her very much, but the prospect of having a life outside of this orphanage away from all these younger girls and attending a school that was far from the dreary one I now attended was truly exhilarating for me.

"I'll show you our gardens," I told Ami.

She practically leaped across the office to thread her arm through mine.

"Good. I hate boring business talk anyway," she whispered.

She was my prospective foster mother, but I felt like I had joined arms with one of the younger wards in the orphanage. We stepped outside into the warm early September afternoon. Summer wasn't over, and anyway, it did look like we would have an extended one. A military jet had drawn a trail of milk white exhaust across the darkening blue, but other than that, there wasn't a cloud in sight.

Ami was right. The orphanage wasn't very large, and the grounds were narrow toward the front, the boundaries of the property shaped more like a parabola. To the right was an old fieldstone wall with mold on the stones and weeds growing out of crevices and cracks. Between the building and the wall were some modest attempts at creating gardens. The people who worked on it were volunteers, and the flowers and plants were pathetic in contrast to those I remembered on our farm. Sometimes, almost as a way of reliving those days, I would work on the gardens here, and when I did, I thought I sensed Noble standing behind me, even though it had been quite a while since he had shown himself to me. It's only a memory, I told myself, just a memory, and I don't need it. I'm stronger. It was a chant my therapist had suggested I repeat every time I was tempted to call for Noble.

"I have a confession to make," Ami began. "I've seen you before."

"Oh?"

Was she referring to something in my past? I wondered. A picture in a newspaper? A magazine? What did she actually know about that?

"I did a bit of a survey of the orphanages and foster homes in our area, and when I learned about you, I parked my car across the street there one afternoon and waited for you to return from school."

I wasn't sure I liked being spied upon, so I was silent.

"Of course, I knew it was you immediately. I can tell a lot about someone from the way she walks, holds her head. You looked like you didn't belong here, and I said to myself, Ami, there's a girl who will appreciate what you can give her."

"Thank you," I said, even though it sounded more like she was patting herself on the back than patting me on mine.

"Anyway, our house could use some youth and excitement in it. As you heard, we have been married for over four years. Wade works with his father, but they are like water and oil. You know what that means?"

"Yes," I said, smiling.

"I bet you're very, very smart. I mean, I heard about

your grades, but getting good grades in school doesn't mean you're necessarily really smart, worldly smart," she said. "I was an average student, but I knew where it was at. Especially," she said, leaning so close I thought she would kiss my ear, "when it comes to men. Do you have a boyfriend?"

"No."

She looked pleased.

"Did you have one, break up or anything?"

I shook my head.

"Good. Are you a virgin? It's all right. You can tell me things," she quickly followed before I could react. "I want us to be like lifelong friends right from the start. I know you haven't had anyone here in whom you could confide your deepest secrets, right? Of course I'm right," she added before I could even think of an answer.

I had to laugh.

"Yes," I said. "I am a virgin."

"That's so great. I was a virgin when I was your age, too. All I hear these days is young girls are losing their virginity at earlier and earlier ages. Not that I'm saying I'm old-fashioned and believe in the golden treasure or anything. I just think sex is something you have to take very, very seriously. If you're smart, you'll use it like a weapon, a tool. That's what I did, and look where I am. We'll talk about all that later. We have lots of time.

"So," she said before I could make any comment or question what she meant by such a statement, "what we'll do first is go shopping for new clothes for you. This Monday, I'll get you enrolled in the school. Don't expect Wade to do much. I'm not saying he wasn't all for this," she added quickly. "He was. He's just . . . a little narrow," she concluded. "Not that I

don't love him. I do. I just think it's important to recognize your husband's strengths and weaknesses and
not be like some of these women I know who have
their heads buried in mud baths at spas. Why, they
could see their husbands with a beautiful woman on
their arms and pretend it was a business associate. See
no evil; hear no evil; as long as you give me my allowance. Some women are like children instead of
wives, but not yours truly, and that's what I'm going
to teach you: how to hold your own with any man you
meet.

"Oh, it's just going to be a wonderful time," she
declared.

We stopped walking. She looked out at the road,
and then she took a deep breath.

"So, now tell me about all this nonsense about your
coming from a crazy family."

I tilted my head slightly and looked at her. She
laughed.

"You were brought up by a boy who turned out to
be a girl?"

"I wasn't brought up by him," I said sharply.

"Don't worry. I don't believe a word of any of
that," she said, flicking her hand as if to dismiss someone. "Whatever happened, it obviously hasn't done
you any great harm. I've spoken to your teachers, and
I've read the nice reports people have made on you.
Wade has no idea how much time I've already spent
on you."

"You've spoken to my teachers?" I asked, very surprised.

"Yes, yes," she said, waving it off. "Anyway, the
truth is," she said, now whispering, "our family is the
crazy family. Wade's mother died at the age of forty-
eight. She had heart failure, but I can tell you now it

wasn't exactly heart failure. It was more like a broken heart. Wade's father is a true womanizer, and his mother was confronted with evidence of one extramarital affair after another. It embarrassed her to death. She got so she hated going out in public because she thought everyone was laughing at her. Some days she didn't even get dressed, didn't even get out of bed. Wade's told me all about it, but he never talks about it in front of his father.

"Wade's father is still quite the man about town. I'll admit he's handsome and doesn't look his age, but you'd think he'd settle down, especially after losing his wife.

"Wade's sister Bethany has refused to have anything to do with him since their mother's death. She's married and lives in Washington, D.C. Her husband works for a United States senator. If anyone's a snob in this family, it's Bethany, but Wade would never say anything against her. He doesn't say anything about anyone, and he hates gossip. I can't even talk about movie stars!" she exclaimed. "If I start, he slaps his hands over his ears and cries, 'Turn it off,' as if I was playing something horrible on the music system."

We walked along.

"But all that's gong to stop," she said. "I mean, I'll have you. Of course Wade will, too, but I'm warning you now, Wade's a workaholic. Even his father, who built the business, criticizes him. The truth is," she said, pausing again, "I'm often lonely. Oh, I could have gotten involved in the business, but who wants that? And I wasn't going to go out and become one of these career women. I don't need the money or the prestige. I come from a wealthy family myself. I was an only child, and so of course Wade calls me spoiled.

"So what? I'm spoiled. A woman, women like us, should be spoiled. We're made to be spoiled, and their job is to spoil us. Oh," she said suddenly, turning to hug me. "We'll really be like sisters. I mean that," she said, pulling back and looking firm. "Don't ever think of me as a mother, even though that's what I'm claiming I'll be. I couldn't stand the thought of it. I mean . . . a mother to someone as old as you? Really, how ridiculous I would look to anyone I told such a thing."

I stared at her. I had never seen or spoken to anyone quite like her, someone so full of energy and excitement. It was as if she had been kept under lock and key for years and was finally permitted to go out and meet people. I'm sure my look of curiosity and amazement confused her.

"I guess I'm talking too much. Wade is always accusing me of that and slapping those hands over his ears. Am I talking too much? Just say so and I'll shut up. Just don't slap your hands over your ears like Wade does. He has no idea how much I hate that. Or maybe he does and does it anyway. Men."

"No," I said, smiling. "I don't mind your talking at all."

She beamed.

"I knew that you wouldn't. I just knew it. Wade, I said, a girl like that is probably just dying to have someone like me to talk to. She's like a flower kept growing in a pot too small. Oh come on," she said, seizing my hand and turning back toward the orphanage. "Let's tell them we're tired of waiting and anxious to get going. Why should it take so long, anyway?"

She took a few steps and paused, turning back to me.

"You are anxious, aren't you? Anxious to get going, I mean?"

I looked at her, at the orphanage, at the meager gardens, and then smiled and nodded.

"Yes," I said. "Very anxious."

She squealed with delight and practically dragged me toward the door.

It did feel like a whirlwind, but I didn't mind it. I packed and said my good-byes in less than an hour. Mother Higgins took me aside before I joined Ami and Wade, who were waiting in the lobby.

"You have been with us a long time, Celeste," she began. "I've always known you were a special girl. You have learned to cherish and guard tightly what you hear inside yourself and what you see. That takes wisdom. I have watched you in prayer, and I know you have a maturity and direction inside you. These people might not be right for all that, but you have to be generous. Do you know what I mean?"

"Yes, Mother Higgins."

She nodded.

"I think you do, dear. I think you are truly wise beyond your years. Most of the time, that's a blessing; sometimes it can be a burden. It is a burden if you are intolerant of those who do not have your insight and maturity."

"I understand, Mother Higgins."

She smiled.

"I know you do. I'm very proud of how you've grown and overcome your difficulties. I only pray that this is the opportunity you well deserve. Best of luck, dear," she said, and hugged me. "Call me whenever you want."

Wade helped carry out my suitcases. I had two good-sized ones now. I remembered when I had only a carry-on bag. Ami waited beside their big black Mercedes. It looked like the limousine I had once dreamed would come to take me away, but to take me back to the aromas that lingered in my memory, the tastes that dwelled on my tongue, and the whispers that lived inside my ears.

"I'm going to ride in the back with Celeste, Wade," she told him. She smiled at me. "We'll feel like we've got a chauffeur then, Celeste. You don't mind being our chauffeur, do you, Wade dear?"

"What's new about that?" he quipped, and she laughed.

"Oh, you're just going to love us," Ami said, and practically pushed me into the car. She closed the door quickly and sat back to catch her breath. She saw the way I was gazing at the old orphanage, and I knew that it displeased her.

However, I couldn't help it. The cold stone front somehow had become so familiar and comfortable, I felt like I was leaving an old friend. For most of the last year I had been the oldest girl there, and often I found myself acting more like a house mother. I didn't mind it so much. In fact, I wondered how sad the other girls would be when they learned I had left.

"You're not even a little unhappy about leaving that place, are you?" she asked, a note more of fear in her voice than of disgust.

"It's been home for a long time," I said. It was the last place I had ever seen Noble, too, I thought; although now the vision was foggy in my mind.

"Oh, it hasn't been a home. It's been a . . . a place. You're about to enter a home," she said, almost snapping at me. She smiled quickly. "At least, I hope with all my heart that you will believe that, Celeste," she added in a far softer tone of voice.

Me too, I thought.

But somehow, despite all the time that had passed and how much I had grown and learned, the concept of home still remained very vague. It was more like a partially formed dream, a flurry of images yet to be connected, feelings yet to be felt, promises yet to be kept.

On the ride to their house, Ami told me about her own youth, the places she had been with her parents, and her schools. She described her social life in great detail, especially the grand parties. Then she listed her boyfriends. She began when she was only ten. It amazed me how she remembered their names and the order of their appearance. She was up to twenty when she paused.

"I was never long without a boyfriend," she bragged. "My father used to say he should have named me Honey because there were so many boys buzzing around our house."

"Bees aren't attracted to honey. They make honey," Wade said.

"Whatever. Don't be so pedantic," she chastised, and then turned to me. "Wade and I met at my coming-out party, but I didn't fall prey to his charms immediately. He had to work on me, but he was persistent, no matter how difficult I made it for him," she said. "And I did make it difficult," she said, raising her voice.

"Difficult's her middle name," Wade quipped.

"Very funny. He had to do a lot to win my hand in marriage, and even more to win the rest of me," she added with another giggle.

I saw the back of Wade's neck turn crimson.

"Stop it, Ami," he warned.

"I will not stop it. I'm going to begin giving her the benefit of my experience immediately." She turned to me, her face very serious. "You must never let a man think you're easy, no matter how much you want him. Once a man takes you for granted, he forgets all his promises."

"Oh, brother," Wade moaned. "Celeste, I don't know what you know about men and what you don't, but you better get a second opinion on everything she tells you. Consider it the same as a medical problem. You need a second opinion."

Ami laughed. Then she leaned toward me to whisper.

"He'll never admit it, but I was his only real girlfriend."

She sat back, smiling.

"Where are we going?" I asked, the realization striking me that I didn't know the name of the town or city. I wasn't even paying attention to what direction we were heading. "I mean, where is your home?"

"Our home, Celeste. From now on, call it *our* home. Peekskill. We live outside of Peekskill because that's where Wade's company is located," Ami said. "The school you'll attend is just south of us about, what, Wade? Five miles?"

"About," he said.

"How will I get there every day?" I asked. From the orphanage, I just walked to the public school. "Is there a school bus?"

"There is, but I'll take you every morning," Wade said. "Drop you off on my way to work. Ami will either pick you up or arrange for a pickup."

"Maybe we'll get you your own little car to use. We can do that, Wade, can't we?"

"We'll see," he said.

She patted me on the arm and winked.

Was this all a dream? After all these years, how could they just come out of nowhere and present me with this exciting new opportunity and all of this luxury? Surely, they'd been sent, and my future was truly beginning.

I really had to pinch myself when I saw their house. Ami was not exaggerating, I thought. This was truly a mansion. The driveway looked like it was a mile long. First we approached the ornate gates with seven-foot-high pilasters, each capped with a large square light fixture. Wade pressed a button over his visor, and the gates began to open very slowly.

"It's like entering heaven," Ami said. "It always gives me chills when I drive in, even after four years."

"Hardly heaven," Wade muttered.

"It is to me," Ami countered. "Wade's father actually owns the house, although he doesn't live here anymore. He doesn't want us knowing his comings and goings. He bought it years ago and had it renovated," she continued as the house and grounds came into better view. The landscaping was elaborate. There were flowers and bushes and trees, fountains and benches, spaced perfectly everywhere I looked.

Off to the left, I saw a large swimming pool, a cabana, and a large gazebo. Just to the right of that was a tennis court. I was like a little girl in a toy store. My eyes were going everywhere, until finally I settled on the house, which seemed to literally rise up before me, looming over us. It was as grand as any house I had ever seen.

"It's what is known as a Second Empire Victorian," Ami continued, assuming the tone of a guide as she talked about it. "It's two stories with a large attic. It's the only house in the area that has a cupola."

On the left side of the house was a one-story porch,

and on the right I could see bay windows. Ami pointed at them.

"That's our dining room, so we can look out at the gardens when we eat. Your bedroom will be on the second floor, just across from ours and above the bay windows. Those two windows on the right are yours. The house has four bedrooms upstairs and two downstairs in the rear. We keep one bedroom for Wade's father whenever he has the inclination to stay over, which means whenever he's here and he drinks too much," she added.

"Which is almost every time he's here," Wade added.

The entrance to the house looked just as ornate as the driveway gates. There were paired entry doors with glass in the top halves and about five marble steps up to them.

"It's just the sort of house you don't see built anymore," Ami added. "All those decorative brackets, the cornerstones, the cresting along the roofline. No one can afford to build such a home. I think we should give it a name, don't you? Famous houses all have names, like Tara in *Gone With the Wind*. Maybe you'll come up with an idea. Wade doesn't even try," she added critically.

"How about calling it Our House?" he said, and smiled into the rearview mirror.

"Ha, ha," Ami returned. She shook her head at me. "Wade has about as much creativity as one of his elbow pipes or whatever they're called."

"Fittings, Ami, fittings. You should at least have some idea about the business that provides all this."

"Right," she said. "I'll take a class on it."

We went around the house to what looked like a definite add-on, an attached garage in the rear.

"I'm dropping you two off, Ami, and heading back to the company," Wade said.

"Couldn't you take some time off today?"

"I'll be back early. I promise."

"Promise? When Wade makes a promise, it's like the weather report. Twenty percent chance of rain," Ami said.

"Very funny. I will be home early," he stressed.

"You better. It's a special evening tonight," Ami warned him.

The rear door of the house opened, and a stout woman emerged, dressed in a light blue maid's uniform with white lace trim. She looked about sixty, sixty-five years old. Her hair was dark brown with gray strands throughout, cut very short. She wore no makeup, not even lipstick, which she could have used; her lips were almost as pale as her complexion. I noticed that her forearms were heavy, and her hands quite large for a woman's hand. She moved quickly to the trunk of the car. Wade had pushed the button that opened it automatically.

We stepped out.

"This is our housekeeper, Mrs. Cukor," Ami said. "She's been working for the Emersons ever since she came from Hungary, which is a long time ago."

Mrs. Cukor paused and turned to us.

"This is Celeste, Mrs. Cukor. She's coming to live with us, as you know."

"Hello," she said quickly, barely looking at me, and turned back to my suitcases.

"Wade used to call her Mrs. Cookie, didn't you, Wade?"

"When I was four," he said.

"Wade's father still calls her Mrs. Cookie," Ami told me.

"My father often acts like he's still four," Wade muttered.

"I never heard you tell him so," Ami teased.

Wade grimaced.

"I don't have to tell him. He knows it."

"I can carry that," I said when Mrs. Cukor took out the second suitcase.

She held them both in firm grips, gazed at me a moment, her dark eyes narrowing as if she thought I was out to take her job and was warning me off. Then she turned without speaking and walked toward the door. If they were heavy for her, she didn't reveal it. There was no strain in her shoulders.

"Mrs. Cukor never likes to seem incapable of doing anything," Ami said. "It's rubbed off on the Emersons because she's worked for them so long. Emersons are perfect in every way, in their bodies and their minds, right, Wade?"

"Right. So long, Ami," Wade sang. He leaned over to kiss her on the cheek, which she immediately fanned as though a fly had landed on her face. He turned to me. "Welcome to our nameless home, Celeste. I hope you'll have a good experience here," he said.

"Thank you," I told him, and he got back into the car.

"Come on," Ami said, taking my hand. "I have a big house to show you, and your room, and then we'll talk about your new wardrobe and everything or anything you want to talk about."

We started toward the door.

Wade backed out, waved, and drove off. The garage door began to come down.

It was like a curtain dropping on my past. For just a moment, a split second in fact, I thought I heard Noble call out to me, his voice shut off by the closing of the garage door. I stared at it and listened.

"Come on, silly. We have a lot to do," Ami urged. She tugged me, and I followed her into what seemed to me to be a storybook world, looking back only once, but fearfully, as though I would be turned into a pillar of salt.

4

A Level of Temptation

♊

Although I had never been in a mansion, I thought
again that Ami wasn't exaggerating when she catego-
rized her home as one in Mother Higgins's office. If
anything, she had been understating. The only compa-
rable place I had visited was a museum I had gone to
on a school trip. I had never seen doors so tall and ceil-
ings so high in someone's home. Two people could
live in a house this big and not see each other all day, I
thought.

From the garage, we stepped into an entryway that
took us past a pantry the size of the kitchen at the orphanage. I wondered, how could only two people need
so much? All of the shelves were stocked neatly with
cans and packaged goods. The shelves were so high
that a ladder on rollers was needed to reach the top.
Toward the rear was a walk-in freezer that I imagined
was normally found only in good-sized restaurants.

"It looks like enough food for a hotel," I said. "We

don't have as much back at the orphanage for all the girls and all the nuns."

Ami laughed, then shook her head and smirked.

"Wade likes to get things cheaper by buying them in bulk. We do have a cook who orders the food, Mrs. McAlister, and she's good at that and a wonderful chef, but Mrs. Cukor hovers over her so closely, she's threatening to quit. Of course, she's been threatening that every other month for as long as I've been here," Ami explained with a smile. "Those two are always complaining about each other, not that anyone pays much attention."

As if taking the cue from the sound of her name, Mrs. McAlister stepped out of the kitchen and into the hallway to greet us. Draped in an ankle-length white apron, she was wiping her hands on a dish towel. Looking behind her, I saw what appeared to be a very modern kitchen for a house this old. The appliances were all stainless steel, and the floor looked newly tiled in a pale yellow limestone.

All I could think when I saw Mrs. McAlister was, either she was too skinny to be a cook, or else she didn't like her own food. Our cook back at the orphanage, Mrs. Putnam, weighed at least two hundred pounds and was only five feet tall.

A good three inches taller than both Ami and me, Mrs. McAlister was thin, with long spidery arms and a long, narrow neck upon which her head rested like a weathercock, making jerky little motions to the right or left when she looked from Ami to me and back to Ami.

She wore netting over her dark gray hair, pinned so tightly around her head that it resembled a helmet. Under a wide forehead dotted with brown age spots, she had untrimmed dark brown eyebrows that nearly grew into each other. Because she was so thin, the features of her long face were hard and very unfeminine. Her nose came to such a point that it looked like it could be used to punch holes in cans, and the dark line between her narrow lips made it seem as if her mouth had been cut out with a razor. I thought she had terrible posture, turning her shoulders inward and making her chest and small bosom look concave.

"Oh, Mrs. McAlister. This is Celeste, our—" Ami paused and looked at me. "What should I call you? I'm not calling you daughter, and referring to you as an orphan is terrible. What is the word I want?" she asked me.

"Guest?" I offered with a shrug. I was half kidding, but she leaped at it.

"Yes, that's wonderful. Guest. We're looking after her until she reaches the age of eighteen. I'm sure Wade has explained."

"He has. I've already set the table for four tonight. Mr. Emerson himself is coming to dinner, seeing as you've brought home a permanent guest to live in his house," she said dryly. "He called me directly," she concluded, adding to her sense of importance. "Welcome," she said, nodding at me, and then she jerked her head toward Ami. "I'm putting up the beef filet for tonight with my small potatoes, the ones Mr. Emerson himself likes so much," she added.

"And something wonderful for dessert, I hope."

Mrs. McAlister tightened the corners of her mouth a bit and looked at me and then back to Ami.

"I thought perhaps my strawberry shortcake," she said.

"Doesn't that sound wonderful, Celeste?"

"Yes," I said.

"Mrs. Cukor said you would prefer that apple cinnamon cake, but I think it's what she would prefer for herself," Mrs. McAlister added, twisting the right corner of her mouth up so sharply I could see her pinkish gums.

Ami shrugged, threw me a conspiratorial glance, and then pulled me along.

"Did you hear the way she refers to Wade's father? Mr. Emerson himself? It's as if Wade isn't really Mr. Emerson too. And imagine Mrs. Cukor and her arguing over what to have for dessert. I sometimes wish the house was small enough for us to have just one maid who could cook," she told me.

If there was only one maid, she would be working so hard, she would drop in a week, I thought. Not only were the rooms very large, but the hallway was twice the width of the one at the orphanage. There were windows placed everywhere it was possible for natural light to come through, all of them the small-paned kind that took forever to clean. I knew. We had to clean them at Madam Annjill's orphanage, and if we missed a spot in one, she made us do all of them over as a lesson.

"Well, she does set a beautiful table," Ami reluctantly admitted when we stopped at the dining room, a room that looked like it was meant for royalty. The table wasn't longer than the one at the orphanage, but it was certainly wider, oval shaped with thick gilded pedestals. There was a matching buffet and an armoire with gilded trimming as well. The chairs were high-backed and decorated in what looked to be a cream silk fabric. There was a grand teardrop chandelier and two sets of brass candelabra on the table. Beneath it was an oval area rug with colors that matched the furniture, the curtains, and the walls.

"We have rugs in practically every room," Ami said.

"Basil, Wade's father, favors hardwood floors and hates carpeting. He permitted stone in the kitchen, but nowhere else. Wade had our bedroom floor carpeted, and for weeks that's all he and his father argued about. Imagine talking endlessly about the pros and cons of carpeting! I really didn't care what was on the floor. I don't vacuum it.

"I do like eating in this dining room, however. It makes me feel . . . special, like I'm eating in the White House or a castle. You'll feel the same way. You'll see," she said. "I want you to enjoy the good life, Celeste, just like me. I really do."

There were two settings on one side, one across from them, and one at the head of the table. The bay windows looked out on the gardens and fountains, just as Ami had described when we first approached the house. Whoever sat at the setting across from the two would have her back to the windows. I assumed that would be my setting.

"The floors look brand-new," I commented, noticing how they shone. "Were they just recently put in?"

"Oh, no. Once a month we bring a team of floor cleaners with machines in to do our wood floors," Ami continued. "It would be too much for Mrs. Cukor, especially at her age."

"How old is she?"

"We don't know for certain, but we estimate she's in her mid- to late seventies, even though she doesn't look it. You can't believe what she has on documents, but we know she's at least that old."

"Why doesn't she retire?" I asked as we continued down the hallway.

"To what? She has no family in America, and she won't return to Hungary. She hates the thought of a rest home. She calls them God's Waiting Rooms, no thank you. She always says she'll retire in the grave. And then she adds, maybe. Personally, I think she'll live forever. The truth is, I'm a little afraid of her at times. I think she was brought up by gypsies, and that's why she has no family. She's very superstitious, always muttering some chant or another, throwing salt over her shoulder, crossing herself. One of the funniest things she does is stop walking, back up, and then start again with a different foot. Ignore her as best you can," Ami advised. Then she leaned toward me to whisper, "I do believe both Wade and his father are a little afraid of her themselves."

I grimaced skeptically. How could grown men as wealthy and as influential as Ami had described them be afraid of an elderly maid?

"Our living room, or great room, I should call it," Ami declared, looking into a truly grand, ornate room with red satin drapes edged in gold, oversized sofas facing each other, and an oval ivory table in the center. There were lamps everywhere, a dark wood grand piano on the right, and walls of bookshelves stacked with leather-bound volumes. I saw a glass case filled with what looked to be expensive ceramic figurines. Ami saw what I was looking at.

"Those are Lladros," she said. "They come from Spain, and there are about twenty thousand dollars worth of them in there. Wade's mother used to collect them. That is about the only expensive thing Wade will buy. It's a way of keeping her memory alive or something. I'm not particularly fond of them. I'd rather spend money on clothes. He buys one and then pretends he's doing it for me, and for his sake, I let him pretend. That's what a marriage is, you know, little compromises, sacrifices. The trick is to make sure he does most of them," she added with a laugh. "Anyway, there's the living room."

As she had described, area rugs were scattered across the floor; they were all very expensive Persians, she said.

"You don't play piano, do you, by any chance?"

"No, but I've always wanted to," I said. The memory of piano music in the farmhouse was always strong.

"Well, I'll see about getting you lessons," she said.

"Really?"

"Yes, of course. It would be nice to really use this room instead of keeping it like some sort of shrine. Wade rarely spends any time in here, but he inspects it regularly, and God forbid there be a spot of dust, or something out of place. It's all the way his mother kept it. Even those old magazines in the magazine rack are the magazines she was reading at the time of her death. Maybe he thinks if he keeps it this way, she'll return."

"Maybe she will. Maybe she has," I said softly. Contact with the dead wasn't something I could just brush off completely.

Ami laughed.

"Talk like that will get you in the good graces of Mrs. Cukor. She takes her responsibility to keep the room spotless and perfect very seriously."

"It's a beautiful room," I said.

A second set of smaller sofas faced an enormous fieldstone fireplace, above which was a landscape with a bubbling brook. The colors were so vibrant, the water looked as if it would literally run over the frame. It brought back an image of the brook that ran near the farm.

"Yes, it is. The whole house is. Look at the elaborate molding work," she pointed out. "I'm not kidding.

A house like this one just isn't built anymore. No one takes all that care about construction. It was built when houses were still works of craftsmanship. At least, that's what Basil is always saying. Just ask him one question about the house, and he'll go on and on for hours. That's a warning," she added with a wink.

I recalled the molding in the farmhouse. That house was as intricate as this, I thought, just not as big or as ornate.

"Every piece of furniture in here is a work of art, imported from Spain or Italy or France, even that backgammon game that no one plays. Do you?"

I shook my head.

"I don't know anything about it."

"None of us do. Of course, Wade's mother did. The board is also exactly the way she left it right before she died. Wade's father bought all the art you see hanging. Except for the Lladros, Wade isn't much of a collector of fine things. I'll give Basil credit for that, but he doesn't buy things for their beauty as much as for their financial value. Everything has always been an investment first to him. He's very open about it, too. He isn't ashamed about his pursuit of wealth. I think he even thought of his children as an investment. Wade's been worth it to him, but Bethany—that's a bust, as far as Basil is concerned. He made her a very expensive wedding, of course, but all he's gotten back in return is disdain from both Bethany and her husband. He isn't attached at all to his grandchildren. He doesn't remember their birthdays. Mrs. Cukor reminds him, or he wouldn't get them a gift. When is your birthday?" she asked. "I forgot."

I told her, and she nodded.

"I'll give it to Mrs. Cukor, and we'll have a big

party. The woman doesn't forget anything, no matter how small. This is Wade's office now," she said, pausing at another grand doorway. "Although Basil uses it whenever he wants. Wade's always complaining how he stinks it up with cigar smoke. Occasionally Wade meets with the company business manager in there. Neither of them smoke. Wade doesn't have any vices except one."

"What is that?" I asked before I could hold myself back.

"Me," she replied, and laughed. "I'm kidding, of course. He has his vices, and I have mine, and we don't share them." She laughed again, but it was a drier, more thoughtful laugh.

What an odd thing to tell me, I thought.

She opened the office doors, and we stepped inside. Large windows with shutters rather than curtains looked out on the north side, where I could see the pool, cabana, gazebo, and tennis courts. A pair of grounds workers were pruning bushes and cutting grass.

"His father's personal things are still all locked in that safe—jewels and guns and money and who knows what else. Wade doesn't even known the combination," she said, nodding at a standing safe that looked like it came from a bank.

The furniture in the office wasn't any less impressive than the furniture in the living room. The centerpiece was the grand dark cherry-wood desk and the leather office chair. Everything on the desk looked neatly organized. There were bookcases here as well, computer equipment on separate tables, and another desk to the right and a fax machine. Behind the desk on the right were wooden file cabinets. The floor was slate with two area rugs. On the wall directly behind the desk was the picture of an attractive, elegantly dressed woman wearing a string of pearls. Dressed in an off-shoulder black gown, she was standing in what looked to be the front entrance of this house with a smile like the Mona Lisa's, a smile that fills you with questions.

The first question was obvious.

"Who is that?"

"That's Wade's mother when she was in her twenties. The stress and worry isn't written into her face yet."

"She was very pretty."

"Yes, but when a man has eyes that wander, a pretty wife makes almost no difference." She laughed. "Some men are just not meant to be in monogamous relationships. Of course, Basil always says he has so much to offer a woman, why waste it on only one? Typical remark from a male chauvinist. Sometimes I think men are born insecure from the moment the umbilical cord is cut, and they then have to spend the rest of their lives proving themselves bigger, smarter, better."

She held her gaze on the desk and chair as if someone was sitting there, and then she clapped her hands and turned to me.

"Why are we spending so much time on all this? Let's get right up to your bedroom. I can't wait for you to see it!"

We left the office and turned left to the gently curved stairway. It had dark wood steps and a beautiful mahogany balustrade with spindle inserts. As we approached the bottom steps, Mrs. Cukor appeared at the top. She stood there, looming over us. The sight of her, appearing as though out of thin air, stopped Ami instantly.

"Oh. Is everything ready, Mrs. Cukor?"

"All her things have been put away, and her bed's turned down," she replied.

"She unpacked my suitcases?" I asked.

"Of course," Ami said. "I told you. You're going to be spoiled here."

She started up.

"Wait," Mrs. Cukor cried, holding her hand out like a traffic policeman.

"What is it?" Ami asked.

"Let the girl go first," she said. "It's her first time coming up."

"Oh, Mrs. Cukor." Ami sighed and turned to me. "Her damn superstitions. Go on. Make her happy, or she'll end up sprinkling some sort of powder over the floor, and we'll never hear the end of it."

I smiled in confusion and then started up the stairs. All the while Mrs. Cukor fixed her eyes on me with great scrutiny. I had the sense that she wanted me to ascend the stairway first so she could concentrate on me. I didn't turn away. Instead, I met her gaze with my own. Suddenly, I saw her eyes widen and her eyebrows lift slightly as I drew closer. When I was very close, she stepped back quickly so I wouldn't brush against her. I heard her whisper something in her native language.

"Satisfied?" Ami asked her, following me up quickly.

Mrs. Cukor said nothing. She crossed herself and then hurried down the stairs.

"I've got to speak to Wade about her," Ami said, looking after her. "She's getting very odd in her old age, very odd. She's always talking to herself."

Maybe she's not as odd as you think, I thought. Maybe she could see through my eyes at the spiritual memories I kept locked within me.

"To your room!" Ami cried, and charged forward as if we were on an attack.

I hurried to catch up to her down the hallway, which was lit by a line of evenly spaced smaller chandeliers because there were no windows.

"Your room is directly across from Wade's and mine," she said, pausing.

All the bedrooms had eggshell white double doorways with gold moldings and brass fixtures, and all were as tall as the ones below, at least nine or ten feet.

"Ready?" Ami said, turning to me with her hands behind her on the doorknobs.

"Yes," I said, smiling.

"Ta-da!" she cried, and opened the doors.

Could the princess of any country sleep in a more grand and beautiful bedroom? I wondered. It made my room at the Prescotts' house look like a room in a bungalow. I had never slept in such an elaborate king-size canopy bed. It had white and pink bedding, the blanket turned down at a perfect folded angle. In front of the arched headboard, which had a pair of angels embossed on it, were more pillows than I had ever seen on a single bed. There was a white netting down the sides of the bed, which was set on a very large, fluffy mauve rug. And there were soft-looking fur-lined slippers as well.

The windows she had pointed out to me when we first drove up to the house were draped in sheer white curtains with sun-blocking shades to pull down. To the right was a beautiful antique vanity table with a gilded oval mirror, on the frame of which were also embossed angels. I saw new brushes and combs and a hair drier.

I simply stood gaping. It was as if I was afraid that stepping forward would make it all disappear.

"Well?" Ami asked.

"It's . . . beautiful, the most beautiful bedroom I've ever seen."

She laughed.

"I think I enjoy the look on your face more than anything." She ran her hand over the vanity table. "I didn't get you any makeup yet. We'll do that together, and we'll get you perfume and body talcum powders, all the things you've probably never had," Ami said.

I was speechless, caught in a storm of promises and luxuries.

"I want you to be as equipped out there as I am," she continued. "That way, we will be more like sisters."

Sisters? She had said that in Mother Higgins's office, too, but something about the way she said it this time caught my attention. I looked at her, at the way she was smiling at me. Was that what she really wanted? I wondered. Was that why she was doing all this? Where were her close friends, her own surrogate sisters? She hadn't mentioned anyone to me, or anything she did with other young women.

"Your clothes look pathetic in this walk-in closet," she said when she opened the door. They did, because there was so much empty space, so many empty hangers. "We'll correct that right away. I expect to take you to the finest restaurants, and maybe we'll attend some of these charity functions I keep getting invited to. Usually they're boring and full of phonies, but I think you and I can have fun, don't you?"

"Yes," I said, even though the way she said, "You and I can have fun," made it sound like far more than just attending a charity event. I tried to look excited and happy about anything she suggested. At this moment I wanted to please her every way I could.

"This is your private phone line," she said, lifting

the pink phone receiver on the matching bedside table. "There's another phone on your vanity table," she pointed out. "I had them installed just yesterday. The unlisted number is five five five, four two four two. Be very select about whom you give the number, especially selective about the boys you meet at school. There are many vipers in the garden," she warned.

I raised my eyebrows.

"Oh, you're wondering how I went ahead and set all this up for you, how I knew you'd agree to come, or how I knew it would all work out? It didn't matter," she said, answering her own question. "I was determined, and when I'm determined, I usually get what I want. Again, Wade thinks that's because I'm spoiled, and again, he's right." She laughed and then opened a cabinet on a wall across from the bed. "Your television and sound system, Your Majesty," she said. "I just love lying in bed and watching television, don't you?"

I shrugged. I had never done it. Even the Prescotts hadn't put a television set in my room for me. What could I say?

"Oh, that's right. You probably never had a television set where you slept. Well, you're going to have a lot of things you've never had before," she said, almost like a threat.

She walked to the bathroom door and opened it, stepping back, a wide, almost clownish smile on her face. I approached slowly and looked. Beside the marble tub there was a separate, tiled shower stall, mirrors everywhere, a bidet as well as a toilet, and another vanity table. The floor was all marble tile. A terrycloth robe hung on the wall beside it, and there was another pair of slippers under it.

"I had this bathroom redone just a month ago," she said. "Well? Do you like it?"

Did I like it? What could I say? For years I had been sharing a bathroom with a half dozen other girls. We actually had to schedule our showers and baths.

"It's—"

"Fantastic?"

"Yes."

"Good. Make a big deal of it at dinner. Wade's such a tightwad. I call him a Tight Wade for fun. Nothing is ever necessary, according to him. He'll argue with someone over a dollar and tells me constantly that just because we're wealthy doesn't mean we have to be stupid about spending money. Well, I like being stupid when it comes to spending money. I dream sometimes of casting it about like chicken feed in malls. It was never important to me, and I've never lived on a budget. You should see the way Wade keeps our books. I think he knows exactly how much each fixture costs to run, each light. He's always going around the house turning off lights, but he better not think he can come in here and invade your privacy," she warned.

"And don't think you have to eat every morsel on your plate tonight, or any time. I know how they made a big deal of waste at your orphanage, but this isn't an orphanage. Those days are gone for good for you. Wade will come up with silly old expressions like Waste not, want not. And don't let Mrs. McAlister intimidate you with her glaring looks, either. If something doesn't taste right, spit it out on the plate. I do. Sometimes," she confessed, "I do it even if it does taste good, just to keep her in her place or to annoy Wade.

"Don't misunderstand me. I love him, but I also love teasing him. He's so . . . teasable. Is there a word like that?"

"I don't think so," I said.

"I don't care. We can make up our own words here if we like. In fact, there is nothing we can't do if we feel like doing it. Don't be shy. Ask for anything you want or need. I do, and as I promised, we're going to be like sisters," she emphasized. "Do you have to go to the bathroom or anything?"

"I suppose," I said. "Yes."

"Well, go do your business and then come to my bedroom immediately. We don't have time to go shopping before tonight's special dinner, but I have some things that will most definitely fit you. I'll start sorting them out and pick out a couple I think would work," she said. "Welcome to your new home," she added, and hugged me quickly before hurrying out. I stood looking after her, gaped about at everything for a moment in disbelief, and then went to the bathroom.

Afterward I followed her to the master bedroom. It was twice as large as mine, with a separate sitting area and another large-screen television set. The bed looked even bigger than king-size. It was draped in a gold canopy with red silk bedding. There was a large, more decorative chandelier hanging in front of it. The walls were done in a technique she called faux paint. It made them looked like pink-colored leather.

Her vanity table extended almost the length of the wall on the right, with mirrors all the way. There were two master bathrooms, a his and a hers. She laughed and told me Wade kept his much neater and cleaner than she kept hers.

"He's very prissy about his things," she explained, and opened his walk-in closet to show me how he had all his clothes arranged by colors and styles. "You see how all of his shoes have a perfect shine as well," she pointed out. "He'd rather have heels and soles redone than buy new ones. I have to shame him into going shopping for himself. I ridicule his styles and tell him he's so out of date he'll make a bad impression on business associates. That works most of the time. You'll hear him complain about me and tell you he has to be thrifty about his own things because I'm not about mine. Don't believe a word of it. We're very, very rich," she declared, making it sound more like a condition than an achievement.

"You see our bed," she continued. "I had it made special. There isn't another like it anywhere, and it cost five times what something close to it would cost in a store. Wade has actually figured out how much it costs us per sleep. I think it's something like five dollars a night for fifty years. He can be so ridiculous when it comes to money, but I love him," she added, almost as though she had promised never to say anything negative about him without adding that at the end.

"I have everything sorted out," she said, taking me to her walk-in closet. It was larger and longer than Wade's, but it looked like one more dress or even a skirt would cause it to explode.

She held out two dresses, one black and one a kelly green.

"Try them on," she instructed, and stepped back. "You're not shy, are you? I'll step out if you are."

"No," I said. "Where I've been, you lose that pretty quickly if you've ever had it."

"Oh, of course. You poor, poor dear. I'm so happy we can do this for you. No one should have to go through what you've been through," she said.

She stepped forward and toyed with my hair for a moment.

"We're going to my beauty parlor immediately tomorrow. You need conditioning and then some styling. Your forehead is a little low and narrow, and your face broadens at the jaw just like mine. You need to give the impression of a wider forehead and eye area. More bounce in your bangs, or maybe a longer, collar-length bob would do it. What do you think of my hair-style?" she asked, turning to show me the rear and sides.

"It's nice."

"Yes, it is. It works. We'll have my personal stylist, Dawn, do yours. I get the best people to work on me, and so will you. Well, go on, silly. Try the dresses."

She stepped back again. I began to undress. I wasn't lying about not having the luxury of modesty while living most of my life in orphanages. Privacy was rare. As soon as a girl got her first period, the whole popula-tion who could understand what it meant knew. We showered and even went to the bathroom in front of each other.

And yet there was something about the way Ami was looking at me as I took off my clothing that made me a little nervous. I could feel her eyes examining my body.

"Oh, you don't wear a bra with these dresses," she told me. "It's all right," she added when I hesitated. "I haven't worn a bra with any dress for years."

I reached back to undo my bra, and she immediately moved forward to help. Still a little hesitant, I slipped my bra off slowly.

"You have wonderful, perky breasts," she said. "Just like me. That black dress is going to look very sexy on you. Any man who looks at you will feel his eyes pop-ping. I love that feeling, that power over the so-called stronger sex. The truth is, we can lead them along like puppies on a leash."

I held the dress up before me. The slinky halter gown had a laced-up front and double-sided ankle-length slit skirt. I had never worn anything remotely like it.

"Go on, try it," she said. "I have matching thongs for it, too."

It fit me snugly, but it seemed to me that half my bosom was revealed. Was that proper, what she wanted me to look like for my first dinner here with her husband and father-in-law?

"Oh, you look great in it."

"But is this okay for a family dinner?" I asked.

"Of course it is." She smiled. "Wade's father, Basil, loves to see women in sexy clothing. But if you're uncomfortable, try on this one," she said, holding up the slinky green tube dress with rhinestone detailing.

It looked like almost nothing to me. How could it be any different?

"I have thongs to match this one, too. Go on, try it on," she urged.

I slipped out of the black dress and then put on the tube. It was even tighter. Without a bra covering them, my nipples were practically popping through the material. It made me very self-conscious. She sensed it immediately.

"You have a beautiful figure, Celeste. Don't be afraid to show it. As they say, if you have it, flaunt it. I do.

"So, which one do you want to wear tonight?" she asked, stepping back and waiting as though my answer would determine the direction the rest of my life would take.

I looked at the first dress and then looked up at the clothes on the racks. Wasn't there anything else, anything less revealing?

"Those are my two favorite," she said, seeing where my gaze had gone.

Not wanting to hurt or disappoint her, I decided on the first.

"Good. I would have made the same choice," she told me. "Now you can go and rest up, shower, and fix your hair the best you can. We'll have dinner at seven tonight. I like to rest up, too, and then give myself a facial. I'll show you all that later, but you've got to walk before you run," she said, walking me to her bedroom door. "Just call down if you need anything. You dial ten, and Mrs. Cukor's phone rings."

Call for what I need? Have servants cater to me? This was more like a grand hotel than a home, and considering where I had just come from, it was all still more like a dream.

"Thank you," I said.

She smiled, hugged me, and then stepped back into her room and closed the door.

For a long moment I just stood there in the hallway, gazing at the chandeliers, the paintings on the walls, the glimmering wood floors. It was impossible not to be dazed by all the opulence rained upon me so quickly. I was thrilled, excited, and happy, but memories of my first foster home returned. I had such fears then, fears that I would lose myself, my identity, my family. I had such guilt over every little luxury I enjoyed. Every pleasure was a small betrayal in my child's mind. And the Prescotts were paupers compared to the Emersons.

I knew what Noble would say. He would say, "Celeste, the devil has decided to raise the level of temptation until he has you where he wants you."

I could feel that same guilt raining itself down upon me, each drop another tiny sting of conscience, trying to get me to turn away from all this, to reject it.

I don't care, I thought defiantly. I deserve this. I've

suffered enough, and I want it all. Why shouldn't I? Besides, it has to be my destiny. It has to be something meant to happen.

I knew no matter what I said or believed, if Noble were here, he would not approve. He was afraid of anything that could make me forget my past, forget the farm and what waited for me back there. However, I was sure that if he was trying to come chastise me, he was finding it more impossible than ever. The lights were too bright in this house. Shadows could hide nothing.

At least, that was what I hoped.

5

Little Lies

♊

Next to the television set was a cabinet in which had been placed a number of music CDs. Another drawer had a video collection as well. There wasn't one I had seen, even on television. From the titles and the pictures on the covers as well as the blurbs about each, it was easy to see every one of them was about romance.

I chose a CD and played it while I continued to explore the room and the view from my windows. Having so much private space was as luxurious to me as soaking in a warm bubble bath. I couldn't stop walking around and around, into the bathroom and out, back to the closet to admire the size of it, and then to bounce on my bed and let myself fall back on the fluffy pillows as if I was falling from an airplane and floating.

I was lying there staring up at the ceiling and enjoying my music when I heard a knock on my door. Before I could get to the door to respond, Ami burst into the room. She was in a pink silk robe, her hair wrapped in a towel. Her face was flush from her skin treatment, and she was carrying a small red leather pouch under her arm like a football player carries a football.

"I decided you should look the best for your first formal dinner here. For now, here are some of my favorite cosmetics," she said.

She placed the pouch on the vanity table and opened it. I stepped up beside her.

"We have similar complexions, and all this always looks great on me," she said. I wasn't sure that was true, but I wasn't going to disagree. "What do you know about makeup? I noticed right off that you don't use any."

"No," I said, laughing. "We weren't even permitted to wear lipstick at school. Mother Higgins didn't approve."

"Not even lipstick! That's so ridiculous. What did she think would happen if you did? Sin would follow? Forget about it." She shook her head hard as if she had to get rid of a horrible, painful thought. "Forget about all of it," she said quickly. "Pretend your past is written on one of those magic toy pads where you lift the sheet and everything disappears so you can start anew.

"Make believe that you've always lived here; we've always been together. There was no yesterday. There is only tomorrow, and tomorrow is always more important than today anyway."

She looked at her watch.

"Okay, we have time for a short lesson. We'll do eyes tonight. Sit," she said, pulling out the chair at the vanity table.

I did so, and she came around behind me and looked at me in the mirror. She tilted her head as she thought and then nodded at a decision she had made.

"We need to make your eyes appear larger, just like I have to do with mine. Keep one eye open while I do the other so you can see how it works and do it yourself afterward, okay?"

"Sure," I said, even though I didn't think we had the same shape and size eyes, just like I didn't think we had the exact same complexion. However, I was intrigued with the whole idea of making up my face. Not only weren't we permitted to wear lipstick at school, I had never owned a tube of one or ever borrowed anyone else's to put on after school.

She reached into the bag and produced a tin of eye shadow. Using the brush on the table, she dipped it into the tin and then brought the brush to my eye.

"From the lash line to the brow," she said, and did it.

She opened another tin and took up another brush.

"We'll use a medium-tone color for the crease beneath the brow," she said, and blended it in. Then she reached for an eye pencil. "Work from the outer corner to the inner corner and stay close to your lashes. Then line the bottom lid from the outer corner only about one-third of the way, see?" she asked as she demonstrated it all.

"Yes."

"Okay," she said, and took up the eye-shadow brush again. "Let's add another layer of light eye shadow from the lash line to the brow bone, blending like so." After that she picked up a cotton swab. "Be sure to get rid of any excess makeup and dust away any loose powder. I just hate it when those old ladies come with makeup dripping all down their cheeks. They look like their faces are coming apart right before our eyes, shedding like snakes or something.

"Now," she said, returning to the pouch, "we just apply the mascara. Pull the wand straight up like this, see? Don't pull it out. Then lightly do the bottom lashes. Voila!" she cried, stepping back after she had done it. "Look at the difference between your made-up eye and the other."

I nodded, impressed.

She stepped up and put her arms around my shoulders, bringing her cheek next to mine as she spoke to me through the mirror.

"There are lots of little tricks I'm going to teach you, Celeste. It will be like just doing it for the first time again for me. Your face will be my face, and vice versa." She stepped back. "Go on, do your other eye yourself. I'll watch," she said, folding her arms.

I did it, following the steps she had demonstrated. When I was finished, she clapped.

"That was perfect, and the first time, too. You are a fast learner."

It's not brain surgery, I thought, but didn't say it.

"The next time we'll work on how to make your lips look fuller. We'll experiment with different shades. We'll put on different eyes. We'll do all of it! I can show you how to put makeup on so your whole face is sexier. Good girls can be devilish, too," she said, laughing.

She returned to her small leather pouch.

"For now, try this lipstick. It's subtle," she said, removing the top. It didn't look subtle to me. "Oh, wait," she said, reaching into the bag again. "Put on this lip gloss first. It will keep your lips from looking dried out. Go on," she said when I hesitated. I did it and then applied the lipstick. "It does look like you're doing it for the first time," she said, snatching the tube from my hand. "Don't press so hard."

She took a tissue and wiped the corner of my mouth. Then she looked at me and nodded.

"You're a perfect candidate for improvement," she said, which raised my eyebrows. "Anyone can use improvement, Celeste. Even me," she said with a laugh. "One more thing." She reached into the bag. "Use this cologne. Basil loves it on me. Okay, get dressed. We'll go down to dinner together, but we'll go down at least ten minutes late. Never, ever be on time for anything that involves men," she advised. "The worst thing you can do is let a man take you for granted. And here's a secret my own mother taught me."

She leaned toward me to whisper, as if the room was bugged and it really was a big secret. I held my breath in anticipation.

"Always make a big deal over the smallest things. If your boyfriend forgets to open the door for you or bring out your chair at the dinner table or walks ahead of you, pounce on him as if he committed murder."

She pulled back and smiled.

"He'll think to himself, If she makes so much of that, what would she do if I did something significant? It's always good to keep them retreating."

"It sounds like a war, not a romance," I said before I could stop myself.

She stopped smiling, thought a moment, and then her smile returned like a wave of glee, undulating down from her temples, around her eyes, and over her lips.

"Well, that's exactly what it is, Celeste, a war. Haven't you ever heard that expression, All's fair in love and war?"

"Yes," I said, but I thought to myself that if there were so many little battles going on between a husband and a wife in their home, what made it a family? What made it warm and wonderful? What kind of a garden did it provide for love to flourish and grow stronger? I often thought of places and people in terms of a garden. In the world Ami was describing, the children would be growing in turmoil.

"Don't look so pensive and serious, Celeste. Men hate that. You know why?" she asked. I shook my head. "Because they're afraid you're smarter, and you can see through them. As I told you, they are very insecure. You'll discover quickly that I'm right, I'm sure. You'll see for yourself that Wade's father isn't really as confident as he makes himself out to be. Selfish, yes, but secure, no. As I said," she repeated, as though it was the most important lesson of life, "that's why he is such a womanizer. He has to prove himself to himself all the time. Men," she said, and shook her head. "They never grow up.

"Not that I want us to behave like two mature and responsible women all the time. Heaven forbid the thought." She looked at her watch. "I'll start dressing. Don't rush, but if you're getting antsy, come to my room. Wade's already dressed and downstairs in the office with his father, discussing boring business things. Not that you'll see much difference in what he wears.

"Oh, this is so wonderful," she said, gazing about the room and then at me. "I have someone I can whisper secrets to in my own home. There is nothing as sad as a secret dying on the vine, wilting away unspoken. I read that in a romance novel once and never forgot it."

She paused, pressed her hand to her heart, and looked up as if she was on a stage.

"She was filled with unspoken secrets, dead and gone, shaking about like ashes in the chambers of her lonely heart," she recited, laughed, and hurried out.

It was as if I had shut a window and stopped the wind from blowing everything around the room.

Less than a minute passed, however, before she was back.

"I realized you definitely need some jewelry. Here," she said. "Let's get this necklace on you, and you can have one of my dress watches." Before I could say anything, she looped the string of pearls over my head and fastened them. She held her hands over them for a moment and sighed.

"We'll be such a hit," she declared, and left again.

I stood there staring at the door, holding my breath and waiting to see if there was something more she had forgotten, but this time she didn't return. After I put on the dress she had chosen for me and the matching thongs, fixed my hair, and put on the beautiful dress watch, I stood before the full-length mirror and gazed at myself. With the makeup, the jewelry, and the clothes, it was truly as though I were looking at a different person.

And then suddenly, I thought I saw Noble standing just behind me. He looked devastated, about to cry. He didn't look any different, any older, but obviously I looked very different to him.

"Noble?"

I spun around, but the moment I did so, he was gone. Was he there, or had I imagined it? I had no doubts about what Dr. Sackett would say. "You're just unsure of yourself and a little nervous and frightened. Get stronger. Close your eyes and get stronger."

"Yes," I whispered. "I will."

Before I could think any more about it, my door opened, and Ami burst in once more. She was wearing a buttercup yellow dress with a pair of see-through shoes. She turned to show me the low-cut back.

"I just bought this," she said. "It's a charmeuse gown with embroidered mesh and, as you see, a sheer chiffon kick pleat in the back. Makes it sexier, don't you think? Look," she said, raising her right foot, "I'm wearing Cinderella's glass slipper. Only I'm not going to turn into a poor young woman at twelve," she added. "Well?" She spun and looked at me. "What do you think?"

"It's beautiful, Ami. What's charmeuse mean?"

"It just means a see through shiny fabric. Oh, I have so much to teach you, but it will be so much fun for me. You look beautiful, too. Come on. We're properly late," she said, hooking her arm through mine.

We went to the stairway, where she stopped, corrected her posture, and then started us down. I heard the sound of a man's laughter reverberate down the hallway below.

"Basil must've told Wade one of his off-color jokes. Wade doesn't laugh at them, so Basil always laughs loudly himself to make up for it," Ami explained.

As we approached the bottom of the stairway, Wade and his father appeared in the hallway, coming out of the den-office. Basil looked a good two inches or so taller. He obviously had dyed his hair. There wasn't a gray strand in the dark brown, which was styled more for a much younger man. He was handsome, with a firm mouth, hazel eyes, and a nearly perfect nose. However, there was nothing pretty-boy about him. The lines in his face were what people called character lines. I thought he looked like an older movie star.

He had twice the shoulders Wade had, and a thicker neck. His dark blue sports jacket and slacks looked tailored to his athletic body. He wore a matching blue tie and black shoes. I saw the diamonds twinkling on his gold watch. He stared up at us with a slight wry smile on his lips.

"Well, now, who is this budding beauty next to our own princess?" he asked.

"This is Celeste," Ami said. "Celeste, meet my father-in-law, Basil Emerson."

"Hello," I said.

He widened his smile and stepped forward, reaching out to take my hand to guide me down the remaining steps. Then he turned to Wade.

"You made her sound like some poor, sad-faced, lost orphan girl."

Wade's face filled with blood so fast, it looked as if the top of his head might lift off. "I did not," he protested.

"Ami, you're looking as ravishing as usual," Basil said, ignoring his son. "What a pair of beauties. Much too much for Wade to handle by himself. If I were married to you, Ami, you'd have a couple of kids crawling all over this place for sure by now."

He glanced at Wade and then turned back to us.

"I might just move back into the house to make sure these women are treated as they should be treated," he added, and laughed. Wade dropped his eyes quickly to hide his embarrassment.

"Oh, Basil," Ami cried, "you're such a flirt."

"I hope I'm more than that. Teenage boys flirt. Real men seduce," he added with another laugh.

Wade turned away.

"Ladies," Basil said, holding his arms up and out. "May I escort you to dinner?"

Ami took his left arm, and I took his right. Then he glanced at Wade and spoke over his shoulder.

"Cover the rear and watch how it's done," he told him as we started for the dinning room.

Ami was beaming.

"My, you both smell delightful," Basil said, bringing his nose close to my cheek. "I feel like I'm drowning in a beautiful lake reeking of female aromas. Who will save me?"

"Not us," Ami replied, and he laughed as we entered the dining room.

As it turned out, Wade was the one made to sit in the chair with his back to the windows. Ami and I sat across from him, and Basil Emerson sat at the head of the table. Mrs. Cukor served the dinner, with Mrs. McAlister looking in from time to time. I gathered that she did this only when Basil Emerson came to dinner. I noticed that whenever Mrs. Cukor brought something in, she avoided looking at me as much as she could.

"So now," Basil Emerson said, "tell us all about yourself, Celeste. How long have you been in an orphanage?"

"About eleven years, with a short break when I went to live with two elderly people."

"Eleven years! I bet if they had dressed you like Ami has, you would have gotten adopted real fast," he said, and laughed. "Hell, I would have adopted you." He turned to Wade and said, "Sad-faced, poor orphan girl?"

"I didn't say that, Dad," Wade countered. "Stop saying I said that."

"Well, what did you say?" Basil snapped back. He was drinking his wine quickly and had apparently already had a few drinks in his office-den with Wade.

"I merely said she was unfortunate."

"Unfortunate." He turned to Ami, who smiled and nodded.

"That's true, Basil. She was unfortunate," she said, "but she isn't anymore."

"I'll drink to that," Basil said, lifting his glass.

"You'll drink to anything," Wade muttered.

Basil smirked and then looked at me.

"Hey," he said, "let the kid have some wine. She looks old enough."

"We're supposed to be setting a good example for her," Wade complained.

"Well, that's what we're doing." Basil laughed. "We're showing her how to dine properly, right, Ami?"

"Yes, we are," she sang.

"Mrs. Cookie, another wineglass, please," Basil ordered. She stepped into the room, took another wineglass out of the cabinet, and put it down in front of me so hard, I thought it would shatter.

"You drank wine at her age, didn't you, Mrs. Cookie?"

"I drank a lot more than wine at her age," she replied.

Basil and Ami both roared with laughter. I looked up at Mrs. Cukor. She stared a moment and then walked back into the kitchen.

Wade shook his head and then dropped his eyes to the table and concentrated on eating his salad in silence. There is a war going on in this home, I thought. The bullets are only words, perhaps, and the only thing wounded might be pride, but nevertheless there was tension all around me, tension between Mrs. McAlister and Mrs. Cukor, tension between Wade and his father, even some tension between Wade and Ami, and now something unspoken between Mrs. Cukor and me, something perhaps only I would notice. In the midst of all this Ami frolicked about as if nothing mattered but her own happiness, and nothing could disturb or prevent it. Was she someone to admire or to pity? I wondered.

Basil continued to dominate the conversation at dinner. Perhaps because of me, he told story after story about his own teenage days.

"I was never much of a student. Fact is, I never got my high school diploma," he said, making it sound like an accomplishment. "The real school is out there anyway," he bellowed, waving at the window. He had finished off an entire bottle of red wine himself and was working on a second bottle. Ami was flushed from the two glasses she had drunk. I had barely drunk half of mine, and Wade had one glass and then stopped drinking wine altogether.

"Dad, please," Wade said softly.

"What, please? What, am I saying something that ain't true? I put you through college and got you all the fine clothes you wore and your car. Not too shabby for someone who didn't graduate high school. Don't you forget it," he warned, his thick right thumb up and his long, thick right forefinger pointed at Wade like a pistol.

"No one is saying anything bad about you. It's different today. Harder for young people to get those opportunities without a good education."

"Oh, right. Young people today. Poor unfortunate young people."

He muttered something under his breath and went back to his food.

Wade looked up at me with apology in his eyes. I smiled, but he looked away quickly, afraid his father might catch our exchange.

Mrs. Cukor brought out the strawberry shortcake as if she was carrying poison to the table. She put it down as hard as she had put down my wineglass and then brought in the coffee. I thought it was delicious, and apparently so did Wade and his father. Ami didn't eat any, I noticed.

In fact, she ate sparingly the whole time, leaving food on her plate. I wondered if she was doing it delib-

erately, as she had told me she did sometimes. I
couldn't help but eat everything given to me. The food
was wonderful, and I finally drank my wine and had a
second glass. Was I being a pig?

"You don't want to ever finish all the food on your
plate," she whispered afterward. "Even if you're taken
to an expensive restaurant. Only men finish everything.
Some because they're paying for it and would eat saw-
dust if they paid for it."

We all went into the living room, where Basil had an
after-dinner drink, and then another. He made speeches
about business today, politics, the school of hard
knocks, and how easy we all had it compared to what he
had to go through. Wade sat quietly listening, while Ami
fidgeted. It was apparent that Basil was just talking and
wasn't even aware if anyone was listening or not. Finally Ami suggested she and I be excused; I had experienced such a dramatic day, I was surely exhausted.

I told Basil I was happy to have met him. He looked
confused for a moment and then smiled and gave me a
kiss on the cheek, a little too close to my lips, I
thought. He kissed Ami good night as well and then
turned back to Wade to continue his lecture. I looked at
Wade as we left the room and felt sorry for him, a
trapped audience.

"I hate it when Basil gets that way," Ami said. "I
couldn't wait to get out of there."

I had started for the stairway when she seized my
arm.

"No, no, silly. We're not really going to go to bed
this early. I just used that as an excuse. Come on," she
said. "We're not wasting all the work we did to look
this good on a dinner with the Emerson men."

"What?"

I didn't understand, but I let her pull me along,

through the hallway, past the kitchen, to the door to the garage. She opened that door and told me to get into her red Jaguar sports car.

"Where are we going?"

"To burn some of that candle on both ends," she said, laughing.

I got into the car, and she backed it out and drove quickly away from the house.

"What about Wade?" I asked.

"What about him? He'll have to help Basil to bed as usual, and then he'll go down to his office and work on his books until all hours of the morning," she explained.

"Won't he be upset that we've left?" I asked.

She looked at me without speaking and then turned back to the road.

"No," she said finally. "Wade won't be a bit upset."

I didn't want to ask, Why not? How much of their personal lives should be my business the first day I moved in with them? I thought.

"Where are we going?"

"There is this really nice hotel only five miles away. They have a great lounge, a talented piano player. Don't worry. You look old enough, and I know the manager anyway. We won't have any trouble. How many times have you used a fake ID?" she asked, her eyes twinkling in expectation.

"None," I said.

"None? C'mon, Celeste. We're going to be like sisters. You don't have to worry about telling me anything, remember?"

"I'm telling you the truth. I went to a party once where they had whiskey and beer, but I didn't drink any."

She raised her eyebrows.

"I thought girls who lived in orphanages were a lot looser than that."

"They have a lot of rules, and I didn't want to disappoint Mother Higgins. She's always been very kind to me," I said.

She looked at me askance again, and then she smiled.

"You just haven't had the opportunity for fun yet. Now you will," she vowed.

Somehow, it sounded more like a threat.

We rode on. She turned up the radio and laughed.

"Yes, my Celestial one, an opportunity for fun."

The hotel she took us to was called the Stone House. It wasn't very big, and it actually looked more like a motel to me because of the way the rooms were spread out from either end of the main building. The main building had a fieldstone facing, an overhang under which we drove to the valet to park the car, and two large glass doors that opened to a tiled lobby. The walls inside the lobby were also faced in fieldstone, or perhaps imitation stone. I wasn't sure. There was lots of dark wood, beams and paneling. The reception desk was on the right, and behind it was a large aquarium filled with beautiful colored fish. The woman behind the counter recognized Ami immediately and smiled.

"Good evening, Mrs. Emerson," she said.

She looked to be about fifty, with very poor hair coloring that made her hair look too orange instead of blond.

"Good evening, Mrs. Stone," Ami said.

Mrs. Stone stared at her a moment and then smiled.

"Oh, Mrs. Emerson. I didn't recognize you for a moment. You've done something new with your hair, the color."

"Just a touch," Ami said, and I looked at her. What change had she made? Had she made it more auburn? More like mine? "Meet Celeste. She's come to live with us a while."

"Hello, there," Mrs. Stone said. "Are you from a foreign country, an exchange student?"

"She's not from a foreign country, but from the way she's been living, she might as well have been," Ami kidded. Mrs. Stone looked confused.

I said hello, and then Ami turned me toward the entrance to the bar and restaurant. We could hear the music. The piano player was singing what I recognized to be an Elton John song.

"She and her husband own the place. That's why it's called the Stone House, but people kid about it and say it's because everyone who comes here gets stoned," Ami told me.

Unlike the owner, the maître d' was able to recognize Ami, but made a comment about her hair as well.

"I hope it's flattering," she told him, and he quickly said it was.

"We'll just go to the bar tonight, Ray," she told him. He fixed his eyes on me suspiciously. "Don't worry. Everything is copacetic," she added

He nodded, but his smile indicated he didn't believe her.

"I spend too much money here for anyone to give us any trouble," she whispered.

At the bar she ordered herself something called a Cosmopolitan and then looked at me and told the bartender to make it two.

"You'll like it. It sort of sneaks up on you. I hate those overpowering drinks. Don't look so nervous," she told me.

"I can't help it. I've never sat at a bar before."

"You really are so much of a virgin," she remarked, as if she hadn't believed the things I had told her about myself. "I think the first time I sat at a bar I was fourteen. It was at a dump, of course, but we were all very excited and drank some cheap gin that made us all sick. But it was fun," she added.

How could that be fun? I wondered.

The bar wasn't crowded, but two men at the far corner had been watching us from the moment we entered. Ami saw that, too, and to my surprise, she smiled at them. It was like putting up a welcome sign. They were off their stools and around the bar instantly. Neither was very good-looking, I thought. One looked like he cut his dirty blond hair himself. It was stringy and uneven. Although both wore sport jackets, they looked like they'd slept on them first.

"Hi," the taller one with dark brown hair said. "You guys just arrive?"

"Do we look like guys?" Ami immediately teased. The other one laughed through his nose and elbowed his friend.

"Hardly," he said.

The bartender brought our drinks.

"Fancy drink," the shorter man said.

"Yes, but we're used to fancy things," Ami told him. She sipped her drink and kept her eyes on him. I could see how it excited him. "We did just arrive," Ami continued. "We're on our way to Grandma's house. I hope you're not wolves. Remember Little Red Riding Hood?"

They laughed.

"Naw. We're more like tigers," the taller man said. "What's your names?"

"I'm Laurie, and this is my sister Virginia. I take it you two are local fellas."

"Oh, no. We're passing through ourselves."

"And where are you heading?" Ami asked.

I kept my eyes down and fingered the glass containing the Cosmopolitan.

"Paterson, New Jersey. We got new jobs in a auto parts factory there."

"Oh, how exciting," Ami said. She looked at me and winked. "I just love hearing about auto parts, don't you, Virginia?"

I didn't say anything.

"Care to dance?" the taller man asked Ami.

She looked at the piano player, who was watching us as he played without singing.

"A little too slow for me," Ami said.

"Oh, you're the fast type, huh?"

"I'm not a type," Ami said. "I'm indescribable," she added.

Both men laughed.

"Can we buy you another drink?" the shorter one said.

"We haven't finished this one yet."

"After that," he said, nodding.

"We only have one drink a night," Ami said. "We like to keep our wits about us."

"That's a waste," the taller man said.

"No, you have it backward. We don't get wasted," she told him, and they laughed again.

Why was she teasing them, flirting with them?

"Mind if we sit next to you? I'm Steve Toomer, and this is my friend, Gerry Bracken."

Ami looked at me and then turned to them and said, "Well, we don't mind." He started to sit on the stool and then froze when Ami added, "But our husbands might. They'll be in soon, and you know how men can get jealous."

"Oh, you're married," Steve said, his voice dripping with disappointment.

Ami flashed her wedding and engagement rings. I didn't see how it was possible for them not to have noticed anyway, but I realized she might have been keeping it out of sight just so she could tease them.

"Happily," she said.

"What about you, Virginia?" Gerry asked me. "Where's your ring?"

"She's allergic to gold. Makes her finger swell," Ami said.

The two of them looked at us and then at each other. Steve's face turned sour, his eyes like dark darts.

"You're going to get in trouble one of these days, fooling like this," Steve warned. "Husbands or no."

"Life's more exciting when you live in the danger zone," Ami told him.

He grunted, looked at his partner, and then nodded toward their corner of the bar.

We watched them retreat, Steve holding his shoulders up as if he wanted to keep a cold wind from going down his back.

"Why did you do that? They got very angry."

"I like to test the waters. See if I still have what it takes," Ami told me. "Besides, I wanted to show you how to handle men like that. Just like I promised, I'm going to teach you a lot, Celeste, and I'm going to have fun in the process."

Steve and Gerry left the bar after another ten minutes, but they paused near us.

"Your husbands must be awful stupid, leaving you two out here so long," Steve said.

"Oh, but they have so much trust and faith in us," she replied. "That's the kind of woman you need."

"I don't need any woman," he growled, and walked out.

Ami laughed.

"See? Men are such boys. They're more gullible than women, and so much more vulnerable. As long as the woman knows what she's doing."

We stayed nearly two hours before Ami decided we should go home. She had another Cosmopolitan, but I'd barely finished my first one. What I had drunk had made me dizzy already, and I was very tired.

"It's been a full first day for you, but you've enjoyed every moment of it, haven't you?" she asked.

"Yes," I said, even though I could have done without the flirtation at the bar. I couldn't help but wonder how Wade would feel if he had seen it.

"You're not upset about what I did back there, are you?" she asked me.

I shook my head, but not as firmly as she would have liked.

"This is all so new to you." She looked really worried suddenly. "All that religion didn't get into you back at the orphanage, did it?"

"I have my own beliefs," I said.

"Good. I mean, I hope you're not a prude at heart."

I said nothing. What was I? I had to wonder myself. She laughed, a little nervously.

"Oh, you'll be fine," she decided. "We're going to have so much fun. It'll be the best time of your life," she promised. "On Monday I'll take you over to the school myself. You can go with Wade after that, and then I'll talk him into a little car for you. I'll show him how it will be what he calls cost-efficient, and he'll agree."

She laughed.

"I can twist him around my little finger. You'll see."

"When do you plan on having your baby?" I asked. I couldn't help but wonder how becoming a mother would change her.

She looked at me as though I was asking a ridiculous question.

"I mean, you'll be pregnant before I leave, won't you?"

She smiled at me without speaking.

"What?" I asked.

"Really, Celeste, I would have hoped you had picked up on that by now. I have absolutely no intention of becoming pregnant."

"But . . . I thought you said . . . Mother Higgins said . . ."

"Little lies. Like dust on a window. Just brush it away, and no one remembers it was there.

"Or," she said after a pause, "cares."

She turned up the radio and laughed.

"Steve and Gerry," she said. "They were like putty in my hands. Soon I'll have you capable of doing the same thing to any man you want to do it to. You'll see."

We drove on.

"You'll be sorry you agreed to this," I heard what sounded like Noble whispering in my ear.

I turned.

But there was no one there.

Not yet.

6

A Dead Bird

♊

Ami didn't seem the least bit worried about our being discovered entering the house this late. She didn't walk softly or whisper when we walked through the hallway. Perhaps the drinks had made her more flamboyant than she wanted to be. In fact, I thought she was talking very loudly.

"Do you want anything before you go to bed?" she asked at the kitchen door. "Not that I know where anything is in there," she added, and laughed. "Matter of fact, except for my own things, I don't know where anything is in this house."

The lights were dim, and there was no one in the kitchen, or anywhere downstairs for that matter. I didn't even know where Mrs. McAlister and Mrs. Cukor slept, but I imagined the door that came after the den-office led to downstairs bedrooms at the rear of the house. I was curious as to how those two slept near each other and what, if anything, they had to share. Probably a bathroom, I thought. Living in an orphanage most of my life, I knew what it was like not to get along with someone who was in your face so much. From what Ami had told me, and what Mrs. McAlister had said, she and Mrs. Cukor seemed to dislike each other intensely.

"Mrs. McAlister has gone to bed long ago, of course," Ami said, "but if you want a glass of milk or something cold to drink, I'm sure we can find the refrigerator."

"No, I'm fine, thank you." I was really too tired to even drink a glass of water.

"You won't hear or see Mrs. Cukor moving about either. Once she goes into her room and locks her door behind her, she couldn't be roused even if the house was on fire. I don't know what she does in there. She has no television, and I've never heard a radio. Actually, I've never been in either of their rooms, not that I would ever want to be in them," she said as we walked to the stairway. Just as we reached it, the grandfather clock bonged to tell us it was one in the morning. I could see a light pouring into the hallway from under the den door.

"Is Wade still working in the office?"

"I don't know what he's doing, but I imagine he is," she replied without much interest. She yawned. "This has been a big day for me, too. I'm sleeping until noon, so you're on your own in the morning. Sunday is a dead day around here anyway. Basil will have a hangover and droop about the place before he leaves, if he's here at all tomorrow, and Wade will camp out in the den and watch news and financial programs all morning after he has his breakfast. He belongs to some investment club, too, and will go there for lunch.

"After I get up, we'll go shopping," she said.

"The stores I want to go to aren't open early anyway."

"What about Wade? Does he ever go to church? At the orphanage, we all had to attend church every Sunday."

"Church? Not Wade, and I'm there only for weddings and funerals. Actually, not too many funerals. I don't like sad events. Why, do you want to go to church? I thought you said you had your own beliefs, but if you want to go, I'll have someone take you," she said, dropping the corners of her mouth.

"It's all right. I just wondered about Wade."

"We'll all wonder about Wade," she muttered, and kept walking. We paused in the hallway in front of her door and mine. I saw her look to the door of one of the two other bedrooms.

"Basil's probably passed out," she muttered, "Well, have a good first night's sleep here in your new home, Celeste."

"Thank you."

"Welcome," she said, hugging me. "We're going to have so much fun together." She kissed me on the cheek and then went to her bedroom, closing the door softly behind her.

I went to mine and undressed slowly, my arms and shoulders feeling so heavy. It really had been a long day, full of so many different emotions. I wiped off the makeup and crawled into the luxurious bed, sinking happily into the soft mattress and fluffy pillows. I thought I heard a door open and close and then footsteps in the hallway. I listened for a moment, expecting Ami to come to my room to tell me something she had forgotten. There were more footsteps and then another door, sounding more like it had been slammed closed.

I listened. Despite my fatigue, my curiosity was too

great to shove aside. I rose and went to my door, opening it slowly and peering into the now dimly lit hallway. I saw no one and was about to close my door when I spotted something on the hallway floor to my right. It looked like an article of clothing. I stepped out and approached it slowly. What was it?

I squatted beside it and lifted it to look at it. It was the bottoms to a man's pair of pajamas. Why was it out here like this? I wondered. Confused as to what to do with it, I dropped it where I had found it and started to turn back to my room. I heard muffled voices behind Ami's door, and then what I was sure was the sound of her whimpering. It froze me in my steps. I listened harder. It was whimpering.

The sound of someone coming up the stairway sent me flurrying back to my room. I closed the door softly, my heart thumping, and listened. If anyone had come up that stairway, he or she was floating over the hallway floor. I heard nothing. After another long moment, I returned to bed.

Still, there was only silence now, and my eyelids were so heavy, I couldn't keep them open anyway, even when I imagined I saw Noble at the foot of the bed.

I called to him, but I didn't hear him speak the way I used to. I thought I heard the sound of a piano, but even that seemed distant and vague. I'm so tired I'm dreaming already, I thought, and whispered his name once more. His name remained on my lips until the morning light slowly lifted my eyelids and introduced me to a new day. My first thoughts were about him. Was I seeing him again? Would I see him now? I gazed around, but he wasn't there.

Then I thought about the pajama bottom. What did that mean? Whose was it? Why would it be in a hallway?

With some effort, I sat up and scrubbed my cheeks with my dry palms. My throat felt just as dry. I was just not used to drinking so much alcohol, I thought. How could Ami do it and look so vibrant and fresh all the time? Or was that all just the magic of makeup? The small heart-shaped clock on the night table read 9:00. Could that be? I couldn't remember ever sleeping that late. At the orphanage, sleeping until seven was a luxury.

I rose and went to my door. Opening it slowly, I peered out and saw that the pajama bottom was gone. How curious, I thought, and wondered if I should even mention it. Perhaps it was just something Mrs. Cukor had dropped when she had brought recently washed laundry upstairs. But I hadn't seen it when Ami and I had returned from the nightclub. Why would Mrs. Cukor be doing wash that late? I shrugged. She was strange enough to do anything, I thought. Maybe it was all a dream. It certainly felt that way at the moment. So much of the evening seemed vague to me now.

I went to the bathroom to shower. Afterward, I dressed, putting on my best one-piece dress. The only shoes I had to wear were what I called my clodhoppers, the ones with the big wide heels. They were ugly and not very comfortable. Maybe they had been designed by Puritans to torture sinners.

Ami's bedroom door was shut tight. I thought about the whimpering I had heard and wondered if that hadn't been part of a strange dream as well. After all, I had drunk more alcohol than ever before in my life.

The house was very quiet. I quietly descended the stairs and went into the dining room. Wade was there, dressed in a jacket and tie, reading the *Wall Street Journal*. He didn't hear me enter, lowering his paper only when Mrs. McAlister stepped into the dining room, saw me, and exclaimed, "I wondered when you would wake up and come to breakfast! I hope you don't think of this as you would some hotel and expect room service."

"I'm sorry I got up so late," I said.

Wade stared at me, a slightly amused look on his face. Did he have to dress so formally even on Sunday? I wondered.

"I usually don't sleep this late. In fact, I can't remember ever sleeping this late. At the orphanage—"

"I'll bet," Mrs. McAlister said sharply. "Well, what do you want? Eggs, oatmeal, what?"

"I'm not that hungry," I said. "I could get it myself."

"Not in my kitchen," she remarked, putting her hands on her hips and standing in front of the kitchen doorway as though she would fight to the death to prevent me from entering.

"Good morning," Wade finally said. "Mrs. McAlister has her set way of doing things," he added. "Just tell her what you would like for breakfast."

"Orange juice. Do you have any cereals?"

"Only oatmeal," she muttered.

"Okay," I said. "And coffee, please."

"Coffee is on the table," she snapped, nodded at it, and went into the kitchen.

I sat at one of the settings and reached for the coffeepot.

"Don't mind her," Wade said. "She hasn't been happy for years."

"Why not?"

"When her husband died, he left her pretty much destitute. He hadn't paid the premiums on his life insurance, and he had fallen so far behind on the house mortgage that the bank foreclosed on her. He worked for my father, and when he found out, he gave her a job here. She's been here ever since."

"She doesn't have any children?"

"No. So, how was your first night here?"

For a moment I was going to mention what I had seen and heard, but thought it was better I didn't.

"Very nice, thank you," I said, pouring my coffee and adding a little cream. I wondered if he would ask where Ami and I had gone. He had to have known we had left the house. I didn't want to be grilled about it, but before he could ask anything, Mrs. McAlister burst in with my orange juice.

"Oatmeal's coming," she said.

"Thank you," I told her, and sipped my juice.

Suddenly I heard the vacuum get turned on down the hallway.

"Doesn't anyone take Sunday off?" I asked.

Wade smiled.

"Only Ami," he said. "Actually, they could take any day off they wish. Sometimes, Mrs. Cukor leaves on Sunday to visit an old friend in Peekskill, but I think she's been ill lately. She might even be in a hospital. So, what does Ami have planned for you today? Once our princess rises, that is."

"She wanted to do some shopping," I said, afraid I shouldn't be the one to tell him.

He snapped his paper.

"What a surprise. Another day of shopping. Too bad they don't give out awards for professional shoppers. Ami would win, hands down." He thought a moment and then smiled, as if he didn't want to leave a bad impression. "She's good at it, though. She always buys something special. If it wasn't for her nagging, I would probably look like a refugee from some Third World country. I suppose I'm just too absentminded to care or remember.

"My mother used to tell me I would wear the same clothes day in and day out for weeks if she didn't come and scoop them up to be washed. What about you? Are you a clothes freak, too?"

I shrugged.

"I never had the opportunity to find out," I said, and he smiled and nodded. He glanced at the paper, and then he put it down and looked at me with more interest. "How much do you remember about your early life at that farm?"

"Some," I said, wondering what he wanted to know. Was he going to begin asking me questions about what had happened and what people believed about us? Would it turn him against me? "I was only six when I left."

"Um." He thought a moment and then nodded. "I'll have my financial people look into the property for you, if you like. Just to be sure it's all being handled properly. You don't want to inherit something that has a tax debt on it."

"Thank you. All I know is, it's being rented out to pay the upkeep and taxes. I saw the first papers on it just this year."

"Right," he said. "Well, I'll have my attorney check on it. You'll be fine, I'm sure. Ami said she's going to enroll you at the school tomorrow, but if she's not up in time, I'll take the time out to do so myself. Don't worry about it."

"Thank you."

Mrs. McAlister appeared with my oatmeal and a platter of toast.

"There's honey or maple syrup on the table," she remarked, nodding at the bottles.

"Thank you," I said. I tasted the oatmeal. She stood just to the side, watching. "It doesn't need anything," I remarked.

She showed pleasure and approval in her eyes only. The rest of her remained stiff, especially her thin lips. She jerked her head toward Wade, nodded as if to say, "There," and then returned to the kitchen.

"That's about as happy as she gets," he said, and we both laughed. His eyes moved off me and toward the doorway to the hallway. The smile left his face, and I turned to see Mrs. Cukor standing there staring in at us, mainly at me. A long moment passed without her saying anything.

"Anything wrong, Mrs. Cukor?" Wade said.

"A bird," she remarked.

"Pardon?"

"A bird died on the front stoop this morning."

"Really? What happened to it?"

"From the look on its face, it looks like it was frightened to death," she said. "I'm just going out to bury it with some garlic," she added. She narrowed her eyes at me and then walked off.

"That make any sense to you?" Wade asked me, trying to hold on to his smile. "Burying a bird with garlic?"

I thought a moment. Garlic was something that stimulated all sorts of early childhood memories. Just at the mention of it, I could smell it. I recalled how it was used as a medicine, and how it was hung about sometimes to ward off something dark and unpleasant.

"Yes," I said softly. "It does."

Wade raised his eyebrows.

"Really?" He looked at the empty doorway and then back to me. "Perhaps you and Mrs. Cukor will get along just fine."

No, I don't think we will, I thought, but didn't say it.

"Making such a deal over a dead bird. I swear. Maybe Ami's right about Mrs. Cukor. My father will keep her until she keels over, however. Now, what I would like to know—"

"What would you like to know, Wade?" we heard, and turned as Ami entered the dining room. She was in her robe and slippers and looked like she wasn't quite awake, but she had put on some makeup.

I looked at Wade. Had he been about to ask me about last night?

He stared at her a moment.

"What would you like to know?"

"Nothing," he said, and snapped his paper.

"What are you eating?" she asked me, grimacing. "Oatmeal? Ugh."

"It's very good," I said.

She poured herself a cup of black coffee. Wade lowered his paper.

"Hangover?"

"Hanger-on, I'd call it," she said.

"I take it you showed Celeste a little bit of our nightlife?" he asked. He didn't sound at all angry about it.

"A little bit," Ami said, not offering any real information. "Basil gone?" she asked in what I thought was a nervous tone.

"Yes," Wade said, "but he threatened to return in a few days. I'm sure he won't," he added. He looked at his watch. "I've got some things to clean up at the plant, and then I'm going to lunch at the club. Maybe we should eat out tonight."

"Oh, what a good idea," Ami cried. "I'm surprised I didn't have to suggest it first, Wade."

"I just thought—" He smiled coolly. "Unless you're too tired from last night, that is," he said. "I didn't hear you come home. I lost myself in bookwork," he added, mostly for my benefit.

"Too tired to go out to dinner? Never," Ami replied. "It's a wonderful idea. Let's go to Hunters."

Wade grimaced.

"Don't you think something more like Billy's Hideaway? The food's good and it's not pricey and—"

"No," Ami said firmly. "Hunters."

Wade nodded.

"Okay. I'll make a reservation for seven."

He stood and looked at me.

"Enjoy your shopping spree," he said.

"We will," Ami promised. It sounded more like a threat.

He folded his paper, glanced at me to smile and nod, and then left.

As though she was constantly in the doorway watching and listening, Mrs. McAlister appeared instantly and began to clear off his dishes and silverware. Ami nibbled on a small piece of my toasted muffin.

"Please get me a piece of diet-bread toast, Mrs. McAlister," Ami told her. "The one with the raisins."

She nodded and returned to the kitchen.

Ami shook her head and turned to me.

"See," she said, "see why I need you to help me liven up this dreary place? Billy's Hideaway. If you ever go there, you'll understand why it's a hideaway. All he cares about are the prices on the menu."

It was on the tip of my tongue to ask her about the pajama bottom and about her whimpering, but I thought if something had made her sad, she wouldn't want to talk about it. I never liked to do that at the orphanage, no matter how the nuns pleaded for me to reveal what had darkened my eyes and brought tears to my cheeks. I was more comfortable with silence, so I just assumed she would be.

Ami sipped her coffee. As suddenly as the depressing note had come into her voice, it was gone, and she was excited again.

"First, we'll go to my beautician and do your hair. I've got that all arranged. Then we'll go to my boutiques and get some fun clothes for you. We'll have lunch at an expensive restaurant, too."

She slapped the coffee cup down so hard, I was surprised it didn't shatter.

"Mrs. McAlister!" she shouted.

The cook appeared instantly.

"Forget about my toast. I don't have time. Come on," she told me as she rose. "Get ready to leave. We have too much to do to waste time here."

She squealed with delight and hurried out of the dining room. I felt funny leaving dirty dishes and glasses on the table. All my life, it seemed, I'd helped clean up, especially after myself. I looked back at Mrs. McAlister. She was shaking her head in those small jerky motions that reminded me of a weathercock.

As soon as she was dressed, Ami appeared at my door and held out a pair of designer sunglasses.

"Take them. I have two pair," she said. "Don't lose them either. They're five hundred apiece."

"Five hundred?" I hesitated, my hand frozen in midair.

"I'm just kidding." She pushed them into my hand. "If you lose them, we'll get them replaced instantly. Put them on," she urged, and I did so. Then she put hers on. They were exactly the same. "We're killers," she said. "Let's go hunt."

I hurried after her out of the house and into her

sports car. As we pulled out of the garage, I looked to the left and saw Mrs. Cukor standing in the field, a shovel gripped in her hand. She looked like someone holding a flag on a field of battle. She watched us leave before returning to her task. Ami hadn't seen her. She was talking quickly, describing her boutiques and the great relationships she had with all the sales personnel. With the money she spent at each shop, that didn't surprise me.

All day Ami moved me from one place to another as if she didn't want me to stop and think about anything. If that was her intention, she was right. I was caught up in a whirlwind of her excitement. At times I thought what I looked like was more important to her than it was to me.

First, we went to her beauty salon.

"I see where you got the idea for the tint," her beautician, Dawn, said when she set eyes on me. Ami just nodded and then went into a discussion of my hair. Dawn wanted to do something different from what Ami wanted to do, but she gave in when she saw how determined Ami was. When Dawn had completed the cut and style, it looked like I had a carbon copy of Ami's hairdo. She stood beside me checking out what looked to me like every single strand to be sure we matched.

"I can't take you to lunch at Mario's dressed like that and wearing those ugly shoes," she said and drove quickly to Ooh-La-La, a boutique in the mall.

What surprised me was that the salesgirl had the dress all set out for me. Ami had apparently called ahead and picked out a charmeuse and chiffon knee-length spaghetti-strap dress. It had tan charmeuse ties at the Empire bustline and was ruffled at the hem. When I put it on, it felt like tissue paper against my body.

The shoes that matched were natural wood wedge slides with buckles. Ami said I had to have a handbag to go along with it and bought me a distressed handbag with whipstitching. I felt like such a nerd; I knew practically nothing about style and the latest fashions.

"It all looks as good on her as it does on you," the salesgirl, Deirdre, said, and I realized Ami had the exact same dress and shoes, as well as the handbag. Why was she duplicating her own wardrobe for me? I wondered.

"I'm starved!" Ami suddenly exclaimed. Of course, considering how little she had eaten for breakfast, that didn't surprise me. "We need fuel before we can continue. Buying the right things is work. Few people realize how hard it is, especially Wade. Which reminds me. Deirdre, put it all on my bill," she cried with a wave of her hand while she hooked my arm and rushed me out the door.

"I left my clothes and shoes in the changing room!" I screamed.

"Good, and good riddance to it all. Who wants to take that ugly stuff back to our house anyway?" She laughed, and we drove off to have lunch at her favorite upscale restaurant.

I couldn't believe the prices on the menu. Everything was so expensive. Ami ordered a fancy chicken salad, but for someone who said she was starving, she ate very little. I didn't eat much either. I was very nervous. My sexy dress made me so self-conscious, I was sure everyone's eyes were on me, especially the men, who were all dressed in sport jackets with ties or suits. Many knew Ami and stopped by to say hello, and when they did, I could feel their eyes moving over my breasts. She introduced me as her young companion. Just as with Mrs.

Stone at the hotel, she made me sound like some sort of exchange student.

I hadn't had all that much experience being with an older, pretty woman who was married, but I couldn't help noticing how Ami flirted with every man, no matter what he looked like. Some took her hand and kissed her cheek, but no matter what, she teased with her eyes, held on to their hands practically until they walked away, and said many things that were suggestive, turning even the most innocent words into something sexual. When one man, Chris O'Connor, said he hadn't seen her for a while, Ami replied, "You're just not looking hard enough, Chris. It's important that it's hard enough."

He turned crimson, right to the tip of his nose, stuttered and stammered, and hurried away to join his group. Ami followed his retreat with a laugh and winked at me.

"See how men are so easy to manipulate? They could be made of putty, for all I know."

Why did she take so much pleasure in teasing them? What if her behavior got back to Wade? I thought. Wouldn't he be very upset? Why didn't that concern her? It was on the tip of my tongue to ask when suddenly Basil walked in with a woman who looked half his age holding onto his arm.

"Well, isn't this a co-inky-dink," Ami muttered, and gave Basil a big smile.

He nodded at her, but walked on to a table in the far corner of the room.

"You think he's embarrassed?" Ami whispered, leaning toward me. "He's not embarrassed. That's not why he's not coming over to us. He just doesn't want the girl to know he has a daughter-in-law older than she is."

She glared at him, her eyes narrowing darkly.

"Why does it upset you so much? I thought you told me you knew he was like that," I said, and she looked at me sharply for a moment before smiling.

"Oh, it doesn't upset me. Not really. Well, maybe a little. He is family, and what he does can bring embarrassment to us all," she explained.

But what about what she did? I thought. No. There was something else. It was like a message coming from somewhere, a message growing louder, louder. I looked about the room. Was that Noble by the kitchen doorway?

He turned, and I saw it was just another waiter.

"Oh, let's get out of here," Ami declared. "We have a lot more important shopping to do, and I want to get home early enough to have a massage. We're going out tonight, remember. Wade's splurging on an elegant dinner, whether he likes it or not."

She signaled for the check.

The food she was leaving on her plate would feed two young orphans lunch, I thought. I couldn't help thinking about it. After spending so much of my life counting pennies, saving old ribbons and paper bags, mending socks, and washing clothing until it all faded, it was hard to witness someone spending dollars unwisely or too loosely. I suppose it would always be that way for me.

At every boutique and department store we visited afterward, the salesgirls immediately knew what Ami wanted for me. They brought us directly to the garments, the shoes, the blouses and skirts, and in every case, what we were buying was either very close to something Ami had or exactly the same. Before we left the last department store, she took me to the jewelry counter, where she picked out what she called an inexpensive dress watch.

"You gave me one already," I reminded her.

"Did I? That doesn't matter. You need more than one dress watch, Celeste."

I thought the one she had chosen resembled the one she was wearing. It had tiny diamonds at the 12, 3, 6, and 9, and was shaped like an almond.

"There," she said, "you're almost complete."

She moved us down to the window case housing earrings and chose three pairs, each with matching necklaces, and each set meant to fit a particular one of the outfits we had bought previously.

"You're spending so much money on me," I finally gasped. "Wade will be so angry."

"What of it? I've been so angry, too," she snapped, and then smiled. "It's nothing. I told you. We're rich. Money is not any concern. I can't send you to the Dickinson School underdressed. I won't have anyone referring to you as some poor waif, which is exactly what those snobby girls would do once they looked at you in ordinary clothing without any decent jewelry on you."

"If they're such snobs, perhaps I should attend the regular public school."

"Of course not. I know they're snobs, but they have the best teachers and the best facilities, and why shouldn't you have the best as well? You're living with me, and I won't hear of your attending some inferior school. You don't have to like the snobs, but you can learn things from them. Some day, just like me, you'll attract the attention of a wealthy man, and you'll want him to think you're someone with class, someone elegant and sophisticated, won't you?"

I shrugged.

"I don't think about my getting married so much," I admitted.

"Of course you do. You're like me. You go to sleep dreaming about handsome princes and castles, wonderful dances, and a storm of jewels forever falling about you. We're—royalty—and it's not from any bloodline, either. We're royalty because we're beautiful," she declared, laughing and hugging me.

Then she turned serious and held me out at arm's length.

"Just enjoy every moment of all this, Celeste. You've waited too long, and you deserve it. Don't you think you deserve it after what you've been through in your life?"

Why did I deserve it any more than the other orphans in all the orphanages in the world? I wondered, but smiled and nodded anyway.

"Of course," she said.

She fluttered her eyelids, smiled, and sighed.

"Let's do one more thing," she said, gazing at her watch. "I'll sacrifice my massage. I want to take you to my makeup adviser. We have to be sure I'm showing you the right things to do and giving you the makeup that fits you. I'm not really as much of the expert I pretend to be, and I don't want to make any mistakes."

Before I could agree or disagree, she grasped my hand, ordered the boxes of clothing we had bought sent to her house immediately, and pulled me out. Ami's makeup adviser was at a different department store. Once again, I had the distinct impression he had been told we were coming. His name was Richard Dunn. Ami said he had worked on television shows and for runway models.

He immediately went to work on my eyebrows and then began to experiment a bit with some makeup shades before concluding that what Ami was using was perfect for my complexion after all. The same went for the shades of lipstick, eye shadow, and liner. Just as she had done with the clothing she had bought for me, Ami duplicated much of her own makeup and bought that for me as well. When we left the department store, I felt like a clone. I was wearing the same outfit, had the same hairstyle, wore similar makeup, and had the same watch and similar earrings, necklaces, and rings.

I had no idea how much she had spent on me, but I knew it was a great deal of money, and she had taken all this time as well. How could I ever complain or question any of it? She was obviously so pleased.

"I just knew you were a truly beautiful girl, Celeste. The moment I set eyes on you that first day I saw you walking up the street, I knew and told myself, this is a deprived young woman who could rise to great heights if she had only the opportunity, and that's what I am going to give you, opportunity. And don't feel you have to thank me all the time. I feel so good doing it. I love to defeat evil fate. That's what happened to you, you know," she said. "Evil fate made you a victim. Mrs. Cukor would agree, I'm sure. I don't usually place much value in those things, but I do like having an influence on someone's future, helping her, I mean. You understand, don't you?" she asked quickly.

"I think so," I said.

"Good, good. Because if you weren't happy with everything I was doing, I'd be simply devastated, Celeste, and very disappointed. You're happy, aren't you?"

"Yes," I said.

"Good."

She looked relieved. Was I happy? How could I not be? Yet there was something, that old sense of my being followed, that sense of foreboding, that something dreadful was following me, stalking me.

As we sped along to home, I saw a young man leaning back against a parked car. He raised his head as we passed, and I was sure it was Noble. He was shaking his head slowly. I turned around quickly to look back.

"What is it?" Ami asked.

"Nothing. I mean, I thought I saw someone I knew."

"Really? How could you know someone here?"

"Right," I said. "How could I?"

She looked at me with a confused smile on her face.

"Don't start pulling Mrs. Cookie stuff on me, Celeste. Not now, not after our wonderful beginning."

"Mrs. Cookie stuff?"

"Never mind," she said, and a moment later she began to talk about what we should wear on our first evening out with Wade. She wanted me to wear the red tube dress we had bought at Le Monde, one of the boutiques. It had a slit skirt and rhinestone trim on the top.

When we returned to the house, we learned Wade hadn't returned home yet. Ami was annoyed.

"He better not appear and tell me he forgot to make our reservation at Hunters," she warned. "Not that it would matter," she added. "I know the owner too well. He'd go out and buy another table if he had to, to please me. To dress!" she shouted like a battle cry, and charged into her bedroom.

Mrs. Cukor brought up all the packages and bags and boxes that I couldn't carry. Hardly glancing at me, she began putting everything away.

"I can do that, Mrs. Cukor," I told her.

She ignored me and continued to hang up the dresses, skirts, and blouses. Rather than argue with her, I went into the bathroom to take a quick bath, taking great care not to mess up my hair or my makeup. When I emerged, she was gone. Even the makeup had been set out neatly on the vanity table. I shrugged and thought to myself that I shouldn't look a gift horse in the mouth just because the horse acted strange. I'll just avoid her, I thought. It wasn't critical to my living here that she like me, or I like her.

I thought I would just take a short rest and lie down on my bed. After a few moments, I realized I smelled something new, something redolent. I sat up, and the smell diminished. More curious than ever now, I lowered myself to my pillow and sniffed. Then I lifted the pillow and saw leaves I recognized as dill, basil, and clove. The clove was the strongest smell. I scooped it all into my palms and stared at it.

The odors and the sight of the herbs revived old images and memories, like similar leaves tied on doors and on windows. I remembered why my mother put them there. To find them here, under my pillow, made me angry. It wasn't difficult to understand how these herbs got here. I carried them all in my palms to the doorway.

When I opened the door and stepped out, I saw Mrs. Cukor closing the door of the bedroom Basil Emerson used. She had just finished cleaning up in there. I waited for her to turn and look my way.

"Did you put this under my pillow?" I asked, and held out my hands to show her the leaves.

She glanced at them but said nothing and started toward the stairway.

"I know what this is supposed to mean," I said, chasing after her. "Why did you put it under my pillow? Why?" I demanded, raising my voice.

At the top of the stairway she turned, her eyes darkening as she narrowed them and peered into my face.

"I knew it when I saw the dead bird. It was a sign, a warning. You brought it into this house, the evil eye. I must drive it out before it does even greater harm," she said, turning and starting down the stairway.

"Brought . . . what?" I cried after her. "What are you talking about? What evil eye did I bring into this house?"

She paused and looked up at me, a wry smile on her pale lips.

"You know," she said. She nodded. "You know."

She continued down the stairway and didn't look at me again until she reached the bottom. Then she turned, looked at me, made the sign of the cross over her breasts, and walked away. My heart didn't beat fast as much as it beat hard, pounding under my breast. A cold feeling passed over the back of my neck and then, like a melting icicle, dripped and ran down my spine.

I thought for a moment, and then I spun around.

And he was standing there.

Noble.

He had returned, and he was more than simply a memory, more than Dr. Sackett had described, more than merely a projection of guilt or fear.

He was there!

What frightened me, however, was that he was smiling with glee.

7

Appearances
Are Everything

♊

"To whom are you speaking?" Ami asked.

She stood in the bedroom doorway in her bathrobe. Her face was covered in a white skin cream, luminescent in the hallway light.

I glanced back at where I thought I had seen Noble, but he was gone.

"I—" I looked toward the stairway. "Mrs. Cukor . . . she put this in my bed under the pillow," I blurted, and extended my arms to show Ami the leaves.

"What is that?" she asked, grimacing and stepping back as though I had a handful of bugs.

"Dill, basil, and clove, herbs."

"What? Why would she put that under anyone's pillow?"

"These are herbs that have certain magical qualities," I said. "She put them under my pillow to drive away evil, the evil eye."

"The evil eye? Is that what she told you? That

woman. Something has to be done about her. I'm
sorry. I'll speak to Wade about her. This has just got to
stop."

"I don't want to be responsible for anyone losing
her job," I said quickly.

"I wouldn't worry about it. I doubt she'll lose her
job. Throw that junk away and get ready. We have to
look like dynamite on heels," she said, backed into her
room, and closed the door.

She doubted she would lose her job? What was the
hold Mrs. Cukor had on this family? I wondered. I returned to my room, crumpled the leaves in my hand,
and flushed them down the toilet. I immediately felt
guilty about it. Maybe it was important, I thought.
Maybe she was trying to help me by keeping the evil
eye away. Maybe I shouldn't have been so angry.
Maybe . . . visions flowed by, memories of Mama,
shadows over the lawn, an owl perched on a grave-
stone.

I shuddered.

"Noble?" I whispered. "I know you're here. Where
are you? I need to speak with you. I need your advice."

It felt strange calling to him, speaking to him. It had
been so long.

The curtains on the windows fluttered, even though
the windows were closed. I waited, but he did not appear. He's punishing me, I thought. He's punishing me
because I have ignored him so long.

After another moment, I felt my heartbeat slow and
my breathing get more regular.

Get hold of yourself, Celeste, I told myself. Don't
spook Ami. Don't risk losing all this now.

I put on the rhinestone-trimmed tube dress and
looked at myself again. I wasn't sure whether I looked
beautiful and sexy or simply sexy. Was this a good

makeover that I was permitting Ami to accomplish for me, or would I be sorry? Being brought up under such dire and in many ways strict circumstances at the orphanage, I rarely, if ever, thought of myself in the way Ami thought of herself and me: sticks of dynamite, ready to explode in the eyes of every man who looked our way. I never experimented with clothes, with my hair, or of course with makeup. What people saw was what they got.

How different it was now. In Ami's world, just like her, I could cast myself into different roles, move through life as if we were in a movie of our own making, treat clothing more like costuming, and listen to our own music in our heads. Every time we left our bedrooms, dressed to go out, we were literally making an entrance onto a stage, imagining a spotlight always on us. I didn't have Ami's confidence yet, and I might never have, but I saw how she anticipated and expected applause, admiration, attention. I had only been here a few days, and I was already moving in lockstep with her.

Was this what I really wanted? Was I so desperate for love and for family that I would willingly trade my own identity to have it? Or was this my true identity, hidden and waiting all this time for the opportunity to rise to the surface? Was I more Ami's sister than I imagined I was or could be?

I was usually so good at seeing what lay in waiting for other people. Why was I so poor at doing it for myself?

I heard a knock on my door and grabbed the purse Ami had bought for my dress. One more glance at myself in the mirror sent me to the door, my heart pounding. I opened it and stepped out. At first I didn't see Ami, and then she stepped forward on my right, and I felt my jaw unhinge.

I was expecting her to be wearing something similar to what I was wearing, what she wanted me to wear, so we would look like that pair of dynamite sticks she had described. Instead, she looked years older and far more conservative in her jacket and ankle-length violet column dress. The jacket had three-quarter-length sleeves, and the dress a straight neckline. It was far from a revealing garment. What was the most shocking, however, was the wig she was wearing. We no longer had similar hairstyles. Her wig was shoulder length with straight bangs and a slight curl at the shoulder. Most surprising, however, was the color. It was black.

"Oh," she said, smiling. "You're looking at my hair. Well, I just couldn't get it to do what I wanted in so short a time. That's why I have my collection of wigs. Sometimes I like being a black-haired woman. It's more mysterious, don't you think? Watch, Wade won't say a word. He never does. He'll never question why I wear something or don't wear something.

"But look at you!" she exclaimed, seizing my hands to hold up my arms and turn me about. "You're absolutely a heartbreaker. I can't wait to see how the men look at you."

"I feel half-dressed compared to you," I said.

"Nonsense. I dress to fit my moods, and this just happens to be my mood tonight. That's probably why I chose the black hair. I'm more secretive about everything, even my body, whereas," she added before I could say anything, "you've been kept a secret far too long."

She took my hand.

"And we're putting an end to that!" she cried, leading me to the stairway.

I looked back, expecting to see Wade. Why was he always dressed and downstairs before us? I wondered. I had the answer before we reached the bottom step.

"Wade will meet us at the restaurant," Ami said. "He got tied up at work. And if he's late," she sang, "we'll start without him."

When we reached the bottom of the stairs, I turned to look down the hallway; I could feel her eyes on me. There she was, Mrs. Cukor, standing just to the right of the den-office doorway with her back to the wall as though she was making room for someone to pass in front of her. Her head was turned my way. She glared in my direction.

What? I wanted to shout at her. What is it you want from me? What is it you expect I'll do?

"C'mon, silly," Ami chided, and headed to the garage.

We got into her sports car. She smiled at me and touched my face softly with her right hand.

"You look beautiful, Celeste," she said, "more beautiful than even I imagined you could be."

She stared at me a moment, her eyes looking as though they were watering with emotion. The depth of her feeling caught me by surprise. I loved the compliment, but something inside me sounded alarms I did not understand. She saw the confusion in my face and laughed.

"Sorry, I was so dramatic," she said, opening the garage door and backing out. Then she sped down the driveway, the car wheels screaming as we whipped out of the entranceway and around to continue on the street. She turned up the music.

"You don't know how to drive yet, do you?"

"Why would I? Who would have taught me? What would I have driven?"

"Yes, I just thought of that. We need to get you

some private driving instruction immediately, along with those piano lessons I promised. I'll tell Wade tonight. When you drive up to the school in your own fancy car, you'll become Miss Popular instantly. You'll see how many new friends you'll have then."

"If they're becoming my friends just because I have a fancy car, they can't be very good friends," I said.

"Oh, stop. That's not you talking. That's one of the nuns or some goody-goody you were under all these years. Just like any princess, you're going to need your entourage," she continued. "When I was in school, I always had a half dozen or so girls surrounding me, wanting to do whatever I wanted to do, hanging on my every word. It will be the same for you soon. You'll see."

"How do you know that's what I want?" I asked. I didn't mean to be mean or contrary. I was simply curious as to what she had seen in me to give her these ideas.

She looked at me and smiled.

"Because underneath that dreary shell the state and these agencies and orphanages put over you, I know there beats the heart of a real woman just like me. I saw it in the way you moved, the way you held your head high, the way you looked at people and especially the way men looked at you."

"But how long did you watch me before you came to the orphanage?" I asked.

"That's for me to know." She laughed. "For a while," she confessed. "I couldn't just take any young woman into my life, could I?" she added in defense. "You understand, don't you?"

"Yes," I said, even though I didn't quite understand. It had bothered me before to know she had been spying on me at all and had spoken to my teachers, but now that she had confessed to doing it for a while, it was even more disturbing. Why hadn't I felt her eyes on me? Why wasn't I warned?

This was Noble's doing, I vaguely thought. He had dulled my senses to punish me for deserting him.

Now there were all these tiny alarms going off inside me continually, but I thought they might be there simply because I was doing so many radically new things. Perhaps she was right. Perhaps I had been living under some shell all this time. Perhaps I had been kept emotionally and socially retarded. I deserve all this excitement and fun, I told myself. Be quiet, my troubled heart. And my tongue . . . stop coming up with platitudes that belong more on the lips of people like Mother Higgins.

What would be so terrible about being popular among my peers, having boys compete for my attention, and having girls want to be my friend? When had I ever experienced such a thing? When had I even dreamed about it? Ami wasn't tempting me toward some pit of disaster. She was giving me opportunity, opportunity to become just what she had described, yes, a vibrant, sexy, and confident woman. And wasn't that what all young girls hoped to be, whether they admitted to it or not?

Go back, my conscience, my paranoid fears, my visions of dark places. Go back into the vault and let me be. I'm not going to cry out for Noble and look for him in every corner. I don't need him now, I told myself. I strengthened my determination.

"Want a cigarette?" Ami asked suddenly.

"A cigarette?"

"Don't tell me you've never smoked a cigarette," she said.

I didn't say anything.

She laughed.

"Well, then," she said, "I guess you've never done pot either."

"No," I said.

"Sister, you're going to feel like you've been reborn," she said.

Voices again tried to clamor inside me, but I shut them down before they could really begin. What good was being alive if you couldn't take some chances some time, experiment, step over the line?

"Don't tell Wade I even mentioned any of that," Ami warned. "He's Mr. Clean when it comes to that stuff, but he doesn't have to know anything about what you and I do together. You know what really ties two people like us together tightly?" she asked me.

"What?"

"Secrets," she said. She nodded. "Secrets. Revelations, getting naked with your thoughts, your ideas, your memories. And you know what, Celeste, it doesn't happen until you have trust. We've got to trust each other first."

"Yes," I said.

"I thought you would understand. See," she said, "I do know you."

She laughed, but her words hung in the air like the odor of smoke, of something burned.

Minutes later, we pulled up to the front of Hunters, and a valet came rushing out to open our doors and park our car. The restaurant itself looked like it had once been a private residence and later I would find out that it really had been. The owners had torn apart the bottom floor and created one large dining room and two small private dining areas. The decor was rustic, the walls covered with old farm implements, historic signs, beautiful mirrors. All the panels and wood were dark oak. There was a beautiful bar on the right

with brass fittings and very comfortable-looking
stools, tables, and an area for dancing. A trio was playing, and the bar itself was very busy. Two bartenders
were hurrying to fill every order.

The main room of the restaurant was nearly full.
Waiters and waitresses dressed in hunter green outfits
moved gracefully between the tables. There were
servers as well. Everyone eating there was well
dressed. I saw some young women who I thought were
about my age, but none of them were dressed like I
was. They all wore more conservative clothing, less revealing dresses, pants suits and light sweaters with
jackets.

The moment we entered the dining room, people
turned their heads. Some stared, some whispered, and
some laughed. The maître d', an elderly, distinguished
looking man in a tuxedo, hurried to greet us.

"Hello, Mrs. Emerson."

"Hello, Aubrey. I'd like you to meet our houseguest,
Celeste Atwell."

"Please to meet you," he said, his eyes sweeping
over me as discreetly as he could. Even so, I caught a
gleam of disapproval at how I was dressed.

"Mrs. Emerson. Your husband called and left a message he would be late, but he said you shouldn't wait
for him," Aubrey told Ami.

"That's because he knows we wouldn't anyway,"
she said, and Aubrey nodded, smiling.

"Right this way," he said, leading us through the
room to a prominent table near the bay windows.

I felt as though I was walking through thick cob-
webs. Everyone was still looking at us, especially me.
What it really made me feel was naked. I tried not to
look at anyone, but I couldn't help catching smirks on
the faces of some of the younger men and reproach on

the eyes of most of the older women. Some of the young women looked envious, if not a bit annoyed that I was capturing the attention of every male in the room.

Aubrey pulled out our seats for us and then handed us the menus. The waiter, a dark-haired, dark-complexioned young man anxiously holding in the wings, rushed forward the moment Aubrey left the table.

"Hello, Mrs. Emerson," he said. "Welcome back."

His name tag read "Anthony." Although he had addressed Ami, his eyes went to me.

"Good evening, Tony. This is my house guest, Celeste. She's quite fond of Cosmopolitans, so bring us two," Ami ordered.

"Is she of age?" he asked, tucking in the right corner of his mouth. He had nice features, especially his ebony eyes and firm lips and jawline.

"Doesn't she look it?" Ami retorted.

"If you say so, ma'am," he replied. "Be right back."

"But I'm not of age," I said as soon as he left our table.

"It's not what you are; it's what you appear to be," Ami said. "Appearances are everything. Look at these people, all watching us. We've given them something to talk about," she said, and nodded at an elderly woman with blue-gray hair glaring at us. Her bald-headed husband, with a face that looked squeezed between two giant fingers, appeared mesmerized, his right hand holding a fork in midair as if he had been frozen instantly. The woman returned a quick nod and shifted her eyes away, saying something under her breath to her husband, who immediately stopped looking at us.

Ami laughed.

She studied the menu.

"Let's share a salad. What would you like to eat? What about lobster Thermidor?"

"I've never eaten lobster," I said. She swung her eyes to the ceiling and then shook her head.

"Okay, then that's what you'll have. I have so much to do with you to get you caught up that I have decided to devote all my time to it," she told me.

All her time? What did that mean? Where were her friends, her other activities? I know I should have felt grateful, but instead I had those pangs of fear again.

Our waiter was returning with our drinks, the cranberry-tinted liquid in large martini glasses carried as if he were bringing crowns on a silver tray. Once again, conversations stopped and all eyes turned in our direction. Ami sponged up the attention as if it nourished her very being.

"Should I take your order, or are you waiting for someone?" our waiter asked.

"Really, Tony, do I ever wait for anyone?" Ami teased. He laughed, his eyes moving quickly to me again. "We'll share the house salad. Celeste will have lobster Thermidor, and I'll have the shrimp cocktail as an entrée. Also, put in an order for a chocolate soufflé," she added.

"Absolutely," Tony said, reaching for the menus. "May I?" he asked me.

"Oh, yes," I said, leaning back.

He nodded, held his gaze on me a moment longer and then hurried off.

"He's drooling," Ami said. "See?"

I couldn't help blushing and looking down.

"You have to get rid of that modesty as quickly as

you can, or rather, get control of it. There are times to appear modest and innocent and times when it's a disadvantage," Ami instructed. "For example, in a room full of stuffy, snobby people like this one, you want to look as confident and return their condescending expressions as quickly and as firmly as you can. You tell yourself there is no one in here who is better than you are, and you let them all know it with the way you hold yourself, look at them, and even speak to them. Never give anyone the satisfaction of thinking he or she is better than you are, Celeste.

"I know, for a girl who has been living as an orphan in hand-me-down clothes and for someone sleeping, eating, and breathing on the proceeds of charity, that's difficult to accomplish at first, but you're my spiritual sister now, and you live in my house. It's good to be somewhat arrogant. If you have it, flaunt it, and you have it," she said.

Her pep talk made me feel better. I lifted my head and looked out at the patrons of the restaurant, meeting every stare head-on. Just as Ami had predicted, they all quickly turned away.

Ami lifted her glass and nodded at mine.

"To us," she said, and we tapped glasses. I sipped my drink and then took a deep breath. When would I stop feeling like I was sinking deeper and deeper into some pool of sin? Every little change in me that Ami engineered seemed tainted, whether it be the use of makeup, the hairdo, the clothes, the drinking, or now the lessons in demeanor and attitude. Was she changing me into a better, more confident young woman, or dragging me down to some awaiting disaster?

Wade didn't appear until after we had eaten our salad. On his way to our table, he shook hands with and spoke to some of the other restaurant patrons. The conversation was obviously about me, as he looked our way and then spoke again.

"I hope he isn't describing you as some orphan," Ami muttered.

"Sorry I'm late," he said when he reached our table. "We had a small crisis at the plant, a truckload of wrong parts, and we had deliveries to do tomorrow."

He sat. Ami shook her head.

"You have a general manager, Wade, whom you pay a good salary to, don't you? Why don't you let the man fulfill his responsibility?"

"The plant has my family name on it, not his," Wade replied drily, looking at the menu Anthony hurried over to give him.

"Family name," Ami muttered, "on plumbing parts."

"I'll skip the salad," Wade told Anthony. "Just bring me the filet mignon, medium well."

"Very good, Mr. Emerson," Anthony said, taking his menu but smiling at me.

From the expression on his face when he looked at me, I didn't think Wade approved of the way I was dressed and made up. He finally noticed the Cosmopolitan in front of me.

"You ordered her an alcoholic beverage?"

"It's her first big night out with us, Wade. What's the big deal?"

"The big deal? Ami, she's underage. You can't do that. You'll endanger the restaurant as well. Please slide that over to me," he told me.

I did as he asked, and Ami immediately went into a pout.

"I'm sorry, Celeste," he said. He turned back to Ami. "You know that Mrs. Brentwood, the principal of the Dickinson School, is sitting by the fireplace with her husband?"

Ami glanced in that direction, and I looked as well. An attractive middle-aged woman with light brown hair sat facing us. Her husband had his back to us. I thought she had a nice smile, and unlike most of the other patrons, she didn't seem at all interested in us. She laughed at something her husband said and then wiped the strands of her shoulder-length hair away from her right cheek.

"So what?" Ami muttered.

"So what? So she'll know Celeste is not old enough to be served alcohol and that you ordered it for her. What kind of a foster mother are you? Not smart." Wade sipped my drink. "It's too sweet," he said. "How can you drink this anyway?"

"Sweets for the sweet," Ami quipped. Wade shook his head, but settled down and smiled at me.

"Excited about tomorrow?" he asked.

"Yes," I said, although nervous was a better term to apply, I thought.

"You'll do well," he told me. "I'm sure you have better study habits than half the school population, most of whom are spoon-fed everything. What subjects interest you the most?"

"Boys," Ami offered for me.

Wade looked at her and then slowly turned back to me.

"I guess English," I said. He nodded.

"Yes, that was my favorite, especially English literature."

"Yes, well, you get lots of opportunity to use that knowledge in a wholesale plumbing plant, don't you?" Ami snapped at him as if she hated all education, regardless of the subject.

"You'd be surprised," he said. "Pipes have to be grammatically correct to fit correctly, and elegant sink, tub, and shower fixtures have to be described poetically."

We both laughed. It was Ami's turn to smirk, but before she could comment, our food was served. Wade looked surprised by my dish.

"She's never had lobster before, Wade, so don't start talking about the cost."

"I'm not. It looks very good, in fact. I probably should have ordered it myself."

"It is good," I said, tasting it. "It's delicious."

He smiled.

"Who's your favorite author?" he asked.

"I don't know as I have one favorite," I told him. "I didn't expect to enjoy reading Mark Twain as much as I did this year. I love *Huck Finn.*"

"So did I," Wade said.

Ami groaned.

"Really, Wade, next thing you'll do is get her reading the *Wall Street Journal.*"

He shrugged and looked at me.

"Maybe I will," he said. "Why shouldn't she understand the financial world?"

"She'll have more important things to do."

"More important? Like what, Ami?"

"Oh, please," Ami said, and pushed her plate away. She had eaten barely half of her dinner. "I'll be right back," she said. "I have to powder my nose. Actually," she said after she stood, leaning toward Wade, "I have to pee."

She giggled and started away, deliberately pausing at a table to speak with a man who had been smiling at her, to the displeasure of the woman he was with. Wade watched her and then turned back to me.

"I'll give you a wake-up call tomorrow," he told me as he continued to eat. "Ami will say she'll do it and you shouldn't worry, but she won't."

"Thank you."

"I'll admit that taking you in was all her idea, but once I agree to do something, I do it right," he continued. Then he leaned toward me to whisper, "This food is good, but it's just as good at Billy's Hideaway and half the price. You'll learn. You'll see what's really important," he promised.

Everyone's trying to teach me something, I thought. Everyone wants to be right about what is most important in life. I just hoped I wouldn't come between Ami and Wade or cause some new troubles. Then Mrs. Cukor would be the one who was really right about me. I would have brought the evil eye into the Emerson home after all. I did have some dark curse attached to my very being.

After Ami returned, and our soufflé was served, she wanted us to go into the bar and listen to the trio, but Wade told her she should take me home to get a good night's rest.

"She's starting a new school. It's not easy, Ami."

"Oh, it's not hard either. An hour or so longer won't matter."

"The bar's no place for her," he emphasized.

She raised her eyes to the ceiling and then stood up abruptly.

"Come along, Cinderella. Wade thinks my car will turn into a pumpkin any moment."

She started away, miffed. I looked at Wade, who was staring down at the table.

What had brought these two people together? I wondered. What did they like about each other? For Wade, beauty was apparently not enough, and as far as Ami was concerned, Wade was uninteresting. Were they different once? Had something changed them? Perhaps this was the way most married people behaved after a while. What did I really know about husbands and wives, families?

"I'll be right home, myself," Wade said as I came around the table.

Ami was already waiting at the restaurant entrance, pouting. I hurried after her. Most of the patrons were already gone, but the bar was filled and the music was loud. People were laughing and drinking. Ami looked at the scene longingly. I almost thought I should suggest Wade take me home and she stay, but she stepped out of the restaurant quickly and ordered her car.

"I really enjoyed everything. Thank you," I said, hoping to help her to feel better.

"What did I tell you?" she asked, spinning on me. "He didn't even comment about my hair."

She raised her arms.

That's right. That was odd, I thought. Why didn't he?

"Maybe he's seen you in the wig before."

"Of course he's seen me in it before, many times before, but that's not the point. Men," she said, and started for the car when it was brought up to us. She tipped the valet, and we got in and drove off.

Suddenly, she laughed.

"It's all right," she said. "I'm really not upset. I just wanted him to think I was."

"Why?"

"That way he'll be nicer to me. Always let them think you're mad at them, even if you have no reason to be. It puts them on the defensive, and there is no better place for a man to be put than on the defensive," she lectured. "By the way, that goes for boys your age as well. It makes no difference. As I told you, all men are boys," she said. Then, under her breath, she added, "In one way or the other."

When we arrived at the house, she insisted we go into the living room and have what she called an after-dinner cordial.

"You have to know about these things, Celeste," she said. "You'll be invited to rich peoples' homes now. Their children have been brought up exposed to elegant, expensive things, have traveled to all sorts of exotic and beautiful places. You should know about the good life, appreciate what you can have, will have.

"I don't want any of them to know you're an orphan, a girl who lived in orphanages most of her life," she added firmly as she poured a black liquor into what she called brandy glasses.

"How am I to prevent them from knowing?"

"Simple," she said. "We'll tell them a different story."

She gave me the drink and sat across from me. I looked at the glass.

"Go on, try it," she said.

I did. I thought it tasted like licorice. Actually, I enjoyed it.

"It's Opal Nera, black sambuca," she said. "Now then, who are you, and why are you here?"

She sat back, thinking. I sipped more of my drink and sat staring at her.

"Okay. You're my niece, understand. Your parents are in a nasty, nasty divorce. Most of those snobs will understand and appreciate that," she told me. "Half of them come from divorced parents. I volunteered to take you in for the remainder of the year so you would have a more stable environment. Now where do you come from?"

She sipped her drink and tapped her fingers on the arm of the chair.

"Can't be from the South. You have no accent. We

have to be careful. These kids have influential relatives everywhere. Where have you been?"

"Nowhere," I replied.

"Where was that farm of yours?"

"It's in the Catskills."

"Okay. What's your father do?"

"What about a pharmacist?" I suggested. Maybe it was the alcohol, the food, the excitement of the whole evening, but I was suddenly enjoying this.

"Pharmacist? No, that's not wealthy enough, unless he owned a chain of stores. Let's keep it a little vague. He's an international entrepreneur, and he's away from home so much, and that's why the marriage failed. Your mother might have had a lover. Yes, she has a lover and you knew it and it was painful for you because even though your father is away so much, you love him and feel sorry for him. However, he might have lovers, too. In Europe. Perfect. If anyone asks anything specific, you get sad and say you can't talk about it. It's all still so raw and painful. Oh, this is terrific," she said.

I laughed and finished my sambuca.

"You like that?"

"Yes."

"I'll teach you everything about good wine, good whiskey. You'll have eaten in fancy restaurants, so we'll talk about food. And we'll eat in good restaurants, frequently, so you'll know what I mean. This is going to be so much fun!" she cried.

We heard footsteps in the hallway.

Wade paused in the doorway and looked in at us. I put my glass down quickly.

"What are you doing, Ami? You were supposed to come home so she could get a good night's rest."

"We have to unwind, Wade. Women like us just

don't hop into bed, close our eyes, and drift into Never-Never Land." She turned to me. "Wade falls asleep in seconds."

"Not always," he said in a dark tone.

Ami's smile faded.

"All right. We'll go to bed, Daddy," she agreed, put down her glass, and stood.

I did too, and we started out of the room. Wade stepped aside. I glanced at him quickly. He raised his closed right hand to his ear to indicate he would make my wake-up call. Ami and I headed up the stairway.

"Of course he's right, I suppose," she admitted. "What are you going to wear tomorrow?"

"I don't know. I hadn't thought about it."

"Wear the blue skirt and the blouse we got at Femme Fatale. You have that blue cardigan sweater. It's smart. Oh, and wear the dress watch, too. Here," she added, pulling a gold band filled with diamonds off her left hand. "Wear this too. You have to look the part you're playing."

I hesitated, and she grabbed my hand and put the ring on me. It fit well.

"Tomorrow, we conquer new worlds," she declared, hugged and kissed me, and went into her bedroom.

I remember thinking I must be more like Wade. Almost as soon as my head hit the pillow, I was asleep. I did wake up in the middle of the night, but I thought I was still asleep and dreaming. I heard what sounded again like Ami's muffled sobbing. I listened, and then it stopped. I was just too tired to get up and see if anyone was out there. In seconds I was back to sleep and didn't wake until my phone rang and I heard Wade say, "I knew she would oversleep and not call you. It's time to get up and dressed. I'll be taking you to school and enrolling you," he added.

"Thank you," I said.

I lay there for a moment or two, trying to make sense out of the night, the dreams, and then got up.

When I opened my bedroom door to go downstairs to breakfast, I found a small head of garlic tied to the handle.

This time, I left it there.

8

A New School

♊

"**A**mi will be full of apologies later," Wade told me after we got into his car and started for the Dickinson School. "Of course, she'll also tell you it wasn't that serious to miss your first day. You could have enrolled just as well later in the day or the next day. Schedules, rules, appointments, were never that important to Ami. I'm afraid her parents were what are euphemistically called permissive parents these days. She was practically on her own from the day she could walk and talk.

"She doesn't mean to be hurtful, however. And I am trying to change her, get her to be more responsible. I wouldn't admit it to her," he added, smiling at me, "but I actually enjoy the way she handles some of my and my father's more conceited acquaintances. She has a lot more courage than I do when it comes to things like that.

"Anyway, I'm sure you'll like the teachers at this school. A student like you will be a breath of fresh air to them, believe me. Just don't pick up any of the bad habits littering the hallways, lockers, and girls' bathrooms. Everyone has bad habits. Rich kids simply have more money to spend on them."

"Did you attend a private school?" I asked him, assuming he was giving me the benefit of his own experiences.

"Me?" He laughed. "No, my father believed a school was a school was a school. What difference did it make where you attended? 'One and one is two in any school in the country, Wade,' he was fond of saying. My family could easily have afforded to send me to a private school," he added with some bitterness running through his voice. "I was always a good student, so he thought it didn't matter, but the truth is, I would have gotten a better education. My teachers were too occupied with discipline problems. The one good thing about private school is they can throw you out more easily. Whenever there is money involved, even permissive parents suddenly take more interest.

"I was accepted to Harvard Business, but my father made me attend a far less expensive institution in Albany. 'You're going to end up working for me anyway,' he would tell me. 'What difference does it make what's written on your diploma?' My mother was on my side, but by then she was sickly, and I didn't want to cause any more havoc around her."

He looked at me and smiled.

"I know. Here I am describing how difficult my life was, and there you are probably wishing you had my opportunities."

I didn't want to say, No, never—I don't envy you at all. I thought it would hurt his feelings if I said such a thing, so I simply smiled back.

"So you do remember a lot of your early life, living on that farm?"

"Remarkably, yes," I said.

"One of these days I'd like to hear about it. I read stuff, of course, and to be honest, I thought you would be quite different from the way you are, having been brought up in a world full of mysticism and superstition. To her credit, I suppose, Ami never had any reservations about you. From what I see so far, she might be smarter than I am."

"Thank you," I said. I hesitated, but since he had made reference to mysticism and superstition, I asked about Mrs. Cukor.

"Other people might not keep her on so long with her so-called peculiarities," I commented.

"Probably not, but she's very protective of the Emersons. She was truly a second mother to me at times, and Dad believes she brings him good luck. Keeps the evil stuff away," he added. "He's more into that sort of thing than you'd think, and Mrs. Cukor has ways of convincing him she's protecting us all."

"I know exactly what you mean."

"Yes. Ami told me what she put under your pillow."

"Today I found a piece of garlic on my door handle," I said. I didn't tell him I had left it there after I had found it.

"I'll talk to her, but she'll do things like that from time to time. Just ignore it if you can, unless she starts putting garlic in your makeup," he added, and we both laughed. "There it is," he said, nodding.

The Dickinson School was directly ahead on the right. The tan brick one-story building was sprawled over acres of beautiful land, with a large, beautiful fountain in front. The three steps that led up to the entrance were long and coffee-tinted, with wide pilasters on both sides. There was a flagpole with a flag snapping in the breeze. To the right was a parking lot with dozens of late-model cars. Some had just pulled into parking spaces, and students emerged, many moving in slow, reluctant steps toward the side entrance.

"There are only a hundred or so students here, if that many," Wade said. "It's just a high school, grades nine through twelve."

"Really? My class at my public school had nearly eighty students alone."

"Well, this is special. I think the teacher-student ratio is something like nine to one. My father never understood how that sort of situation allows for more personal attention. I suppose it has its pros and cons. If you burp, the whole student body hears about it," he added, laughing.

We pulled into an empty parking space and stepped out.

"Despite its size, or because of it, this really is an impressive school. They don't have much of a basketball team, and they're too small for football, but they do have winning golf and tennis teams."

"I never played either," I said.

"Oh? Well, we have our own tennis court, so I'll break you into the game, not that I'm much of an athlete. My father is actually quite the tennis player, even now. He loves playing against me to prove he hasn't lost his youthful vigor," Wade said as we walked up to the front steps. "I attended a play here once, so I know they have a good drama club. The daughter of a friend was the lead. That was two years ago. She's graduated and attends Vassar. They usually get their graduates into top schools," he said.

He opened the front door. I took a deep breath and stepped into the small but plush school lobby. The gold-tiled floors glimmered as did the three black marble columns. There were dark wood and glass display cases filled with trophies, and paintings of beautiful rustic scenes on all the walls. Etched on the far wall was THE DICKINSON SCHOOL. Underneath that was a bust on a black marble pedestal. Wade quickly pointed out that the bust was of Zachary Dickinson, the founder of the school and its original benefactor. He told me Zachary Dickinson was a businessman who had made a fortune in the furniture industry. When we drew closer and I could look at the bust better, I thought he looked like Bob Hope.

There were two hallways, one on the far left and one on the far right. The one on the left had a plaque indicating that the administrative offices were there. I was quite struck by the silence in the building. Unlike any school I had attended, this seemed deserted. Even when classes were in session at my former high school, there were students moving about, making noises, shouting to each other, going to bathrooms, or simply wandering without permission.

At the beginning of the hallway was a door on the left; a gold plaque beside it read "Central Office." I gazed down the remainder of the hallway. All the classroom doors and other office doors were closed. There was no one in the hallway, and it was just as quiet as it was in the lobby. The walls were clean, without any posters or signs, and the hallway looked as if it had just been washed and polished. A series of tubular neon bulbs down the center of the hallway ceiling cast a yellowish white light over the walls and floor.

Before Wade reached for the office doorknob, we heard another door open and some voices echoing up from the rear of the building. Two boys walked in from the parking lot. I could see that one had hair close in color to mine, though in the yellowish light it looked somewhat redder. In fact, for a moment it looked to me like his head was on fire. The other boy had dark hair and was a few inches shorter. They laughed at something, paused to look our way, and then entered a room.

I entered the office after Wade opened the door. Unlike the offices at my old school, this was like stepping into a library. The two women working at their desks behind the counter were speaking softly to each other. Everything was neat and orderly; even the bulletin board on the immediate left had announcements perfectly pinned in straight, even columns. There was none of the turmoil and frantic activity I was used to seeing in a central school office.

One of the women appeared about sixty, the other more like thirty. They both looked at us, and then the older woman stayed at her desk while the younger woman approached the counter.

"May I help you?" she asked, and smiled at me.

"I'm Wade Emerson. My wife and I spoke with Mrs. Brentwood about Celeste's enrollment this morning," he said.

It didn't occur to me until then that Ami would have wanted to tell them I was her cousin. After all, she and I had gone through the fabrication of my history just the evening before. But wouldn't the office personnel know the truth anyway? I wondered.

"Oh. Just one moment," the woman said, and returned to her desk to use the phone. She spoke as softly into it as she had been speaking with her associate.

Almost immediately, the principal's office door opened, and Mrs. Brentwood appeared. Dressed in a charcoal skirt suit and white blouse, she looked as elegant and as pretty as she had when I saw her in the restaurant.

"Mr. Emerson, how nice to see you. Please, come in," she said, stepping back.

"Thank you," Wade said. He waited for me to go first.

"Hi," Mrs. Brentwood said, smiling. "You must be Celeste." She offered me her hand.

"Hi," I said, shaking it, and we walked into her office.

If she had seen Ami, me, and Wade at the restaurant the night before, she didn't care to mention it.

"I was under the impression your wife was bringing her around," she told Wade when she noticed Ami wasn't behind us.

"So was I," he said drily. "Actually, this works out well for me. It's on the way to work."

She raised her eyebrows, softened her smile even more, and went behind her desk.

"Please," she said, indicating the chairs in front of her desk.

I sat, and Wade did the same.

"First, let me welcome you officially and informally, Celeste," she said to me. "I'm impressed with your school record. It's nice to have a straight-A student come here, and I see you won an essay contest at your school last year as well."

"You have all that already?" I asked.

"Oh, yes. Mrs. Emerson arranged for that last week."

"Last week? But how—" I clamped my lips shut and glanced at Wade, who swung his eyes toward me and then turned back to Mrs. Brentwood.

"I just hope you're not so far ahead of the other students in your classes that you get bored and impatient. All of your teachers know about your arrival, by the way. They are all anxious to meet you. Here is your schedule," she said, handing me a card. "I'll take you around and familiarize you with the building. You'll find we can do that in minutes," she added, her eyes twinkling. "We're probably a third of the size of your former school, but we like being cozy."

"You have all the phone numbers, all the information you might need, then?" Wade asked her.

"Yes, we do." She looked down at an open folder. "Including dates of her inoculations. Very complete. It's all here," she emphasized. "This is a booklet about the Dickinson School, Celeste," she continued, handing a blue-and-gold-bound pamphlet to me. "Those are the school colors, by the way," she added. "The booklet will tell you our history, explain our policies, our rules. There is also a list of all the electives available for our seniors. And that is really the only decision left for you to make concerning your official schedule. You have period five free, and you can choose art history, drama-speech, or creative writing and journalism. That class does the school paper. Any of that catch your interest?"

"I think creative writing and journalism," I said.

"Yes, that's right. You won that essay contest. Wonderful. Mr. Feldman will be so pleased. He needs more soldiers in his troop. Well, then," she continued, and reached for another pamphlet on her desk. "This is for our parents, Mr. Emerson. It lists the school activities, open houses, events that we hope our parents will attend. We're rather proud of the support our parents give the school."

Wade took it, glanced at it, and nodded.

"Of course. We'll do what we can."

"Good." She glanced at her watch. "Well, we have about ten minutes before classes begin. All the students are in homeroom at the moment. Yours is room twelve, the senior homeroom. We'll get started immediately. I'll show you around. Care to join us, Mr. Emerson?"

"I think I have to get on to work. Seems like I'm leaving her in good hands," Wade said, rising quickly.

"You are," Mrs. Brentwood said. "Please don't hesitate to call me if you or Mrs. Emerson have any questions."

"Will do," Wade said. He turned, paused, and then turned back to me. "Good luck, Celeste. Something tells me you won't need it, however," he added, and left.

For a moment I felt abandoned. It was only a passing feeling, but it shot through me like a sharp knife cutting through a marshmallow. I was dangling. Not just a fish out of water, but a fish with no sense of where she belonged in the first place. Who were these people? What kind of a world had I entered? How could I possibly fit in and be comfortable?

"Now then, Celeste," Mrs. Brentwood said. Her voice was suddenly sterner, harder. I turned with some surprise. "Let's you and I have what I call my Come to Jesus meeting. We have plenty of time. Sit again," she ordered, her eyes no longer soft blue, but a cold gray.

I sat and waited while she went to the window, closed the shade, and then turned back to me.

"I am pleased to see you have achieved such good grades at your public school," she began, pronouncing the word *public* as though it soiled her tongue to do so. "But I am also aware of how good grades are sometimes given out charitably or simply to take the easier route. I know how burdened and stressed out the teachers are in our public schools and how they avoid any conflict they can."

"I earned my grades with hard work. No one has ever given me a pass unless I deserved it," I countered. "For almost all of my life, I had no one to defend me or stand up for me if I was treated unfairly, Mrs. Brentwood. My teachers had no fear of any conflicts."

Her eyes sharpened, narrowed, but her lips remained taut.

"Yes, that might be true, but I am also aware of how children without proper parents and home lives can contaminate those that have them," she said.

To me it felt as if she had reached across the desk and slapped me across the face. I winced and pulled myself back in the seat.

"I've been called all sorts of things, Mrs. Brentwood, but never a disease."

"I'm not accusing you of anything or saying anything like that about you in particular. I don't judge people on what they look like. I wait for them to show me who and what they are through their behavior. I simply want to make you aware of my full responsibilities here. The welfare of the student body as a whole is paramount. I have promised that to the parents who have entrusted me with the welfare of their children and who pay a great deal of money to have this extra TLC."

From the way she spoke, I couldn't imagine that care to be tender or loving.

"Never will any individual take on more importance than that, no matter how wealthy his or her benefactor might be," she emphasized.

She cleared her throat and relaxed her stiff posture.

"Now then, you are starting here under the cover of a deception I have agreed to because of how concerned your foster mother is about your well-being and assimilation into the family at the Dickinson School. I assured her there was no reason to have such fears, but she was very concerned and beseeched me to go along with the story."

"Story?"

"Frankly, everyone's personal business is everyone's personal business. This is not one of those public school general offices where things are leaked out through the gossip pipeline. We eschew gossip, and any one of my staff who perpetuates it will be let go instantly.

"In short, what you tell your fellow students about yourself is your business, as long as it does no one else any harm. I have no problem with your being Mrs. Emerson's cousin, if that makes her feel better. I have made this promise to your foster mother, and now I am making it to you, but I am adding that point, Celeste. Don't do anything that will bring harm, disrespect, or bad publicity to the Dickinson School. Am I understood?"

"Yes, ma'am," I said, holding my eyes on her the way I used to hold them on adults when I was much younger, even though my mind was reeling. How could Ami have done this before last night? She had obviously already planned out our spontaneous fiction about me.

Mrs. Brentwood looked immediately uncomfortable under my glare and stood up. She came around her desk and headed for the door.

"Follow me, then," she commanded, opening the office door and stepping out.

The two women in the office glanced up at us but quickly dropped their eyes back to their work as we stepped into the hallway.

"Our school is small enough that I can fulfill the responsibilities of what guidance counselors, principals, and deans of discipline do at public schools," she began as we walked down the hallway. "If you have any problems or questions, you can make an appointment to see me, regardless of the issue.

"This," she said, pausing at a doorway, "is our science lab." She opened the door, and a bald-headed man with just some gray fuzz around his ears, dressed in a lab coat, looked up from his desk, which was built higher than the student desks. He adjusted his glasses on the bridge of his nose and lowered the flame on a Bunsen burner.

"Good morning, Mr. Samuels. This is Celeste Atwell, the new student whose paperwork you were given at the end of last week. You'll recall that she will attend your period-three chemistry class."

"Yes, of course. I saw you were already in chemistry at your old school. I hope we'll match up," he said.

I could feel Mrs. Brentwood bristle.

"I have no doubts about that, Mr. Samuels," I said. "My class was so large, we had to take turns using the manuals."

"Yes, well, welcome to Dickinson, Celeste," he said, smiling. His round cheeks bubbled out.

"Thank you," I said.

"I'm giving her a very quick tour," Mrs. Brentwood said, and backed up, closing the door. "Mr. Samuels has been with us twelve years. He has written a significant paper on genetics that was published in a prestigious science journal. He also sponsors the science club after school, should you be interested," she added, her words like nails pounding her pride into my head.

"This is the ninth-grade homeroom," she said, nodding at room 9.

"And the tenth, eleventh, and your homeroom," she continued, but didn't pause.

We followed the corridor to the cafeteria, which was less than half the size of the one at my old school, but with far nicer furniture and much cleaner looking. Two elderly ladies and a young woman were working vigorously on the day's menu.

"You don't pay for anything, so there is no cashier," Mrs. Brentwood explained. "It's all part of the cost of the school. We ask only that you clean up after yourself properly and don't waste food."

We continued on to the gym, which, although smaller than my school's, was again cleaner and newer looking; even the bleacher seats looked more comfortable. The girl's physical education teacher was setting up a volleyball net.

"Morning, Mrs. Grossbard," Mrs. Brentwood called, her voice echoing.

Mrs. Grossbard, short and stout for a physical education teacher, turned. She had very thin, closely trimmed light brown hair and wore a uniform with a skirt and blouse in the school colors.

"This is Celeste Atwell."

"Oh, yes. How's your golf game?" she immediately asked me. "I have a spot on the team."

"I never played," I replied.

She looked dumbfounded.

"Maybe she has natural talent," Mrs. Brentwood offered. "You can test her."

"Yes. Of course. Yes," Mrs. Grossbard said, but without much enthusiasm. She returned to her volleyball net, and we continued. I looked out the rear doors, which opened to the ball fields, the tennis courts, and a golf driving range and putting green. None of that had been visible from the front of the building, and I was surprised at how big the school grounds were and how beautifully kept.

"The courts were a gift from one of our anonymous benefactors," Mrs. Brentwood commented.

The corridor took us around to additional classrooms and the library. A tall, lean, dark-haired man was working at the file cabinet.

"This is Mr. Monk, our librarian," she said, and he paused. "Our new student, Celeste Atwell."

"Welcome," he said. "I'll give you a tour on your study period. We have a half dozen computers and twenty thousand volumes," he said proudly. "Students from the community college come here often to do research. With written permission first, of course," he added, nodding at Mrs. Brentwood.

She nodded without speaking, and he returned to his files as if it were brain surgery and he couldn't spare a second of his attention.

"Thank you," I said, and we walked to the lobby and then down to her office, where she paused.

"I guess that's easy enough to navigate. You can go to your homeroom. You still have three minutes, and your teacher, Mr. Hersh, who is also your math teacher, will enter you in his books. Good luck and welcome," she said, her pretty smile and soft eyes returning.

I thought of a deer in the woods and how it could blend in so well it could almost disappear. Like a chameleon, she could change colors, but in her case it was moods, appearances, whatever fit the moment. Perhaps that was the skill of a successful administrator, a politician. She was telling me she could be all things to all people. Satisfy her, and she'd be Mrs. Sweet. Cross her, and she'd be Mrs. Executioner.

"Thank you," I said, and continued down the hallway to my homeroom. Even though she had spent time giving me a quick tour of the building, a lecture full of veiled threats, and introductions to some of the teachers, I felt tossed into the unknown. At my old school, the student body provided what we called Big Sisters or Big Brothers, who would at least show the new students about for a while and introduce them to other students. They had someone to talk to so that they didn't feel completely alone and strange. I guess everyone here is assumed to be independent and sophisticated enough not to mind, I thought. What choice did I have anyway?

Despite what I had been told about the size of the student body, I was still surprised to see only about eighteen students in the entire senior class. All eyes were on me the moment I opened the door and entered the room. The redheaded boy I had seen down the hall was in the first row, slumping, his long legs sprawled under the desk so that his black running shoes protruded in the front. He had patches of freckles on the crests of his cheeks and a dimple in his left cheek. The sharp bright blue of his eyes and the orange tint of his lips gave him a colorful face. He was smiling impishly, as if he knew all about me.

Beside him sat, I thought, a far more interesting and good-looking dark-haired boy, whose ebony eyes announced his sensitivity and intelligence. He sat straighter, firmer, and, without radiating arrogance, looked more athletic and self-confident. His eyes held mine for a moment, and then he softened his lips and looked at the teacher again.

I gazed at the rest of the class and thought the girls had as much interest in and curiosity about me as did the boys. One girl in particular, a pretty brunette with hazel brown eyes, looked a little upset at my entrance.

It was as though I had interrupted something she was saying or doing. She glared at the dark-haired boy and then back at me as I approached the desk.

Mr. Hersh was standing with his hands on his hips, his jacket unbuttoned. He looked at least in his fifties, with curly black hair sprinkled with gray and blue-gray eyes. I could sense he was in the middle of reprimanding the group. He straightened up quickly and turned to me.

"Welcome," he said. "Class, this is Celeste Atwell, who was just enrolled this morning." I waited as he jotted something in his register. Then he looked up and smiled. "Why don't you take the empty desk at the end of the first row, Celeste. I was just finishing up today's announcements, and we have only another minute or so before the first-period bell rings."

"Thank you," I said.

"How polite," the redheaded boy quipped. Some of the other boys widened their smiles, but not the dark-haired boy beside him. He simply shook his head.

I walked across the room and turned up the aisle, gazing at the pretty brunette girl as I passed her. I looked at her with some interest because of how hard she was staring at me, but she didn't smile back. As soon as I took my seat, Mr. Hersh continued.

"And so, as I was saying, Mrs. Brentwood wanted me to point out that someone has been careless about throwing paper towels into the garbage can in the girls' room in this corridor. If anyone sees a paper towel on the floor, she should put it into the bin."

"Ugh," a short, light-brown-haired girl moaned. "Who wants to pick up someone else's dirt?"

The girls around her nodded.

"Why can't you girls be as neat as we boys?" the redheaded boy cried. The other boys cheered.

"You don't wipe your hands on towels, Waverly. You wipe them on your pants," the short girl retorted, and there were cheers and hisses.

"All right, that's enough," Mr. Hersh said firmly. The students quieted down instantly. "You all spend most of your day in this building. You should be treating it the way you treat your homes."

"That's the problem," another boy shouted, and there was more laughter.

"If it continues," Mr. Hersh said firmly, "you might find no towels in the bathrooms. Then you'll all be wiping your hands on your clothes, and considering how expensive some of your outfits are, girls, you should think about that."

If that's the biggest problem here, I thought, this will really be a new experience. The girls' room in my school always smelled of smoke and had towels crunched and thrown about, graffiti on the walls and mirrors, and often toilets overflowing or full of cigarette butts, gum wrappers, and even tampons.

The bell rang, and everyone stood up. The dark-haired boy gazed back at me and then started out. The pretty brunette stepped toward me.

"I'm Germaine Osterhout," she said. "I'm the senior class president. Welcome to Dickinson," she blurted.

"Thank you," I said, but before I had finished, she had turned away and started out of the room.

"That's more than I got when I entered this school for the first time," said a very tall girl with long, straight, brown hair. "It was weeks before anyone would say hello or even recognize I existed."

I stared for a moment, and then she laughed.

"C'mon, stupid, I'm just kidding you," she said, seizing my arm and starting us after the others. "I'm Lynette Firestone. My mother and your cousin are good friends."

"Oh?"

Ami had never mentioned her, but she had never mentioned anyone for that matter, and what was again surprising, she hadn't mentioned that she had told our fiction to anyone else already.

Lynette paused and turned to me in the hallway. I noticed that just about everyone passing by us looked at me with some interest.

"Sorry about your parents. Lucky you weren't much younger when it happened. It's really nice of your cousin to take you in like this," she recited, "even though it makes you feel like a refugee."

"Pardon me? A refugee?"

"Just kidding. It's nice of her to care about you, and nice of me to volunteer to help you get acclimated."

She had a long mouth that dipped in the corners, as though her facial muscles collapsed with fatigue around her lips. Her dark eyes were a little too large for the narrowness of her face, and her nose had an arrogant turn that looked recently constructed by a plastic surgeon. She was shapely, but not pretty enough to become a model. Her height, which looked to be at least six feet, had to be a detriment considering the rest of her, I thought.

"You could say thank you," she added drily when I didn't say anything in return.

"What?" That's all I need, someone to remind me of when to say thank you, I thought.

"Nothing," she said, smiling. "Just kidding. No one says thank-you much around here. And no one apologizes for anything, so don't expect it."

"I don't," I said. "I don't expect anything from anyone. That way, if something good happens, it's a wonderful surprise."

She smiled.

"Actually, my mother made me promise, hand on the Bible, to be your friend. She had promised that to your cousin."

"Oh, don't worry about that," I said, glancing at my schedule card to confirm the classroom for my first period. "I don't expect to make any friends here."

"Huh?" she said, her mouth opening with surprise.

"Just kidding," I told her, and walked on.

"Nicely done," I heard on my right and turned to see the dark-haired boy flash me a smile and walk on toward the same classroom. I had no idea he had been standing nearby and listening to our conversation.

As it turned out, he sat across from me. It was our class in economics taught by Mr. Franks, a spry little man in his forties with prematurely gray hair, whose flow of energy and excitement was designed to fill his students with enthusiasm and interest. Sometimes he looked like he was teaching to the back of the room, to an imaginary perfect class of students. I was amused by the way he would ask a question and then, anticipating no response, answer it himself as though someone in the class had done so. I could see that the dark-haired boy was just as amused by him as I was.

"Hey," he said when the bell rang to end the period, and we stood up to leave. "I'm not the class president, but welcome to Dickinson."

"Thank you," I said, and then quickly put my hand over my lips. "Oops. Didn't mean to say it."

He laughed.

"I'm Trevor Foley. Don't believe anything Lynette tells you," he warned. "She's a pathological liar and the least popular girl in the school. In fact, if anyone wanted to get you off to a bad start with the kids at Dickinson, she'd be the one he'd recommend you become friends with.

"Take your time. Do what everyone else does here: window-shop first."

"Is that what you're doing?"

"Sure. And I like what I see," he told me, smiled, and walked on.

There was something about him that reminded me of Noble. Was it the way he looked at people? The way he smiled? The mystery in his eyes? Or was it just my wishful thinking?

After all, there was nothing I feared more than being alone. And something told me that could happen here as easily as it could anywhere.

9

My Mother's Child

♊

Ami was waiting for me at the end of the school day, but despite Wade's prediction, she was not full of apologies. She was angry instead. She stood by her sports car waving as I stepped out of the front entrance. Trevor was beside me. He and I had spent most of the day together. He had sat with me at lunch, introduced me to other students, and given me advice about some of them and some of our teachers.

Waverly, who was obviously the class clown, teased him mercilessly about me.

"You finally found a girl who would give you the time of day, huh, Trevor?" he said at lunch. "Wait until tomorrow," he warned. "When she finds out you just got over a sexually transmitted disease."

"Shut up, you idiot," Trevor told him, trying not to give him the satisfaction of sounding too angry.

I could see that Lynette was upset about my not

clinging to her offer of friendship. She tried to get me to sit with her at lunch and was both surprised and disappointed that I was already spending time with Trevor.

"I'm just trying to be nice," she quipped indignantly, but it looked like tears were imminent.

I invited her to join us. She thought about it for a moment and then opted to sit with two other girls who were at least twenty pounds overweight and shared her disdain for most of the student body. Together they formed a perfect picture: *Misery Loves Company.*

"Celeste!" Ami called, even though she knew I had seen her waiting. "Hurry up, we have some things to do and we're already late."

I turned to Trevor.

"Thanks for spending so much time with me," I said.

"Another thank you? I'm sorry, but there is nothing I can do about it now. I'll have to report you tomorrow," he joked.

I started away, laughing.

"Hey," he said, catching up and seizing my arm to turn me back. "Seriously, if you have any questions about any of the work, here's my number," he said, and gave me a card. "We all have cards," he added when he saw my surprise. "It's a thing here. Gives you more prestige."

"Thank yo—never mind," I said, stopping myself and putting his card in my purse.

"Hey, that's not fair. How about giving me your number?"

"I don't have a card," I said.

"But you have a number."

I laughed and told it to him.

"See you," he said, and hurried toward his car in the parking lot. I looked after him a moment and then hurried to Ami, who looked after him as well.

"Is that Trevor Foley?" she asked.

"Yes."

"You made friends with him already?" she asked. She didn't sound as much impressed as she sounded disappointed.

"I think it was the other way around," I said. "Why? How do you know him?"

"I know who the Foleys are. His father owns a dozen car dealerships between here and New York City."

She looked pensive and then smiled.

"I knew you would have no trouble here," she said. "Get in. I have a surprise waiting for you at home."

"A surprise?"

"Yes, just be patient. So, Wade called," she said, her anger flaring as she got into the car and started the engine, "to bawl me out for not getting you up and getting myself up early enough to register you this morning. Big deal. We could have done it tomorrow just as well."

I smiled to myself. How did he know her so well and yet not know her at all? I wondered.

"C'mon. Don't just sit there like a stuffed toy. Tell me about your first day. Do you like the school, the teachers? Did you meet other boys beside Trevor Foley?" She fired her questions in rapid succession. However, the answer to all the questions was a simple yes.

"What about the other girls?" she followed. "Oh, I know they can be very snobby at first. They want to see what you're all about before they commit to any friendships, but we'll take care of that ASAP.

"Oh, did you meet Lynette Firestone?" she asked.

I laughed at how she was more excited about my first day than I was.

"Yes," I said. "She introduced herself right away." I recalled all she had said. "How did she know our story so quickly? I thought you and I made up the actual details together last night," I said, curious. "Mrs. Brentwood knew what you were going to tell people, too."

"Oh, I had already planted some ideas around, and we just fleshed them out," she said, waving her hand to toss off the answer as insignificant. "Actually, I tried it out on Lynette's mother first to see how it would fly. Occasionally, we have lunch. Lynette would be a nice friend for you," she added. She smiled. "I'm so happy you have gotten off to a good beginning," she said.

She went on to tell me about charity events that were upcoming, shopping sprees she had planned for us in New York City, and some possible ideas for vacations.

"If I can ever get Wade to take one," she added. "Maybe now that you're with us, he'll have to."

We paused at the gates, and then she said, "Close your eyes."

"What?"

"It's the surprise," she said.

I laughed and did as she asked. We drove in.

"Not yet," she said. "Not yet. Okay," she said when I felt us stop. "Now."

I opened my eyes. A car was parked in front with a man sitting in the driver's seat. Across the sides of the car was emblazoned SAFETY FIRST DRIVING SCHOOL.

"Your first lesson," Ami squealed. "He'll be here every day for two weeks, or until he feels you're ready for the driving test for your license. See. I live up to my promises," she declared. "Go on. He's waiting for you, silly," she said.

I was just sitting there, staring stupidly.

"Now?"

"Of course now. What kind of a teenage girl doesn't drive? Go on," she urged, practically pushing me out of the car. "I'll take your books into the house for you and put them in your room. Go on. Don't keep him waiting. He gets paid by the hour, and you know how Wade is about money."

Clothes, jewelry, hairdos and makeup, a private school, and now driving lessons, and all this in a matter of days, I thought. I am truly finally lucky.

My first driving lesson went well. The instructor was nice but almost robotic, repeating instructions, driving regulations, and criticisms frequently in a dry monotone. I thought he had concluded I was simply spastic, but when we returned to the house, he told me I had done exceedingly well for someone who had no previous experience.

"And unlike my other teenage students, you listened and didn't treat the car like a new toy."

I thanked him and went into the house through the garage, since the door was still open. Mrs. McAlister was working at a frantic pace in the kitchen, preparing the evening's meal. She barely glanced at me as I passed by. I didn't see Mrs. Cukor about, but I wasn't disappointed. I hurried upstairs, intending to get right into my homework. I wasn't in a panic, but I did realize that in every class, I was behind. In the back of my mind was Mrs. Brentwood's face and her words concerning my good grades at the public school. If I did poorly here, she would certainly feel justified, and I would see it in her face every time I looked her way.

When I reached my bedroom, I noticed immediately that the garlic was gone from the door handle. Perhaps Wade had spoken to Mrs. Cukor after all, I thought, and went into my room, changed my clothes, and started my homework. I hadn't been at it ten minutes before I heard a knock on my door, and Ami appeared.

"I'm sorry, I was on the phone. How was your first driving lesson?"

"I think it went well. He seemed pleased."

"Good." She hesitated and then said, "You had a phone call. I heard your phone ringing and ringing, so I answered it for you."

"A phone call."

"Trevor Foley." Her face turned a bit sour. "You gave your number out rather quickly, didn't you? I advised you to be very selective about that. I mean, you hardly know the boy, and that number is unlisted so that you won't be bothered by every Tom, Dick, and Trevor."

"Oh." I said. I hadn't thought about it being so precious and restricted. The truth was, I had never had a phone I could call my own, and it was quite exciting to be able to give someone the number.

"I don't mean to be so critical of you so quickly, Celeste, but I do want to look after your welfare and give you the benefit of my years and years of experience, especially when it comes to men. Boys," she added.

"I know. I'm sorry."

"What happens is, you give it to one boy and then he gives it to another and another, and before you know it, they're all calling and saying stupid things to you to try to get you into bed with them. You have to understand from the start that their reason for calling you, for talking to you, for being friendly, is purely to get you to sleep with them. It's their nature. They can't help it."

She continued into the room and sat on my bed.

"Maybe I should give you a first lesson about boys. I know how isolated from the real world you've been. Those nuns wrapped the Bible around you, built walls between you and boys."

"Well, not entirely," I began. "The wall wasn't that high."

"It was high enough," she said sharply. "As soon as a boy's hormones develop, they take over completely. You can see it in the way they look at you, if you're observant. They're looking right through your clothes, imagining your breasts, your stomach, between your legs, everything. They make love to you in their minds over and over until their tongues hang out."

I caught the note of bitterness in her voice, and she saw that I had. She smiled.

"I don't mean to make them sound so horrible. I just want you to be aware. My mother was always quoting, 'Fools rush in where angels fear to tread.' And for good reason. So many girls younger than you ruin their lives for a few moments of physical pleasure. They lose their reputations and then finally their self-respect. They become cynical and depressed and end up hating either themselves or everyone around them. Many become mentally ill. Yes, they do, Celeste, and you have had a very difficult childhood to overcome. Look how far you've come, too. I would just hate myself if I put you in harm's way. You can appreciate and understand that, can't you?"

"Yes, of course," I said.

"Good." She looked down at her hands and then up at me, her eyes glowing with tears held firmly back. "I just hate having to sound like I'm chastising you. I always hated it when my mother did that, or especially when my father did. I know it makes you feel small and empty inside."

She smiled.

"Just like me, you feel certain you can take care of yourself. I know. It's the arrogance of youth," she added, holding her head high. She laughed. "You feel nothing bad can happen. It makes you reckless. I can tell you I was, but I was lucky to have such strong parents."

I listened, but I couldn't help raising and bringing my eyebrows together. Wade had told me her parents were too permissive, and careless about their obligations. Why did he believe one thing and she another so dramatically different?

"Come here a moment," she asked, smiling. She reached out for me. I rose and took her hand. She patted beside her on the bed for me to sit. She still held onto my hand.

"You don't realize how beautiful you are yet, Celeste. Where you lived and how you lived made that difficult for you to appreciate, I know. They probably told you it's a sin to think of yourself as beautiful, to concentrate on your looks, right?"

"Sort of," I admitted.

"Of course they did. That's what they do because they're so unhappy about their own appearances themselves. Misery loves company," she said, as if she had heard my thoughts earlier in the day and wanted to show me we thought alike.

"I don't think it was quite that way, but—"

"It was. Believe me," she practically commanded. Then she smiled. "It doesn't matter. What matters is what's true, and it's true you are beautiful. Now, when a girl is already out in the world, the normal world, and she grows into her own, into her own beauty, she has had some preparation and at least has some idea of what to expect.

"But you . . . you were kept under lock and key, shut away in that place or one like it previously, and then suddenly, here I come along and emancipate you, just like Lincoln emancipated the slaves."

I started to smile.

"Don't laugh. I'm not making a foolish statement. It is like that. You're so free to do practically anything you want. In fact, you have more freedom, because you have the advantages now. You have your own things. You have beautiful clothing, a magnificent new home, and soon"—her eyes twinkled—"you'll have your own car. You will."

She squeezed my hand harder.

"However, with freedom comes responsibility. You must promise me on your soul, on your heart and your soul, on your very life that you will not give away your treasure quickly and foolishly. You must find restraint. You must—"

"I wouldn't do that, as much for myself as for anyone else," I said firmly.

She stared a moment, and then she smiled and nodded.

"No, you wouldn't. I knew that about you the moment I set eyes on you. You are very special, Celeste. You have something those other girls don't have. I'm so happy about that."

She took a deep breath of relief and let go of my hand. Then she stood up.

"Let's make a pact for now. Until you're really settled in and you have a firm understanding of what I would call the lay of the land, you won't go on any dates or spend any time alone with any of the boys you meet. You can talk to them on the phone, of course, but for a while, let's keep them all at a safe distance. Not that you would be too weak or that I don't trust you," she quickly added. "I just would feel better. I can't imagine how I would feel if I had brought you into some danger instead of improving your life."

I stared at her and thought to myself, wasn't she throwing up walls even higher and thicker than all the Mother Higginses in the world had done or could do? Wasn't she imprisoning me in a real sense?

"When you say for a while, how long do you mean?" I asked, full of disappointment.

"Oh, not long at all, but long enough to be certain you're on solid ground. If I didn't look after you properly, Wade would be all over me anyway, Celeste. He might even want me to send you back," she concluded, a thick sense of threat underlying her final words.

It brought blood to my face.

Behave and do as I want you to do, or we'll send you back, was the message, clear and strong.

This was a day full of threats, I thought, recalling my moments with Mrs. Brentwood in her office after Wade had gone. Was there something on my forehead, something about me I couldn't see but others could? Was it the dark cloud of my past that hovered over my head? When had I been anything but a good girl, a proper girl, obedient and responsible and trustworthy? Mother Higgins appreciated me, but was that for the reasons Ami suggested? Was it because I was so shackled by the orphanage, by the religious chains? If someone is locked away for her whole life, is she far less likely to be a sinner?

"Just show me you can handle the freedom," Ami finally said. "That's all I ask. Okay?"

I nodded.

"Okay."

"Good. Good. Let that be the only serious, mean conversation between us ever." She pressed her palms together as if it was a prayer, hugged me, and then started to leave. "Oh, Basil is coming to dinner again tonight. Mrs. McAlister is preparing Irish stew, one of his favorite meals, especially the way she prepares it. Wear the outfit I got you at Oh-La-La, and don't forget the cologne he likes. After all," she said, trailing a thin laugh, "he's really paying for all this in one way or another."

She left, closing the door softly behind her. It wasn't until that moment that I realized my heart had been pounding. Why was it so important to always look sexy for Basil? He was truly like the king of the manor.

I returned to my schoolwork, but I couldn't stop thinking about Trevor and wondering why he had called me so soon. Despite all the warnings Ami had given me about boys, I still felt it was simply impolite and ungracious to ignore his call. Ami had not taken down his telephone number to give to me. Perhaps he knew he didn't have to give it to her. I reached into my purse and took out his card. As I tapped out the numbers, I couldn't help feeling like I was doing something forbidden. He answered on the first ring.

"Trevor Foley," he said. "At your service."

"Hi. It's Celeste Atwell."

"Hey. How are you doing? Recuperating from the first day in the pits?"

"The Dickinson School would hardly qualify as the pits," I said, laughing. "You haven't ever attended a public school?"

"No, I went right from preschool to a private elementary school. I spent summers at a camp designed to turn us into preppy little men. Do I seem preppy to you?"

"I don't know what that means."

"Yeah, well, you're better off not knowing. Anyway, I called to see if you would like to attend a party with me this weekend. It will be a good opportunity to get to know some of the other students. Waverly is having a birthday party for himself."

"He's making a party for himself?"

"No one else will, including his parents. They believe birthday parties end after the age of five. Fortunately for us, and unfortunately for them, they are taking his ten-year-old sister to an audition for child television positions in New York City, and Waverly resisted going along. Since it's his birthday, they granted him his wish."

"They're leaving him on his birthday?"

"Like I said, they don't carry on much about birthdays, but we will. You'll have a great time. Can I pick you up about eight?"

"I'd like to go. I really would, but I can't," I said. "My . . . cousin has asked me not to socialize until I've settled into life here."

"How long does it take you to settle in?"

"Not long. I hope," I added.

"What a bummer. So until then, you have to sit at home with the cousin watching television or something?"

"I'm sure my cousin has activities planned for me."

"Activities? What are you, in a camp or a home?"

he asked, making no attempt to hide his disappointment.

"I'm sorry. I'm at a . . . a disadvantage."

"Yeah," he said, and was silent. In a moment he
calmed down, however. "I suppose you are. I don't
mean to sound like such a dork about it."

"They're being very generous. My cousin arranged
for me to have formal driving lessons. I had my first
one today."

"You mean you've never driven a car?"

I bit my lower lip. Already I was putting my foot in
my mouth. One lie always led to another, and as if you
were weaving a web around yourself, you were suddenly trapped in deceptions of your own making. I had
never strayed from the truth before I came here to live,
I thought. I was never afraid of it.

"No. My mother is a very nervous person," I told
him, quickly thinking of a way out.

"I'll say she is. Maybe you're better off living with
your cousin."

"I hope so. I mean, they're nice people, and they
have so much."

"Yeah, I know the company. Actually, the Emersons
bought all their cars from my father's dealerships. If
you need extra driving lessons, I'd be happy to give
them to you," he added.

"For now I had better stick with the formal ones."

"Right," he said. "Okay. I'll see you tomorrow."

"Yes. And Trevor . . ."

"Yes?"

"At the risk of endangering myself with the in-
crowd, thanks for thinking of me."

He laughed.

"Drop the past tense," he said. "I am thinking of
you. See ya."

I held the receiver to my ear for a few moments longer, like someone who wanted the taste of something wonderful to last as long as possible. I had no way to judge, of course. Ami was right about my inexperience, but my instincts were telling me not to be afraid of Trevor, that there was an underlying goodness about him, and he wasn't simply looking at me as he would look at one more conquest.

It was surely times like this when I missed Noble the most, missed the sound of his voice in my mind, the sight of his spiritual being. Had I drifted too far from him, from them all, from my past, from my family? Would I never touch or hear them again?

"All children," my psychologist Dr. Sackett had told me, "have their imaginary, innocent world, and then they grow out of it. I suppose we always mourn the loss of childhood faiths, of that willingness to believe in something more, but it's how we were meant to be in order to function in the adult world," he said.

For me, it was too great a sacrifice and loss, I thought. And yet I was afraid to work hard at regaining it. I was afraid of being considered as crazy as my mother and my family. I was afraid of being stigmatized and forever branded weird. Where would I go under those conditions, and whom would I love and who would love me? How could I find a compromise, hold on to the wonder I once knew and enjoyed, and yet live among those who never had and never could?

I'm tired of being lonely, I thought. I'm tired of being shut up in one world or another. Gazing around at all that I now had and would have, I wondered if I was willing to wait. Trevor's soft dark eyes called to me.

I wanted so much to answer.

For now, I had to still my inner voices, keep my heart from beating too fast and too hard, and pretend I didn't yet care.

With all this turmoil spinning in my brain, I had a hard time getting back to my homework, but I managed. In fact, I was so involved in my studies, I lost track of time. Ami was shocked to see me still sitting at my desk.

"What are you doing? You have to get dressed! It's not something a woman does in ten minutes. We don't shave a little and splash on some scented lotion, put on a shirt and pants, and run out brushing our hair. Preparations, preparations, preparations, are so important, Celeste. I thought I had taught you that already."

"I'm sorry. I just got involved in my schoolwork. I'll get dressed quickly."

"I'm not asking you to do it quickly. I'm asking you to do it perfectly," she said. "Don't be such a student," she warned, nodding at my books. "You'll miss out on the important things. I'll be back in a half hour." She glanced at her watch. "Actually, it's all right for us to be a little later than ever. I'm still mad at Wade for opening his mouth to me about not getting you to school this morning," she said, and left.

I started to dress immediately, again wondering why it was always so important to look sexy and attractive for Wade's father. When I had finished and went to her room, Ami was surprised at how quickly I had gotten myself together. I stood there waiting for her to criticize something, but she smiled and nodded at me instead.

"Very nice. You look terrific, Celeste. I'm proud of how quickly you've picked up on everything. You've done a wonderful job on your lips and eyes." She tilted her head. "You're not lying to me, are you? You didn't do all these things before you arrived here?"

"Hardly," I said, smiling.

"Well. It doesn't matter." She sprang to her feet. "What matters is, we look fantastic once again. Wade's already called to see where we are. He says his father is drinking too much too fast. He needs me, you see. Next time he won't be so quick to pick up the phone to chastise me for something. Take note. These are little lessons you'll appreciate when you finally settle down with your own Wade," she said, and hooked her arm through mine.

My own Wade? Whomever I fell in love with and married, I thought, I hoped our relationship would be far better. Was that a silly dream? Were all marriages eventually the same, with two people eventually finding ways to tolerate each other, rather than hold on to something magical and special?

"You're teasing me," Basil Emerson accused the moment we entered the dining room. He pointed his thick, long forefinger at Ami, and his expression of anger actually nailed my feet to the floor for a moment and stole my breath. His eyes were blazing.

Wade had his head down and his hands clasped like some penitent hoping for mercy. I saw the full glass of whiskey in front of Basil on the table.

"Moi?" Ami said, pretending grand innocence. "How so, Basil?"

"Keeping us waiting like this. You know what they call women who do that, don't you?" he asked, and then he smiled, reached for his glass, and took a drink. "Women who tease?"

"We just can't rush our preparations, Basil," Ami

said, leading me to the table. "Imagine if someone tried to rush Renoir or da Vinci."

Basil roared with laughter, and Wade looked up.

"You're comparing putting on makeup to a world-class artist?" he asked.

"Yes," Ami said without hesitation. "Basil, am I right?"

"You're always right in my book, Ami," he said. "Now look at you," he said, turning to me. "Every time I see you, Miss Unfortunate, I am more and more confused. How could you have been passed up all these years?"

"The people coming to the orphanages weren't looking for concubines, Dad," Wade muttered.

"Conk you what?"

"They're looking for needy children, children they could help find family lives," Wade explained. "Not lovers and mistresses and the like."

Basil pulled the corners of his mouth in and shook his head.

"You ever relax, Wade? You ever crack a joke with the crew at the plant? Sometimes I wonder if I had anything to do with your birth at all."

"I often do too, Dad."

Basil stared a moment. I thought he was going to blast Wade with his anger, maybe even strike him, but instead his face collapsed into a smile, and then he roared with laughter again.

"That's good. Now there's a good joke. Imagining Jeanie Emerson having an affair and getting pregnant. Why, that woman was so modest, she wouldn't even undress in front of me, and I'm talking about after twenty years of marriage. We had to make love with the lights out, for crissakes. Come to think of it, we made you in the dark, Wade. Maybe that was the problem, huh, Ami? What do you think? Is it easier or better to make love with the lights on or off?"

"Can we talk about something else?" Wade pleaded.

"Yeah, we can talk about something else," Basil said, waving his glass at Ami. "We can talk about when I'm going to have a grandchild, made in the dark or in the light."

It was as though lightning had streaked through the room, just over our heads, singeing our brains and thundering in our ears. Both Wade and Ami froze.

"Aaah, forget about it. Let's just enjoy a good dinner, a good Irish dinner," Basil shouted, and Mrs. Cukor appeared with Mrs. McAlister behind her, bringing in the food.

It was all delicious, but the tension at the table made it hard to enjoy. Wade tried to turn the conversation to my first day at school, but his father went into a rant about wasting money on spoiled children.

"A girl with her looks don't need to worry about fancy schools," he declared. He smiled at me, intending it to be a compliment, but I didn't see it that way, and neither did Ami. She went into a lecture about women's rights and a woman's place in the business and professional world.

The tips of Basil's ears grew redder and redder, either from the combination of wine and whiskey or from Ami's snappy criticism of male chauvinists. Wade was quiet most of the time. By the end of the dinner, everyone was quiet, however, and a heavy atmosphere pressed down on us all. Basil made some excuses about having to leave early.

"I got something to do early tomorrow," he said, "so I can't stay over tonight."

When he kissed Ami good night, he put his hand around her waist and dropped it to her rear. She grabbed his forearm and turned him away quickly, but I caught the whole scene. If Wade saw it, he pretended he didn't.

Basil then turned to say good night to me, but when he stepped toward me, I thrust out my hand. He looked at it as if I had a knife in it and then at me and smiled.

"I see why Ami's taken to you so quickly," he muttered, shook my hand slightly, and then left.

"Let's go for a ride," Ami said immediately. "I need some fresh air."

"But I have so much homework," I pleaded.

I saw how disappointed she was, but I didn't know what to do. Wade came to my rescue.

"Where are you going this time of night, anyway? And besides, you've enrolled her in an expensive school. Why waste the opportunity for her?"

Ami pouted, and I excused myself to go back to my room. As I started for the stairway, Mrs. Cukor appeared as if she had been waiting in the wings for me.

"Darkness is falling on this house," she warned. "You know it is, too."

"I don't know anything about any darkness," I shot back at her. "I don't know who or what you think I am, but I'm getting tired of being treated like something evil."

"You're the snake in the Garden of Eden," she muttered, not retreating.

"This was hardly the Garden of Eden before I arrived, Mrs. Cukor, and for all I know, you might be the snake."

That took her back.

She brought her hand to the base of her throat.

I am my mother's child, I thought. I will not cower before anyone. I stepped toward her.

"Beware of the darkness that is in your own heart," I

said, and left her standing like a statue at the foot of the stairway.

My heart was pounding, but I felt stronger.

Maybe you're not showing yourself anymore, Noble, I thought, but you're inside me. You're inside my heart. And from that place, you will never escape.

Until I am able to let you go.

10

A Half-Naked Guy

♊

There was a knock on my door hours later. Before I could say, "Come in," Ami entered, dressed in her nightgown. She still wore all her makeup. However, her hair looked like she had been running her fingers through it madly.

"I'm sorry about tonight," she said, pacing in front of me. "Maybe it wasn't such a good idea to leave Basil waiting and drinking so long. We'll remember next time. He can be terribly obnoxious." She paused to look at me. "Were you very upset with him? Did he hurt your feelings?"

"No, it's all right," I said, but on the subject of hurting my feelings, I wondered if I should mention anything about my confrontation with Mrs. Cukor. I quickly decided enough was enough for one night, and I was getting tired. I had done a great deal of reading and note taking and had written a short essay for my writing class.

"Look at you," Ami said, perusing my desk and seeing the opened books and papers. "You really are quite
the student, aren't you?"

I shrugged.

"I guess so. When I was little, my brother and my
mother read to me often. They say that works the best
when it comes to getting someone to become a good
student."

"Your brother? You mean your sister, don't you?"

"Yes," I said.

"How weird all of that must have been. One day I
would like to talk to you about it all, but not if it will
be unpleasant for either of us," she added quickly.

"I don't remember enough to talk about it," I
replied, turning away quickly. Except for Flora and Dr.
Sackett, I had never really talked about my past with
anyone. Everyone else usually had what I felt to be an
almost pornographic interest in the details.

"That's good. Forgetting is sometimes a blessing.
Like I'm going to forget all about the nasty things
Basil said tonight." She snapped her fingers. "Just like
that. See, the ugliness and unpleasantness is gone.

"This is a magical place. We can drive away sadness
with the click of fingers or just by going out and buying
something new, which is what I plan to do tomorrow
while you're in school. I'll get you something special,
too."

"You've gotten me so much already, Ami."

"So what? It pleases me to get things for you, things
I know will make you look good."

She touched my cheek softly.

"It's like I'm doing it all for myself, anyway. I'm reliving my youth through you, Celeste. So don't worry.
You're giving me something very precious in return,
very precious," she said, and then leaned over to kiss

my forehead before turning to leave. "Sweet dreams," she called from the door. "I insist that all dreams in this house be sweet, and nightmares stay outside the doors and windows where they belong."

I watched her leave and then I rose and prepared for bed myself. Before I went to sleep, however, I decided to go downstairs to get something cold to drink. The water from my bathroom sink was not very cold, and I had a craving for something sweet, like juice or even some soda. I knew there was some in the refrigerator behind the bar, if not in the kitchen.

The halls were dimly lit, and all the rooms downstairs were dark. I hesitated at the kitchen doorway, thinking about Mrs. McAlister and how she guarded it with such determination. I was positive she would know if I disturbed one little thing in that refrigerator, so I went to the bar and found a can of ginger ale. I opened it and took a sip before hearing something in the hallway. Slowly peering around the corner of the door, I looked into the dimly lit corridor. Was it Mrs. Cukor? Did she hover about this house like some sort of ghost?

I didn't see her, but I sensed her. Perhaps she was standing in a shadow near the far door or just inside the den-office. She wasn't haunting this house, I thought. She was haunting me. I waited a few more moments, then started back up the stairs to my room. When I reached the top and turned toward my bedroom door, I heard whimpering coming from Ami and Wade's bedroom.

Wade's voice was muffled, but I could tell he was pleading, cajoling, practically begging her about something. Her response was merely to cry and whimper and then finally to burst out with a scream that made my very bones vibrate with its shrill, terrifying sound.

All was quiet after that, and I felt very guilty about eavesdropping. I hurried into my own bedroom and closed the door as softly as I could, so no one would know I had been out there listening.

What was that all about? I wondered. Was Ami sick? Was Wade doing something that hurt her? Thinking about it and about Mrs. Cukor sliding like a shadow over the walls below kept me awake for a while, but finally I drifted asleep.

I was woken again by my phone.

"Your wake-up call," Wade sang.

Once again I was surprised I hadn't woken up myself.

"I should just use an alarm clock."

"It's all right. I don't mind."

"I never sleep this late usually. I don't know what's gotten into me."

"Wine at dinner," he replied drily. "Ami's dead to the world again, so as I expected, I'll be your chauffeur once more."

"Thank you," I said, rose and dressed, and went down to breakfast, where he was sitting and reading his newspaper as usual.

It made me wonder about living a life as regimented and as organized as his, doing the same things day in and day out and seemingly enjoying it. Some people simply didn't appreciate spontaneity and were uncomfortable with changes, no matter how small, I thought. Wade was one of those people. He wore the same clothes, brushed and styled his hair the same way, arrived at his business at the same time, and read the same paper. Ami, who was so unpredictable, was surely like an extraterrestrial to him.

Mrs. McAlister appeared in the doorway and waited for my breakfast order. I wondered if I would ever get used to having people do so much for me—cook for me, clean up, and clean up my room as well.

"I think I'd like some eggs this morning, please. Sunny side up."

"Sunny side up," she repeated. "Fried eggs or poached eggs?"

"Fried, I suppose."

"Humph," she said, as if that's what she expected, and backed into the kitchen.

Wade lowered his paper.

"Sorry about Dad last night. He came half tanked as it was, and then waiting for you guys, he drank a lot more. Not that he's much better sober," he added.

"It was all right. He didn't bother me that much," I said, feeling I had no right to complain about anyone in this house anyway.

"No, I don't think he did bother you. You're quite a kid, Celeste. Maybe living in orphanages hardened you more than Ami thinks. I don't suppose you can grow up too dainty there, or too soft-skinned. Whatever Ami thinks is just terrible or horrible, you probably brush off like an elephant brushes off a fly."

"Things might bother you just as much in the or-phanage," I suggested, "but you can't complain, and you don't get much sympathy anyway, so you find ways to cover up or hold it inside you."

He nodded.

"What doesn't destroy me makes me stronger," he then said.

"Excuse me?"

"Nothing. It's a statement a philosopher wrote, a statement I like."

I thought about it and smiled.

"I like it too," I said. "I'll have to remember that. Thank you," I said, and he smiled.

Funny, I thought, but that was something I hadn't seen him do much of in his own home, smile.

"Is Ami all right?" I asked, thinking about the whimpering I had heard.

"Ami? Sure. I don't know if she told you she would be up early every day to have breakfast with you or what, but it would surprise me if she ever does."

"I don't want to be a burden to anyone," I said.

"Why do you say that?" he asked, a softer smile on his face. "It's no problem for me to take you to school. Really. I have to go past it to get to work, and I'm up this early all the time, even on weekends."

"Okay," I said, and drank some orange juice.

He reached over and poured the coffee into my cup.

"So, tell me now, now that my father's not bellowing over us, how was your first day at school? Did you meet some nice people?" He smiled. "On occasion, rich people can be nice, too."

"Yes, I did," I said.

"A boy, perhaps?" he asked, tilting his head.

"Yes," I said.

"Well, then, I expect you'll have a real social life, get invited to parties and everything pretty soon," he said.

It was on the tip of my tongue to say I already had been invited to a party here, but I thought that would be a betrayal of Ami and her wishes; Wade might question her restriction, and she might think I had gone complaining to him about it.

"I guess," I said.

Mrs. McAlister entered with my eggs. Once again she practically stood over me while I began to eat. I was afraid to reach for the pepper and salt, even though it needed some.

"Thank you," I told her between bites. "It's just the way I like them."

"It's the way Mr. Emerson himself likes them," she replied, as if that was the gold standard. She nodded at Wade and returned to the kitchen.

Immediately I reached for the salt. Wade watched me with a sly smile. I didn't hear any vacuum cleaner or any other noises in the house and wondered where Mrs. Cukor was. Once again I thought about describing my confrontation with her after dinner, but once again I felt it wasn't my place to start any trouble in this house.

Instead, I talked more about the school, my impression of the teachers, most of whom did impress me, and the nice facilities. He asked me more about my public school experience and listened like someone really interested in young people today.

Later, in the car and on the way to school, Wade continued to tell me about his own youth and how his true secret ambition was to be a college English professor.

"Like you, I read a great deal," he said, "and even tried to be a professional writer. My mother encouraged me, but my father thought I was wasting money on postage, sending my short stories and poems out to magazines. He might have been right; I never published anything anywhere except the school literary magazine and newspaper, and of course Dad always degraded teachers and the teaching profession because of their poor salaries. He would boast that he made more in one month as a plumber than my high school English teacher made in six. I think that was true, but to convince him that there were other considerations in choosing your career was a waste of time.

"When you do start writing for the school paper, I'd like to see it, if that's all right," he added.

"Of course, although I don't make any claims to be anything special."

He turned and smiled at me.

"But you are special, Celeste. You don't have to make any claims. I can see it already."

I don't know how many moments I had already enjoyed in my life where I would blush at a compliment tossed my way, but I knew my face was on fire. It brought a laugh to his lips and brightened his hazel eyes so that they looked more like polished stones under clear brook water.

"Have another great day," he told me when we reached the school. "Oh." He took out a business card and handed it to me. "In the event our Ami doesn't get here in time or completely forgets to pick you up, call the cell phone number on this card and I'll come get you."

"Thank you," I said, and headed for the school's front entrance.

Feeling his eyes still on me, I turned once to wave good-bye. He nodded and drove off, but his face was framed in such melancholy, it made me sad for a moment.

Everyone I meet outside of the orphanage seems covered in layers and layers of mystery, I thought. Children were naked, their fears and hopes obvious for anyone to see, especially orphan children who were alone, cast on the water like leaves no longer tied to the branches of any tree, unable to remember the tree from which they had fallen.

Both Wade and Ami had families, had heritage, had a foundation under them, a foundation from which they could grow, but inside their world there were so many unheard voices, too. How ironic, I thought. They had one disadvantage we didn't. From the day they could understand, talk, and walk, they were under pressure to please their parents. No matter how much Wade disagreed with his father, I could sense that he still wanted, craved, his father's approval. Why else would he have trapped himself in his father's business?

What sort of approval was Ami seeking, and from whom? I wondered.

How could it be that having a real family was any sort of disadvantage? How foolish it was for me to even think it.

And yet I remembered too well how guilty I used to feel as a child, afraid that I wasn't living up to the expectations my mother, my wonderful spiritual family, had for me. Now that I was out in what we orphans called "the real world," what awaited me? Who would I disappoint now?

I entered the school and began my day. Trevor was with me at every possible opportunity. I saw immediately that Germaine Osterhout was annoyed and upset over the attention he was devoting to me. She glared at me across aisles, whispered to her friends while keeping her eyes burning my way, and turned her back on me whenever she could, especially when I was walking or talking with Trevor.

"I really wish you could come to the party," he told me at lunch. "Maybe I could speak to your cousins about it. I'd promise to bring you home early. They should be happy you're getting to know people. It's one of the hardest things to do when you start a new school. Should I try?" he asked.

I thought about it. I wanted to go very much, but I

also still felt Ami would see it as some sort of betrayal, some form of ungratefulness. I had agreed to her restrictions and hadn't whined or complained.

"I don't think it would be a good idea. I have to be sure they're comfortable with everything I do. They're doing so much for me," I said, hoping he would understand.

"If they really want to help you, they'd let you make friends," he muttered, refusing to be denied.

He saw my troubled look. I liked him. I really did. I think he saw that too.

"I know what," he said, suddenly brightening. "Forget Waverly's birthday party. I'll pay you a visit instead. How's that sound?"

"What? Pay me a visit? What do you mean?"

"You'll invite me to your house Saturday night, and I'll show up there instead of the party."

"It's not my house."

"So? You're living there. Invite me."

"I don't know." I couldn't help sounding flustered. "I'll—"

"What's wrong with that? People can visit you, can't they? They're not shutting you away in some attic or basement on weekends, are they? Your cousin can be our chaperone the whole time if she likes."

"But you'll miss your friend's party."

"So what? It's not going to be anything great. I've been to parties at Waverly's house before. Don't you want me to visit you?"

"Yes, of course, but . . . okay, I'll ask," I relented, seeing any other answer would make no sense.

"Great."

Later, between my creative writing class and the last period, Lynette Firestone caught up to me in the hallway and bumped my shoulder to get me to stop walking.

"You're moving pretty quickly on Germaine Oster-hout's boyfriend," she muttered. "Everyone's talking about it and teasing her."

"No one told me he was her boyfriend, and I think he has a mind of his own."

"Just warning you," she said. "She's not the one to turn into an enemy. I know from experience," she added, the corners of her mouth drooping.

"Actually, you have that backward."

"What? What do you mean?"

"I'm not the one to turn into an enemy," I said, and sped up to my last class of the day.

At the end of the day, Trevor walked me out, both of us expecting Ami to be waiting there as she was the day before, but she was nowhere in sight.

"Are you sure she's picking you up?" Trevor asked after a good ten minutes. Most of the other students had gotten into their cars or had been picked up quickly by their parents. We were practically the only ones standing around. The parking lot had nearly emptied out.

All day the sky had shifted from partly cloudy to complete overcast to an occasional sprinkle, and it looked like it was gathering bruised clouds from the east to deliver more of a downfall. The breeze picked up and blew dust across the drive. Trees wavered and shivered. I could see the humidity in the air. Even the birds were in retreat.

Where was she? I wondered. Maybe she really had gotten sick last night, but why wouldn't she let me know she wasn't coming for me? I fingered the card in my purse that Wade had given me. He had offered it with an expression on his face that told me to expect to

need to call him, but I couldn't help thinking I would
be taking him away from his work, and maybe cause
trouble between him and Ami, if not between Ami and
me, especially if she was on her way and I jumped the
gun.

I strained my neck to look down the street, but there
was still no sign of her, and I did have another driving
lesson to begin in twenty minutes. What about that?

"Should I run you home?" Trevor offered.

"I don't know. What if she comes and I'm not
here?" I said, practically wailing.

"We'll look out for her on the way. If we see her,
I'll blow the horn and get her to stop."

I shifted from one foot to the other. My nerve endings felt like guitar strings twanged and vibrating
through my heart. The first heavy raindrops fell.

"C'mon," Trevor said, seizing my left arm and
pulling me toward his black Mercedes sports car. "I
just got this car recently anyway, and I want to show
off. It's silly to wait in the rain, and it looks like it's
going to be quite a downpour."

My reluctance weakened, and I permitted him to
take me to his car, open the door, and help me get in. It
did smell new, especially the leather.

"It's a beautiful car," I said when he got in.

"Yeah. Dad gives me one to use, and then he sells it
as a used car, but gently used, if you know what I
mean," he said, smiling. He started up and backed out
of the spot.

I kept my eyes on the street, still searching for signs
of Ami, but there were none. How odd, I thought.
Where was she? How could she forget me? Why didn't
she call the school and have Mrs. Brentwood or someone tell me she would be late?

We started away from the school. It was too late to

change my mind, and I really wasn't doing anything terribly bad, I thought. She would understand.

"Actually, your cousin will be happy if I take you home every day," Trevor said, rushing us into a relationship, at least in his mind. "I can even pick you up in the morning. It's nothing to swing by their house."

"I don't think so," I said gently. "My cousin goes past the school on his way to work."

"Not really. It's a longer way for him."

"Whatever," I said, surprised to hear that. "He wants to do it."

"Okay. So tell me more about where you used to live and the school you attended. It wasn't a private school, right?"

"No."

"Did you leave someone behind, some lover pining away like in that Shakespearean sonnet we read today?" he asked with a coy smile.

"No."

He grimaced and then looked at me skeptically.

"What did you do, break up just before you left or something?"

"I've never had a steady boyfriend, Trevor."

"Afraid of relationships because of what your parents are going through? Can't blame you," he said before I could respond. "You know, three out of every five kids at our school come from divorced parents. My parents are doing fine," he made sure to add. "I'm not afraid of having a serious relationship."

"Were you going steady with Germaine Osterhout?"

"What, did she tell you that? I never—"

"No, Lynette Firestone warned me today that I was making an enemy by stealing her boyfriend."

He shook his head.

"Just like Lynette. She has to live through everyone

else because she doesn't have a life of her own. I've taken Germaine out, but we're hardly going steady. You're not really afraid of her, are you?" he asked with an impish grin.

"Hardly," I said.

He glanced at me and then stopped smiling.

"So when are you going to tell me your life story?"

"As soon as I finish writing it," I said, and he laughed.

Many a truth was told in jest, I thought, thinking about my diary.

A little while later we pulled up to the gates. It was really pouring. The wipers couldn't keep up.

"I guess they won't hear me blowing my horn. I'll go to the call box," he said, pulling his jacket over his head.

"You'll get soaked."

"Anything for a fair damsel," he said, imitating one of our poems in English class.

He got out and went to the box. The rain was coming down in sheets. His jacket, which looked like an expensive leather one, was getting soaked. Whoever was to respond to the call box was taking her time. It could only be Mrs. Cukor or Mrs. McAlister, I thought, unless Ami was home, but why wouldn't she have called the school?

He turned and shrugged, the rain streaming down his cheeks and soaking his pants and ruining his shoes.

"Get back into the car!" I shouted.

Suddenly, the gate started to open.

He rushed back, throwing his soaked jacket behind the seat. We started up the drive.

"You're absolutely soaked through," I said.

"I know. If I die . . .'tis better to have loved and lost than never to have loved at all."

"You're such an idiot," I said, laughing. I didn't see my driving school instructor and his car, and I was already ten minutes late. "Go around the house. There's a side entrance that's right off the garage."

"Oh, servant's entrance, huh?"

He pulled up.

"I'm sorry you got so wet. You want to come in and dry off?"

I felt I had to offer that. It was only right.

"Sure," he said.

"Okay, follow me," I said, took a breath, opened the door, and charged for the side entrance with him following right behind.

We burst into the house, both laughing.

"Now that's a rain," he said.

Mrs. McAlister stepped out of the kitchen and looked at us.

"Hello, Mrs. McAlister," I said. "This is Trevor Foley. He brought me home because Ami didn't show up. Do you know where she is or what happened to her?"

"Hardly," she said.

"What about my driving instructor?"

"He called to say he wasn't coming today because you weren't experienced enough yet to drive in such weather. Now, beside being a cook, I'm the message taker here. People who call usually call Mrs. Emerson's direct line and leave messages on her machine."

"I'm sorry," I said. "I didn't . . . I mean, I don't have a machine or . . ."

"You'd better not continue to stand there dripping on Mrs. Cukor's floors. She'll cast a nasty spell on you," she warned, and returned to the kitchen.

"Who's that, and who's Mrs. Cukor?"

"Hopefully, you won't find out," I muttered. "Take

off your shoes and socks and at least get yourself dried off. I know how to use a drier. The laundry room is right off the hallway down here," I said. "That's a very cold rain."

"Brrr," he said, exaggerating, but he did look uncomfortable. His pants were soaked through and through.

He slipped off his shoes and socks and followed me down the hallway. I took him to the downstairs powder room first.

"What a house! I thought ours was something special," he said, looking everywhere.

"Go in there and take off your wet clothes," I said, pointing to the powder room. "I'll get you a robe to wear until I get them dry," I said.

I hurried upstairs, fetched the thick terry-cloth robe off the hook in my bathroom, and hurried down. Then I tapped on the bathroom door and handed him the robe when he opened it, standing in his briefs only and smiling out at me. He handed me his wet clothes. He laughed at the look on my face and began to put on the robe.

"Smells great," he said, sniffing.

"I'll be down in the laundry room," I said, and started for it.

After I put his clothes in to dry, I gathered up my schoolbooks and then found him standing in the hallway in his bare feet, looking through the den doorway at Wade's mother's portrait. Mrs. Cukor finally appeared, stepping out of the living room, where she had been polishing furniture. The sight of him stopped her cold.

"Trevor," I called. "I'm sorry I forgot a pair of slippers. Come with me until your clothes dry."

He looked at Mrs. Cukor, whose glare could send

anyone running for company and safety, and then joined me at the foot of the stairs.

"Who is that?" he whispered. "She was looking at me so hard, I felt her eyes burn into my face."

"The housekeeper. She's a little strange," I offered, and led him up the stairway to my room.

"Wow," he said, looking in on it. "This is really nice. I like your bed."

I put my books on my desk and slipped out of my shoes. My hair was a little wet, but I hadn't gotten anywhere near as soaked as he had standing out in the rain by the call box, waiting for someone to open the gates. He walked around my room, looking at everything. Then he flopped on the bed, stretching out his arms and falling backward.

"Comfy," he said.

I stared at him. It occurred to me at that moment that I had never ever been alone in a room with a boy aside from a second or two in a classroom at public school.

"What's wrong?" he said, sitting up and looking at me. "You look absolutely terrified."

"I'm not terrified," I snapped back, gathering myself quickly. "I'm just—"

"Nervous?" he teased.

"No."

"Bashful?" he suggested, rising off the bed. "Don't tell me a pretty girl like you has never been in a room with a half-naked guy," he said.

"I haven't," I confessed.

He smiled and stepped up to me.

"Why is it every girl wants every boy to think she's Miss Proper, innocent and pure, these days?" he asked, his face now inches from mine. "Is it because so few are?"

He put his right hand on my waist. I didn't back

away. I felt like I was under a spell, caught like a deer in the headlights, captured by Trevor's eyes, Trevor's inviting lips, his handsome smile and the promise of pleasure that lay just beneath.

With his left hand, he undid the robe so it would open and then he pressed himself against me and kissed me, softly at first and then harder, pressing his building sex against my leg so that I felt the passion moving through his body and into mine the way electricity traveled. My head spun.

"You are delicious," he whispered, and was about to kiss me again when we both heard the door thrust open and turned to see Ami standing there. Her hair looked soaked through, and her shoulders rose and fell with her heavy breathing. She had obviously run up the stairway. Her face was full of shock and surprise, her eyes wide, and her lips stretched back as her jaw fell open. She looked as if she was in the midst of a great scream.

She brought her right hand to her heart as if she had to press down to keep it from pounding through her chest, and then she leaned against the doorjamb as if she was about to faint. Trevor quickly stepped away and closed the robe.

"What . . . are you doing?" she managed between breaths.

"Trevor took me home," I quickly blurted. "We waited and waited, and he offered to take me home. But he got soaked at the call box trying to get someone to open the gates, so we put his clothes in the drier, and . . ."

She stepped forward as if she was going to charge at the both of us.

Trevor was so embarrassed standing there in my robe, he turned away and looked down at the floor.

"I was only fifteen minutes late, Celeste. I would have let the school know if I wasn't coming for you. I was frantic, and I got pretty wet myself running from the car into the school to look for you. Mrs. Brentwood was upset because no one came to ask her to call me. I do have a cell phone, you know. I could have been reached. She has my numbers to use in an emergency."

"We didn't know what to do," I offered weakly. "I didn't mean to cause any problems. I'm sorry."

Ami pulled herself together.

"It looks like Trevor volunteered to do a little more than simply take you home," she said sharply. It was as if she had thrown darts at him, only some hit me as well. I felt the same pain. "I'd like you to march yourself downstairs, young man, and we'll ask Mrs. Cukor to get your clothing for you. I'm sure it's all dry enough."

"Yes, ma'am," Trevor said obediently. "I didn't mean to cause any problems. I—"

"No. Men never mean to cause any problems," Ami said. "But they do. Oh, how they do."

Trevor looked at me with confusion. I could hear his thoughts. *Is she for real?*

"Whatever," Trevor said, and walked toward the doorway. Ami stepped aside.

"Go on. Mrs. Cukor is waiting for you," she advised him sternly.

He looked back at me.

"I'm sorry, Trevor," I said. "Thank you."

"Right. You're welcome," he said, and then left.

Ami watched him go by, pulling herself back farther as if she was afraid he might touch her, and then she looked at me.

"I'm so disappointed in you, Celeste, so very disappointed," she said, shaking her head.

She stepped out and closed the door, leaving me trembling in a pool of embarrassment, confusion, frustration, and anger. I felt pulled in every direction, felt myself coming apart like a figure of clay.

I would soon know how I would be put together again.

11

Wishful Thoughts

♊

I changed my clothes and was about to go downstairs to talk with Ami to see if I could calm things down when she returned to my room. Her whole demeanor was different. She wore a smile and looked relaxed, more like the Ami whom I had first met.

"I'm sorry about all that," she began, waving her right hand behind her as she entered. She had a large shopping bag in her right hand and put it on my bed. I recognized the Ooh-La-La logo. "Just look at what I got you today," she said, and took out a pair of jeans. "They're low-rise. You don't have a pair, and I got you this short-sleeved button-up shirt to go with it." She held it up against herself. "See, it has these cute elastic-gathered puffed sleeves with a floral pattern. It's perfect with the jeans. And I thought you'd love this floral stone chain belt," she added, scooping it out of the bag. "All the girls your age are wearing them these days."

"Thank you," I said. "I did see girls wearing jeans like that at school."

She put it all aside and sat on the bed, folding her hands in her lap.

"I didn't mean to sound so angry before, but I was so surprised to see him in your robe, and from what I saw, he was moving fast on you. Look how clever he was to get undressed that quickly and into your room."

"It wasn't his idea. I thought he would catch cold in his wet clothing, Ami. I was the one who suggested we get them dry, and I couldn't think of anything else to give him to wear in the meantime than my robe. I certainly didn't want to give him one of Wade's. That's a very cold rain, and he did get soaked through and through."

"Yes, of course. You did the right thing there. I know I shouldn't get angry at you. I know your intentions were pure and good, but I'm just afraid for you, Celeste. I know you've had nearly zero experience with boys."

"How do you know how much experience I've really had?" I asked, slightly annoyed, even though it was true.

"Oh, I can tell about a girl's experience. Believe me, it's not hard to separate the very experienced from the innocent babes these days," she said.

Was I that obvious? I wondered. Was that what Trevor saw as well?

"That's not the point, though," she said. "The point is, I have taken on a big responsibility, and I want to be sure I don't mess up. I should have known the boys would be after you at the starting gate, especially one like Trevor Foley."

"He's very polite and very nice, Ami."

She shook her head.

"You can't go by that. If someone was a serial killer, would he walk around with an unshaven face, dirty clothes, knives or guns obvious? No. He would look like the boy next door and be polite and courteous and get you to come into his room, get you alone in your room, or whatever trap he had set."

"Then how do you ever tell the bad from the good?"

"That's the trick," she said, smiling. "That's the skill that comes with experience, and that's why I want you to move slowly, very slowly, Celeste. I'm not trying to stop you from having fun. Look," she said, nodding at the new clothes, "I've bought you the latest fashions according to my salesgirls just so you wouldn't be left out. Would I do all this if I didn't want you to be happy and enjoy yourself? Well, would I?"

"No," I admitted. It would be like advertising to sell something and then not having it to sell. Why advertise?

"No. Of course not. What I do want to do, however, is be sure you have the best preparation, the best training, so you won't be caught in any situations from which you can't gracefully exit, and most important, Celeste, so you don't fall into any mantraps and end up like so many young girls do these days . . . running off to get an abortion.

"That's right," she added quickly when I looked up at her. "You'd be shocked at who in that school has already gotten herself into big trouble. News like that gets around, especially in this community of jealous alley cats."

She rose and began to pace in front of me like some teacher starting a lecture.

"Now, I'm not stupid about it," she said. "It wasn't

all that long ago that I was your age, and just as I said in front of that nun in your orphanage, I want to give you the benefit of my experience and provide some important guidance in these matters, guidance you would never get in that place. How can a nun lady tell you what it's like to have a man kiss you and touch you and promise you things as his hands move all over you?"

I started to speak, but she had obviously been preparing to say all these things to me and wanted to get it over with quickly.

"I know you think you're very smart, too bright to be fooled by any boys, but it's not your brain they're after, believe me. Unfortunately, your own body is not to be trusted. You don't know it at the moment, but you're probably your own worse enemy."

"What? Why do you say that?"

"You can't trust yourself, trust that you'll always do the right things. There are places on your body, erogenous zones or something. I forget what they call them. Places that when touched or kissed," she said, putting her hands over her breasts, "start to open the doors to your treasure, and if you don't put on the brakes, if you don't stop them before they go too far with you, you suddenly find yourself unable to shut the doors.

"In fact," she said, leaning toward me and speaking almost in a whisper, "you find yourself just as willing and as eager to do what they want."

Her eyes were wide, brilliant. She blinked and stepped back.

"Of course, it feels wonderful at the time. Or at least that is what we're always told by men and women who've sunken low, but it doesn't feel wonderful each and every time!" she cried. "From the way men describe it, it almost doesn't matter whom they're with. They even say disgusting things like every woman is the same in the dark.

"Worst of all, maybe, is if you did do it with someone you didn't love, you could be so disappointed that you would never enjoy it afterward. You might even become frigid or something," she said, looking away.

"So you see," she continued, turning back to me after a moment, "I'm really concerned for you. I worry about you. All of my energy is spent on your behalf these days, and willingly so."

"I know, Ami. I appreciate it."

"Good," she said, smiling and then sitting beside me on the bed again. She took my hand into hers. "Good. Now then, I'm a realist, too, however. I know that no matter what I say, how much I teach you, how much you understand and promise, things happen."

She thought a moment and then shook her head.

"I can't imagine growing up and never being taught about these things. No wonder girls like you get into so much trouble. The first thing I want to do is get you started on birth control pills. I'll speak to my doctor about it first chance I get."

"Birth control pills?"

"I'm sure the nuns never even suggested it to you," she said, "but it's something you should do for your own protection, protection, as I say, against yourself, and to help me feel better and more at ease about you."

I didn't know whether to laugh or cry, and she saw it in my face.

"Don't go thinking you're better than anyone else, Celeste. No matter how you were brought up or how you lived in the orphanage. I'm well aware of all the spiritual and psychic things you were exposed to and you supposedly inherited, but you've still got the same equipment every other girl your age has, and as I said, there are buttons men, boys, know to push. Sometimes, no matter what, we can't help ourselves. We can't stop! Think of the pills as a safety valve."

She looked like she would simply burst into hysterical sobbing if I didn't agree.

"Okay, Ami," I said. "I'll take them as a precaution, as you say."

"Thank you. Thank you. I'll see about it."

She folded her hands in her lap.

"Now tell me, what did Trevor Foley say to get you to take him up to your room so fast? You've been in that school only two days. I'd say you're either overly ripe fruit or he's one helluva magician."

She sat back anticipating some juicy story and description.

"He didn't say anything to get me to do that. I just thought he would be embarrassed sitting down there in my robe."

"No," she insisted, poking her finger in front of my face, "he made you feel he might be embarrassed. He put the idea into your head, whether you realize it or not, believe me. He probably planned it all from the moment he offered to take you home. Maybe even before."

"I don't think so, Ami," I said softly. "Really, he was just being polite and helpful. It was raining hard, as I said, and you hadn't come, and I did wait. We thought if you were coming along, we might see you and stop."

She shook her head.

"It's my fault; it's my fault. I got too involved with what I was doing and didn't pay attention to the time. I won't let it happen again. I can't leave you out there vulnerable and alone in this . . . this jungle."

I hated the way she made me sound so helpless, but I didn't argue with her.

"What happened to your driving lesson?" she asked.

"He canceled because of the weather. He said I wasn't prepared yet to drive in such a torrential downpour, which is what Trevor got caught in when he got out to push the call-box button," I emphasized.

"Okay, okay, enough of that," she said, standing. Then she smiled. "One more surprise. I have a music teacher, Mr. LaRuffa, coming to begin your piano lessons. He'll be here at seven-thirty on Saturday."

"Seven-thirty in the morning on Saturday?"

"No, in the evening. I'd like to watch, and he's agreed to the day and time. You have nothing else to do," she added. "Right?" she asked, her eyes scrutinizing my face. It wasn't a question as much as an order.

I thought about Trevor and his hope I could invite him over. With what had happened and with this, that idea was out the window. He might be gone as well, and I couldn't blame him.

"You don't look happy about it, but when I mentioned it before you were very excited. You said you always wanted to learn how to play the piano."

"I'm happy about it. Yes. It has been something I've wanted to do for a long time. My mother used to play for us, and she could play well."

"Oh? You remember that vividly, do you?"

"Yes. Even the music. She played every night after our dinner. My brother and I would sit and listen."

"Brother?"

"I mean, my sister."

She smiled. Why was it so important for her to correct me all the time? I thought.

She took a deep breath and smiled.

"Okay, wonderful. Now, let's keep all this business

with Trevor Foley from Wade. He doesn't have to know. It will just make him nervous and turn him into a nagging nanny or something. Okay? Secrets, remember? The glue that binds two friends together is how they share and keep their secrets."

"Both Mrs. Cukor and Mrs. McAlister saw Trevor here," I reminded her.

"That's all right. They won't say anything. You don't last in this house if you gossip about anyone in it. They both know that." She patted me on the knee and got up. "I'll leave you to do your homework. I know how serious you are about all that. We're going to another special place for dinner this Friday night, too, so put that on your calendar. Wade won't be coming. He has some stupid pipe or bolt and nut convention to attend. How grown men can sit around and talk about fittings and new tools is beyond me, but men are another animal altogether, aren't they?"

She walked to the door, where she paused a moment and then turned.

"I'm not saying Trevor Foley isn't a good-looking boy or someone who doesn't come from a fine family, but he is a boy with raging hormones. It's the age. For women like us, beautiful and special, they are like bulls seeing red. It takes some grace and clever maneuvering to avoid getting gored, if you know what I mean? I'll see about those pills," she added, and then smiled. "Olé," she said, laughing and turning like a matador avoiding a charging bull. Then she left me staring after her in more wonder than ever.

I envisioned Trevor standing before me just after he had kissed me, and in my secret heart of hearts, I wished I would need this pill. The very thought of it brought blood to my cheeks and heat to my neck, but despite the warnings and the horrors Ami had described, I couldn't help enjoying the fantasy. Maybe she was right about one thing. Maybe I, like any girl my age, could be my own worst enemy.

True to her word, Ami kept the incident with Trevor a secret from Wade. When at dinner he asked her about picking me up after school, she went into a long description about how hard it was to drive back in the downpour and how she had called the driving instructor to tell him to postpone the lesson until I had more experience at the wheel. Wade listened without expression, but when he looked at me, I was unable to hold his gaze. He knew she wasn't telling the truth, but he didn't challenge her story.

When two people learn to accept each other's lies, do they grow closer or further apart? I wondered. It was surely one thing to tolerate each other's weaknesses and yet another to endure each other's deceptions. At the orphanage we were often generous with each other when it came to lies. They were more like wishful thoughts anyway. Girls would invent a past or a reason for their being alone in the world, a reason we all saw through—at least, I often did—but we didn't challenge them. Sometimes, I thought, we wrap ourselves in illusions and fantasies to keep us safe from cruel realities. Surely there is nothing terrible about that. I was positive that in her mind, Ami thought her lies were good, good for all of us.

Wade, on the other hand, looked like someone who didn't need or rely on lies. He had few illusions and made no excuses for himself or even for Ami, and especially not for his father. Some people accepted the darkness in life and did nothing to deny it. Did that make it impossible for them to ever be happy? Maybe, but happiness appeared to be something Wade had long ago lost hope of having, at least in the sense of it Ami had.

What would make him happy? I wondered. Did Ami really care? Did he want the child they originally claimed they would have, which she told me she wasn't in any rush for? Did he know that?

It suddenly occurred to me that I might be another way for her to postpone her motherhood, that she was using me and might continue to use me to that purpose. I hoped that wasn't true. Wade would certainly come to despise me if it were so, I thought.

He caught me alone just before I went up to my room to finish my homework.

"How did you really get home today?" he asked with a smile of anticipation.

For a moment I thought I would just confirm all Ami had told him, but I saw clearly that he wouldn't believe it for a moment, and he wouldn't let me get away with any lie.

"A boy I met," I told him quickly.

He laughed.

"It's all right," he said. "We'll keep your revelations secret," he added, and walked to his den.

Now they're both doing it, I thought. They're both using secrets to bind me to them.

I wasn't in my room twenty minutes when the phone rang. I practically lunged for it to keep it to a single ring. I knew who was calling, of course.

"Did you get into a lot of trouble?" Trevor asked me as soon as I said hello.

"No. It's all right."

"I was stupid. I should have thought about it and expected that might happen. See what you do to me?"

"And what's that?"

"You throw a spell over me and make me act stupid. If anyone else ever saw me in your bathrobe or found out—"

"I doubt very much that my cousin will say a word about it to anyone. Don't worry."

"I guess my being invited over Saturday is out of the question now, huh?"

"My cousin arranged for me to have my first piano lesson Saturday night."

"Saturday night? Who has a piano lesson on Saturday night?"

"I do, apparently."

"Hey," he said. "I'm warning you, and you can warn your cousin. I'm not giving up on you. No one has ever dried my clothes better."

I laughed.

"Let things calm down," I told him.

"Things can. I won't," he vowed. "See you tomorrow," he said.

"Okay."

I was still smiling after I hung up. Was I getting a crush on him too quickly? Was Ami right about my inexperience and vulnerability?

It wasn't all that long ago that whenever I was confused or frightened about something, I could resurrect Noble and have someone who loved me help me. Dr. Sackett made me believe it was only another part of myself, born out of insecurity and fear. Maybe that was true, but at least I didn't feel as alone as I did now, I thought.

How silly, I told myself. Just cope with your problems like any other mature person.

Shutting my ears to any voice but my own, I returned to my homework and read as much as I could to get myself tired enough to fall asleep quickly.

I was already in bed when I heard a soft knock on my door.

"Come in," I called.

Ami opened the door partway and gazed in at me. She was already in her nightgown.

"Just checking to see how you are."

"I'm okay," I said.

"Good. You did real well at dinner. We're going to be real pals. You'll see," she said. "Sweet dreams. Once I start you on the pills, you'll have fewer nightmares, believe me."

She backed out and closed the door softly.

Was that what she was doing? I wondered. Taking the pill perhaps without Wade knowing? Had she promised to stop and not stopped? Suddenly their intimacy was of great interest to me. Like a little girl who couldn't imagine her parents having sex, I had difficulty seeing them in a passionate embrace.

Wade might still be wearing a shirt and tie, I thought, and giggled to myself.

I looked across the room at the shadows in the corner. They seemed to take Noble's form. How I wanted a companion. If I call out to him, he'll be there, I thought, and then . . . then it could all begin again.

I shut my eyes hard, shut them like someone locking a pair of jewelry boxes. I could almost hear my eyelids slam closed. I fled into sleep.

Despite the obstacles standing in his way and mine, Trevor was true to his word the following day. He spent every possible moment with me at school. It got so we sat alone in the cafeteria, and twice he managed to find a secure place in which to kiss me. He pulled me into the empty science lab once, and the second time he stopped walking, let the people behind us go ahead, and then pulled me behind the door to the English classroom. Of course I was nervous about being caught, but that just seemed to make his kiss sweeter and my heart pound fast and harder.

The remainder of the week, Ami was right there at the end of the school day to pick me up promptly, rushing me off so I would not be late for my driving lesson. On Thursday, she even came into the building, which prevented me from walking with Trevor to the front entrance. Of course, she was continually asking me about him.

"Is he still after you?" was her initial question. "Pouncing on you every chance he has?"

"You make it sound like a hunt or a chase," I replied.

"That's exactly what it is at your age, Celeste. You're prime prey for them," she insisted. "And what do you think would happen once he has his way with you? I'll tell you," she said before I could even think of an answer. "He'll drop you like stale fruit, because that's what you'll be in his mind."

"Why?" I asked. Was she right? Was she as wise about the relationship between men and women as she claimed?

"Why? Because the mystery of you is gone. That's what intrigues them. They all think there's something different about this girl or that, something that will give them a wondrous orgasm.

"That's right," she said, blushing a little herself. "That's what men are hunting for, the mythical wondrous orgasm, because they don't have what we have."

"What's that?"

"The ability to have multiple orgasms during intercourse," she explained in the tone of some health and science teacher. "For them it's more important. They just can't start immediately on another one.

"Weren't you taught any of this?" she asked. "Ever? I can't believe you weren't exposed to something."

"A little," I said. It was one thing to learn about

reproduction in biology class and another to learn what would actually happen to you personally.

"Well, now you know more, and you can understand more why I'm so concerned, right?"

"Yes, Ami," I said, but not with the enthusiasm she hoped for. I could see the disappointment in her face, but I really didn't sense these sort of base motives in Trevor, and I had always depended upon my own instincts when it came to people. They had always proven reliable for me when I was younger and confronting one sort of threat after another at the orphanages. Of course, I was afraid my therapy had taken me far away from those abilities. I had long ago stopped being Baby Celeste, the gifted little girl. Perhaps I truly was as vulnerable as anyone else.

"You'll come to appreciate me," she predicted, more to herself than to me, I thought.

That Friday we dressed in what she called our "killer outfits," and she took me to dinner at a restaurant nearly thirty miles away. She explained that Wade never liked driving that far just to eat.

"To him it's simply eating. To me, it's an evening out," she explained. "He'd be just as happy going to some diner, believe me."

Once again, I saw that the maître d' knew her and told her he would hold a good table for us. The restaurant was an upscale Oriental restaurant, featuring Thai food as well as Chinese and even some Continental dishes involving steaks and lobster. There was a very busy bar where we went first to have our cocktails. For a moment I thought they would insist on checking my identification, but Ami slipped the waiter some money, and he brought the two Cosmopolitans. She ordered two more and had them delivered to our table when it became time to eat.

Before that, just as she had done at the Stone House, she flirted with some single men, giving them the impression they might be able to pick us up and then, just as before, at the last moment flashed her wedding ring. I realized that she had slipped it off and then slipped it on, and that was probably what she had done at the Stone House.

"Don't you think they might get very angry at you one time and make lots more trouble?" I asked after she had justified herself the same way she had before, claiming she just wanted to have fun and see if she could still "run with the bulls," as she called it.

"No," she said. "They won't bother. They'll just turn to another target, believe me," she said. "I know men."

She saw I wasn't happy with the answer, and I couldn't help thinking about Wade. Being Ami's partner during all this made me feel guilty.

"What's the matter?" she asked, a little impatient at the way I was playing with my food and looking down. "Aren't you having a good time?"

I thought a moment and then decided to tell the truth.

"No," I said. "I keep thinking about Wade. I'm sure he would be hurt if he knew about all this, no matter what he pretends. It doesn't seem right to be such a tease, anyway," I told her. I didn't care if she accused me of being a prude, or being too much under the influence of the nuns at my orphanage.

"Oh, Wade," she said, sighing deeply. She looked away for a moment. When she turned back, I saw there were tears in her eyes.

"You think I'm just some tease, some sick flirt, just like Basil says I am, is that it?"

"I don't feel comfortable doing it with you, Ami," I

admitted. "I'm sorry," I said, "but I do have the experience to know enough that men call women names like tease when they do what you're doing and what I'm doing when I'm with you.

"I mean it's like someone putting her finger close to a candle flame and pulling back just before it gets burned. First, you tell me to be extra cautious, and then you bring me to places like this and attract all sorts of men to us, just to shoo them away. I'm sorry," I said, realizing how harsh I sounded. My heart was thumping, too. Maybe she would just throw me out of her house now.

She looked at me long enough for me to realize she actually was making some major decision. Did she want to send me back to the orphanage, tell me I was hopeless after all? I girded myself for rejection. It was, after all, something I had lived with ever since I had been brought to my first orphanage. I was no stranger to it. At times I thought we were old friends, in fact.

"All right," she said, "I'll tell you something. It's my biggest secret, and I wanted to wait until we were even closer, but I'll rely on your promise to keep everything between us locked in your heart. Can I?"

"Yes," I said, holding my breath. Was she going to tell me she was having an affair? What would I do if she did, and what would I say? How could I hide that from Wade? He'd see it in my face for sure, I thought.

She sipped her drink and sucked in her breath. Then she straightened up and looked at me hard.

"The reason I was late picking you up that rainy day was because I ran over my time with my therapist. That's right, I see a therapist. We were making significant progress, according to her, and she didn't want to end it even though my hour was long over. I was so involved in what we were doing that I didn't pay any attention to the clock.

"Anyway, these nights out alone, this flirting I do, it's all part of my therapy," she claimed.

"What? How could this be therapy?"

"I know you'll find this hard to believe, but I've always been quite bashful and introverted. I didn't tell you the truth exactly when we first met. I exaggerated and made things up just so you would think more of me and we could get to be friends faster. I didn't really have that arm-long list of boyfriends. Actually, they were my wish list of boyfriends."

I shook my head in disbelief.

"I can see you don't believe me because I know so much and I'm so good at what we do now, but it took a lot of therapy to get me to be this self-confident. I do this flirting just to reinforce myself. It's really harmless, but it boosts my ego and reinforces my self-image."

"I don't understand. Why would you need to boost your ego?" I asked. "You know everything about style. You know you're beautiful. Men are always looking at you."

She laughed.

"Right, now they do. I was quite a thin and gangly girl growing up. My nice features didn't develop until late in my adolescence, and my mother did little to help me develop any self-confidence. She had this stupid expression, 'You have to play with the cards you're dealt.' That was like telling me, You're not pretty. You'll never be pretty. Boys will never be interested in you, so face it and live with it. I didn't go out on a real date until I was a senior in high school! Well, you can just imagine what effect all that had on me. I told you how my father always called me Mon Ami, as if I was a friend and not a beautiful daughter.

"I saw the way other fathers doted on their daughters, treated them like little princesses and told them how beautiful and precious they were every chance they had. That wasn't my father's way. Between the two of them, I felt like your famous ugly duckling."

"But didn't you tell me you were a debutante?"

"Yes, and that was some disaster. The only reason my mother insisted I do it was to get herself on the society pages. We actually had a hard time filling up the guest list. I hated every moment of it. Wade wasn't aware of all this when we first met, and as he wasn't exactly a lady's man himself, it was easier for me to put on an act. To this day he believes I was the most popular girl at school. It's all right. Your husband should have some illusions and fantasies about you."

"Does Wade know you're in therapy now?" I asked.

"Yes. It was actually his idea," she said.

"But . . . I don't understand. If he still believes you were so popular, why would he want you to be in therapy?"

"There's more to my story," she said, waving the waiter away as he started to approach to see if we wanted anything more. "Because I was so desperate to be accepted and wanted, I let myself have a very bad experience."

"What kind of experience?"

"It's complicated," she said. "I've confused you enough, and you've been exposed to enough nitty-gritty in your life. Just know you can stop worrying about Wade. Worry about me or . . . actually, you don't have to worry about either of us. We're both fine. I'm fine," she insisted. "I hope you don't think that because of my own insecurity problems, I don't know what I'm talking about when I give you advice. One thing has nothing to do with another. It's like teachers often say,

'Do what I teach, not what I do.' And besides, I have learned so much in the process of becoming assured and confident that I really can give you the benefit of great wisdom. Understand?"

I didn't, but I nodded.

"It's all right. Believe me. I'm fine now. I have a wonderful therapist. She's brought me a long way. It wasn't easy being the way I was and living with Wade and having Basil around. You can imagine how Basil would treat a woman with my kind of insecurity."

She paused.

"You're not shocked, are you?" she asked me. "Anyone can have these sort of problems, and lots of people see therapists these days."

"No," I said. "You know that as a child and even a teenager, I was in therapy, too."

"Yes, I do know that, and that was why I thought you and I would get along so well. We both know what it means to place all your trust in someone, someone who is really a stranger. Because of what I see in you, I have no problem placing my trust in you. You are a very sincere person and I know you mean it when you say you won't hold any of this against me, even the flirting."

"Thank you," I said, and she smiled.

"Yes, that's what I hoped to hear. You are a wise young lady. We're going to be great friends, forever and ever." She reached over the table to take my hand into hers, squeezed gently, and then, as if she had said nothing, began to talk about a couple to our right, complaining about the way the man was looking at every other woman but the woman he was with.

"They always think the grass is greener somewhere else. Men," she said disdainfully.

Knowing all this about her now actually made me

appreciate her behavior more. I would never have guessed this was a woman in therapy for insecurity when it came to men, and I was sure no man, not even Basil, would be able to guess it.

However, these complications and contradictions left me reeling inside. She wanted men to appreciate her, but she was so distrustful and even hateful at times toward them.

"You see," she continued, "the way a man treats you can make you feel insecure about yourself. That's why it's so important to understand their motives and to be strong yourself. I won't let that happen to you. I won't," she vowed. "That's why I don't mind telling you all my secrets, and why I hope and pray you'll tell me yours as well."

I smiled and nodded, but I couldn't help wondering if her revelations brought us closer, as she had hoped, or drove us further apart. I wasn't sure about the answer myself. In my heart I knew that it would take some time to find out.

Neither of us ate very much, and I was happy when she suggested it was time to go home. Wade would be home from his meeting, she told me, and we left.

Once we were in her car and on our way, she reviewed the men she had attracted in the bar, predicting what each one would be like as a husband. It was as if all the things she had told me about herself, her therapy, her insecurity, were put into a trunk and buried under old furniture in some attic. She was back to being the Ami I had first met.

When we got home, she had an entirely different story about the restaurant to tell Wade. Then she started to tease him about his meeting, just the way she teased men at the bar.

"Did you all talk about your newest nuts? What's new in bolts?"

He turned beet red in front of me, and Ami laughed. It occurred to me then that she had married Wade precisely because he was so inexperienced when it came to women and sex, and so very shy himself. He was no threat to her. How different it was when she confronted Basil. She needed therapy almost for that alone, I thought.

Wade and I finally got into a conversation about the required reading I had to do in English class. He took me into his library to give me a book he thought I would enjoy, and Ami grew bored. When she went up to the bedroom to go to sleep, Wade soon followed. I started to read the book he had given me. Before I knew it, I'd been sitting there nearly half an hour. I got myself something cold to drink and started up.

Once again, when I reached the upstairs hallway, I heard Ami whimpering. I was sure of it. Wade sounded angry, however, and I distinctly heard him say, "You're not trying."

In response, Ami continued to sob.

Suddenly, I did catch a movement in the shadows down the hallway near the bedroom Basil used. I held my breath as a figure stepped forward. It wasn't Noble.

It was Mrs. Cukor.

The surprise stopped my heart. She started toward me, and I turned quickly and went into my bedroom, closing the door behind me and waiting there. What was she doing in the shadows? Would she tell Wade and Ami that I had been eavesdropping at their bedroom door?

If she walked past my bedroom, she did it on air, I thought. I didn't hear a footstep. After a few more moments, I went into the bathroom and prepared for bed. It was very hard to fall asleep; I tossed and turned, listening every moment for the sound of someone at the door. Finally, out of near exhaustion, I sank into a deep sleep.

Trevor called me first thing in the morning the following day, and we talked for almost an hour. He threatened to sneak onto the property and climb up the wall to my room after my piano lesson, and he made it sound so possible that I had trouble concentrating when my piano teacher arrived. Apparently, Mrs. Cukor did not report me to either Wade or Ami. Neither asked me about my listening at their bedroom door.

Ami sat watching me take my first piano lesson, and Wade stopped in to listen and observe as well. Afterward, Ami had Mrs. McAlister serve tea and cakes.

I liked my teacher. He said that he could tell immediately if a prospective student had any potential, and he assured both Ami and me that I did.

"She has a musical ear," he said.

"She might have inherited it," Ami said, looking my way and winking.

"Quite possible," Mr. LaRuffa told her, and we scheduled two lessons a week, one always being on Saturday night. He wondered about that himself. "Surely a young lady this pretty will have dates and parties."

"Not right away," Ami assured him firmly. "We'll change days and times later."

"Whatever you wish," he said, and left.

Afterward Wade, Ami, and I sat together and watched television. It was really the first time we had done something remotely social together, and I saw that Wade was relaxed and happy. We laughed at the comedy show we watched. For the first time, I felt as though I was really part of a family. It was also the first time I had seen Wade and Ami show any affection toward each other. She sat beside him on the sofa and leaned against him, and he put his arm around her.

What could possibly have been their problem the night before? I wondered.

Watching them made me think of Trevor. I wondered if he was having a good time at Waverly's party and if Germaine Osterhout had dug her nails deeply into him again. She surely had to be encouraged by my not attending the party. Wade saw the sadness in my face.

"Why are we getting her lessons on Saturday night?" he asked Ami. "Maybe she wants to go to a movie with her friends or something."

Ami looked at me, her expression urging me to answer.

"It's all right," I said. "I didn't have anything planned."

"Yes, this Saturday maybe, but what about next week?"

"If something comes up, her teacher will reschedule, Wade. We've already discussed it. Not to worry," she told him. "Right, Celeste?"

I nodded.

He looked skeptical but dropped the subject. After another ten minutes or so, I excused myself to go up to my room.

"I want to take you to the new outlet stores tomorrow," Ami shouted after me. "Plan for it."

"She must have other things to do beside go shopping constantly with you, Ami," I heard Wade tell her. I paused to hear her reply.

"We might see a movie, too," Ami told him.

"I'd like to see her go places with kids her age," he insisted.

"She will. Don't worry so much. Just give her some time to make sincere friends. She's very perceptive and very particular," Ami replied.

They were quiet, so I continued up to my room. I went right to the bathroom and then took off my clothes and put on one of the sheer nightgowns Ami had gotten me. I suddenly realized, however, that I wasn't that tired. I pulled back my blanket, but instead of crawling into bed, I felt myself drawn to the moonlight and went to one of my windows.

I sat on the edge of the sill and looked out at the moonlit lawn and trees, all silhouetted and silent like dedicated sentinels keeping guard over the house and grounds. Sitting there reminded me of my life on the farm before I was permitted to be outside during the daylight hours. I felt as imprisoned and as aloof from the real world. I was a girl locked in a bubble again, wishing I could simply open my window and fly away like one of the beautiful birds I used to watch. How wonderful it would be to have that freedom, I thought, and recalled the heavy blanket of sadness and self-pity I wore on my tiny shoulders back then.

I wasn't even aware that I was crying until I felt a tear fall off my chin and touch my face. Suddenly, in the window, I thought I saw Noble's reflection, saw him standing behind me, looking sad, but before I spun around, I heard what sounded like hail hitting the glass.

In an instant Noble's image was gone.

But I saw something better, something I wanted to see even more, something I had wished for and fantasized so hard, I made it come true.

When I looked out and down, I saw Trevor Foley standing in a pool of moonlight, looking up at me.

12

Sweet Sorrow

♊

I opened my window and poked my head out.

"What are you doing here?" I called down to him.

"The party stunk," he said. "I thought I'd drop by. I saw your piano teacher leave, and I was watching you through the window so I would know when you went up to your room."

"How did you get through the gate?" I asked. I knew no one would let him in.

"You think mere gates could stop me from seeing you?"

"You'd better go. Someone will see you or hear you, Trevor."

"So? Didn't you ever read *Romeo and Juliet?* Like Romeo, I'm willing to risk life and limb. I'm here to climb up to your balcony." He turned as if there was an audience watching and cried, "But soft! What light through yonder window breaks? It is the east and Celeste is the sun."

"But I don't have a balcony," I said, laughing.

"Really? Well, then the roof of these bay windows will have to stand in its place," he declared, and began to climb, pulling himself up to the bay window roof.

"Trevor, stop. Go back. You can't do this," I warned him, turning to be sure no one had overheard, no one was coming into my room.

He hoisted himself to his feet and was now standing with his face inches from mine.

"Hi," he said.

"You idiot. You're going to get us both into big trouble. Get out of here before it's too late."

"I wouldn't think of leaving without a kiss," he said.

"You're absolutely crazy."

"Crazy for you," he replied, and leaned on the windowsill, closed his eyes, and pursed his lips.

"If I kiss you, will you go?"

"Probably not," he said, "but it's worth a try."

When I leaned in closer to kiss him, I smelled whiskey on his breath and snapped my head back.

"You've been drinking!"

"Just enough to boost my courage," he said, and held up his thumb and forefinger. "Waverly's parties get a little wild. Booze comes out of the faucets. It's like a Roman orgy."

"So how come you left?"

"I quickly realized you weren't there," he said.

"No one tried to take my place?"

"Many tried, none succeeded," he declare. He closed his eyes again and wavered. I thought he was going to fall off the narrow roof and reached out for him.

"Trevor! You're making me nervous," I said, gripping his arm.

"Have a drink," he said, "and boost your courage."

He reached into his back pocket and produced a small metal flask. He offered it, then he opened it and took a sip. "Now, I can face anyone and anything," he declared, and moved to crawl through my window.

"Trevor!" I cried in a hoarse whisper.

"My kiss, please," he said halfway in.

I kissed him quickly. He kept his eyes closed.

"A little too fast," he said. "Didn't have time to register. Replay, please."

"You fool," I said, but I kissed him and held my lips to his longer and firmer.

When I pulled away this time, he opened his eyes and looked at me with such affection and clear desire, I felt what Ami said I would feel, a loss of control, an eagerness to continue, a tingle down my spine that swept all caution away.

"I'll be as quiet as a feather," he promised, and kept coming. I stepped back and waited until he was completely inside. He was already inside my heart. I couldn't help but be amused by his antics and charm.

"You're going to get us both into big trouble," I said, but not with much firmness.

"Really great things, important things, are always full of risk, but usually worth it," he replied, and reached for my hand to pull me closer to him.

I realized how thin and flimsy the material between my naked body and him was when his hands moved up from my waist and slowly came around to caress my breasts while we kissed again, this time longer.

"You know, Celeste," he said. "I would never tell anyone I believed in love at first sight until I saw you walk into homeroom the other day. It was as if my heart had been sleeping in my chest, pretending to beat, because suddenly it thumped like someone pounding his fist on my bedroom door to wake me up.

"And when you looked at me, held me in your gaze like you did, I was ready to kiss your feet."

"You're just saying that because you're drunk, Trevor Foley."

"I don't have to be drunk to tell you what's in my heart," he replied, and kissed me again.

All Ami's words and warnings hovered about my head flapping their wings like hysterical butterflies, trying desperately to get an audience with my whirling brain, but I refused to pay attention. I didn't stop him from backing me up to my bed, and when he kissed my neck and moved his hand over the nightgown, guiding it off my shoulder, I didn't stop him.

I sat on my bed and let him lower the nightgown below my breasts. He fell to his knees and for a long moment just drank me in. I didn't move. The excitement exploding inside me seemed to make me more and more helpless. He brought his lips to my breasts, to each nipple, kissing and licking, and then he slowly guided me back until I was lying there looking up at him with wonder in my eyes. It felt so much like one of my dreams that for a moment or two, I really did believe I would blink and he would be gone. The window would be closed, and all that had occurred would prove to be fantasy.

The sound of his belt being unbuckled brought me back to reality.

"Trevor," I whispered, more as a weak plea for him to stop than an invitation.

But that was how he took it. He smiled and lowered himself beside me, kissing me, holding and petting me as he completed the removal of my nightgown. How could Ami's words and warnings be so ineffective? Why wasn't I heeding any of it? Was it because I saw her as hypocritical since she had revealed her deepest secrets? Or was I using that to rationalize my own promiscuous behavior?

As Trevor continued to kiss and touch me around those erogenous zones Ami had described, I continued to think and debate with myself. It was truly as though I had lifted myself out of my body and was sitting on the bed watching all this take place. Perhaps I had replaced my precious Noble.

Are you trying to make up for lost time, missing romantic experiences? Does it bother you so much that Ami saw you as a complete innocent, bother you enough to cause you to surrender yourself so quickly and completely? What are you trying to prove, Celeste Atwell? Do you really believe that one experience like this will make you just as sophisticated as all those other girls at the private school?

I almost laughed aloud when I heard myself think, *Are you going to respect yourself in the morning?*

"We shouldn't do this so fast," I offered weakly as Trevor shifted his body to place himself between my legs.

"It won't be fast," he whispered, his lips touching my ear. That tingled too.

Everywhere he touched me and kissed me, even breathed on me, lit up as though my body were filled with thousands of tiny candles and he had the power to light them. I was glowing, illuminated as brightly as a star or the moonlight that had drawn me to my window and hypnotized me so quickly.

I heard him unwrap something and started to sit up.

"No," he said. "Don't ruin the moment."

"Trevor," I uttered, my voice shaking weakly.

He was at me again.

"I really love you, Celeste," he said, and began to enter me.

Yes, I was tight, and at the start it threatened to be a very painful thing, but my body's willingness to accept him overcame all that, tolerated the pain. Once again, the moans and even the sobs I heard seemed to be coming to me outside my body. I was sitting there, watching it all with an almost scientific detachment.

What happens next? How do I react?

Although it wasn't at the top of my concerns, I did think about the fact that I was disappointing Ami, letting her down and turning my back on all her advice and admonitions. Was I being ungrateful? This was, after all, her home. I was wearing the clothes she had bought me. She had put me in the private school where I had met Trevor, and in return, here I was, locked in the most intimate embrace with him right across the hallway from her room.

I opened my eyes and looked at Trevor. He looked like he was in his own world. No longer kissing me and whispering his love, he kept his eyes closed and had his head back as he moved his body to bring him the most possible pleasure. He uttered a short cry and then a groan as he exploded inside me and then dropped his head to my shoulder, floundering for a moment like a fish pulled out of the water. Gradually, he wound down and became still, his breathing and mine more regular.

He opened his eyes and looked at me. The expression on my face and my having my eyes wide open and studying him brought a smile to his face.

"Hello," he said. "Fancy meeting you here."

I didn't laugh. It had happened so quickly, and I was so confused and worried about every feeling that I wasn't sure it actually had occurred. Was that it?

"Are you all right?" he asked.

"You'd better get dressed and go," I said.

"But I just came," he replied, and laughed. He turned over and lay there beside me. "I like this bed." He bounced on it. "It's like sleeping on a giant marshmallow."

"You've got to go, Trevor," I urged with more insistence. "Sometimes Ami stops by before she goes to bed."

"Stop calling me Trevor. My name is Romeo," he said, propping himself on his elbow.

He traced his left forefinger down the middle of my bosom and then under my breasts as though he wanted to memorize ever curve in my body.

"You're as beautiful as I thought," he said. "I was a little surprised, however, to discover you've not been with anyone else like this."

"Well, don't be," I snapped, and pushed his hand away from my breasts.

"Don't get upset. I'm not being critical."

"You sounded critical," I said. "You made it sound like I was emotionally retarded or something because I have never slept with a boy."

He shrugged.

"Hey, there has to be a first time for everyone, and I'm happy to be yours. They say every time you make love from now on, you'll always be comparing him to me."

I sat up and reached for my nightgown. Would I do that? He shouldn't be so confident, I thought. These circumstances made it most likely that it would be better the next time, either with him or someone else.

"I don't intend to be going to a sexual supermarket, Trevor," I said, bothered by his arrogance and that he was still under the influence of the alcohol he had drunk.

"A sexual supermarket? I like that," he said. "Hey,

c'mon, don't be upset. I really do feel very strongly about you, Celeste."

He watched me put on my nightgown.

"That's a pretty sexy nightgown," he commented. "Looks like one of those Fredericks of Hollywood things." He started to reach for me again, and I pulled away.

"Trevor, you really have to get dressed and get out of here," I insisted, practically pleading.

"Okay, okay," he said, and sat up. He scrubbed his face with his palms and looked around a moment before reaching for his own things. He went into the bathroom. I heard the toilet flush, and then he came out, still not fully dressed.

"Trevor."

"I'm going. I'm going," he said, and continued putting on his clothing. He moved very slowly. His drinking and everything he had done was finally registering in his drooping eyelids.

I thought I heard someone on the stairs, heard voices.

"Hurry, Trevor," I cried.

"I am. I am," he said, putting on his shoes. "You know, we might have hit upon something here. If your cousin continues to keep you locked up like this, I'll just come by nights. We'll make up a signal or something. You know, like a candle in the window. Instead of crying, 'The British are coming. The British are coming,' you'll cry, 'Trevor is coming. Trevor is coming.' "

Despite my nervousness, I had to smile.

"You really are incorrigible," I said.

"Wow. Incorrigible. I haven't been called that since kindergarten."

He stood up.

"Okay," he said. "It's good night, good night, parting is such sweet sorrow . . ."

"Just go, Trevor," I said, pushing him toward the window.

"One more kiss," he insisted, turning on me. "I need to seal it with a kiss and take it home to my dream factory."

"Kiss me and go," I said.

He smiled and ever so slowly brought his lips to mine. As he did so, he slid his hands up the sides of my body and across and over my breasts. I stepped back.

"You're making it impossible," I told him.

"It will be better the second time," he said. "I promise."

"If you don't get out of here, there'll never be a second time," I warned.

"Never say never," he joked, touched the tip of my nose, and started to climb out the window.

He had just put his right foot on the narrow roof above the bay windows when my bedroom door was thrust open. I turned to see Ami standing there with Mrs. Cukor at her side. Ami's shrill scream spun Trevor around awkwardly, and his left foot caught on the sill. He fell forward, trying to break the fall with his hands out, but he missed the edge of the roof and went tumbling over.

I screamed after him.

"Trevor!"

"Go get Wade and tell him to go out there," Ami told Mrs. Cukor, who glared at me and then hurried away.

Ami came rushing in to look out the window. She pulled me away and stuck her head out. I leaned to look over her shoulder. I couldn't see Trevor. I had hoped to see him running off, but he was nowhere in sight.

"He fell off!" I moaned.

"What have you done?" Ami asked, her eyes wide. "How long was he here?"

I bit down on my lower lip, not knowing what to say. She looked about the room frantically and settled her eyes on my bed. Then she walked to it slowly and pulled the blanket back. There on the sheet was a sizable blood stain.

"Oh, my God," she said, turning to me slowly. "You've been raped!"

"What?" I looked up, shaking my head. "No."

"It's nothing more than that. He entered this house without permission. He climbed into your room like a burglar, only what he burgled was your innocence, your virginity. He's nothing more than a common thief."

We heard a commotion below, and both looked out the window. I saw Wade, Mrs. Cukor, and Mrs. McAlister now, but I still didn't see any sign of Trevor.

"What is it?" Ami called down to them.

Wade stepped out so he could look up.

"He broke something. Maybe his shoulder," he said. "We'll have to call an ambulance. I don't know how to move someone who's broken a bone. I don't want to make it worse."

"You should call the police," Ami told him. "Not an ambulance."

"No!" I screamed.

"I'm calling an ambulance, Ami. Calm things down up there," Wade ordered.

"Calm things down," she muttered, and turned to me. "How could you let this happen, Celeste, and so soon after I caught him up here with you? I did all that I could to prevent it. I trusted you."

"I'm sorry," I said.

She thought a moment.

"Do you know if he used any protection? Well," she screamed when I didn't respond immediately. "Do you?"

"Yes," I said, "I believe he did."

"You believe?"

"I'm sure he did, I mean. I'm just so confused. Please."

"Oh, God. And I was just going to see my doctor on Monday and get the pills for you. We'll have to have you examined."

"I'm all right, Ami. I'm worried about Trevor more than I am about myself at the moment."

"You shouldn't worry about him. He should be worrying about himself. When did you have your last period?" she asked, her eyes narrowing.

"It ended just about a month ago. I'm due any day."

"Good. I want you to tell me the moment it starts again. Do you understand, Celeste? The moment it starts," she said, staring out of my bedroom.

"But I told you he was wearing protection," I said.

"That doesn't always matter. There's always that small percentage, and you don't want to be one of them."

She turned at the door. "Take that sheet off the bed. I'll send Mrs. Cukor up with a clean one. Go take a hot bath," she ordered. "Thank goodness Mrs. Cukor came to me to tell me what was going on. Otherwise this might have continued. I know what men do when they gnaw a path to your heart. They travel it until they wear it out. Clean yourself up," she concluded, and left.

Mrs. Cukor? I thought. If she had seen Trevor climbing the roof and entering my room, why had she waited so long to tell Ami? Why wasn't Ami here sooner? It was almost as if Mrs. Cukor wanted terrible things to happen first, and what was more frightening, almost as if she knew they would.

I looked out the window again. I should go down to him, I thought, but then I thought it might just make things harder for him. Who knew what he might say and what he might reveal had occurred between us? Feeling dazed myself, I began to strip the bed.

A little more than twenty or so minutes later, I heard the ambulance approach the driveway gate, and I rushed back to the window to watch it come up the drive and park. The paramedics hopped out and unloaded a stretcher. Wade heard them too and rushed to them. They quickly approached the bay windows. I was still unable to see Trevor. Finally, they lifted him onto the stretcher and began to carry him away. I saw how he held his right arm, but it was too dark below now to see much else. I watched him being loaded into the ambulance. Wade and Mrs. McAlister stood by. The paramedics spoke quickly with him, and then they got in and drove off.

I collapsed onto my desk chair and stared at the floor.

Ami came charging back into my room.

"Why aren't you in the tub already? You haven't even run the water!" she cried, looking into the bathroom. She went in and started the bath.

Mrs. Cukor was right on her heels with a clean new sheet for my bed. She began to put it on, avoiding looking at me while she worked.

"Get in here," Ami commanded, "and get into the tub. You're a mess."

I felt so helpless and distraught, I did what she asked. I complained about the water and then added some cold while she stood by in the doorway watching me and watching Mrs. Cukor. Finally, Mrs. Cukor left, and Ami entered.

"How could you let him sneak into your room like that?" she asked, her voice sounding more curious than angry now. "Didn't you think something like this might happen? Are you really that naive, even after all I told you? I thought you were smart, a good student. How could you do this with the first boy you met?"

I didn't respond. I sat there staring at my legs. It still all felt like I was outside my body, like this was happening to someone else. When would I wake from this dream?

"I don't know if we can keep this quiet," she said, pacing and thinking. "He's been taken to the hospital. There'll be questions and questions. Some nasty gossip mongers, jealous bitches, will probably say I was a bad influence on you or something stupid like that. They just love making trouble for people who outshine them. You know what I'm talking about. I'm sure it's happened to you repeatedly at the orphanage . . . jealous girls making up stories about you. It's dreadful. What to do, what to do," she muttered, still pacing.

Suddenly she stopped and looked at me, her eyes filling with an idea that excited her.

"What?" I asked.

"No one has to know he actually got into your room. He could have fallen off trying. That's it. That's the story I'll give out and the story you'll support when the other students at the school ask you about it, which they're bound to do. I'll even tell that to Wade. He doesn't know the full story yet. Trevor was just moaning and groaning."

She pointed her right forefinger at me.

"And you had better not say anything different," she warned. "If you do, your only defense will be to accuse him of rape, just like I said."

"I wouldn't do that."

"I have no idea what Wade would do if he knew the whole truth," she added, not really listening to me. "He'd probably want me to send you right back to the orphanage, even if we did accuse Trevor of breaking in and raping you. Wade is not capable of handling domestic problems, only business problems," she said.

I looked at her with skepticism. My impression of Wade was that he could deal with family issues far better than she could, and he should know the truth.

"He puts on a good act," she said, seeing my doubts. "You have to remember what his youth was like, how Basil treated him and still treats him. In many ways Wade is immature. That's right, immature. He's socially immature. Just take my word for it. He might not show it to you, but if he learned all of this, he would be in a panic, worrying it would somehow impact on his precious plumbing business, and I'd hear about it behind closed doors. Can you listen to me and do what I ask finally?" she nearly screamed.

I nodded and looked away.

"Good. Now as soon as you're finished in here, go to sleep and leave the rest to me," she said. "We'll have a quiet sisterly talk about all this tomorrow."

She approached the bathtub and put her hand on my head, caressing me softly. Surprised, I looked up at her and saw her smile.

"I'm not blaming you as much as you think, Celeste. I know how conniving and clever men are. I knew from the very beginning that you would be a target. You're so beautiful. I probably should have put bars on your windows," she said. "I'm sorry we don't utilize chastity belts anymore. Some social progress for women has only made them more vulnerable and left them with more disadvantage."

When I looked up at her, I saw she was dead serious.

"Just try to get some rest," she added, and leaned down to kiss the top of my head before leaving. "In the morning after breakfast, you and I will have a real sisterly heart-to-heart talk."

Try to get some rest? What an impossible request that was, I thought, rose from my bath, dried myself, put on a different nightgown, and crawled back into the bed. The new sheets smelled starchy, but I also detected the faint aroma of something else. I sniffed and recoiled.

Garlic again! What had she done, filled the sheet with it before bringing it up here? How could I sleep with that in my nostrils? And yet how could I complain?

I heard a knock at my door. Ami wasn't going to knock first anymore, I thought. I was sure it was Wade, or perhaps Mrs. McAlister, sent up with a cup of some herbal tea.

"Come in," I called, and Wade opened the door.

"How are you doing?"

"I'm okay," I said. How could I mention the sheet without revealing what really happened in here? I thought.

"Teenagers. It's a form of insanity," he said, shaking his head. "I had to call Chris Foley and tell him what happened to his son. The irony is, he'll probably sue me. Did you see Trevor fall?"

"Yes," I admitted. Was he going to ask me more and force me to tell him the whole story?

"He's lucky he didn't get even more damaged. I

found this on him," he said, holding up the silver whiskey flask. "I thought it would be better if I was the one to find it. I'll have to tell his father, though," he added. "Maybe that will keep him from starting any sort of stupid legal action."

"I'm sorry about it all. I didn't tell him to come here," I said, which was true.

"Hey, young love. We'll get over it. Ami will calm down. I'll handle the Foleys. Don't worry. One of these days, we'll all actually laugh about it," he said.

Just as I had thought, he was taking it all far better than Ami.

"I'm sorry," I said again.

"Try to get some sleep. You'll need your strength for what's to come. I'm sure you'll be the center of attention tomorrow, and especially the next day, when you return to school. News travels fast around here, especially news like this."

I nodded. He hesitated, looking awkward, as if he wanted to say something more.

"Well . . . good night," was all he added, and then he turned and left, closing the door softly behind him. I lowered my head to the pillow. A few moments later, I could hear Ami and Wade mumbling in the hallway. She was whining and sobbing, and he was comforting her. Then I heard their door close, and all become quiet again.

I felt so terrible having brought all this trouble to their home, and so soon after I had arrived. I thought I would start crying again, but that quickly made me feel melancholy and alone. Memories stirred as if they were nudged out of hibernation.

A long time ago, Noble and I sat by the front window in the living room and looked out at a moonlit night not much different from this one. He had just finished reading me a beautiful story about a caterpillar who fell in love with a butterfly, and promised her that as soon as he turned into a butterfly, they would fly off together. The butterfly stayed beside him and waited and waited. The strength of his love for her finally sped up his metamorphosis, and at the end of the story, he had beautiful new wings and they flew away together, carried along by a warm breeze.

"Where did they go?" I wanted to know.

"To a place where they would always be together and always beautiful," he said.

Where was this place? I wondered.

Was he looking for it now when he gazed so hard out of our window at the dark forest across the way? Was there a beautiful butterfly waiting for him, and did that mean he would leave me forever and ever?

He saw the worry in my face and smiled.

"What?" he asked me.

"You're going to go away, too," I told him. It was just before it all happened, and he did go away.

"No, I won't."

"Yes," I insisted. "You will."

He stopped smiling. He always paid attention to the things I said. I remember that. He made me feel important. Mother would, too. Now, when I thought about it, I realized I didn't really know why I said some of the things I said. They seemed to know more about that than I did. How strange!

The day he left, I thought about the butterfly story.

He'd always known in his heart he would go, I thought. He'd lied to me.

Maybe that was why I was so angry then.

It was another betrayal in the long line of many to trail behind me for the rest of my life.

All I wanted to do in the days that followed was

turn into a butterfly, wave my wings, and fly away to wherever Noble had gone, to that magical place.

I'll spend my whole life looking for it, I thought as I closed my eyes.

In minutes, I was asleep, dreaming of apple blossoms rising slowly to return to their branches, until I realized that they were all white and red butterflies, stirred by something.

What was it? What stirred them up?

Somewhere just outside the door, the answer hovered, just as Mrs. Cukor hovered in the shadows of this strangely beautiful house with walls woven in mysteries better left untouched—but mysteries that would touch me.

I knew that as well as I knew my own name.

I could almost feel them swirling about my bed, drawing closer and closer until . . .

I woke with a scream, a desperate cry for Noble.

Always, for Noble.

13

A Sense of Danger

♊

True to her promise, the next day after breakfast, Ami asked me to go out with her and sit in the gazebo near the pool for her so-called sisterly heart-to-heart, which I thought would simply be one of her long lectures about the evils of men, especially after last night. She surprised me, however, with her decision instead to reveal the second biggest secret of her life. She had already revealed the first by telling me she was currently in therapy.

She actually didn't come down to breakfast, but had Mrs. McAlister bring something up to her instead. Wade, reading in my face that I thought she was sick over what had happened the night before, urged me not to be upset.

"She often has breakfast in bed on Sundays," he said; "she's come down recently only because you're living with us now. She says I have my face buried in the newspaper, especially on Sundays, and she'd rather watch television than the back of the business section," he added, shrugging.

What struck me about Wade was his utter lack of rationalization or attempt to excuse and justify himself. He was who he was, and he couldn't deny it or change. He was basically telling me he didn't blame her for remaining in bed to have breakfast. She was right. He ignored her.

He left earlier than he had before to join his business associates at their club, but told me to tell Ami he would gladly take us to dinner if she wanted to do that. Despite appearances, he was concerned about her happiness.

Mrs. McAlister returned from Ami's bedroom to tell me Ami wanted me to know she would be down shortly to speak with me, and I should wait for her.

When she did come down, she was still in her robe and fluffy pink silk slippers. She looked like she had slept even less than I had, but she was determined we have our talk, and she wanted us to go outside. I thought she would be cold dressed as she was, but that didn't seem to concern her. She looked like she was in some sort of daze, as if she was still in the midst of some dream. She moved like a sleepwalker over the tiled pathway through the lawn, with me following close behind. My head down, I felt like a child about to be reprimanded.

For a while she simply sat there, her eyes blinking, her lips twitching slightly.

"I gave all this a great deal of thought last night, Celeste, and I made some very serious and important decisions," she began. "I hesitated to tell you everything about my own youth," she continued, "because I really didn't want to give you the impression that everything I've told you and tried to teach you about

male-female relationships stems from any one horren-
dous experience. I would have had these insights to
offer you no matter what. These were all things I had
learned before I was . . . before my traumatic experiences occurred. I hope you believe me." She took a
deep breath.

We were beside each other on the built-in bench,
looking out at the pool, which was now covered to prevent it from being filled with the crisp orange, red, and
brown leaves of autumn rushing over the property on
the backs of northern winds. It was far from freezing
yet, but the air had begun to take on that underbelly
of coolness that warned us winter was not far behind.
It hovered anxiously and eagerly under the ever-
lessening weight of time, casting days and weeks off
its shoulders as it closed in around us.

I could remember first snows in upstate New York
falling as early as mid-October. The flakes would cast
a thin white blanket over everything, but in the morning they would be gone under the warm breath of sunlight. When I was little, it seemed quite magical, a
"Now you see it, now you don't" trick Nature pulled. It
reinforced my belief that the world outside my windows was a world full of illusions, which of course
made the possibility of spirits hovering around us even
more credible.

"I know you're sitting there now and thinking about
the things I told you the other night at the restaurant
about my therapy and reasons for it. I know you're
probably thinking I'm about to tell you I was raped or
I went too far with a boy when I was younger and I got
pregnant and had to have an abortion, or even gave
birth and gave the baby up for adoption. Those stories
are typical, and far too common. I know they happen
often, too often, but that's not what happened to me,"

she said. "That's not why I've been in and out of therapy so often and why I am involved with a new doctor right now."

She looked down, and when she looked up, I saw her eyes were filled with tears. They looked like two tiny glass balls under water, and she had her lips pulled so tightly, they lost all color. Her chin quivered.

"Ami, you don't have to tell me anything," I said quickly. "I don't want to hurt you or see you suffer. I'm sorry for what happened last night. I won't let it happen again. Please, don't put yourself through any more pain on my account," I pleaded. Her face was bringing tears to my own eyes.

"No, no, I've got to do it," she insisted. "I have to tell you everything so you don't think I'm just some ogre who doesn't want you to have fun and enjoy your youth. You must believe that I am sincere when I tell you I want you to be aware of every minefield out there, and believe me, there are many.

"Parents," she said, suddenly filled with anger, the word seeming to be spit out of her lips instead of spoken, "for one stupid reason or another, let their children go forward in this world without warning them of the dangers looming or in waiting. They are either too embarrassed themselves or simply Pollyanna. They expect or hope that nothing terrible will happen to their children. They bury their heads in the sand and pretend that none of the evil exists, and certainly none of it will touch or affect their children.

"It's what happened to me," she added in a softer tone. "My mother was quite unsophisticated actually, despite the airs she put on in front of others. She was protected and spoiled most of her life, and my father behaved as though sex was something married people had only once, and just to make children. He never

ever brought up anything remotely close to the subject with me, and neither did my mother. And if I asked him anything that remotely suggested male-female relations, he would always answer with the same words:

" 'Ami, remember, sex is just a trick to bring people together, just Nature's trick. Don't make anything more of it and you'll always be fine.'

"That was his advice. Those were my parents. Why, my mother didn't even prepare me for the advent of my first period. When I had it, she looked as shocked and surprised as I was. It was almost as if she had forgotten I was a girl.

" 'Oh dear,' I remember her saying, 'we'll have to get you properly equipped right away.'

"Properly equipped? I remember thinking. What was I doing, preparing for a mountain climb or a hike? What about the cramps, the reasons for it? Are we just to go by those words in Genesis my grandmother liked to quote: 'I will greatly multiply thy sorrow and thy conception; in sorrow thou shalt bring forth children'? We were being punished forever because Eve gave Adam the fruit of the Tree of Good and Evil? Was that the only explanation for the blood and pain and the sick feeling? And were we simply to accept it as that and grit our teeth?

"In my school we didn't have health-education classes to do for the young girls what their parents failed to do. Everyone had to learn everything on her own.

"Decent young women didn't talk about those things, you see. That was how my mother was brought up, and how she was bringing me up. Do you know that never once in all the time I was living with my parents did I ever hear my mother say the word 'bathroom,' much less 'toilet'? It was always 'the powder room.' When I was little, I used to look for the powder. What powder? I wondered.

"Until I was bathroom trained, we had a nanny. My mother never once changed a diaper. Can you imagine that? If I ever said I have to pee, she would correct me instantly with, 'No, say you have to go to the powder room, or just say I have to powder my nose.' You can't imagine how girls and boys my age would laugh at me when I did say that. Every other girl would raise her hand in elementary school and ask if she could go to the bathroom. I would ask to go to the powder room. Finally I stopped, but I never let my mother know."

She smiled.

"Once I got very angry at her and stood there reciting the forbidden words: 'urine, toilet, penis, vagina . . .' She had my mouth washed out with soap.

"Anyway," she said, waving her hand, "I seem to be getting off the track. I'm not. I'm just trying to get you to understand how young people your age are left on their own to handle the experiences and traumas they will confront. No wonder so many get into trouble.

"We are," she continued after another deep breath, "comprised of all sorts of contradictions. That's why so often we will do things that will even surprise ourselves. There are depths and depths of contradictory emotion in us all, in you, Celeste, and definitely in me.

"Oh, dear," she said, biting her lower lip. "I just realized you might be so turned off by what I'm about to tell you that you and I will never be able to be close."

"Ami, don't—" I began, but she put up her hand and shook her head vigorously.

"I can't be concerned about that now. I can't be selfish. If that's what results from all this, then so be it. At least I would feel I had given you everything I could, everything my own mother didn't give me."

She pulled herself up again and took another deep breath. My heart was thumping. Around us, birds were chirping, and somewhere on the far end of the property, the grounds people were beginning to mow grass and trim bushes. The monotonous hum of their engines sounded like hives of bees.

"I was very close with a girl in my class, Gail Browne. She was practically my only close friend. Almost from birth, she had poor eyesight, and she was wearing glasses by the age of two. I was far prettier than she was. Almost any girl was, even some of the boys. It wasn't even a contest when it came to our facial features, even though, as I told you, I was a somewhat late developer myself.

"Unfortunately for Gail, she took after her father, who was a big man with a thick nose, iron jaw, and heavy lips. She wasn't that bad, of course, but her features made her look plain, actually masculine. And under those glasses, her eyes were always teary and red. However, she did have beautiful hair, which other girls thought was a complete waste framing a face like Gail's. She didn't even take as good care of her hair as most of the other girls did, much less do anything about her rough complexion.

"She knew nothing about cosmetics, in fact, and her mother did little to instruct her. She looked uncomfortable wearing lipstick and always chose a shade that did little for her. She was messy about it, too, always going too far in the corners and even smudging her chin.

"I became friends with her because she was such a good student, and I enjoyed the way she followed me about in school like some puppy dog. I was her celebrity friend in her eyes, I suppose, and it made me feel good to have someone look up to me. I could depend on her to help me with my homework, and whenever we did study together, I got better grades on tests. Nothing distracted her from the work like so much distracted me.

"Anyway, not until the last half of our junior year in high school did she develop any sort of womanly figure, and when she did, it literally seemed to happen overnight. At least mine came along gradually and sensibly. You can imagine what it was like for a girl like her who was flat-chested to suddenly have a much bigger and better-shaped bust than most of the other girls, and her rear end puffed out so that all her pants and shorts became impossible to wear. I remember her mother telling my mother how much she was costing them in new clothes all of a sudden.

"Boys noticed, of course, but because she was so unattractive, their interest was purely prurient, lustful. They made up dirty jokes about her and teased her whenever they could. They called her a double bagger. The only way to make love to her, they said, was to put a bag over her face and then over your own. She was that ugly, they claimed. It was a terribly mean joke. Disgusting and cruel, that's what they were.

"Gail was embarrassed about her voluptuous new body, and because of the way these boys were treating her, she did all sorts of things to detract from it, including wearing bras that were more like straitjackets and oversized one-piece dresses to hide her curves.

"I was going through this great period of doubt about myself about the same time, and I was quite interested in how she dealt with all of this, too. Soon our study sessions became more personal. She wasn't as shy as she appeared to be when it came to talking about intimate things. She revealed to me that she wasn't just putting on a mature body. She was in some inner turmoil with her new feelings.

"She even admitted to having spontaneous orgasms, sometimes, even in school. Since that hadn't happened to me, I was very intrigued, of course, and our discussions grew bolder, more intense.

"One night, when we were supposed to be studying for an upcoming literature exam, she told me about her masturbating. I remember feeling absolutely mesmerized by her description. I told her I had not done that, and she looked at me skeptically. 'You should,' she said. 'It's not as unnatural as you might think.' She went on and on, describing some of the books she had read and the things she had learned.

"Of course, I was rapt. Living with parents like mine, especially a mother like mine, and not being as chummy with the girls at the school as I would have liked, and not yet having any sort of real romance with a boy, I was hanging on Gail's every revelation.

"Finally she put down her notebook and proposed that I do it right then and there. I remember feeling as if I had stepped into a gigantic bowl of hot honey. Just the mere suggestion of doing such a thing made my body tingle and warmed my private places. I felt as though my arms and legs were stuck together.

" 'It's just like an experiment,' Gail said, 'with yourself. It's not that big a deal.'

"I started to shake my head, and she said, 'I'll do it, too.'

" 'First,' she said, 'we should undress.'

"I watched her stand up and begin to disrobe, unbutton her blouse and unzip her skirt. She paused and looked at me. 'Well? What are you waiting for, Ami? You're not afraid, are you?' she taunted.

"I was afraid, but I wouldn't admit it, and I hated myself for being afraid. So I began to undress, too. When Gail removed her bra, I was shocked to see how big she really was, but she had a flat stomach and nice hips. In other words, it all did seem to fit together to form a body every girl at the school would desire, even me.

"I won't go into every detail about what followed, but I became so self-conscious and felt so foolish, I stopped. Especially when I saw how she was watching me, looking at me. 'Why are you stopping?' she asked. I told her I felt foolish, and she took on this look of great concern.' 'You've got to get over it,' she said. She was so caught up in being the teacher when it came to these things. It was her way of lording it over me, you see.

"I hated feeling so insecure and so inadequate. Even Gail, the double-bagger, was ahead of me when it came to these things. That's what went through my mind.

"And then . . ." Amy paused. She put her hand on her chest and looked like she was struggling to breathe. She took another deep breath before continuing.

"And then, Gail said she would help me."

I held my own breath, listening to her story. The world truly seemed to grow silent and very still. Even the mowers and trimming machines became mute.

"And I didn't stop her," Ami finally blurted. She paused to see my reaction.

When I said nothing nor changed expression, she thought I didn't understand, but I had already pictured the scene she was describing and anticipated what she was about to tell me. For me that made the actual hearing of the words less traumatic. It had always been this way for me, and most people interpreted my reactions as lack of interest when in fact I was merely thinking ahead.

"I let her touch me, excite me," she confessed. "Afterward, she kept reassuring me, telling me I should think of it as just an experiment, but I couldn't ignore the fact that she enjoyed it as much as I did.

"While she was exciting me, she excited herself! We were, in fact, having sex with each other.

"I didn't sleep that night. I was filled with a mixture of guilt and memories of pleasure. I thought I could never look at Gail again. I even thought I had better stop being her friend.

"But I did look at her, and I didn't stop being her friend, at least, not for a while longer.

"I didn't want to enjoy it, and I didn't want to do it or be with her, but I was. It just seemed to happen spontaneously, and of course, every time it did, we did, I went through these deep depressions of guilt, my sleep filled with twisted nightmares. I was convinced something was now seriously wrong with me. And then . . . a terrible thing happened."

"What?" I said when her pause ran too long. I could feel the darkness closing around the images in my mind. I didn't want to hear about it, and yet I couldn't help being drawn to it.

"I wasn't aware of the fact that Gail was friends with another girl like she was friends with me. Actually, they were not exactly friends like she and I were. It was a younger girl, her neighbor, Rhonda Lindsey, the fourteen-year-old sister of a boy at our school, Oliver Lindsey. She had done the same sort of sexual things with her, only Rhonda Lindsey was so disgusted with herself and so frightened about it, she told someone who told someone until it got to Oliver, who confronted Gail in school in front of a crowd of our classmates. It was a terribly ugly scene, and I remember how Gail looked to me to come to her aid and defend her, but I turned and ran away.

"It was a big scandal. Rhonda's parents found out and confronted Gail's. Everyone was talking about it every day at school, and I was terrified that they would learn about me as well. Fortunately, no one knew how often Gail had come to my house, but some of the girls were beginning to ask questions because they knew how she followed me about and idolized me. However, before any of that could go further . . . Gail overdosed on her mother's sleeping pills. Before anyone discovered what she had done, she died. She took the whole bottle, so there was no question that it wasn't an accident. Everyone's attention was on the horror of that. Oliver Lindsey had no remorse, nor did many of the other kids at school feel sorry for her.

"Another example of how men can be so cruel," she muttered. She wiped an errant tear from her cheek and sucked in her breath. "There was to be no mercy, no understanding, just nasty, mean talk. Everyone seemed to have teeth as sharp as vampire teeth, chomping down on the memory of Gail. The Brownes eventually sold their home and moved away."

"I'm sorry," I said. "It must have been hard for you, but I hope you didn't blame yourself."

"I tried not to. I kept it all locked away, but I was haunted by our encounters and by what I had done. I even began to wonder if I wasn't the one who had caused it all, actually caused Gail's suicide by being so willing a partner and thus setting her off and onto another girl."

"But from what you've described, you didn't initiate it. She did."

"I know, but I didn't reject her as I should have. The shame I felt made it more difficult to get into a good relationship with a boy. I was always afraid anyone I did go out with would immediately know what I had done. All you have to do is resist a boy's advances sometimes, and he immediately accuses you of being a lesbian. Don't let any of them try that on you!" she warned. "You can be sure they will.

"Anyway, after time passed, I did start to date, and eventually I met Wade. Before you ask, he knows all of it," she followed, "but of course Basil knows nothing. If he did, he would make something disgusting out of it. He's actually jokingly proposed I make love to a woman. He said he could arrange it as long as I permitted him to watch. He said it when he was drunk, but I don't doubt he'd like that or has done things like that.

"They're so different," she said, shaking her head, "Wade and his father. Sometimes I think it really is possible for a child to be more like a clone than the offspring of two people. Of course, I sense that Basil suspects Wade might not even be his son, even though he laughs at such an idea. He couldn't face the fact that his wife could have had interest in any other man, but he's as much as made that accusation in drunken rages from time to time. It bothers Wade when he does that, of course, but I told him he should be hoping it's true.

"Well," she said, sitting back, "there you have it: all the skeletons in our closet. The point of all this is, I want you to understand how deep and how lasting mistakes in relationships, sexual mistakes, can be." Before taking another breath, she added, "I'd like you to promise me that you will avoid Trevor Foley now.

"Because," she said, leaning forward quickly, her right forefinger up, "make no mistake about what he's going to do next. He's going to try to get you to feel terrible about what happened to him. He's going to get you to feel guilty about it, and then he's going to play on that guilt and seduce you again."

She nodded after her prediction.

"Don't worry about that, Ami. I won't feel guilty, and I certainly wouldn't permit a boy to make love to me out of some sense of guilt," I said firmly.

She studied my face a moment and then smiled.

"Good. Good. Because I want you to be a happy girl, a wholesome happy girl," she said.

She sighed and looked around, but I could tell she wasn't looking at anything. She was locked in her own head, listening to her own thoughts. I saw her tears emerge like prisoners quietly escaping over a wall.

"Ami . . ."

"I suppose you think I'm weird and strange and horrible after learning that story."

"No, I don't. I really don't," I said, and she turned and looked at me.

She smiled at the sincerity in my face.

"Oh, Celeste, you are special," she said, and hugged me. "Thank you. Thank you."

She pulled back as if she thought I would read something salacious in her embrace.

I reached out and took her hand.

"Thanks for trusting me with your secrets," I told her, and she relaxed and then smiled.

"So," she said, standing after another silent moment, "why don't we wash away all this sadness and stupidity by going to the Nest for lunch? It's a popular restaurant on Sundays. I feel like a lobster salad and some wine and maybe a chocolate soufflé. Go get dressed. It's too beautiful a day to waste on regrets," she declared firmly. Then she looked at me and asked, "Okay?"

I smiled.

"Okay, Ami. Sure," I said, and we both started for the house.

"I hate to be a complainer this morning," I added as we walked, "but Mrs. Cukor—"

"Now what?"

"She must have thrown a chunk of garlic into the washing machine when she did the sheet she put on my bed last night."

I couldn't help laughing after telling her.

"She didn't? Really?"

I nodded.

"Oh, brother," Ami said. "I'll have it changed while we're at lunch. Why doesn't that woman go off and join a circus?"

Maybe she thinks she has, I thought, but I kept it to myself.

Ami shook her head.

"You're right to laugh about it, too. We've got to look on the bright side of things. It's actually very funny," she declared.

She did have the amazing ability to forget unhappiness and become ebullient and jovial. I decided she was an emotional chameleon, able to blend into any atmosphere, wherever she was and whatever she was doing. Anyone looking at us when we entered the Nest, especially looking at her, would think the events at our house the night before were surely fiction. She knew many of the people who were having Sunday lunch there, but only one woman, Joy Stamford, a round-faced redhead, had the nerve to ask her outright if the story she had heard this morning was true.

"The Foley boy fell off your roof and broke his shoulder last night?"

Ami didn't even bat an eyelash, nor let her smile slip off her face.

"It was so stupid, Joy, it's not even worth discussing," she said. "I'm sure the Foleys are so embarrassed they'll go into hibernation."

"Well, what happened?" Joy insisted, playing now for the two other women at her table.

"We really don't know. There was a commotion, and then Wade found him lying there and called an ambulance."

All the women looked at me.

Ami saw where their attention had gone.

"And poor Celeste is just as much in the dark as everyone else. Maybe he was just a Peeping Tom," she added. "Poetic justice. How's the lobster salad today? I just hate it when it's stringy."

"Oh, it's wonderful," one of the other women said, and we went to our own table, where Ami held court much the same way she did everywhere she went.

"You see," she said, smiling and nodding at anyone who looked our way, "you don't show how upset you are. That's what they're hoping to see. They so enjoy someone else's troubles. You take their mean comments and just deflect them a bit and laugh, and thus you frustrate them. I know how to handle them. They are my mother's people. I've been in their world and lived in their country and spoken their language.

"And so will you, Celeste. You'll be even better at all this than I am. I'm sure of it," she said, and ordered us our lobster salads.

Early that evening, before we were to go out to dinner as Wade had proposed, my phone rang. It wasn't Trevor, as I expected, however. It was Waverly.

"He's in some pain," he said, "and asked me to call you for him. They have him under some sedation, but he managed to get out his plea like a dying man's last request," Waverly said in overly dramatic tones. "You should see the cast they have him in," he added. "He won't be driving for some time, and he won't be climbing up to your room either."

"Tell him I hope he gets better quickly," I offered.

"Sure. If you want, I'll take you over to see him tomorrow. He's home. We can go right after school."

"I can't. I have a driving lesson, and then I have a piano lesson," I added.

"What about the day after tomorrow?"

"I can't," I simply said.

"That's not being very nice. He risked his life to see you, and left my party to boot," he added. I envisioned his impish smile.

"From what I heard, he risked his life going to your party," I countered, and Waverly laughed.

"Hey, I just wanted you to know I'm available to serve you in any way you'd like. Any way you think I might be of some assistance," he added, with sexual overtones that could not be ignored.

"I'll keep that in mind if they start asking me to take out the garbage," I threw back at him. "Thanks for calling."

I hung up before he could respond, but I was sure his ears had turned red.

Despite all that and despite Ami's warnings, I did feel sorry for Trevor, and I had every intention of finding a way to visit him, if I could. I wasn't sure how his parents had reacted and whom they blamed. I didn't want to complicate the situation any more than it was, especially for Wade, but I couldn't help wondering what stories would be made up about me now.

As if she could hear my thoughts, Lynette Firestone called minutes afterward. I had just started my homework.

"Hi," she said, and before I could even say hello,

added, "everyone's talking about what happened to
Trevor at your house. Was he drunk? Did you let him
in, or did he fall trying to get into your room? Did you
invite him?" she asked, not pausing or taking a breath
between questions.

"How did you get this phone number?" I asked first.
I was sure Trevor wouldn't have given it to her, and
now I wondered if Waverly was giving my number out
to everyone as a joke.

"Your cousin gave it to my mother," she replied.
"She thought we could be friends and that you needed
a friend, especially now."

Why was it so important to Ami that I be friends
with Lynette Firestone, one of the most unpopular girls
at the school?

"So tell me. What really happened?" she pursued.

"I just heard this morning that something did. I was
asleep the whole time. Thanks for calling," I said.

"What?" I heard her say as I hung up.

Soon after, Ami came by to remind me to dress for
dinner. She was making Wade take us to what she said
was one of the more expensive steak houses.

"I need meat tonight," she declared. "I have to build
myself up."

She pretended to flex her biceps, laughed, and went
to get dressed herself.

When we descended the stairs together, Wade came
out of the living room, and we were both surprised to
see his father beside him.

"Dad's decided to come along with us tonight,"
Wade said. The look on his face and the way he said it
made it perfectly clear that it was Basil's idea entirely.

Ami stiffened and pursed her lips.

"We're not discussing what happened here last
night, Basil. It's over and done with."

"I'm sure it is," he said, smiling at her. His eyes, however, went quickly to me, and the smile on his face told me exactly from where his thoughts were coming.

For the first time since I arrived, I truly felt a sense of danger.

14

Driving Lessons

♊

Basil insisted that he be thought of as my escort for the evening.

"Celeste is my date tonight," he said, and directed Ami to sit in front so he and I could sit in the rear. Before we reached the restaurant, he was holding my hand and talking like a teenage boy, bragging about his skiing ability, the trip he took to Europe last winter, and how he's always been a great athlete, which he said, kept him young.

Although Ami had insisted he not talk about the events of the evening before, he teased us both about them, claiming our castle walls had been scaled, and the fair damsel within was in great danger.

"I can see I might have to spend more time at the house as long as we have this fair beauty living behind our walls and gates," he said.

"That's like having the fox in the chicken coop,"

Wade commented, and to my surprise, Basil roared with laughter instead of being insulted.

When we arrived at the restaurant, he did try to be charming, opening doors for me, holding my arm when we entered, pulling out my chair for me, explaining and reviewing the best things on the menu, and recommending what he thought I'd like the most. He talked about other places he had been since his wife's death, describing his visits to Asia and Africa, where he went on a hunting safari, their foods and wines and scenery. At times it felt as if only he and I were at the table. Both Wade and Ami were left out of the conversation. "There's nothing more enriching than traveling, Celeste," he told me. "And traveling in style."

"Yes, well, that takes money," Wade muttered, finally interrupting his father. Basil turned around slowly and replied in deliberate and strong tones.

"Which she's going to have. I can tell," he said, winking at me. "I know the winners from the losers, Wade, and this girl has winner written all over her." He leaned toward me and whispered, "All over."

I felt myself blush.

Our meals were served, and mine was as delicious as Basil had predicted it would be. I was served a glass of the wine from the bottle he had chosen, too. While we ate, Basil went on and on about the great restaurants he had been in, and continually taunted Wade about his failure to enjoy life. The only places Wade had been to that Basil had been to were the places he had been taken when he was a child and young boy.

"Someone has to mind the store," Wade offered in his own defense.

"Yeah, you do that, Wade. You mind the store while me and Celeste here enjoy ourselves, right, Celeste?"

I didn't respond, and he laughed. Occasionally I

looked at Ami to see if she was getting annoyed or angry with Basil's flirtatious antics and total concentration on me, but she seemed withdrawn into her own thoughts. Eventually Wade asked her if she was all right, and she said she was just more tired than she had anticipated.

"We've got to make it an early evening anyway," Wade said. "There's school tomorrow, and I have a lot to do at the plant, Dad. You know that shipment from Burlington came in all wrong. There is so much incompetency these days. I've got to go through the invoices line by line, item by item."

"Right, right," Basil said, waving the air as though Wade's conversation was full of flies instead of words. "Don't you remember what your mother used to tell me?" he added, leaning over toward Wade. "Don't discuss business at dinner. It's not polite. The women will be bored. I can't imagine this young woman having any interest in your pipes," he added, his words falling like slaps on Wade's now reddened cheeks.

Basil winked at me again, as if he and I had conspired in this attack on Wade. I couldn't help feeling sorry for Wade, and I wanted to come to his defense, but I kept my sharp words under lock and key. I felt like we were all sitting on a powder keg, and all it would take was one contrary word to Basil to set it off. I certainly didn't want to be the one to light the fuse.

Suddenly, however, Ami laughed, a nervous, high-pitched laugh that seemed to come out of nowhere and caught everyone's attention.

"You know, Basil," she said, "you're just impossible. You'll never let anyone contradict you."

"I hope not," he told her. His eyes narrowed, and his impish and flirtatious smile suddenly flew off and left a dark, almost threatening expression there instead.

Ami looked as if her breath had caught. She brought her hand to the base of her throat and then looked away quickly. The tension I sensed between her and Basil confused me for a moment. The memories of old shadows unfolding like clenched fists flooded my brain. I could hear the voices whispering warnings, and I recalled the farmhouse walls pulsating like the walls of a quickened heart. Darkness seeped in under the doors. Asleep in her bedroom, Mama woke with a scream. Owls froze on branches and the moon slipped behind a cloud.

In my memory I was crying and calling for Noble, but he was already gone by then, and my sense of loneliness was second only to the sense of death lying down beside me, tickling and teasing me with its cold fingers. The unmarked small grave in the family cemetery unzipped in my nightmares. Someone was coming; someone terrible was coming.

"Are you all right?" Wade suddenly asked me. "You look a little pale, Celeste."

Now everyone's eyes were on me.

I nodded, weakly.

"I'm okay."

"Let the girl be, Wade," Basil said. "I don't know how or why you turned out to be such a nervous Nellie."

"Yeah, it's a big mystery, Dad. Let's call it a night." He signaled for the waitress. "She's been through a traumatic experience. We should have just spent the night at home."

"Oh, nonsense," Basil said. "She's too young to call that a traumatic experience. She's fine. You're fine, Celeste. You don't have to worry about anything. If my son here doesn't protect you, you can be sure I'll be there. She just needs some good things happening in her life. Now, what's this hesitation about getting her a car?" he suddenly blurted, taking Wade by surprise and certainly me as well.

"Hesitation? She hasn't even gotten her license yet, Dad. She's just started taking lessons."

"Lessons," he muttered. "Nowadays, young people even take lessons in how to eat. For crying out loud. My father threw me into our old truck and said get going and don't hit anything or I'll wack you from here to kingdom come, and I haven't had an accident in forty years of driving. What's so complicated about it, especially today, where you don't have to shift? You point and shoot, for crissakes. Listen, Celeste, I'll be by tomorrow when you come home from school to give you a driving lesson that will qualify you in less than an hour."

"But we have the driving instructor coming then, Dad," Wade said, almost whining.

"Driving instructor be damned. Those people drag it on and on to make more money off you. Cancel it. I'll teach the kid, and then I'll take her to get her driving test. I know everyone over at the motor vehicle bureau anyway. I'll collect on some favors I'm owed."

I looked to Ami to put up an argument, but she simply smiled.

"Don't worry, Wade. She does know the basics already," she said. "And you know as well as I do that it's who you know in this world too often and not what you know."

Wade started to protest, but Basil reached across the table and plucked the bill that the waitress had just given him out of his hand. It took Wade by surprise, and he choked on his reply before he could get out the words.

"I might as well be the one signing for it," Basil said. "I'm paying for it anyway."

I had the feeling he was doing it for my benefit, acting like a bragging teenager. Wade's face was as
flushed as if he had a terrible fever.

Ami laughed again, that same shrill nervous laugh.

Wade's eyes went to me. There was a desperately
sad look in them. I pretended interest in something
going on elsewhere just so he wouldn't be embarrassed.

On the way home, we heard another one of Basil's
lectures about the school of hard knocks.

"You can spend your whole life in classrooms and
not learn half of what you'll learn in the real world,"
he said, practically bellowing now. "Man to man, face
to face with important decisions, knowing how to back
someone down and when to maneuver, that's the
ticket. When you negotiate for potentially prize real estate, for example, it don't matter if your grammar ain't
perfect, Celeste. What you got to know is how desperate the other guy is to make the sale. That's the secret
to everything: learn how desperate the other guy is,
what he wants and needs first, and then take action. As
long as you're in a position to do something for someone else, you'll get what you want in this life.

"Ain't that right, Ami?" he asked.

She looked like she had just been stung by a bee.
She was flustered a moment, then quickly said, "Yes."

"Yes," Basil repeated, nodding.

Wade said nothing, but I could see from the way his
neck tightened against the base of his head that he was
furious. When we arrived at the house, we stopped
next to Basil's car so he could get out before we went
into the garage. I sensed it was Wade's way of making
sure he left and didn't go into the house with us.

Basil took my hands firmly into his and repeated his
offer to teach me how to drive the next day.

"I'll set up your driving test myself," he added. "See you after school."

He leaned over and kissed me on the lips so quickly, I had no time to turn my cheek to him instead. He laughed at my surprise.

Then he reached over and slapped Wade on the shoulder, rather sharply, I thought.

"Get some sleep, Wade. You've got a big day at the plant tomorrow going over item by item, and I expect profits to go up this year, the way I'm spending money. Ami, my dear, sweet dreams," he said, throwing her a kiss.

"Good night, Basil."

He got out, went to his car, and drove off as we continued to the garage in silence.

"I'm tired of apologizing for him," I heard Wade tell Ami as we headed down the hallway.

"Then don't," she said, and walked ahead of him.

"Good night, Celeste," Wade told me at the top of the stairway. He didn't look back. His shoulders slumped, and his head was down. I wished I could say something that might cheer him up, but all I said was, "Good night."

He went to their bedroom. Ami stood beside me, watching him go, and then turned to me.

"Don't be upset about Basil's offer, Celeste. He means what he says. He'll get you your own car. Let him teach you how to drive. You'll have your license in no time, and I know how important it is for you to feel independent. Just put up with him. He's really not that dangerous," she offered, "and he really likes feeling important. It never hurts to stroke the guy with the bank account. Never refuse a favor from Basil Emerson. That's my motto."

She embraced me and kissed my cheek.

"Everything will be better tomorrow. It always is," she said.

Before I could say another word or ask a question, she went to her room and closed her door softly.

I was happy to discover that my bed sheets had been changed, and the garlic odor was gone. Exhausted, I fell asleep almost the moment my head hit the pillow. As usual these days, it was Wade's phone call that woke me. I showered and dressed and hurried down to join him for breakfast. I was anxious to tell him I wouldn't let his father give me driving lessons if he didn't want him to, but that wasn't the way Wade presented it.

"I said last night that I wasn't going to apologize for my father anymore, but I am. I'm sorry he was so obnoxious last night. I can stop him from coming over here to give you driving lessons if you would rather he didn't," he offered.

If I would rather? He would use me as the reason to keep his father from coming.

"It's not important, Wade," I said. The last thing I wanted now was to be the cause of a rift between Wade and Basil, especially after what had happened with Trevor. I'd certainly feel like the one bringing the evil eye into their home, just as Mrs. Cukor predicted.

"You sure you don't mind?"

"I'm okay with it," I assured him.

"I'd offer to do it myself, but I could only do it on weekends. Dad has all this free time on his hands," he muttered. "The truth is, he never ran the company as well as I'm running it."

"It's all right," I said.

"I suppose I should be happy he's doing something productive with his time. It keeps him out of my hair," he added. Then he looked up at me quickly and smiled.

"He did teach me how to drive. He wasn't the most patient instructor, but we got through it. I'm sure he'll be nicer to you than he was to me. He was nicer to my sister."

It was the first time he had ever made a reference to her, I thought. There were all sorts of questions on the tip of my tongue, but I swallowed them back.

"If it's in the least bit unpleasant for you, don't hesitated to—"

"I'll be fine," I said, more confidently.

He nodded.

"I'm sure you will."

Ami didn't get up and come down before it was time for Wade and I to leave. As we drew closer to the school, I could see he was more nervous than I was about how the other students would treat me.

"You let me know if the Foleys made up any stories about you," he told me. "Chris Foley knows his son was drinking, and it was entirely his fault. You'll let me know," he said again when we pulled into the school lot.

"I'll be okay, Wade. Thanks," I told him.

When I entered my homeroom, I saw from the looks on their faces that the other students were chatting about me and Trevor. Lynette Firestone pouted, and Germaine Osterhout gloated.

"I guess you knocked Trevor off his feet," Waverly quipped. "By the time he left you, he was too dizzy to navigate."

The boys laughed licentiously, and the girls looked at me with glee lighting up their eyes.

"If you had confided in me, I could have helped you back there," Lynette told me after the bell had rung and we were off to our first class.

"Help me with what?" I asked her.

After what I had been through in my life, being the object of some juvenile humor was hardly worth a second thought. It was easy to ignore them, to look right though them and let their words bounce off my ears.

"They'll ruin your reputation," Lynette said, "and don't expect Trevor Folcy to come to your aid later on. You'll see. They all stick together."

Maybe they do, I thought, but what was so important about it anyway? Suddenly my time here, living with the Emersons, going to this rich school, didn't seem as desirable as I had hoped it would be. I used to sit in the orphanage and dream about turning eighteen and being on my own. I was like someone who was serving a prison sentence and counting the days to freedom. This life now was supposed to be the start of that freedom—look at all that had been lavished upon me already—but in ways I could never have imagined, I felt even more incarcerated than I had been at the orphanage.

Was this my destiny, always to be under some form of lock and key, always to be in invisible chains? When would I be free? When would I truly be able to breathe?

Ami was there at the end of the school day, naturally full of questions about how the other students had treated me.

"I'm sorry I didn't get up in time to speak to you before you left for school today. I wanted to warn you how catty some of these girls can be. What sort of mean things did they say? Did Lynette help you? Have they begun to spin nasty rumors about you?"

"I ignored them," I said.

"Well, what did they say?" she asked. She had to know the details.

"I really don't know, Ami. I didn't listen."

"But—"

"I just walked away from their smug smiles and whispers and concentrated on my lessons. I had a surprise quiz in math, and I have a project to complete in social studies, so I spent my lunch hour and free time in the library. Oh," I added, sounding as if I was going to describe an accomplishment, "Mrs. Grossbard doesn't think she has a place for me on the golf team. She evaluated my ability to drive and putt, and determined it wasn't my forte."

I smiled to indicate how trivial I thought it all was.

Ami's mouth opened and closed.

"Well, that's . . . how . . . I'll speak to Mrs. Brentwood about that," she vowed.

"I don't care. It's fine. I'm really not interested in being on the team. I do have an interesting assignment for the newspaper, however. I'm going to do all the book reviews. I've been made the book editor, in fact," I said.

Her mouth drooped.

She didn't have to say anything. Her eyes told me what she was thinking: *boring.*

"Oh," she finally uttered. "If that's what you want to do. I mean, if that makes you happy here."

"It does," I said, and she nodded.

When we turned down the street toward the house, she slowed and to my surprise pulled behind a parked Mercedes sports car.

"Basil is waiting for you," she said, nodding at the car.

I leaned forward and saw him step out and wave.

"The driving lessons, remember? I went ahead and canceled the driving instructor."

"Oh, yes," I said, a ball of nervousness tumbling in my stomach and growing bigger with ever roll.

"Go on," she urged. "And be nice to him. You need someone who can do you favors, Celeste, even more than I do," she added with a note of sadness. "I'll take your books up to your room."

She leaned out her window to wave back at Basil.

"C'mon, Celeste," he urged, ignoring her. "We've got a lot to do."

I got out of the car and started toward him. He was wearing a tight knit sweater and jeans and did look handsome, his hair blown into a free-flowing style. He smiled and reached out for me. I took his hand, and he opened the driver's door a bit more so I could slip right behind the steering wheel.

"Let's first see how you do and what that driving expert taught you," he said.

He closed the door and started around the car. Ami remained behind us, watching. Basil barely looked her way. He got in beside me and closed the door.

"Now this isn't a bad car to learn on," he said. "Handles like a baby, smooth and very receptive. It's a high-performance automobile, so go easy on the acceleration. Go on. Let's see what you were told to do first," he challenged, folding his arms and sitting back.

I went through the steps I had been taught, adjusting the seat and the mirrors to make sure I had good views. I quickly studied the shift, the parking brake, and the signal lever. Then I put on my seat belt.

"You look good behind that wheel, Celeste," he said. "You look like you belong in a car like this. You know how much it cost?"

I shook my head.

"It's over a hundred thousand dollars," he said. "I'm thinking of getting a new one. Maybe I'll just give this one to you to use, so don't get us into a wreck," he added, laughing.

Was he serious? Just like that, he'd give me a car this expensive to use?

"C'mon, get the engine started. Let's get moving."

He looked back at Ami, who was still parked behind us. I saw his eyes narrow with displeasure.

"What the hell is she waiting for? Let's go," he ordered more firmly.

I started the car, checked my mirror, made my hand signal, and shifted to drive. He was right about the car's sensitivity compared to the far cheaper vehicle the driving instructor used. We lunged forward so fast and hard, I hit the brake.

Basil laughed as we jerked forward and back.

"Sorry," I said.

"Don't worry. You'll get used to it quickly," he promised.

Gingerly this time, I accelerated, and we pulled onto the road. He moved closer to me, putting his left arm around the back of my seat. I could smell his rich cologne and aftershave as it flowed over my face.

"Steady," he said. "Just keep her steady and keep aware of everyone around you. I always check the rearview to see how close the idiot behind me gets. People tailgate like crazy these days," he warned. "Driving is defensive nowadays. You just have to keep anticipating the other guy will do something stupid, and most of the time, he does."

My pounding heart slowed down as we cruised along. It was a wonderful car to drive, and I was comfortable in the seat. He told me where to turn.

"You're doing just fine," he said. "I'm impressed. This is going to be a piece of cake. I might not even need a favor at the motor vehicle bureau," he remarked.

I said thank you, but never took my eyes off the road, even though I felt his on me all the time. Once in a while his fingers grazed the back of my neck or my hair, and that would send a chill down my spine because I was afraid the touch would last longer or go down my neck to my shoulders.

We practiced parking. To my surprise, he wasn't a bad driving instructor. He had a mechanic's understanding of everything, angles, speed, exactly how to turn the wheel enough, and when to stop.

"That's perfect," he told me after my fourth attempt at a parallel park. "Again. By the time I'm finished with you, you'll be able to do it with your eyes closed."

I did gain confidence with him, and by the end of my lesson, I felt quite at ease. He laughed about it.

"Hell, I might make you my chauffeur," he said, and I smiled for the first time.

"Thank you."

"No problem. Actually, I enjoyed myself, watching you. You know, I taught my wife how to drive. Wade doesn't even know that, but it's true. You remind me of her in some ways," he said. "Especially the way you concentrate, get those eyes of yours fixed on something. I used to tell her she could drill holes with her looks."

We drove through the opened gates and up to the house.

"Why don't you want to live here all the time?" I asked him.

"Too many memories for me," he said. "Besides, it's a house for a family, not a widower. I expect a family here, kids running all over the place, Emersons. I want a grandson before I'm too old to teach him how to drive too," he added, and I thought about Ami and her hesitation about getting pregnant. I wondered if he had any idea.

"I'll come in for a while," he said when we parked. "I need a drink. Not that your driving did it," he added quickly. "I just have a drink about now every day."

As soon as we entered the house, Wade came out of the living room to greet us. Worried, he searched my face quickly to see what it would tell.

"She's damn good!" Basil bellowed. "The poor unfortunate can drive better than you, Wade, and after only a few lessons."

"Stop saying that, Dad. I never called her that."

"Stop saying that, Dad," Basil mimicked, and laughed as he brushed past Wade to go to the bar.

"Was it all right?" Wade asked me quickly.

"Yes, it was. He's a good teacher," I said.

Wade looked skeptical a moment.

"Where's Ami?" I asked.

"She had a headache and went to take a nap. She gets migraines occasionally. She'll be all right, but she might not come down to dinner."

"Oh, I didn't know."

"It's all right."

"What the hell you doing out there, Wade? Come on in here and tell me how much money I made today," Basil shouted from the doorway.

"I got to get onto my homework," I said. "Thanks again, Mr. Emerson," I called.

"Don't call me Mr. Emerson. Call him Mr. Emerson. I'm Basil," he shouted back at me.

I shook my head, glanced at Wade, who smirked, and then hurried up the stairway.

The phone rang almost as soon as I entered. I thought it might be Waverly again, teasing me, but it was Trevor.

"I've been calling you all afternoon," he said.

"Where have you been? Don't tell me you found a new guy already."

"Driving lessons," I said.

"Oh yeah. I was afraid your phone had been disconnected or something."

"How are you?"

"Better, but you won't believe this cast. I look like something from a horror movie. It's not easy to sleep with it, either. Glad you're taking driving lessons. I won't be driving for some time, and I'll need a ride home, so get your license soon."

I didn't say anything. The very idea seemed so remote a possibility to me, it was like talking about a trip to the moon.

"Aren't your parents upset about what happened?"

"Yeah, but they get over things quickly," he said. "My father gave me one of his fast-food lectures, abbreviated into five minutes with his usual lead-off, 'I was young once too, so I know what you're going through.' Why is it they always think we're carbon copies or just walking along a trail they've carved?" he wondered aloud. "Your parents like that?"

I almost said I couldn't remember, but caught the truth before it had a chance to find its way to my tongue and sent it reeling back.

"Yes," I said.

"I heard you took a lot of ribbing at school. Waverly's being Waverly."

"It didn't bother me."

"Good. Because I'm coming to school tomorrow. Of course, I can't take any notes or take any tests for a while, but I have you to take notes for me." He was silent because I was silent, and then he asked, "Are you mad at me?"

"I'm mad at myself," I said.

"Good, because I couldn't stand you being mad at me. You're the first one I want to sign my cast, so think of something great to write, like, 'No pain, no gain.' " He laughed. "Okay?"

"I don't know," I said. "I have to hang up. I have to get to my homework."

"Okay, sleep tight in that great bed of yours, and don't think this cast will keep me from chasing after you," he vowed, and laughed again.

"I'll see you tomorrow," I offered. "Bye."

"Hey?"

"What?"

"We'll get over this. Don't worry about it."

"I'm not," I said.

I didn't mean to sound so casual about it, but how could I explain that I had been through far more traumatic events in my life, and when I was far younger and less equipped to handle them, too?

"Well, at least worry a little," he urged. "It makes me feel more important to you. I am important to you, aren't I?" he pursued.

"Yes, Trevor, but all this happened so quickly after I moved in here. You have to understand what I'm going through, too."

"Yeah, you're right. I'm sorry. I'll go easy. Whatever it takes," he said. "I mean it."

"Thanks," I said. "See you tomorrow."

"Tomorrow," he replied, and we hung up.

Never had *tomorrow* felt so ominous to me. Would it bring on more trouble or less if Trevor and I were together all the time at school? Ami would know for sure. What was I to do? Talk about migraines—my head was spinning. I made the mistake of lying down and closing my eyes. Minutes later, I fell asleep and didn't wake up until I felt myself being nudged.

Ami stood looking down at me. Her face was filled with concern. She was in her robe.

"What's wrong with you? Why are you sleeping? Wade called up to me to tell me you hadn't come down to dinner, and you didn't answer your phone when he called."

"The phone rang?" I asked, sitting up and looking at it. "I didn't hear it." I ground the sleep out of my eyes and took a deep breath.

"Did something happen in the car with Basil?"

"Happen? No. What could happen? He was actually very nice," I said.

She relaxed a little, but still looked at me with the suspicion of a doctor, her eyes perusing my face, looking for symptoms.

"We're going to see my doctor next week. I'd like you to have a physical. I bet you didn't have very good medical treatment at the orphanage. How could you?" she asked before I could respond.

"I've never been seriously sick," I said. "Just a little cold once in a while, but nothing terrible. I didn't need a doctor."

She nodded.

"Yes, I know that, but still . . . I'm worried about you. I'll make the appointment," she said. "And remember, I want to know when your period starts. Immediately," she added. Then she thought again. "It didn't start, did it?"

"No, Ami."

"Okay. Don't forget. All right. I wasn't going down to dinner tonight, but I'll throw something on. It's just us. Basil left," she said. "Just wash your face and brush your hair. We don't need to dress up for Wade. I'll be out in ten minutes," she added, and left.

There was a heavy atmosphere at dinner. Wade barely looked up from his food, and Ami looked like she was still suffering from her migraine.

"You really should go to the doctor about the headaches you've been having lately, Ami," Wade finally said.

"I am going to the doctor. We're both going," she replied.

"Both?"

"Celeste and myself. For a physical. I'm making the appointments tomorrow," she told him.

He looked at me.

"Aren't you feeling well?"

"That's not the point, Wade. We didn't tell you all of it. She was physically attacked."

"Attacked? Now listen, Ami—"

"We want to be sure everything is all right, don't we, Celeste?" she asked, her eyes wide.

"Yes," I said.

"So don't butt into female business, Wade," Ami immediately told him.

He shook his head and looked down again.

"If you start a story like that, we will have some legal problems," he muttered.

"No one is starting any stories. Celeste has not really had a good physical anyway. It's only smart to have one."

"Whatever," Wade said.

No one was in the mood for any desert. Wade excused himself and went to his office, and Ami went back to bed.

As I ascended the stairway to go to my room, I saw

Mrs. Cukor standing in the living room doorway, looking up at me. She didn't look fearful or angry.

She smiled.

But it was the smile of someone who knew she was soon to be proven right.

And that sent more chills into my heart than anything else she had done or said.

15

The Alarms Return

♊

On our way to school the following day, Wade was quieter than usual. I tried to start a conversation about my book assignment for the newspaper. He listened politely, but he lacked the enthusiasm he had shown before whenever I talked about books and my studies and work. He seemed very distracted. I thought he might be worrying about Ami's headaches. When I asked, he said only that she would be all right, but he said it with an underlying tone of bitterness sharper than I had heard before in his voice. I pretended to be involved in studying notes for a first-period quiz.

Trevor was at school, just as he had promised. His cast went over his shoulder and the upper part of his arm so that his arm had to remain somewhat extended. It was quite impressive, and he was the object of everyone's attention. Many of his friends signed it and wrote silly things on it. He showed them to me at lunch. He had smeared over what Waverly had written.

"Too disgusting," he said when I asked him why he had rubbed it out. "When are you signing?"

"I haven't thought of anything yet," I told him. He looked disappointed.

The chatter about us went up ten octaves every time we spoke or walked the halls together, and especially when we sat next to each other in the cafeteria. I was torn between keeping my distance and being with him, helping him. I did copy over notes for him, but I knew our closeness was increasing the gossip, and that gossip would reach Ami.

"I've got to talk to you about the math tonight," he said. "I'm still taking some pain medication, and I wasn't paying good attention."

"You're only going to talk about math?"

"Maybe just about multiplication," he joked.

I laughed too. I couldn't help liking him, no matter what ideas Ami had planted in my mind. He was handsome and funny. Maybe all this will pass over, I dared think. Maybe in time we would be like any other young couple. However, it was apparent that even the faculty had heard and talked about our incident. I could feel the way our teachers looked at us walking in the hallway together or sitting near each other in classes. It made me even more self-conscious. Mrs. Brentwood glared at me with obvious disapproval, and later, before the day ended, she saw me coming out of the girls' room and crossed the hallway to speak to me.

"I see you've already made yourself the center of attention here, Celeste," she said. "I wouldn't advise you to get into any trouble in school."

"Why would I do that, Mrs. Brentwood? I'm so grateful I'm here," I said drily. I held my eyes on her the way I used to hold my eyes on Madame Annjill years and years ago when I was just a child.

Mrs. Brentwood pulled herself back.

"Just be sure you obey our rules and regulations."

"Thank you for the reminder," I said, and I smiled at her so coolly she simply turned and walked back toward her office.

I'm a stranger in a strange land, I thought. It made me pensive all the remainder of the day. At the end of the day, Waverly was to drive Trevor home. He asked me if I wanted to come along for the ride.

"Some other time," I said.

Of course, I expected Ami to be right there waiting for me as I emerged from the building anyway.

But I was surprised when I stepped out. Instead of her waiting for me, there was Basil, leaning against his beautiful Mercedes sports car, waving and smiling at me.

"Whoa," Waverly teased. "She's going home in style."

"Talk to you later," I told Trevor, and quickly walked toward Basil. "Why are you here instead of Ami?" I asked, wondering if she had gotten more ill.

"I thought, why waste an opportunity?" he said. "Get in the driver's seat."

I looked back and saw both Trevor and Waverly and some of the other kids watching. I heard Waverly's whistle as I got into the automobile. Basil smiled their way and got in.

"That's the Foley kid with that monster cast on him, huh?" he asked, gesturing back with his head.

"Yes."

"I'd say he's really fallen for you," he said, and laughed.

I couldn't help smiling.

"I guess so," I said.

"Let's go," he said. "Show me yesterday wasn't just a fluke."

It was truly exciting driving his car, and once again

he told me he was considering getting a new one and leaving this one at the house for me.

"It's all broken in. Why waste it?" he said.

He had me drive on different roads and took me out to a different area to show me some land he had bought four years ago.

"I own forty acres here," he said. "I can see a house on the rise there someday. Of course, not for me. I'm too old and I'll never marry again. You know what they say, 'Marriage is not a word. It's a sentence.' "

He laughed.

"It doesn't have to be that way," I commented.

"Maybe it won't be for you. How would you like to live here one day?"

"I have a farm I've inherited," I told him. "Someday I'd like to return to it."

"Yeah, Ami told me about it. That area of the state isn't doing anything. You won't get much for it. Now here, here property is like gold."

"How could I live here anyway?" I asked. "It's your land."

"You never know," he said.

I checked the time.

"I've got a lot of homework to do," I told him. "And a report to write for the school paper."

"Make a perfect U-turn," he commanded, and I did so.

"Excellent. You handle this car as if you've owned it for years, Celeste. I'm going to have the driver's test appointment set up for you right away. We can get in a few more lessons beforehand, but I don't think you'll need them."

When I drove in through the gates and up to the house, he opened the glove compartment and pulled out a pair of brand-new ruby leather driving gloves.

"For you," he said. "If you're going to drive a car

like this, you should look good doing it. Not that you can be anything else."

"Thank you," I said, taking them. They were butter soft leather.

"You're welcome. I'll see you tomorrow and tell you your date for the test," he said, getting out with me. He reached back, got my books for me, and came around to my side to hand them to me.

"Thanks," I said.

"No problem, sweetie," he said, kissed me on the cheek, and got into the car. He rolled the window down. "Looks like I have to talk to my car dealer about a new car sooner than I expected," he said.

I stared after him as he drive off. He has to be joking, I thought. Just like that, he wants to give me a car that costs over one hundred thousand dollars? I shook my head in disbelief.

When I turned toward the house, I saw a curtain closing, but I caught Mrs. Cukor's face glowing like a skull in the late afternoon sunlight before she disappeared within. There was no one around when I entered, so I went directly to my room and began my work. Less than ten minutes later, however, Ami appeared to tell me she had made our doctor's appointment for the day after tomorrow.

"I'll let Basil know," she said, "in case he's planning to give you another driving lesson after school."

"I think he is," I said. "He said he's going to arrange for my driving test very soon."

She nodded.

"He bought me these driving gloves," I said, showing them to her.

"Very nice. I don't even have a pair as nice as these," she commented, turning them in her hands. She handed them back to me.

"Ami, I don't know if he's kidding me or not, but he told me a few times that he was going to give me his car to use, and he was getting a new one."

"Why should he be kidding?" she replied with nonchalance. "I promised you that you would be happy here, and you will be," she said, sounding more determined than ever. "Just keep in mind that all I want for you is for you to be very, very happy. It's all I want for all of us," she added softly. For a moment she looked like she was going to cry. Then she smiled and left me swirling in a world of wonder and confusion.

Wade didn't join us for dinner that night. He sent word home that he had to remain at work and would stop someplace to eat much later. Ami wasn't upset. In fact, from the way she sounded when she told me, I gathered it was not unusual.

"It's why I end up going out myself to some of the places I've taken you to," she told me.

I sat there, imagining them both eating alone or distracted by strangers. Dinner had always been a sacred time when I was very little, I remember, and it was always our special time of the day at the orphanages. All of us fantasized about having family dinners, being at a table with loved ones, everyone eager to share his or her day's activities. It was the glue that would bind us to whatever new family we had found and had found us. In our minds it was almost a religious event, a session of silent prayers of gratitude. For orphans every dinner was truly a Thanksgiving dinner.

To see it cast aside so casually both saddened and angered me.

Basil was waiting for me the following afternoon to take me on another driving lesson. He put me through every maneuver he could and seemed more determined for me to pass my driving test than I was. When I mentioned it, he said he wanted to be sure he was leaving his car in good hands.

The next day Ami was there promptly after school to take me to her doctor, a female doctor named Dr. Bloomfield. She put me though a full physical, including blood tests and X-rays. She even gave me a gynecological exam. Although not all the blood tests were in, she told Ami I was in perfect health.

"There's nothing wrong with her? Nothing happened as a result of . . ." Ami started to ask.

"No, nothing," the doctor told her. "She's fine. Someday she'll have wonderful, healthy children, I'm sure. You have no worries, Mrs. Emerson," she said.

Ami looked very relieved. I had had no fears about it before we came and expected no other response.

"When are you being examined for your headaches?" I asked her when we started out of the office.

"I was already. It's nothing," she said quickly.

Two days later, Basil took me for my driving test after school. He did appear to know people at the motor vehicle bureau. When I returned with the examiner, I was told immediately that I had passed the test, and I was given a temporary license.

"We'll celebrate tonight," he declared when he left me off at the house. "Tell Ami I'm making reservations at Fishers Lobster Pot."

I thought about all my homework, but he was so excited, and I was in such a happy daze, I dared not mention it. I would just do it all later, I thought. Ami was excited for me, and when Wade returned from work, he was full of congratulations as well, though of course he was more reserved. Later, when I was getting dressed to go out to dinner, I had a bout of cramps and discovered my period was starting. The moment Ami came in to check on my preparations, I told her.

She clapped her hands.

"Thank goodness," she said.

"I told you there was no danger, Ami. Despite what happened, Trevor is a very responsible young man."

"That's an oxymoron," she said. "You know, like cruel kindness, a seeming contradiction? A young man by definition can't be responsible."

"That can't be true for all of them, Ami, can it?" I asked in frustration.

She stared at me a moment and then smiled.

"No, I guess not. You're right," she said. "I shouldn't put all my prejudices into you. You have a right to form your own opinions. I just want you to be careful and not to ruin everything now that you have this wonderful new beginning. Promise me," she asked.

"I promise, Ami," I said, although I wasn't quite sure what it was I was promising.

"Good. Now let's go out and celebrate the hell out of the Emersons," she added, and laughed.

She was suddenly back to being jovial and happy. The migraines were gone, as if the coming of my period was the cure to all her woes.

Little did I know then that it would be the beginning of all mine, but I was never good at predicting anything for myself, only for others.

That was especially true when I looked at Wade. I didn't like what I saw in his face that night, saw in his eyes and heard in his voice. The more Basil offered to do for me, the happier he was for me and the more excited he was about showing me things, the sadder Wade became. I wondered if there wasn't some jealousy. Was he upset that his father was so interested in me, or did it bother him that his father was doing more for me than he was for his own grandchildren and daughter now? All these possibilities rambled through my mind.

Basil surprised me as well as Wade when at dinner he suggested he would put up the money to send me to a fine college.

"Ami told me that school she attends gets their graduates into the best universities. Can't let a little thing like tuition stop her. We've discussed it."

"Since when is one college any better than another to you, Dad?" Wade asked. He glanced at me. "I mean, I've always thought so, but—"

"This is a very bright young woman. We don't want to see her waste her talents and skills in any mediocre place, now, do we?" Basil said. "Huh, Ami?"

"What? Oh, no," she said. "Of course not."

"Well, then . . . what are you looking so long in the face about, Wade? Don't you want good things for your unfortunate?"

Wade shook his head and looked away. He drank more than usual, too, and kept quiet most of the remainder of the evening. Basil insisted I drive everyone home that night and put Wade and Ami in the rear of their own car.

"Not bad, huh?" he said, bragging about my driving. "I guess the old man can still perform miracles, huh, Wade?"

"What's the miracle?" Wade replied, sounding a little drunk. "You've been telling us all night how talented she is."

"Ho-ho, listen to him. No matter what, you still need a good teacher, a guiding hand in this world. Don't you forget it either, buddy-boy. Don't you get too big for your britches."

"No chance of that," Wade muttered.

Basil looked at Ami and then turned his back on Wade for the remainder of the ride home.

He didn't turn over his automobile to me right away, but three days later he was there to pick me up at school and hand me the keys. I didn't know it was permanent until we drove onto the property and I saw his brand-new Mercedes parked in front of the house.

"That's my new one," he said. "In here are all the papers on the car, the telephone number of the service department I use for it, everything you'll need," he added, opening the glove compartment.

"You're really giving me this car to use?"

"Enjoy it, sweetheart," he said, and kissed me just at the corner of my lips. "I'll tell Wade to make room for this car in the garage. He should be happy. He won't have to take you to school every morning, and Ami won't have to pick you up. Good luck with it," he added, and got out.

I sat there running my hands over the leather and the wood. This was mine, mine to drive whenever I wanted. Just a relatively short while ago, I had two small suitcases of clothing to my name and title to an old property I hadn't seen in years and years. Now I had a closet full of designer clothes and shoes, valuable jewelry, a beautiful large bedroom with my own phone, vanity table, and makeup. I attended an expensive private school, went to expensive restaurants, and had a weekly allowance equal to all the money I had possessed in a year at the orphanage. I was given piano lessons and driving lessons, and now a car worth well over a hundred thousand dollars was at my disposal.

How quickly my thoughts and desires to return to the farm, to a restricted and isolated existence, dwindled. Never had my memories of Noble and my family spirits, all of the wonders of my infancy, seemed as vague as they did now. Why shouldn't I attend a prestigious college and develop a career in the business world? Why shouldn't I travel as Basil traveled and meet people, eat wonderful new foods, and see magnificent scenery? Why shouldn't I be as sophisticated as the snobby girls at my school, and most of all, why shouldn't I find a wonderful young man with whom I could share my life? Why was all that coming to those other girls and not to me? Why had I been trapped in orphanages and made to feel less than worthy of having a family and a home?

Too excited to go into the house and start my homework, I started the engine and drove away. I didn't have anywhere in particular to go. I just cruised the side streets, then suddenly found myself turning onto the road that would bring me to Basil's property. I pulled to the side of the road and looked out over the choice acreage. I could see a house on that hill, I thought, a big, elaborate home, a modern-day castle with elegance as well as all the bells and whistles that come with gates and pools and tennis courts. I could be Ami, but I'd be happier than she is, I thought. Was that arrogant of me?

The sun was going down quickly. Days were far shorter now, and winter was just over the horizon, the colder winds and grayer clouds inching forward to announce its impending arrival. As shadows deepened, I thought I saw a figure walking up the knoll where Basil and now I envisioned a house. It looked like Noble. He turned my way, and then he disappeared over the crest.

"You're imagining things," I told myself, took my foot off the brake, and accelerated to put distance between me and the illusion. I turned up the radio to drown out any warnings or dark thoughts, and I sang along as I seemed to float over the highway until I reached home again and drove up to the garage. Anyone who saw me probably thought I was just another crazy teenager.

"Where have you been?" Ami asked as soon as I entered the house. I was still humming the last song I had heard on the radio. She had been waiting in the living room, and she stepped out when I opened the door.

"Basil gave me his car!" I cried. "I just had to take a ride on my own for the first time. I just drove to drive. I didn't go anywhere special."

Ami's hard look quickly softened.

"Oh, how wonderful. I'm happy for you, Celeste. But from now on, especially since you have a car to use, please let me know where you are and when you'll be back, okay? I don't want to sound like Wade, a worrywart or anything, but it's important."

"Of course. I'm sorry, Ami. I should have told you. I should have taken you with me."

"We'll go plenty of places together in your car," she said, laughing. "Don't worry about that. Come upstairs." She hooked my arm. "I have to show you the new coat I got you for winter. It has a fox fur collar."

"A new coat!"

It was truly as if heaven was raining gifts down on me. Hopefully, it would never end, I thought, and hurried up the stairs with her.

Naturally, she couldn't simply buy me a new coat without buying new gloves, new boots, and a pair of pants with a matching sweater. It was all laid out on my bed. I tried it all on quickly and paraded about, modeling it for her. We were laughing and giggling so much we didn't hear Wade come up the stairs and to my bedroom door. He knocked on the partially opened door.

"Dad's here?" he asked, looking in curiously at us.

"No," Ami said. "Unless he came after we came up here."

"His car is parked out front, so I just thought . . ."

Ami gave me a conspiratorial smile and turned back to him.

"It's not his car anymore, Wade. He made good on his promise to Celeste. He gave it to her."

"Gave her his car?" he asked, obviously shocked.

"To use," I said. "I don't think it's actually signed over to me, although," I said, looking at Ami, "I didn't look at the papers."

"Don't be surprised if it is," she told me.

I looked at Wade, expecting him to get over his surprise and be happy for me, but he looked darkly pensive and troubled instead.

"What's all this?" he asked, nodding at the clothing on the bed.

"We have to get her winter wardrobe started," Ami replied, as if it were obvious.

He nodded.

"I'm happy for you, Celeste," he said. "Just be careful."

"Careful?" Ami challenged.

"Driving the car," he explained, nodded, and left us.

"Told you that man is a worrywart," Ami said, waving him off. "Don't let him ruin this wonderful day for you."

Despite the look on Wade's face and the tone in his voice, I didn't lose my elation and buoyancy. Ami's flighty, carefree manner carried over to me. Actually, I relished it. I wanted to ignore the dark faces, the looks I got from Mrs. Cukor, the unhappiness and sourness in Mrs. McAlister's visage, and the stoic intensity and foreboding in Wade's demeanor even at dinner. Ami and I continued to laugh and giggle. I let her woo me with her plans for our trips. We were going to drive to New York City to see the Christmas decorations this year, and it would be up to us to plan a vacation trip during the holidays. She warned Wade not to come up with any business reasons for delays or postponements. I was so excited that evening, I knew I would have trouble sleeping. Later, I called Trevor and told him my good news.

"He really gave you the car? I can't believe it," he said.

"Neither can I."

"But it's great. How about taking me home from school tomorrow?"

"Sure," I said quickly.

I described some of the plans Ami was making for us and told him about my new clothes. I'd never rattled on so over a telephone. Of course, I'd never had anyone like Trevor to speak to on a phone before either. We began to make plans for the future as well, talked about upcoming school events, parties, and trips we might make together.

"For a while," I said, sobering a bit, "we have to be discreet. I still have to work on Ami and convince her you're not Jack the Raper."

He laughed.

"What if I am?"

"I don't care," I said recklessly, and we laughed again. I was in that kind of mood, and I didn't want it to end. It was a natural high that I was positive was as good as any drug or alcoholic high.

By the time I was tired enough to go to sleep, I realized I had neglected some of my homework, and I hadn't even begun the new assignment for the newspaper.

"I'll get by somehow," I told myself. Perhaps I would borrow one of the many excuses the other students had for their failure to do their work at school. Our teachers, for the most part, let them slip through.

Money talks, I thought, and then thought, so what? I'll let it talk for me as well.

I was disappointed to see it raining in the morning. It was a hard, cold rain, too, pounding the windows with drops that were only a few degrees from being hail. Wade immediately insisted that he drive me to school.

"The streets will be slick as hell," he said.

"But I have to learn how to drive in all weathers," I whined.

"Not immediately. With your little driving experience, it would be irresponsible of me to permit it," he insisted. He was so adamant, I dared not oppose him. Ami was still in bed, so I didn't have her beside me to argue on my behalf.

Trevor was disappointed, of course. He had to go home with Waverly again. The rain stopped by midday, but the sky remained gray and oppressive. Ami was there to pick me up. She saw me say good-bye to Trevor, giving him a quick kiss, but she didn't say anything about it. Instead she complained about Wade's worrywart ways.

"You're probably a better driver than he is," she said.

"It's all right. He was only worried for me."

Because of the disappointment over my failure to complete my homework assignments I had seen in the faces of my teachers, especially my newspaper adviser, Mr. Feldman, I went right to work when I got home. Early that evening Trevor and I spoke on the phone, and he told me the weather report was good for the following day.

"Good-bye, Waverly," he sang, and we laughed. "I've always wanted to be driven around by a beautiful girl in an expensive automobile."

As soon as I woke up the next morning, I saw it was a beautiful day. All the clouds were swept south, and the sky had that rich turquoise glaze that made the few remaining small clouds transparent. It was still brisk, reason enough for me to wear my new coat. I didn't realize until I had come out of my morning shower that for the first time, Wade hadn't made a wake-up call to me.

However, what surprised me the most, and of course told me it was fine for me to drive to school, was the fact that Wade was already gone by the time I went down to breakfast. His place had been cleared. For a moment I thought he hadn't yet risen, and asked Mrs. McAlister.

She pulled herself up and pursed her lips.

"He's gone about the time he used to go before you arrived," she said, clearly making my arrival sound like a detrimental thing. "He likes rising early."

I could hear Mrs. Cukor working the vacuum cleaner in the hallways. She usually waited before vacuuming so close to the dining room, but with only me in here now, that wasn't any concern for her. I could barely hear myself think, so I ate quickly and left the house.

At school my teachers were pleased with my work. I eagerly answered questions in class. Mr. Feldman gave me a compliment on my book review, and even Mrs. Grossbard applauded my enthusiasm during the volleyball game.

"Maybe you should think about joining our ski team," she suggested. Once again, I had to tell her I had never done one of the sports she coached here at the Dickinson School. "Never skied?" she asked in disbelief. I shook my head. She looked skeptical and tucked in her lip, as if she thought I was lying just to get out of being on the team. I began to wonder if Ami's fabrications about me were a good idea after all. It was always on the tip of my tongue to tell Trevor the truth, and a few times I had nearly slipped up when he asked me questions about my past.

Lies truly entangle you, I thought. Eventually I would trip, and the truth would come out about me. I was sure of it. I had no idea how Trevor would react once he knew, but for the moment, I thought it better to keep it that way. Actually, when I was honest with myself, I had to admit I simply didn't want to lose his attention.

Finally, our wish was to come true. I could take him home at the end of the day. Waverly stood by watching with his usual wise-guy smirk, whispering to the other boys and laughing about us.

"How can you be friends with him?" I asked Trevor. "He's such a . . . a . . ."

"Dork?"

"Yes."

He shrugged.

"He amuses me, I guess. I don't have trouble giving up my time with him to spend it with you, however."

"I hope not," I said, laughing. "Otherwise, you'd be the dork."

"Hey. You're getting too smart for yourself," he kidded. Then he looked at the dashboard. "It really is a nice car. He kept it like new. I'm still amazed he gave it to you and bought himself another one."

"I was always taught never to look a gift horse in the mouth," I said, and backed out of the parking spot.

"Yeah, well, this is more than a gift from a horse,"

he remarked. "Cousins are usually not that generous toward each other."

Something in the air right after he said that gently shook the alarms inside me. I quieted them quickly. I wasn't in the mood to listen to any.

But as we pulled away from the school, I checked my side mirror, and I was sure I saw Ami parked surreptitiously behind a parked truck, watching me drive off. She had come only to spy on me, I thought. I was sure she would be angry and give me one of her lectures about men later. But what I saw surprised me. I had only a short glimpse of her face, but she looked more frightened than angry.

And what my instincts told me was she was more frightened for herself than for me.

I couldn't imagine why that would be, but the alarms returned.

And this time I couldn't ignore them.

16

Sweet Dreams

♊

Trevor's home was a beautiful sprawling ranch-style house with dark gray stone facing and large picture windows, a house that looked like it had been lifted off a page in a high end architectural magazine. There were two fireplace chimneys in a lighter shade of gray stone. Although there were no "heavenly" gates to go through and the driveway wasn't as long as the Emersons' driveway, it was much longer and wider than the ones at the nearby homes.

The house itself was set back on a two-acre parcel with beautiful landscaping, with some old sprawling weeping willow trees, a kidney-shaped pool, and two large matching bowl fountains in front with water cascading from the smaller bowls down to the base. The property was bordered by impressive fieldstone walls someone maybe over a hundred years ago had taken a long time to build. The garage was attached in a way that made the house look longer because the doors were at the rear, the shuttered garage windows making it look like additional rooms. I pulled up to the mauve tiled walkway in front.

"It's a very pretty house, Trevor."

"Can you come in for a while?" he asked.

The image of Ami planted in her car behind that truck back at the school flashed across my mind. I saw her crunched over the steering wheel and glaring out at me.

"I have a load of work to do, Trevor," I said. "Maybe next time."

"My parents aren't home, if that's what you're worried about. My dad's at work, and my mother's gone with some of her friends to a fashion show. C'mon in. At least let me show you my room. It's not as big as yours, of course, and I merely have a queen-size bed."

"I really should go," I said.

"Fifteen minutes can't make that much difference," he insisted.

I was tempted to tell him about Ami, but the sight of her spying on me was so weird to me, I thought it would spook him as well. My nerve endings were twitching like broken electric wires. For all I knew, she had followed us and was keeping track of how long I spent here.

"I can't," I said, looking away from him.

"You can't? I'll tell you what you can't do. You can't leave a helpless person out here on his own like this," he moaned.

I smiled at him.

"You're not helpless, Trevor."

"Well, one thing's for sure. I can't take advantage of you. Not in the condition I'm in. You'll have to take advantage of me. C'mon," he insisted, reaching for my hand. "Just a little while. We really haven't spent any time together since I returned to school. Everywhere we go in that school, we're being watched. It's no fun being famous," he joked.

I didn't say anything, but inside, I was pulled in two directions.

"I'm right-handed, you know, and I've lost the use of it in this cast," he added, now trying to play on my sympathies. "I have to carry in these books, open my door, struggle to change clothes. Even Waverly helps me get into the house!" he cried.

"All right," I relented. "I'll help you get into your house, but I'm not staying," I warned.

"Hey," he said, putting up his left hand like someone about to take an oath, "I won't ask for much more."

"You won't get much more," I retorted, and turned off the engine.

Then I got out, walked around the car, and opened his door.

"Your Majesty," I said bowing.

"Thank you, my lady."

I took his left hand and helped him up and out of the car. He pretended to stumble into my arms and kissed me.

"Consider that a tip," he said.

"Thanks for being so generous."

"Hey!" he said, pretending to be insulted. "There are a lot of girls who would be grateful. I hope."

I moved him aside gently and reached in for his books. He smiled and walked to the front door, reaching into his left pocket for the keys. I looked back down the driveway for signs of Ami's car on the street, but I didn't see it.

"Could you do this?" he asked, holding up the keys.

I shook my head at his obvious pretense at helplessness, but took the keys and opened the door. He pushed it and we entered his house. I heard music.

"Someone's home," I said.

"No, no. My mother always leaves music on. She thinks that would discourage would-be burglars. Unless, of course, they're music lovers. You want something cold to drink?"

"No, Trevor, I'm leaving. I told you."

"All right, all right. Just take a look at my room. It's right down here," he said, walking through the entryway.

I was reluctant to take another step, but I was curious about the house. The entryway floor was of stone, similar to the floor in Wade's office, but the living room and dining room were carpeted. The kitchen was actually a little bigger than the kitchen at the Emerson house, and it was brighter because of the skylights and the lighter tones in the tile, the wallpaper, and counters. Trevor's father had a beautiful office, too, albeit half the size of Wade's. I liked Trevor's father's furnishings better. They looked softer, more comfortable.

This house didn't have the opulence and size of the Emerson house, but it was smartly decorated, with a subtlety that I appreciated. It felt warmer, more like a home. We just glanced in at his parents' bedroom. It was a large room by any standards, but it didn't have the lounge area Ami's and Wade's did.

I was surprised at the neatness of Trevor's room. There were no articles of clothing lying about, no drawers half-opened, nothing on the floor. He studied my face as I perused his room.

"What do you think?"

"It's a beautiful room, Trevor. Are you this neat, or do you have someone picking up after you?"

He laughed.

"My mother is a cleanliness and neatness freak. Dad jokes that if he gets up to go to the bathroom during the night, she'll make the bed."

I remained standing in the doorway. I knew that if I entered his room, I would be in trouble.

"Hey," he said. "You're so uptight. Relax." He reached for my hand, but I didn't step forward. "C'mon, Celeste. You know how I feel about you, and I know you like me. Why not take advantage of an opportunity?" he asked sincerely.

I wanted to stay with him. I wanted to kiss him and make love to him. My heart was beating with anticipation, but those alarm bells wouldn't be stilled. I saw I had no choice. I had to be honest.

"I didn't want to tell you because I didn't want you to think my cousin was weird or I'm weird or anything, but when we left the school, Trevor, Ami was parked across the street."

"What?" He stepped back. "You mean she was spying on you?"

"Yes," I said. "I'm even afraid she followed us here. She might get Basil to take back the car or something."

He thought a moment.

"Man, she is nuts," he said.

"Maybe not in her way of thinking or even Wade's. After all, what happened was quite a shock to everyone, and they are responsible for me until I'm eighteen. Let's do this slowly," I said. "I have to live there, and they are my guardians, technically."

He looked about his room and sighed.

"What a waste," he said.

"No, it's not. When you call me later, I'll be able to picture just where you are," I said.

He smiled and then stepped forward to kiss me, holding me with his left hand while his right jetted out in that humongous cast, now splattered with stupid sayings and the signatures of our fellow students. Lester Hodes, a very good art student, had drawn a picture of a monkey riding on the back of a goat, an obvious allusion to *Othello*.

I couldn't help laughing at the picture of the two of us caught in his dresser mirror.

"We make some romantic sight," I said.

"Yeah, but don't think a little thing like this or even your paranoid cousin is going to stop me from loving you, Celeste," he said, his face turning serious.

"I won't," I promised, kissed him again, and turned to leave.

He followed me to the door, and we kissed once more before I hurried to the car. He stood there watching me drive off, a look of frustration on his handsome face. As soon as I pulled out of his driveway, I looked again for signs of Ami's car, but I didn't see it anywhere. At least she hadn't gone this far, I thought, but I girded myself to face what would surely be a most severe lecture when I got home.

To my surprise, it wasn't that way at all. She was in another one of her buoyant moods, coming to my room with a bag in hand from one of her favorite boutiques. She wanted to show me a new blouse she said she just had to get for me.

"The moment I saw it, I envisioned it on you," she said, holding it up against me. "It's a color that brings out your eyes. Yes, it does. And you can wear it now. This is a warm material," she added.

"Thank you, Ami."

"Isn't it wonderful having your own car, being able to go and come when you please?"

"Yes," I said, holding my breath in anticipation of what was to come.

"I told you it would be," she said instead. "Just wait until it sinks into the heads of some of those other girls at school. They'll be beating down the doors to become your best friend. Anyway, go do your homework or whatever. I have to confer with Mrs. McAlister on tonight's dinner. Basil's coming. He wants to hear all about your first days with the car. I swear, he's acting like a teenager himself these days.

"Oh," she continued in the doorway, "Wade won't be at dinner again tonight. Seems his manager's wife was in a car accident, and he's had to take her to a New York City hospital. Some serious spine injury or something," she said. "So naturally, Wade has to stay at the warehouse to deal with his new emergency. I think he feeds on these business crises. Like a vampire," she added with a short, thin laugh, and left.

The nervousness did not leave my body, despite Ami's happy demeanor. I knew she had seen me take Trevor home. Maybe she had concluded it was better not to be so negative. Maybe she hoped I would come to her conclusions on my own if she stepped back.

I went right to my homework. A little more than an hour before dinner, Ami returned, and to my surprise, she brought one of her dresses with her.

"I thought you'd enjoy wearing this tonight," she said, spreading it on my bed. "I hardly wear it anymore because I have so many others that are similar. It's practically brand-new."

It looked no bigger than a bath towel.

"But I have so many of my own nice things to wear now, Ami," I said.

"Basil loved me in this dress," she said with a cool smile on her lips. "He'll love it on you, too, and we so want to please him tonight after all he's done for you, don't we?" she asked, making it sound as if everything he had done for me, he had done for her as well. "It's just a little thing," she added, "but sometimes the smallest things please a man to no end."

I looked more closely at the dress. It was a flared black short-sleeved dress with a low plunge front with a strap to hold the breast area together, cut out of a very slinky material. The skirt was really a true mini.

"It will fit you better and look better on you than it did on me," she insisted. "You have a firmer, larger bust than I do, and your hips are fuller as well. Go on, put it on, and don't forget to use that cologne Basil loves. We're going to have a wonderful dinner. Mrs. McAlister has prepared one of Basil's favorite meals, rack of lamb. Scrumptious," she said.

She stepped forward to fluff my bangs a bit and then looked at me with what I thought was more like a mother's pride than a sister's or friend's.

"You're very beautiful. Never be ashamed of it. Never," she admonished, as if she was afraid I had been infected with too much humility.

She checked her watch.

"We'll go down on time tonight. He'll appreciate that," she said.

After she left, I tried on the dress. It was a little more than tight and left little to imagine about my body. I felt constricted, afraid to move, to bend. So much of my bosom showed, my nipples prominent under the thin material. I debated with myself. It makes me look cheap, I thought. I am not a prude, but to wear this to a family dinner? On the other hand, Ami had made it sound so important to please Basil and show gratitude. Wasn't there a nicer way? Wasn't a sincere thank-you enough? I hadn't asked him for the things he gave me. I was excited and overjoyed about them, but there was such a thing as going too far.

"Rip it off," a voice resembling Noble's told me. "It's disgusting on you. It's too tight; it's too short. You actually look ridiculous, look like a caricature of a sexy young girl. It's not you, Celeste, and doesn't Basil like you for who you really are? Didn't he compare you to his wife when she was younger? Ami's wrong."

On the other hand, she is so volatile these days, I thought. Her mood swings are so great. Disobeying her, rejecting her suggestion, could make her maudlin, angry, and the dinner and evening would be ruined. She might get one of her headaches. You'd be the cause of new trouble. Just get it over with, I thought. Wear the stupid dress, spray on the cologne, and get through the evening.

In the end that was what I decided. Of course, when Ami saw me, she exclaimed that she had been right.

"I just knew you would be a knockout in that dress. You could be a movie star easily. How far you've come from that homely, dark-faced waif at the orphanage. They made you sexless and took your self-confidence. Now you have it back, and how!"

That wasn't how I recalled our first meeting, I thought. She made me feel as if we really were sisters, that my features were very attractive, and that I was bright and lovely and simply perfect.

I smiled, but noted that she was wearing a far more conservative dress, with three-quarter sleeves and an ankle-length hem.

We started down together.

"Wade's missing a very special occasion," she said as we descended. "He's such a fool to be so devoted to that plumbing business. He says he hates it, but just try to tear him away during the day. Just try to get him to attend a luncheon or go to a matinee or anything. He acts like it would be a cardinal sin to desert his precious pipes and fittings."

"Maybe, like us, he's just trying to make his father happy," I offered, and she stopped on the steps as if I had tugged her hair. I didn't mean it to sound sarcastic.

She looked at me and smiled.

"We're just being beautiful, appreciative young women, Celeste. We're not hung up on pleasing anyone more than he should be pleased."

"I didn't mean—"

"Well, there you are," Basil cried from the hallway. He wore a black sport jacket, red tie, and black slacks with sporty-looking black leather loafers. "The two of you make my heart race like an Olympic runner's heart. This woman's done wonders with you, Celeste. You're going to conquer the world!" he cried. His exuberance brought a smile to my reluctant, timid lips. "Let's get to that dinner. I'm starving. It smells like gourmet paradise in there."

When we stepped into the dining room, I saw a small, nicely wrapped box by my place setting. I looked at Ami, who wore a conspiratorial smile.

"What's this?" I asked immediately.

"A graduation gift," Basil said.

"Graduation? I didn't graduate from anything."

"Oh, yes, you did, young lady," he said sternly. "You graduated from the world of the unfortunate to our precious little kingdom of happiness. You have become independent and confident and your own young lady, a young lady I'd match against any of those back at your private school or anywhere, for that matter, no matter their upbringing or how much money their parents have.

"Hey," he said in a less laudatory tone, "you're my first complete success in a long time. I wasn't always this good with my own kids. You make me feel twenty years younger. Go on, open the gift," he urged, nodding at it.

I sat and began to undo the thin ribbon. Then I peeled off the paper neatly and opened the box. Inside was a gold key chain with the key to the Mercedes sports car already attached. What's more, the key chain had my name engraved in it.

"It's beautiful," I said, taking it out to admire it.

"Beautiful things for my beautiful ladies," Basil declared.

"Thank you, Basil."

The sight of it brought tears to my eyes now. He laughed, and so did Ami. She hugged me, and then he approached to kiss me on the cheek. He kept his face close to mine, with his eyes closed, as if he could inhale my very essence. I drank in his strong, masculine aftershave and cologne. Then he bounced back and cried, "Let's pour the wine."

He filled our glasses and then proposed a toast.

"To Celeste. Let this be the beginning of many, many successful accomplishments," he said.

The three of us drank. I felt bad about Wade not being here to enjoy all this. It promised to be a very special dinner. There was none of the tension I usually felt when Wade was here. Perhaps Ami had been right, I thought. When Basil was happy, the house seemed to take on more light and be filled with the echo of more laughter.

Mrs. Cukor stepped out of the kitchen to serve us our dinner. Although she looked at me with the same dark eyes filled with foreboding, she didn't seem as aggressive or angry. I wasn't happy about that, however, because she looked more defeated, fatalistic.

There was an air of doom about her as though angry, bruised clouds hovered over her head and followed her about the dinning room, into the kitchen, and back, never leaving her and threatening constantly to rain down a tragic storm. She moved almost listlessly, placing dishes, serving potatoes and vegetables in silence. She didn't appear to hear Basil's laughter and joyous voice, Ami's thin crystal giggles, or my own happy protests at Basil's endless compliments about my learning abilities, my motor skills, my politeness and mature ways.

"When they first brought you to this house," he said, taking on a more serious tone, folding his hands together and leaning forward, "I thought, what a foolish thing to do, bringing a teenager to live here, and only for a short time at that. Of course," he said, nodding at Ami, "I thought it was nice of my children to do generous things, but I know firsthand how difficult young people can be. Why add more turmoil to your life? Just give the orphanage or whatever a donation. Other people are better equipped for this sort of thing.

"Little did I know that Ami was bringing so refined and accomplished a young lady into our lives. I've heard about your piano teacher's compliments already," he said. "And your accomplishments at school, of course, which is why I said I would like to help you continue your education.

"Ami's our little shopper," he continued, smiling at her. "She always buys the right things, gets Wade the right things, gets the right things for the house, whatever. It shouldn't have surprised me that she went out and did her homework when it came to bringing the right young lady into our home. You're to be congratulated, Ami," he said.

She smiled, glanced at me, and looked down, out of not modesty but sadness, I thought, which sounded a discordant note.

Basil slapped his hands together before I could think any more about it.

"No more speeches. Let's eat!" he declared, and Mrs. Cukor brought out the rack of lamb, staring ahead, I thought, like someone assisting an executioner, bringing the victim her final meal.

Later I discovered that Mrs. McAlister had baked a chocolate cake inscribed "Congratulations Celeste" in whipped cream for our dessert.

While we ate, Basil asked me if I had any questions about the car and how I was enjoying it so far. I looked at Ami to see if her face would betray what she knew—that I had taken Trevor home after school—but now she looked amused and happy, her small smile stuck around her lips.

I wondered why Wade wasn't home yet, and hoped he would at least appear for dessert. As if my thoughts could affect events, Basil was called to the phone a few minutes later and returned to tell us there had been an accident at the warehouse. One of their workers had been struck by falling pipes and taken to the hospital.

"It's just one of those days," he said, referring to the manager's wife's car accident.

Mrs. Cukor muttered, "Trouble always comes in threes."

"Please," Ami moaned. "We don't need to add to the sadness with dire predictions."

Undaunted, Mrs. Cukor glanced at me sternly before leaving.

"What's Wade doing?" Ami asked Basil.

"He's gone over to the hospital," he said. He was thoughtful a moment. "I lost a young man once, almost the same way. Someone else was careless, and the pipe struck him in the right temple and killed him on the spot. Second year after I began the business, matter of fact.

"Wade takes it all too personally," he concluded. "Accidents happen everywhere. Anyway," he cried, "let's not permit this to spoil our celebration."

Basil decided we all needed an after-dinner drink, so we went into the living room for what he called "our final toast of the night."

It was a rather sweet, but strong cognac. In fact, it made me a little dizzy.

As soon as we finished the drink, Basil decided he had to go over to the hospital.

"My name is still on everything that happens there," he explained. "It's a family business and will always be."

He kissed me, and I thanked him again for the gold key chain. Ami walked him out, and I returned to my room to finish my homework and begin another newspaper assignment, but as I felt a little giddy from all the wine and the after-dinner drink, I decided it would be better if I just woke up a little earlier and did the rest of the work before breakfast.

Just after I got undressed and ready for bed, Ami knocked on my door.

"Have you heard from Wade?" I asked immediately. "How is the employee?"

"No, he hasn't phoned yet. Don't worry about it. I'm sure they'll do what they can. The Emersons always look after their own. That's why they're so successful," she added, finally giving Wade a decent compliment.

She hesitated a long moment, keeping her eyes down.

"Is there anything else wrong?" I asked.

She looked up at me with tears clouding her eyes.

"I'm so happy for you, happy for us all. But—"

"But what?"

"I know," she continued, "that young love is often blind and relentless. It's the nature of young people that they have to make their own mistakes. My father used to say wisdom is wasted on the old. I know you're still involved with Trevor Foley, and I've already seen how deep that involvement is."

"Ami, I just took him home. Nothing else happened."

"I believe you. We didn't get you a prescription for the pills the other day, but I'd like you to start with this," she said, holding out her palm, in which she had a small white pill. There was something written on one side of it, but my vision was too cloudy to read much of the small lettering beside an R at the beginning of whatever word was embossed. I did see an encircled 2 on the other side.

I realized Ami wasn't going to leave until I took the pill, so I got some water and did it in front of her. She looked relieved.

"I really don't think it was necessary, Ami," I said.

She smiled at me.

"Oh, it was necessary," she said with a strange assurance.

I shrugged.

Whatever, I thought.

"It's so wonderful how Basil has taken to you, Celeste. He'll do wonderful things for you. Let him. It gives him so much pleasure. You know his own daughter won't let him do things for her."

"But you said that was because of what he did when her mother was alive."

"Yes, yes," she said, waving her hand, "but you'd

think children would be more forgiving of their parents."

"You told me—" What had she told me? Everything was so mixed up.

"We've got to go with the flow, silly. We've got to do whatever makes life happier and easier for us. That's what I've been teaching you.

"Don't worry about all this," she said, closing my schoolbooks and my notebook. "You can do it later."

"I know. I—"

She pulled back the blanket on my bed.

"Go on, get some sleep," she said. "You've had quite a day and quite an evening. Come on, silly," she urged, and I laughed and climbed into bed. She tucked the blanket in around me. "Sweet dreams, Celeste, my Celeste," she said as she stroked my hair. "You're always in mine. You've been there for some time. Even before I set eyes on you," she added, which made no sense to me.

But then, nothing was making sense to me. I started to think about things that happened at dinner, things that were said, but everything was so jumbled. I felt her kiss me on the cheek, brush my hair again, and then I heard her walk out, turning the lights off as she slowly closed the bedroom door.

Moments later, I felt as if the room was spinning. I closed my eyes and surely blacked out, but it wasn't for long. I opened my eyes again and tried to move my arms, but they seemed disconnected. The same was true for my legs. A moment later I was drifting back, falling into the bed, sinking deeper and deeper. I closed and opened my eyes, but nothing changed.

It was as though I was asleep and yet still awake. I heard a voice, and I smelled men's cologne, the cologne that Basil wore. Was it so embedded in my memory from when I had smelled it on him earlier? I vaguely thought so. I thought I was moving my arms, moving my legs, but it seemed too much like a dream. I was drifting again. My body shook and then seemed to rise and fall as though I was sliding down an undulating hill, moving through warm and then cold places. The feeling lasted for quite a while, and then it was truly as if all the lights had been turned off, and I was sinking into a dark pit.

When I woke, daylight was pouring through my windows. I was terribly confused. For a while, I couldn't remember where I was. Was I in the orphanage again? It was as if everything that happened to me during the recent past was a dream. I groaned, stirred and sat up, and immediately felt nauseous. I thought I had to vomit, but that passed, and I dropped my head back to the pillow. Gradually, I remembered where I was. When I looked at the clock on my night table, I was shocked to see that it was nearly eleven.

Eleven!

I had slept this long?

I looked at myself and realized I was naked. How did I get naked? Didn't I go to sleep in my nightgown? Where was my nightgown?

I sat up again and looked about, finally seeing it crumpled on the floor beside the bed. Once again, I caught a whiff of Basil's cologne, so strong that I actually looked about the room and into the bathroom to see if he was here.

What was going on? The last thing I remember . . . what was the last thing I remembered?

Wasn't Ami here?

Where was she now? Why hadn't anyone tried to wake me up for school?

I sat at the edge of the bed and tried to get my bearing, get my head clear, but the spinning wouldn't stop, and the nausea returned. What was wrong with me? I had started to stand when the phone rang. I reached for it slowly, my arm seeming to telescope out of my elbow. I'm hallucinating, I thought, as the walls of the room pulsated like the walls of a heart.

"Celeste?" I heard. I guess I had been holding the receiver against my ear but for seconds had not said a word.

"Yes?"

"It's Trevor. Why aren't you in school?"

"School? Oh. I don't know," I said.

"What? What do you mean, you don't know? Are you sick or what?"

"I don't know," I said. "Yes. Maybe I'm sick."

"Maybe? Well, do you have any fever? What's wrong with you?"

"I don't know," I said. "Maybe."

"You're not making any sense."

"I know," I said. "I mean . . . I'm tired. I'll see you later, okay?"

"What?"

I hung up the phone. Take a shower, I thought. Take a cold shower. My body trembled when I stood up. I wasn't cold as much as I was simply unsteady. The room spun again, and I had to sit back on the bed to wait for the spinning to end.

Suddenly I heard my door open, and I turned to see Ami step in, yawn, and look at me.

"I thought you were still here. I thought I heard the phone ring."

"I overslept," I said.

"Obviously."

"I don't know what happened to me. I don't know why my nightgown is on the floor. I don't know why

I . . . I feel strange. I have these visions running through my head."

"Oh, I'm sure it's all just a dream," she said, smiling. "So you overslept. Big deal. I wish I had a dollar for every day I missed school. I'll see that Mrs. McAlister prepares a late breakfast for us." She smiled. "It'll be nice spending the whole day together. Wash up and get dressed. I'll meet you downstairs, okay?"

I stared at her and then nodded.

"You're just having dreams," she insisted. "Stop worrying about it. We both drank a little too much last night, but it was fun, wasn't it?"

"Yes," I said, even though the night before still remained very vague in my thinking.

She nodded and then left. I sat there a while, trying hard to think, to remember. Something terrible was bothering me, something very bad.

I looked down at my naked body and saw what were clearly black and blue marks on my thighs. I touched each of them, and they hurt. It looked like I had been squeezed very hard, like . . . someone had seized my legs.

Images of hands all over my breasts, down my stomach, flowed past my eyes. I felt lips on mine, on my neck, on my breasts and on my stomach.

What had happened to me? What couldn't I remember?

Walking like someone still in a daze, I went into the bathroom and looked at myself in the mirror. There were red blotches on my neck and on my breasts. I closed my eyes. Basil's cologne filled my nostrils again, and again I opened my eyes and looked about quickly. I almost called out to him.

Visions paraded across the mirror. I was being embraced, held, twisted, and lifted. What it suggested struck me so hard, I felt a ball of ice drop into my stomach, sending chills up around my heart. Slowly, I returned to my bed and pulled the blanket back. Then I brought my face to the sheet and inhaled. Basil's cologne reeked.

My head snapped back, and I gasped.

What had happened to me? What had he done?

I felt like screaming. Panic seized my feet, froze me in place. I stood there embracing myself, my mouth open in a silent cry, trembling.

And that was how Ami found me, nearly twenty minutes later.

17

All Orphans

♊

"What's the matter with you, Celeste?" Ami asked, her face twisting before me as if it were made of rubber. I wavered as if I was standing on a ship at sea, tossed about in a small storm.

"I don't . . . I think . . . did Basil come back last night?"

"Basil? No, of course not. He went to the hospital. Remember? The accident at the warehouse? What's this all about? Why ask about Basil?"

Yes, why ask about Basil? I wondered and then remembered.

"Smell my bed, my sheets, my blanket," I said.

"Why? Did Mrs. Cukor put garlic in them again?"

"No, it's something worse. It has nothing to do with Mrs. Cukor."

She pulled in the corners of her lips and lowered her chin.

"Are you still drunk?"

"Smell them!" I cried.

"I will not. That's the stupidest request . . . Go take your shower and come down to breakfast and stop this nonsense immediately," she ordered, and then she smiled. "Later, we'll do something together, take a nice ride, maybe to the discount shopping center they just built."

"Look at my neck, my breasts. Look at my thighs!" I demanded.

"So?"

"I have blotches, black and blue marks," I said, pointing them out to her.

"Oh, I get that often myself," she said. "It's nothing. Maybe you're allergic to something. I'll take you to see the doctor if it continues."

"It's not an allergy. I was . . ."

What was I? Why couldn't I remember exactly what had happened? Had it been a dream? How could it have been?

"You were what, Celeste?"

"Why was I naked when I woke up?"

"How would I know? You probably had a hot spell or something from drinking and tossed your night-gown off. Then you hallucinated, and now you're just confused. It's nothing. It happens to people when they drink too much. You're not used to wine and cognac. It's nothing terrible. Take a shower. Get dressed. Eat something, and it will pass. You'll see," she promised. "Hurry up. I'm actually somewhat hungry myself."

I shook my head. I wasn't making sense to myself. How could I make any to her?

I nodded and returned to the bathroom to shower. Even afterward, I felt listless and still half-dazed. I ate very little for breakfast and found myself dozing off periodically. I noticed Mrs. Cukor studying me with some interest, but saying or doing nothing. Afterward, Ami went up to dress for our ride and told me to do the same, but when I got back to my bedroom, I lay down for a moment, and the next thing I knew, it was nearly four-thirty.

This time, when I woke up, I did feel a little better. I threw some cold water on my face and went to look for Ami. Mrs. McAlister said she had gone, but she'd left a message for me that she had looked in on me, seen I was asleep, and decided to let me rest.

"She said she'll come to you the moment she's home," Mrs. McAlister added, annoyed that she had to pass messages on to me.

Now I felt bad about missing school, so I returned to my room and called Trevor.

"I was afraid to call you again," he said immediately. "You sounded so weird this morning."

"I know. I mean, I can imagine. I don't remember much about the morning. I thought you and I had spoken, but I wasn't sure it wasn't a dream."

"Wow, what did you have to drink last night?"

"We celebrated my passing my driving test. Basil came to dinner, and I drank too much wine and cognac, I guess," I said. Some details began to rush back. "But there were two accidents, one involving the plant's manager's wife and one involving an employee. I haven't seen Wade yet, so I don't know how everyone is."

"Oh," he said, not sounding very interested. "Well, how are you now?"

"Better, I think. What did I miss at school?"

"Not much. A surprise quiz in math. Lynette Firestone was dying to know why you weren't in school. She wasn't the only one asking after you. You'd think some of these kids didn't have a life."

"Maybe they don't," I said.

"You'll be at school tomorrow?"

"Yes, of course," I said.

"Okay. I'm sure it won't take you long to catch up."

I heard a knock on my door.

"I'll call you later," I said. "I think Ami's here."

Just as I hung up, she entered.

"How are you?" she asked.

"Better, I think. I still feel confused."

"Oh, you'll be fine," she said. "Sorry I left you, but you were so dead asleep, I didn't have the heart to wake you. Guess what? Wade's not coming home for dinner again tonight. There's a big brouhaha at the plant. The accident might not have been an accident."

"Why not?"

"Seems two employees were angry at each other, and one might have caused it to happen to the other. The police have been there all day, investigating. Newspapers heard about it already. Wade's overwrought. Basil's been there all day, too. Nothing's ever easy anymore," she said, which came as a surprise out of her mouth. As far as I could tell, everything was easy for Ami.

"How sad," I said.

"It's just the two of us again."

"Again? Basil was here with us last night, wasn't he?" I asked. She had me wondering even about that.

"Oh, yes, but I was referring to Wade. Anyway, let's just have a nice dinner and relax until he comes home with his stories."

She left, and I concentrated on the homework I hadn't finished the day before. Later, as she said, it was just the two of us for dinner. Mrs. Cukor wasn't there to serve; Mrs. McAlister did it all. I had a little more appetite, but nothing like I normally did, whereas Ami seemed ravenous. Despite all the turmoil around us, she was bubbling with energy and very gabby. Actually, my head spun as she jumped from one topic to another, describing new clothes, a new restaurant, a show we should see in New York City, men who flirted with her in the mall, and a bank teller who had the audacity to wonder aloud why she was withdrawing so much cash. I don't think I got in two words.

We went to the den to watch television and wait for Wade's return. Ami said I was dozing on and off again, and it would probably be best for me to get an early night's rest. I thought she was right, so I went up to my bedroom and prepared for sleep. Ten minutes later she came bursting in.

"Oh, I'm so sorry," she said. "I nearly neglected you."

"What do you mean?"

"I've been so selfish all day, shopping, talking to friends, I forgot to see the doctor about your pills. I promise I'll do it tomorrow."

"I'm not worried about that," I said.

"You don't understand, Celeste. It doesn't just work after one pill. You can't take one and stop. You have to be on a regimen. Here," she said, holding out another small white tablet. "Take another one of mine until I set you up. Go on. Otherwise, the first one would be a waste."

I took it and looked at it.

"What does this mean?" I asked.

"What?"

"Roche?"

"Oh, that's just the pharmaceutical company. Here," she said, going to the bathroom to get me a glass of water.

I hesitated a moment, and then, with her standing and waiting impatiently, I took the pill.

"Good. Now get a nice rest," she said, and left.

Soon after I got into bed, I began to feel listless again, but it wasn't unpleasant. I felt more like I was floating, more like what people described as having a nice buzz on. Even with my eyes open, I was dreaming, cruising on a cloud. I wasn't sure how much time had passed or if I was actually asleep, but the sounds I heard around me seemed to become more and more distant. I was then suddenly aware of being sexually aroused. Fingers strummed my nipples, and a warmth began to build between my legs, climbing higher and higher. I moaned and made an effort to slow down the rapidly building excitement within me, but once again, I felt as though my body was not my own. It wasn't obeying any commands. It felt like clay being molded by other hands.

Sounds became confusing. There were grunts and moans, the moans maybe my own. I heard the clicking of lips, the sucking of air, and felt a warm wetness over my neck and face. It made me laugh because it felt like a tongue. The sexual excitement exploded inside me. I thought I screamed, but I wasn't sure. Soon after, I blacked out and sunk slowly into the dark pool of dreams and visions, bright lights and sobs, flowers, Noble's face, a pair of eyes with candles burning in them.

I woke to the sound of my own voice crying, "Mommy!"

When I looked up, I was sure I saw the back of a man who was quietly leaving my room. The door opened, and the light from the hallway quickly identified him.

It was Basil.

I wasn't dreaming.

Unable to stop myself, I began to cry. I sobbed so hard, my stomach ached.

And then I really did scream. I screamed as loudly

as I could. The effort was exhausting. I fell back to my pillow and gasped. I thought I would scream again or get up, but I didn't have the energy to do either.

In moments I was asleep, but this time I woke just before dawn. There was a hazy light in the window. I struggled to sit up and then took deep breaths.

I reached over to turn on my night-table lamp, and when I did, I gasped again.

Sitting there in the shadows and staring at me was Ami. She was in her nightgown and slippers.

"What are you doing here?" I asked in a loud whisper.

"I heard your screams earlier and came," she said. "Fortunately, Wade is dead to the world. He heard nothing. He needs sleep. He's been going full steam and didn't come home until very late."

"You heard my screams?"

"Yes."

Then I didn't imagine it, I thought. I didn't imagine any of it.

"Ami," I said. "I think . . . I think I've been raped."

"I know," she said. "I didn't like doing it this way, but he thought it was best at the start."

"At the start? At the start of what?"

"Of your ovulation," she said. "I'm sorry about what you've gone through, but you've got to do this for both of us, for you and for me," she said with desperation.

I shook my head. Was I still dreaming? Was she really sitting there, and was I really talking to her?

"What do I have to do for both of us?"

"You've got to have an Emerson baby," she said. "I can't. I have trouble with all of it."

She was the one who sounded as if she was talking in her sleep now, not me. Her eyes were dark. Even in the subdued light, they looked empty, glazed. She sat stiffly, clutching her hands against her breasts.

"Trouble with all of it?"

"That's really why I'm in therapy now. Wade's been patient with me for a number of reasons, but Basil . . . Basil thinks his time is limited, and he wants to see his grandchild, his Emerson child."

"But why would you . . . how can he make anyone do such a thing?"

"I haven't told you everything about my family, about my marriage. I'm ashamed of it, if you want to know the truth. My parents got themselves into very deep debt. My father was a terrible businessman, and my mother thought economy was a dirty word. They spent way beyond their means, and we were going to lose everything about the time I met Wade.

"Basil was impatient with him as well. I didn't exaggerate about his not having any real girlfriends before me, and you can see from the little time you've been with us and the little contact you've had with Wade that he isn't exactly a ladies' man. If you want to know the truth, I think he has problems with sex as well, male-female sex. I have my suspicions now because of how infrequently he has even attempted it, and at times Basil practically admits it."

"Admits what?"

I was having such trouble making sense of all this. My mind was still full of globs of murky clouds.

"Wade's lack of interest in women. The embarrassment to Basil of having such a son is too much for him to face. He takes it personally, an attack on his own virility.

"Anyway, he bailed out my parents and offered me this wonderful rich life." She laughed a short, thin, mad laugh. "The truth is, Celeste, Basil proposed to me first, but not to be his wife. To be Wade's. Then Wade proposed, at Basil's urging, I'm sure. Basil was in charge of everything in those days. He even had our prenuptial written. I promised to give him a grandchild within five years. When it became obvious that it wouldn't happen within that time, I became desperate. I came up with this idea, and Basil went along with it."

"What was your idea?" I asked, my heart starting to pound so hard, I thought I would lose consciousness again.

"I scouted you out. Oh, not you in particular. For some time I looked for someone like you. I almost chose a girl from a different orphanage, but when I did my research, I found out she was quite promiscuous. I couldn't take the chance with her, you see. What if she got pregnant before . . . before Basil could have his grandchild? It would have all been a waste. That's why I was so upset about your rendezvous with Trevor Foley.

"When I learned about you, saw you, I knew I had found the perfect young woman. You were virginal and beautiful and intelligent. You would produce a wonderful child if I could protect you."

"You mean you brought me here right from the start to do this, to drug me so I would be a surrogate mother?"

"Would you have agreed to be a surrogate mother?"

"No," I said sharply. "Never."

"I knew that. But I hoped that after you saw the life you could have, the benefits, luxuries, advantages, you wouldn't be so reluctant. Maybe I could talk you into being a surrogate mother. Then—"

"What then?"

"Basil actually fell in love with you and decided he wanted to impregnate you the old-fashioned way," she said, and again laughed that mad, thin laugh. "Of course, he knew you wouldn't be so willing to do that either, so—"

"So you drugged me."

"They call it the date-rape pill nowadays," she admitted. "We waited until you would be in the period of ovulation, but I couldn't see doing this to you night after night, so I agreed to two, maybe three, but when I heard your screams . . . it would be easier if you would just cooperate now," she concluded.

I stared at her in disbelief.

"Cooperate? You mean, lie here waiting for him every night?"

"Yes. Listen to me. Look what he's given you already, what you have and what he will give you. You're going to get pregnant someday anyway. You do this small thing, and for the rest of your life—"

"Small thing? You call this a small thing?"

I felt the nausea returning, my dizziness. I closed my eyes and took deep breaths.

"Why don't you do it, if it's such a small thing?" I snapped back at her. "If you have trouble making love, then why don't you have a doctor plant Wade's or Basil's sperm in you?"

"We tried once, Wade and I, but it didn't take. After Wade told Basil about that, Basil became more determined and aggressive about it. He came to me himself, hoping I would agree to let him seduce me. He even attempted it one night when you were here, because he didn't think we could manage it with you. But I couldn't be with him, and he got so angry and disgusted, I thought he would bring everything to an end, including your wonderful new opportunity."

"Wonderful new opportunity? That's why you made me so sexy for him, to please him? You wanted to get him off your back," I said, not meaning to make it sound like a pun.

"But you do please him!" she said. "More than I do."

"Like that's an accomplishment? The clothes, the jewelry, the school, the car! All of it was like a bribe?"

"Don't you enjoy it all? Don't you want to keep it forever? You don't want to go back to that life you had in an orphanage? Even with that old house and land you supposedly own, you won't have anything close to this. I've taught you how to appreciate the good things, haven't I? You're getting something wonderful in return. You will go to one of the best colleges someday."

"And they thought my family was crazy," I muttered. "You can't just use people like this," I said, shaking my head at her. "It's horrible."

"Are you saying you'd be willing to give all this up?"

"Of course I'm saying that, Ami."

"You're not thinking right," she insisted. She stood up and smiled. "You're still having problems from the pills, and it's affecting your thinking. After a little rest, when you give everything deep thought—"

"I'll never agree to such a thing," I said, as firmly as I could.

My head was pounding. I squeezed my temples with my thumb and fingers.

"I'm tired. I've got to get some sleep," I said.

"Of course you do. Everything will be different once you've had some rest," she said.

I shook my head at her.

"I really do feel sorry for you," I said, and lowered my head to the pillow.

She came to the bed.

"I didn't want to hurt you. I don't. I'm making sure you have the best things in life. Please believe me," she said.

"I believe you. I believe you really think that," I said.

She misunderstood and smiled.

"I knew you would."

I shook my head and licked my lips. They felt so dry, about to crack.

"I'm thirsty," I said, reaching for my glass of water. She handed it to me eagerly.

For a moment I distrusted even that, and first I smelled the water. There was no odor, so I drank it. I didn't realize how dehydrated I was. I nearly emptied the glass, and then she took it from me and put it on the table.

"I'm only doing what's best for both of us," she said. "You'll have to trust me."

I didn't like the way she said that. I glanced at the water glass again. She wouldn't dare give me another pill. She wouldn't, I thought.

But it was too late.

I could feel it taking effect immediately, as I still had some of the previous dosage working inside me. I felt her brush my hair and then lift my nightgown to my waist and fold over my blanket until it was down below my knees, as if she was preparing me for sacrifice in some ancient ritual.

I could feel myself trying to bring a scream for help up out of the depths of my very being, but it was too heavy. It faltered and fell back. I was waving my arms and kicking my legs, but I had no control of where and how they moved. My whole body was in turmoil, in free fall. I was like a pilot who had lost all of his controls and could only sit and watch the winds carry the plane randomly to some disaster. I felt just as trapped and helpless inside my own body.

Sometime after Ami left—I had no idea how long—I felt myself being lifted and was vaguely aware of my feet touching the floor. A very strong arm was around my waist. I was limp, but lying against someone so strong, I dreamed I was leaning against a tree. Once or twice my body left the ground, and I was actually being carried along. I put up no resistance. I remember thinking, It's not my body anymore anyway. Forget about it. It's going away from you. Let him do what he wants to it. It doesn't matter.

I floated into sleep even while I was moving, and when I woke up, I was just as confused as I had been the first time I had been drugged, if not more so. These surroundings were so unfamiliar, I thought I might still be sleeping and dreaming.

I was in a much smaller room with two small windows, the curtains drawn closed, but sheer enough to let in some daylight. It gave the room an eerie glow, a look of dusk.

There was a dark wood dresser with a large black candle flickering on the top of it. To the right of the dresser was a small gray settee. The bed I was in was a quarter of the size of the bed I had in my room, and a cream-colored comforter was pulled up to my chin. Above me a ceiling fan turned very slowly. I closed and then opened my eyes to see if it would all be gone, but it wasn't. Then I turned ever so slowly to my left. I felt eyes on me.

There sat Mrs. Cukor, staring at me.

"Where am I?" I asked her.

"You're in my room," she said.

"How did I get here?"

"I brought you here," she said. "You've been here all night."

"What time is it?"

"It's nearly one o'clock," she said.

One thing I noticed about her right away was there was none of that gloom and doom in her voice. She sounded softer.

"Don't worry," she continued. "They have no idea you're in here. They think you somehow wandered out of the house. The front door was left open. Perhaps your spirit has already left. You have to catch up to it."

"What are you talking about?" I struggled to sit up and my head spun.

She reached to her side and handed me a glass of a strange-colored liquid.

"Drink this," she said.

I grimaced.

"You'll recognize it," she said confidently.

I took it and brought it to my lips slowly, inhaling. There were familiar aromas.

"It's an Old World herbal mixture. Some ivy, some juniper, of course some garlic, and a little of my own ingredients. Drink it fast," she said. "It will help purify your blood."

Memories of Mama's drinks returned, giving me the trust and faith I needed. I drank it all as quickly as I could. Something in it warmed my chest and stomach.

"Rest a while," she said, urging me to lower my head to the pillow again.

"Why did you bring me here?"

She just smiled at me.

"You know why," she said.

My mind was still so cloudy, but I began to recall

my conversation with Ami and all that had happened. It made me want to cry, and I couldn't help but start to sob.

"No, no," she said. "You must be stronger now, not weaker. You can cry later if you want," she said.

"But why are you suddenly helping me? I thought you hated me."

"I didn't hate you. I hate what was coming in here with you, or what was coming back here because of you."

"You knew from the start what they wanted to do with me?"

"No, not exactly, but it wasn't long before I . . ."

"Before what?"

"Was told," she said.

"Told? Who told you?"

She smiled again.

"You know. You had stopped listening to the voices, but I never stopped."

Could it be? Should I ask?

"Was it . . . Noble?"

"I don't know any names. I heard a voice that whispered in my ear every night and told me to be vigilant. That was why I did what I could."

"And that was why you put those things in my bed, on my door?"

"And more that you don't even know about," she said. "It wasn't strong enough. I'm sorry. That's why I brought you here now."

"They'll be very angry at you now," I said.

She shook her head.

"It doesn't matter. They can't do me any harm."

"Why are they so afraid of you?"

"Mrs. Emerson is afraid of her own shadow," she said. "She's up in her room, sedated in fact. I brought her the pills myself. She'll sleep away most of the day."

"And Wade?"

"He left very early for work this morning. He doesn't know any of it yet."

"But Basil . . . why should he put up with you once he finds out what you've done?"

She took on a look that turned her face into cold stone for a moment, her marbled eyes gazing into a memory. When she spoke, it was almost as if someone from beyond was speaking through her. Her voice was that different.

"There are so many different ways to sign over your soul to the devil," she said. "When you swallow a great lie, it festers and eats away at your spirit. That was what happened to the first Mrs. Emerson. I did all I could with her, too, but it was too great a dark secret to keep buried in her craw. I watched her weaken and weaken with time."

She sighed deeply, her voice softening again.

"She was tortured by her own power to love."

"How can that be? How can you be tortured by love?"

"Who she loved was not her own," she said. "What agony it was for her to look upon what should have been her own and mourn the death of a child never born. I stood by and watched her cry inside herself whenever she smiled or hugged Wade or kissed his cheeks."

"You mean Wade was not her son?"

She shook her head.

"He's Mr. Emerson's son, but it wasn't his wife who gave birth to him in this house. I delivered him myself," she said.

"Where is his real mother?"

"In her own hell, I imagine. I don't know where she

is. She was given money and sent away. She was a helpless young girl, not much older than you are. The first Mrs. Emerson did everything to have people believe the baby was her own, isolating herself from society, fabricating a pregnancy she wished so hard was true."

"Why did she do it?"

"She was that devoted to Mr. Emerson, and her heart wouldn't let her cast a child into the wind. Only she and I and Mr. Emerson knew the truth, and now it is only he and I."

"Wade never was told?"

"Never. There's no reason to tell him now," she said. "Mr. Emerson came to believe that he, himself, had been the cause of evil being brought into the house, his wife's death and then his son's and his daughter-in-law's failure to give him the grandchild he believes in his heart will somehow redeem him. From time to time, in one of his drunken states, he'd confide as much to me. I don't disagree, nor do I comfort him in any way."

"So he keeps you here because he's afraid you'll tell what you know, and because he thinks you can protect him with your candles and herbs and powers?"

"I can't protect him against himself," she said. "He's really a very lonely man. So is young Mr. Emerson, and especially so is Ami Emerson."

"We're all orphans in one way or another, aren't we?" I thought aloud.

She just smiled softly and nodded.

"What will happen when they do find out I'm in this room?"

"They won't," she said. "Rest. Let the medicine help you. I'll bring down clothes for you, and things you'll need."

She stood up.

"Then what?" I asked.

"Then you should go home," she said, as if it was the simplest and clearest answer of all. "Surely you know that," she said, and quietly left the room.

I fell asleep again, but when I woke this time, I felt stronger and my mind was clearer. Like Mama's wonder cures, Mrs. Cukor's had done what it was intended to do. I saw a suitcase on the floor to the right of the door and a pair of jeans, a warm blouse and sweater, a pair of shoes, socks, and panties neatly laid out on the small settee.

I sat up slowly and then slipped my feet into the pair of slippers that had been left beside the bed. I was still in my nightgown. Never having been down this side of the house, I didn't know where the bathroom was exactly. I opened the door carefully, making as little noise as I could, and listened first. The house was very quiet, so I stepped out and saw that the bathroom was just down the narrow hallway on the right.

The cold water felt good on my face. I couldn't believe how droopy my eyes were, however. My hair was a mess. It looked like mice had been trampling through it all night. When I came out of the bathroom, I confronted Mrs. McAlister, who was just stepping out of her room. I froze. She looked at me, but then jerked her head in that mechanical way and continued down the hallway as though I wasn't there.

Mrs. Cukor didn't return to her room until after I had dressed.

"You'll need this," she said, and handed me an envelope.

I opened it and looked at a stack of twenty-dollar bills.

"Where did this come from?" I asked her.

"Never mind that. You'll need it. There's a taxicab coming in a few minutes. It will take you into the city to the bus depot. You don't want to touch that man's car again," she added, before I could even mention the possibility.

"Thank you for helping me," I said.

"I'm not helping you as much as I'm helping him," she told me. "You're not the one who needs the help," she continued when she saw the confused expression on my face.

"Thank you anyway," I said.

She picked up my suitcase when I started to reach for it.

"I carried it in; I'll carry it out," she said. I thought it might have some superstitious meaning for her, so I didn't resist. I wasn't exactly feeling like a ball of fire anyway.

"And Ami?"

"Still in her room."

"I wish I could say good-bye to Wade," I thought aloud.

"I'll say good-bye for you when the time is right for such a thing," she said.

I followed her out and down the hallway to the main part of the house. How empty it seemed to me now, despite all its luxurious furnishings, the artwork and expensive accessories in every room. Our footsteps even seemed to echo. I paused at the office door and gazed at the painting of the first Mrs. Emerson. Now I understood that cryptic half smile on her face, I thought. Mrs. Cukor saw what I was looking at and then urged me to continue.

The phone rang, and Mrs. McAlister stuck her head out of the kitchen doorway to tell us that a taxicab was waiting down at the gate.

"Well, let the man in, you fool," Mrs. Cukor snapped at her. "You don't expect me to walk the length of that driveway with this, do you?"

Mrs. McAlister disappeared quickly back into the kitchen. Mrs. Cukor shook her head, glanced at me, and continued toward the front door. I paused once again to look up the stairway, half expecting to see Ami at the top, looking down at me. She wasn't there, of course.

I stepped out behind Mrs. Cukor. The afternoon sun was very bright, making my eyes tear and forcing me to shade them as I watched the glittering taxicab come up the driveway. As soon as it came to a stop, Mrs. Cukor rushed to the rear door and opened it. The driver stepped out and came around to take the suitcase from her so he could put it into the trunk.

I hesitated, trying to think of a way to thank her again.

"There's nothing to say," she told me. She had a touch of clairvoyance, for sure. "What's done is done, and what must be done will be done. Go find yourself and where you belong," she advised.

I got into the taxicab, and she closed the door and folded those heavy arms across her bosom, standing back like a palace guard who'd give her life before surrendering. Her face was that firm, her eyes that determined. I pressed my palm against the window, and she at least nodded at me as the taxicab began to leave. I looked back and saw that she didn't move until we were actually out the gate, and then we made a turn and she was gone.

As was the great house.

And everyone in it.

18

Back at the Atwell Farm

♊

Twenty minutes later I was at the bus depot. I bought the ticket to Sandburg and waited another half hour in the lobby. Every time someone else entered the depot, I looked up quickly, half expecting to see Ami or Wade or even Basil hurrying to stop me from leaving. Finally, the bus arrived, and I boarded. I had to make another change of buses, with another layover. This time it was nearly an hour. I slept on the bus most of the time, but in the second bus depot, I began to question what I was doing. Shouldn't I have just returned to the orphanage and Mother Higgins?

No, I concluded; for better or for worse, Mrs. Cukor was right. I had to go home again. I had to reconnect with my past and with what hopefully still waited for me in the shadows and dark corners of that world. Then I would know what to do.

It was late afternoon by the time I reached Sandburg. I had almost no memory of the village—not that there was all that much to remember about it. It had two main streets, one that ran through the village and one that joined about three-quarters of the way and then ran north. There was a post office, a firehouse, a dozen stores, including a supermarket, and two bar-restaurants. The bus depot was a small confectionery store run by an elderly couple, who had been there for nearly twenty-five years. It was called George's, and the wife's name was Annie. I was actually the only one to get off the bus. There had been only five people on it, and the others had gotten off at Centerville, the village preceding Sandburg.

The streets were nearly empty, only an occasional vehicle passing. I saw some boys at soccer practice on the school grounds as we went past the field. The air was brisk, but the sky was mostly clear, the late-afternoon sunlight making windows glitter. When we turned up toward the bus depot, I saw a man washing a storefront and a dog lying comfortably on the side-walk, as if he knew no one would come by to disturb him. His eyes popped opened with curiosity when I stepped down. The driver got out my suitcase, looking at me and the surroundings as if he was leaving me at the end of the world. He got back into the bus and drove off as I went into the confectionery store to see about getting a taxicab.

"Hello, there," George said. He wore a starched white full apron and was washing down the counter with a large sponge. His wife, who wore a half apron over a bright print dress, was sitting on a stool and reading the newspaper. She turned and glanced at me before returning to whatever held her interest in the paper.

"Can I get a taxicab?" I asked.

"Sure. I'll call Al for you," George said. "He's the

only taxicab operating at the moment. Where you heading?"

"I have to get to the Atwell farm," I said.

"The Atwell farm!" Annie said, perking up. She couldn't contain her curiosity. "Why are you going there?"

"I own it," I said.

George froze with the receiver in hand.

"You own it? Are you . . . you're the baby?" Annie asked, amazed.

"Yes," I said, smiling. "The baby."

They both just stared at me.

Annie realized it first and spun on George.

"Call Al for her already," she ordered.

He quickly tapped out the numbers.

"I have a fare for you," he said over the phone. "To the Atwell farm. Okay." He hung up. "He'll be here in five minutes. Just throwing on his jacket," George said. "He's right down the street."

"Do the Farleys know you're coming?" Annie asked.

I didn't want to let out how little I knew about the tenants at the farm.

"I mean," she continued, "Pru Farley was in here just this afternoon and didn't mention you."

"Not everyone tells you their business, Annie," George told her.

Her eyes went to my suitcase.

"You're staying a while, I see."

"Yes," I said, smiling. "I'm staying a while."

"Well, I . . . how have you been?" she asked, dying to know everything. "Where have you been all these years?"

"I've been . . . away," I replied.

"I can remember your mother carrying you in here

just like it was yesterday," she said. "For an infant, you had such a serious way of looking at people, fixing your eyes on them like two tiny searchlights. Your mother wouldn't let me give you a lollipop, but she did let me give you a carrot. You ate it like a rabbit. Remember, George?"

He grunted and smiled.

"Pru and Brice Farley are a very nice young couple," George said. "He's the guidance counselor at the high school."

"I'm sure she knows all about the Farleys, George," Annie told him. Then she looked at me to see if I did.

I nodded without comment.

Her eyes narrowed with suspicion.

"There's a rumor that Marvin Becker, an attorney, is trying to buy your land and develop tract vacation homes on it. Is that why you've come?" she asked.

"Don't mind her. She thinks she has to write the column for local news," George said.

"I do not. Everyone knows about it," she protested.

A car pulled up in front of the store.

"There's Al," George said. "He got here quicker than I thought. He doesn't get that many fares this time of the year, so he's anxious."

"Don't worry, he's a good driver," Annie said.

"Thank you."

"You were some beautiful child," she said. "It doesn't surprise me to see that you're a beautiful young lady now."

I held my smile.

"I'm not here to sell my property," I gave her in return. She beamed with the exclusive news.

During the short ride up to the farm, the taxicab driver, Al Shineman, filled me in on the property's history since I had left.

"It took your attorney quite a while to get it rented, you know," he said. He lowered his chin and looked at me over his thick-lensed glasses. "Considering what went on there, most people were afraid of the place. On Halloween the teenagers used to go up there and have bonfire parties until the police finally put an end to it. They could have caused forest fires, and someone was always breaking into the house.

"I hear the Farleys have fixed it up nicely inside. Brice coaches the junior varsity basketball team, and Pru works for your attorney, you know. She's a paralegal."

I said nothing to indicate I knew or didn't know. The quieter I was, the more he chatted. All the while my heart was thumping like a parade drum. As we drew closer and closer to the farm, the surroundings became more and more familiar. I was truly falling back through time with every ticking minute, every mile, every tree and field and rock we passed.

"Are you all right, miss?" Al asked when we reached the entrance to the long driveway and I uttered a clearly audible gasp.

"Stop!" I cried when he made the turn onto the property.

"Stop?" He brought the car to a halt. "What's wrong? This is the Atwell farm."

I took a deep breath. To my left I could see the small old stone cemetery, the tops of the three tombstones just peeking over the fieldstone walls. Many times I had held Noble's or Mama's hand at night when we stood there and held a prayer vigil, all of us looking at the unmarked grave that held our deepest secret.

I took a deep breath and gazed around the property. The forest surrounding it had thickened and expanded, as if it had begun a slow march toward the house. The three-story Queen Anne with that oh-so-familiar turret in which I had been hidden so many times looked unchanged. The lawn immediately in front of the house was well maintained, but the fields were overgrown, the weeds raging even up to the walls of the old barn. I saw that the area where the herbal garden had once bloomed was totally overrun by wild grasses and some flowery weeds. A late-model ruby sedan was parked in front of the house, a black pickup truck just to the right of it. To the left of the house, the inhabitants had obviously worked a small vegetable garden. I saw the remnants of pumpkin plants and recalled how Noble and I used to cut out the faces for Halloween. We'd give them names.

"How much do I owe you?" I asked Al.

"Don't you want me to drive you up to the house?"

"No," I said. There was no way to explain it so he would understand.

"Oh. Well, that will be twelve dollars," he said.

I opened the envelope Mrs. Cukor had given me and counted out the money. He took it and stepped out to get my suitcase off the rear seat.

"Sure you don't want me to drive you to the house?" he asked, handing me the suitcase. "It's not light."

"No, thank you," I said.

In a little while he'll be back at the confectionery store talking about this for sure, I thought, but I didn't care.

I started down the driveway.

How many, many times had I walked this driveway with Mama or with Noble and heard them both talking about the spirits of our family standing to the side, smiling at us! Were they here now? I didn't blame them for not appearing, for not trusting me. Look at the detours I had taken. Look at how I had denied and avoided them, treating them as if they were figments of a disturbed young imagination.

In the wind that brushed my hair and flowed past my face, I could recall Mama's singing. Perhaps sounds, voices, words, and music linger just like anything else that hovers about, and when it's proper, when all the forces of nature come together just right, those memories return as echoes, reverberating once again. I was thinking about all this as I walked. I didn't even notice how heavy my suitcase was, nor did I look back at Mr. Shineman, who had yet to back out of the driveway. I knew he was watching me, expecting to see something strange and amazing, something he could take back to the store for gossip.

What he did see was my stopping and standing so still, he surely wondered if I had changed my mind and was about to turn around and flee. I stopped because there was no question, no doubt, that I could hear someone playing the piano. The melody was familiar. It made my heart jump in my chest. Would I knock on that door and find Noble greeting me? Would Mama be at the piano? Would all that had happened ever since disappear like a dream when the sunlight wakens me? Would the forest move back, the weeds be gone, the herbal garden bloom?

Slowly now, each step very deliberate and careful, I walked toward the front door. A large cloud cast a shadow like a fisherman's net over the house. I took a deep breath and closed my eyes.

"Please, please," I whispered. "Let my dream be true."

I knocked on the door, using the old brass knocker that was still there. I heard the piano playing stop. A few moments later the door opened, and a young man with closely trimmed light brown hair and hazel eyes looked at me. Surprise curled his firm lips into a pleasant smile. He was in a flannel shirt and jeans and wore a pair of running shoes. I thought he was easily six feet tall, with a slim, tight build.

"Well, hello," he said in a jovial tone. He leaned out and saw no automobile. Al Shineman had backed away and gone. "Who are you?"

"I'm Celeste Atwell," I said.

His mouth fell open, and his eyes went wide. He looked past me again, and I realized immediately that he was thinking I had somehow materialized out of thin air. It brought a smile to my face, too.

"A taxicab brought me," I explained.

"Oh. I didn't hear it," he said. "My wife was playing the piano."

"Who's there, Brice?" I heard a woman call from the living room.

"It's Celeste Atwell," he called and stepped back. "Come in, come in," he urged.

"Who?" I heard, and looked at the living room doorway to see Pru Farley. She was a very pretty woman about my height. She had green eyes the shade mine often took, and dark brown hair. Her features were small, but she had full lips, and a sharp angle to her jawbone made her high cheekbones seem even more prominent. She was slimmer than I was, and longer legged. Her hair lay softly, curling up at the ends.

"It's our landlord," Brice said with amusement. "Celeste Atwell."

"Really?" Pru said, stepping toward me. "How did you get here?"

"She said a taxicab," Brice explained. "Come in, come in," Brice continued, taking the suitcase from me.

"Yes," Pru said, stepping back. "Come into the living room."

I saw them look at each other with expressions of amazement and confusion.

I paused as soon as I stepped into the living room. The furnishings were different, but the piano was the same, and sat exactly where it had always been. A cream-colored area rug had been placed beneath it.

"Please, sit anywhere," Pru said.

I nodded, but I had to walk to the piano first and put my hand on it.

"That sheet music was part of the collection we found here when we moved in," Pru said.

I kept my hand on the piano. Just for a few seconds, I closed my eyes, and a melody played up my arm and into my heart. It brought tears to my eyes to remember Mama playing and Noble and I sitting on the sofa, listening. After another moment I sucked in my breath and sat on the new soft, light brown leather settee, one of a pair facing each other.

"Can I get you something cold to drink?" Brice offered.

"How about some soda, juice?" Pru suggested.

"I'm fine."

They both stood there gaping at me, until Pru realized first what they looked like.

"Oh, sorry," she said, sitting on the settee across from me quickly. She looked up at Brice, and he sat beside her. "It's just that this is so unexpected."

"What brings you here now?" Brice asked. "We know most of what everyone else knows about what went on here, of course, and how long you've been away."

How do I begin? I thought.

And then, as if the words were always there in the

house, just waiting like ripe fruit to be plucked, I started to tell my story.

Nearly three-quarters of an hour later, after we all had had some cold drinks, I had brought the events up to date, and they both sat looking stunned and saddened.

"How horrible," Pru said. She turned to Brice. "I can understand why the poor girl came here. It's the only real home she's known. We have to do something."

"Yes," Brice said, and then pulled himself up firmly. "First," he began, "you'll move in here with us immediately. I'll take care of getting you transferred to my school, so you can finish achieving your high school diploma. I'll contact the agencies involved and arrange for us to take charge. We can ask your attorney, Mr. Deward Lee Nokleby-Cook, to help with that. Pru works for him."

"I know. The taxidriver told me," I said, and they both laughed.

"It is a small town, you know. Anyway, we'll do all those things first."

"But I didn't come here to throw myself on you, or anyone else, for that matter."

"Understood," Brice said. "I know I'm speaking for both of us when I say we don't see it that way, Celeste. You're not eighteen yet, and we don't want to see you tossed about from one agency to another."

"Exactly," Pru said, standing. "I'll get our dinner under way. I'm sure you're starving."

"I know I am," Brice said.

"Which is nothing new," Pru told me.

I liked them both immediately. It reinforced my faith that I would be comfortable and safe here, for a little while at least.

"Can I help you with dinner?" I asked.

"No, go on. Let Brice get you settled in."

"Sure," he said. "I'll show you upstairs. Which room, Pru?"

"The one on the right when you go up is the nicest," she suggested.

"Right, right," he said.

I stood at the foot of the stairway and looked up after he had taken the first few steps. A torrent of memories rained down upon me, the most shocking and traumatic being the sight of Betsy Fletcher crumbled at the base of the stairway, her neck broken in the fall. It had been forever imprinted in my mind.

"Are you all right?" Brice asked.

"Yes," I said. "Just a little tired, I guess."

"Sure you are," he said. "You rest up. Don't worry about helping with dinner. We've got it down to a science. She cooks, and I do everything else. C'mon," he urged, and I followed him up the stairs and to the room on the right, which had been my room what seemed now more like a hundred years ago than eleven.

They had painted the walls and redone the floors. There was a pretty queen-size bed with pink and white pillows and comforter, a matching dresser, and to the left, a small vanity table with an oval mirror that swung back or forward.

"Some of our old furniture," Brice said, "but the mattress is quite recent."

"It's very nice," I told him.

He put my suitcase by the closet door.

"Get some rest. I'll call you when we get ready to eat."

"Thank you," I said.

I was tired, so tired I was afraid I'd fall asleep for the rest of the night if I did lie down and close my eyes. Instead, I found myself drawn to the small stairway that led up to the turret room. Once again, I hesitated, the memories flashing over my eyes like miniature bolts of lightning. How many times had Noble carried me up and down those stairs?

I took a deep breath and ascended. The door was unlocked. For a moment I stood there with my hand on the knob, debating whether or not I should continue to open it. Perhaps I was rushing back too quickly. Even if that were so, I couldn't help but do it.

The room looked so much smaller to me now. There was more old furniture in it and more cartons piled up, even against the two windows. There was barely any room to navigate too far into it, but I managed to squeeze past lamps, mirrors, and two dressers to reach the center, where I had spent endless hours reading my picture books, coloring, or sleeping on Noble's lap while we waited for whomever had come to the house to buy herbal medicines to leave. This was before anyone knew I existed.

I lowered myself to the small clear space and sat on the floor, my eyes closed, remembering, drawing up images from my past as if I were panning gold out of a stream. I heard a Mozart sonata and recalled discovering a music box that intrigued both Noble and myself, but I also remembered Mama's fear and anger at our playing with it. It was gone after that, and no one would talk about it.

So much of my early life was truly like a knotted ball of string, difficult to unravel so it would make sense.

I leaned against an old dresser and folded my arms under my breasts, keeping my eyes closed as I whispered for Noble, for those comfortable, happy times when I felt loved and secure, even cloistered and hidden, in this small room. I didn't mind whispering. I didn't mind cloaking myself in shadows. It was truly as if I knew it would all change for the worse when I was brought out and into the light.

"Celeste!" I heard, and opened my eyes. I realized I had dozed off. "Celeste?"

I stood up quickly and stepped out of the turret room. Brice was at the foot of the short stairway.

"Oh, I . . . just . . ."

"I know," he said. "This is a great house to explore, especially for you. Anyway, dinner's ready," he said.

He waited for me, a smile on his face.

"You'll be fine," he told me. "Don't worry."

"Why are you doing this?" I asked, as if my returning to the turret room had made me stronger and more wary.

"It's like Pru said. We just feel . . . this house has been so good to us. We've been so happy here that we feel obliged to preserve it and all that belongs with it," he said.

At dinner they told me more about themselves, how they had met and fallen in love, where they had gotten married, and why they had decided to live in this small community. Brice described the school and how much he enjoyed working in one that was still small enough for him to be the guidance counselor to every student, grades ten through twelve. I helped them with the dishes, even though they both insisted I relax.

Afterward, we sat in the living room and talked some more. I answered as many questions as I could about my life at the orphanages. While we were talking, the phone rang, and Pru went to answer it. She returned with a smile on her face.

"That was Mr. Nokleby-Cook," she said. "I made a call to him earlier, and he just returned home and called me back. I told him about you, and he wants to see you first thing tomorrow at the office. You can go in with me. He said since you're here, he has a nice surprise for you. He also agreed to do everything necessary for you to remain here for as long as you wish," she added, nodding at Brice.

"That's great. I'll get right on the school transfer in the morning as well."

"Thank you. Thank you both," I said. Pru saw the way my eyelids fluttered shut and then opened.

"You should go to sleep, Celeste. Let me go up with you and see what you need. I have extra toothbrushes, and whatever else you'll need."

"Thank you," I said, and stood up.

"Have a good night's rest," Brice said.

I gazed around the living room. Although they had changed it in so many ways, the walls still spoke to me.

"It's been a long time since I slept in this house," I said, more to myself than to them.

Brice nodded, and then I walked out with Pru right behind. She brought me toiletries and asked if there was anything else she could do.

"You've done enough," I said. "It doesn't surprise me that you have been comfortable here, that the house has good energy for both of you."

She liked that. She hugged me, wished me good night again, and left.

I stood in my old room for a moment, just listening to the house, to the wind making it creak.

"I've come home, Mama," I whispered. "I've come back to you all."

When I crawled into bed, I lay there with great expectation, but I heard no voices nor saw any spirits. My eyelids grew heavier and heavier until I was unable to keep them open. My sleep came so quickly and so deeply, it was like anesthesia. The sunlight surprised me; it seemed to follow instantly. I could hear sounds coming from the kitchen below, and so I rose, washed, and dressed quickly to join Pru and Brice, who were just setting out breakfast.

"I've whipped up some scrambled eggs with a little cheese in it. Brice likes a big breakfast every morning," she explained. "I hope you woke up hungry. You ate very little last night, but I knew you were probably just exhausted from travel and all that had happened to you."

"Actually, I'm starving," I admitted. The aroma of eggs, coffee, and toast stirred my stomach.

Everything was delicious. I was eating so quickly, I didn't notice until I looked up and saw them both smiling and laughing at me.

"I'm not usually this piggy-wiggy," I said.

"You go right on and oink as much as you want," Brice told me. "Besides, now she might stop making fun of my appetite for a while."

"I wouldn't bet on it," Pru said. "She has an excuse. You don't."

I liked the way they teased each other and then lovingly kissed or just touched hands to reinforce their deep affection for each other. Love is in this house, I thought. Why shouldn't it be calm and satisfied? The darkness has been swept out with the dust.

After breakfast, Brice went off in his pickup truck, again reassuring me that he would handle all the necessary paperwork to get me enrolled in the public school so I could finish up my high school diploma. Pru went up and dressed for work, and then the two of us headed out to Mr. Deward Lee Nokleby-Cook's office. I knew he had been our family lawyer for some time, and he knew all the details of our lives, especially about my sister Celeste. I wanted to see her as soon as I could, of course, but the thought of it made me very nervous. Surely she would have no idea who I was, and I had no idea what condition she was in after all these years. Perhaps he knew what had happened to Panther as well. I couldn't help but be curious about him.

Our lawyer's office was a large ten-room three-story eggshell-white house with Wedgwood blue shutters. The house had been converted, the entryway widened to form the lobby and the bedrooms redesigned into offices for paralegal assistants and junior partners. Pru took me right past the receptionist, telling her Mr. Nokleby-Cook was expecting us. We went directly to his office, which had once been the living room.

Now there were bookcases on the walls, a large dark oak desk, an entertainment center, and leather furniture. I had no memory of Mr. Nokleby-Cook, and so much time had gone by since I had seen him anyway, I wouldn't have recognized him. He had a full head of gray hair that had once been light brown, a color that still clung to some strands of it. His bushy eyebrows were mostly light brown. His face was robust, with deep-set brown eyes and more orange than red thick lips.

When he saw us enter, he leaped to his feet and bellowed a welcome with a burst of energy that made me feel as if a gusty wind had swept into the room. He was barrel-chested, maybe just five feet six, and bull-necked.

"Amazing, amazing," he said, coming around his desk to greet me. "I would have known her anywhere," he told Pru. "She looks like both of them. Come in, come in," he beckoned, guiding us to the leather sofa on his right.

"So," he said, pulling a chair up to face us. "You've made your way home." He shook his head. "I shouldn't be surprised. I anticipated this day. Your grandmother once told me that the land, that farm, all of it was as much a part of you all as—"

"My grandmother?"

I looked at Pru, and she quickly rolled her eyes back to Mr. Nokleby-Cook.

"Oh, my God," he said, sitting back, "of course. How would you ever have known?"

"Known what? I don't understand. What are you saying?" I asked with more authority.

"Well, how do I explain this?" he asked, looking down and thinking aloud.

"Just tell it to her straight," Pru advised, and then looked at me. "She's a great deal stronger and more mature than you can imagine."

"I bet. Sure. Well," he continued, leaning forward now with his hands pressed together. "Your sister, or should I say, the one you thought was your brother Noble, had a relationship with the boy next door, Elliot Fletcher. When she became pregnant with you, your grandmother kept her secluded, and when you were born, as you do know, you were kept secluded and hidden away for some time. Your grandmother eventually married Dave Fletcher, and the world . . . the world," he said, smirking, "I mean the local community, came to believe you were Dave Fletcher's child, a child he had with your grandmother. She wanted it that way. She wanted your mother to remain your uncle Noble, you see."

Somewhere, deep in my soul, I could hear a small laugh, like the laugh of an infant. Should I say I always knew? For surely I did. I sensed it, felt it, and in my way, understood it. We were too close, Noble and I, Celeste and I. I was always more than a sister. I saw it in the way she looked at me when she didn't know I was watching her. I heard it in her voice and felt it in her soft touch.

"I'm sorry you had to learn all this in this manner," Mr. Nokleby-Cook said.

"Who else would be able to explain it to me?" I asked him pointedly. "I had no family, and my guardians, my foster parents, would surely have fled the very sight of me had they known all that."

He nodded.

"Perhaps so."

"What about Panther?" I asked.

"Oh, I don't know all that much about him anymore. He was taken in pretty quickly by foster parents who later adopted him. I had some trust money to forward to him, or to them to keep for him, but all that was done about eight, nine years ago.

"Which brings me to other news for you, good news. There was a man with whom your grandmother had an ongoing business relationship. His name was Bogart, and he had something of a New Age shop. He sold your mother's special herbal mixes and arranged for them to be sold in a more commercial manner. At one time she was producing quite a bit, in fact.

"Anyway, he had no children of his own, and recently he passed away. His attorney contacted me to tell me he had left the bulk of his estate to you."

"To me?"

"Yes, and I might say it's a considerable sum. Makes me want to invest in these New Age shops, with their crystals and stones and herbal magic," he told

Pru. "The fact is, Celeste, when you turn eighteen, you will be a rather wealthy young woman."

"Isn't that wonderful!" Pru cried.

I shook my head in wonder. All this happening now, now that I had returned. Mrs. Cukor would never know how right she was when she said I had to go home.

"Anyway, I want you to give a good deal of thought now to what you want to do with yourself. You have more than just an old farm to consider. For now, the funds are well invested in safe entities. I'll have a full accounting for you in a day or so."

He slapped his own knees and stood up.

"Brice is getting her enrolled in the school?" he asked Pru.

"Yes, he is. She can start tomorrow here if she likes," she said.

He looked at me thoughtfully for a moment.

"Maybe she needs a day or two first. Get reacquainted with everything and everyone."

I looked up sharply. I knew whom he was speaking about, and it made my heart pitter-patter.

"She's reasonably well, you know. I can arrange for you to go see her when you're ready. You'd like that, I'm sure," he added, and raised his eyebrows in anticipation.

"When I'm ready," I said.

"Yes." He glanced at Pru. "Well, then, you'll just let me know."

"I'll run her home and come right back," Pru said.

"Take your time. Take your time," he said. He looked at me again. "Remarkable. When I look at you, I see a young Sarah Atwell. She was a beautiful woman. Just as you are, and as your mother is," he added.

I stood and shook his hand.

"Thank you," I said.

"My pleasure. I know you're going to be all right, my dear."

"Yes," I said, my eyes so tight and hard on him, he raised his eyebrows. "I'll be just fine."

We walked out and got into Pru's car.

"I'm sorry you had to find it all out like that. It just seems there should have been a different way, little by little or something."

I smiled at her.

"I always knew it, Pru. In my heart of hearts, I always knew it."

She smiled.

"When do you want to go see her?" she asked.

I didn't answer.

She didn't ask again.

It wasn't something I knew myself.

Epilogue

Home Again

♊

I didn't attend school immediately. Mr. Nokleby-Cook was right; I needed time to acclimate myself. Although I had never read the novel, my English teacher at the school I attended when I lived at the second orphanage liked to quote Thomas Wolfe and say, "You can't go home again." He meant that so much had changed there and in you that nothing would look or seem the same.

Nothing sounded more irrelevant to an orphan who had never had a home, of course, but I was so different from most of the others. I had had a home once, and I impressed everyone with my remarkable memory. I could recall such detail from my first six years of life, most of it from the sixth year, but vivid enough to astound anyone who listened to me describe my home, our land, and of course, Noble, my grandmother, and eventually, Celeste, my mother Celeste.

Pru and Brice were very patient and understanding.

Neither pressured me to do anything or go anywhere. I spent the next two days wandering about the farm, sometimes just sitting and staring out at the thick forest. Eventually, I wandered into it and made my way to the brook. It wasn't as full and powerful as I remembered it to be. The water still polished rocks and bubbled about, but it wasn't as wide and didn't look anywhere near as deep. Once it had an almost religious significance for us. It was here that Noble had died, and now I knew that the boy who drowned here had been my father.

The land, the water, all of nature, gives birth to so much within us and then absorbs it all, takes it back in one way or another, I thought. It isn't just dust unto dust. Something of our souls, our spirits, surely finds a place in all this, and that was what my grandmother felt and saw, and what she had passed on to my mother and to me. I had lost it along the way, and now I wanted to regain it.

Would I?

Could I?

Only time would tell, but I had faith, not in myself as much as in the land, in every tree and blade of grass, and especially in the brook. I would touch it all and be sure it was all aware I was here again.

I sat for hours in the old cemetery and thought about the prayer vigils we had held in the darkness, with only a candle sometimes to provide illumination under a fully overcast sky. What are graveyards really, but doorways to memories?

Brice and Pru saw me wandering about or sitting quietly and staring out at the forest. Occasionally, Pru asked if I were okay, and I assured her I was.

And then, one morning, a Saturday morning, I announced at breakfast that I would like to go to the institution where my mother still lived so I could visit her. Pru immediately volunteered to take me.

"I'll just take a taxicab," I said.

"You will not. I'll drive you there, and I'll wait for you in the parking lot," she insisted.

I agreed finally, and we set out. It was a partly cloudy day, the sort of day when the sun teases us by peering around clouds or piercing through some of the thinner ones. I felt carried along in the wind as we traveled. What I was doing was not something I could fight or resist.

When I entered the building, I went directly to reception and asked to see Celeste Atwell. It was strange asking to see someone with my exact name, and when I gave my name, the receptionist looked puzzled. She asked me to wait while she went to see someone about it, and a short time thereafter a tall, dark-haired woman with ebony eyes and what I would call a professional smile appeared. She introduced herself as Dr. Morton and told me my mother was under her care.

"Aside from her attorney, you're the first real visitor she's ever had," she told me.

I explained as much as I could about myself, as quickly as I could.

"Yes, I knew you existed and you had been placed in the care of child protection agencies, but that's all I knew."

"This is my first time back here," I said. "Back home."

She nodded.

"Has your attorney or anyone told you anything about her?" she asked.

I shook my head.

"Um. Well, the best way I can describe her to you is, she is frozen in time."

She saw I didn't understand.

"Her way of dealing with the trauma of what I would call her imposed schizophrenia has been to lock herself back in the age she was before it all began."

"You mean she has the mind of a child?"

"She behaves that way, and I suppose for all practical purposes you can say that. It's been very difficult to get her to age in a sense, because when she does, when she crosses over, she has to confront it all again, you see. It's very complicated. Actually, she has been the subject of a number of studies and many different papers published in psychology magazines," she added, as if I should be proud of the fact.

I just stared coldly at her, and she cleared her throat and stood up.

"Yes, well, I can take you to see her. She's in the recreational room. She spends most of her time there."

"Doing what?"

"Coloring books, painting with watercolors, reading children's books, playing children's games. The children we have here like her. She's actually a good influence on them."

"I'm glad you find her situation of some benefit to the clinic," I said sharply.

She bit her lower lip and nodded.

"This way," she said.

She led me down the corridor to the recreational room, a good-sized room filled with tables, games, and two television sets, one at each far corner. Some older people were watching television, and a half dozen children with counselors beside them were playing board games and card games. My mother was near the window, sitting at a desk and painting with watercolors. She had her back to us. Her hair was cut short, and she wore a plain blue dress with sandals.

"I don't expect she will have any idea who you are," Dr. Morton said. "Don't be upset."

"I won't," I assured her, and we walked across the room.

"Good morning, Celeste," Dr. Morton said, and my mother looked up from her painting.

The painting had no recognizable shape. It looked as if she was simply intrigued by the mixing of colors and the odd shapes she could create. Perhaps it made some sort of sense to her.

She smiled at Dr. Morton and my mind did flip-flops at the power of that smile to resurrect a torrent of memories. It actually brought hot tears to my eyes, tears I kept trapped beneath my lids despite how they burned.

"I have a guest for you today," Dr. Morton said, and my mother looked at me for the first time in nearly a dozen years. If there was any recognition, she kept it well locked up behind her childish smile. "I'm going to leave her here a while to talk to you, okay?"

My mother didn't answer. She returned to her painting.

Dr. Morton looked at me with that all-too-familiar arrogant doctor's expression of "I told you so."

I looked away, and she told me she would be nearby if I needed her.

I waited for her to leave, and then I pulled a chair closer and sat.

"What are you painting?" I asked.

She looked up at the window as if the question had come from there.

"Tomorrow," she said.

"Tomorrow? You can see tomorrow?"

"Uh-huh."

She returned to the painting.

"Can you tell me what you see? Is there someone there?"

She lifted the paper so that I could see it better, and she smiled.

"Yes, I see someone," I said.

She widened her eyes.

"She's coming from faraway in time. She's coming back to see you. She's grown up now, and she wants to see you very much. She hopes you'll remember her, if not today, then maybe the next tomorrow or the next. Do you know who she is?"

She nodded and went back to her painting.

"Can you tell me?"

She didn't answer me. I sat there in silence for a while, and then, as if he were whispering in my ear to tell me what to do, I heard him hum, and I began to hum the same tune and then to sing it. It was something my grandmother sang to Celeste and to Noble and eventually to me.

> *If you go out in the woods today, you're sure of a*
> *   big surprise.*
> *If you go out in the woods today, you'd better go*
> *   in disguise.*
> *For every bear that ever there was will gather*
> *   there for certain because*
> *Today's the day the teddy bears have their picnic.*

She turned slowly and looked at me, this time long enough so that our eyes met and held.

"Mama," I whispered. "I'm home."

I reached for her hand and held it.

"I need you to come too. Please, please," I begged, my hot tears now free to pour over my lids and trickle down my cheeks.

As if she was looking into a mirror and had to mirror the image, she brought tears to her own eyes, and soon they were trickling down her own cheeks.

I smiled through mine.

"You want to come home someday soon, don't you?" I asked.

She nodded.

"When?"

She smiled.

"Tomorrow," she said, and showed me her painting again.

"Yes, Mama. Tomorrow. I'll come every day until you see it in your painting. I promise," I said.

I leaned forward and kissed her on the cheek.

She looked troubled for a moment and then smiled and turned back to her painting. I stayed with her a while longer, and then I kissed her again and left.

Pru was standing by her car, looking very nervous and worried, when I emerged from the building.

I smiled at her.

"How was it?"

"It was good," I said. "It was a beginning."

"Oh, that's wonderful, Celeste. I'm so happy for you."

"Thank you," I said, and we got into the car and headed back to the farm. "I'll go to school with Brice on Monday," I said.

"That's great."

"I want to talk to Mr. Nokleby-Cook about getting myself a car. I need it now."

"Oh, I'm sure something can be arranged quickly for you."

"Yes, I'm sure," I said. "I'm sure about everything now," I said.

She looked at me with a smile of astonishment.

"Oh? Why is that?"

"I just saw tomorrow," I said, "and tomorrow and tomorrow. It's a gift I have."

"Really?"

"Yes."

"Who gave it to you?"

"I suppose my grandmother, in a way, and of course my mother."

I wanted to add someone else, but I knew she would never understand.

I wanted to say most of all, Noble.

But that was something to be forever locked in my heart, a secret I shared with no one.

Someday, perhaps, I would share it with someone.

I'd have to go back to Mama and look at her painting to see, I thought.

Tomorrow.

I'll look tomorrow.

POCKET STAR BOOKS
PROUDLY PRESENTS

APRIL SHADOWS

V.C. ANDREWS®

Turn the page for a preview of
April Shadows . . .

Prologue

About six months or so after my thirteenth birthday, my daddy changed into a monster. It was truly as if he woke up one morning with someone else in his body. We didn't take note of the actual day because we all thought he was just in a bad mood, and everyone, especially someone who worked as hard as he did, deserved the right to have what Mama calls, a bad hair day. If my sister Brenda had one or Mama had one, or even I had one, the best advice was to steer clear, nod, walk away, or change the subject. The only thing was we couldn't do any of that to Daddy. He had a way of focusing his eyes like tiny laser beams and he always demanded complete attention. He wasn't to be ignored, and attempting to change the subject with him was like trying to step out of a speeding automobile.

Anyway, about this time, he stopped doing any fun things with us and started complaining daily about everything in sight. He never seemed to be able to get out of a bad mood or throw off this shroud of grouchiness. According to him neither my older sister Brenda nor I could ever do anything right anymore, whether it was the way we made our beds, cleaned up our rooms, or helped Mama with her household chores. Mama started to call him Mr. Hyde from the story, *Dr. Jekyll and Mr. Hyde*. No matter how she protested, it didn't seem to bother him, which disappointed and surprised my sister and me. Up until then, when Mama complained about something Daddy did, especially in relation to us, he softened. He would rather walk barefoot over hot coals than see her unhappy. She was always our savior, but now she was like a fairy godmother who had lost her powers and her wings. She fell back to earth to wallow in the real world with the two of us.

"It's like water off a duck's back," she muttered when he turned abruptly away from her or just left the room after she had protested about something he had said or done. "I might as well have addressed the wall. He was never like this, never," she said, wagging her head like someone who wanted to shake out what she had heard and seen.

It became worse than that for her, however. Eventually, Mama cried a lot over Daddy's new ways and words when she thought we weren't looking. As a result of all this, the three of us changed. Brenda became Miss Angry Face because she left her smile outside the front door whenever she came home from after-school activities, and I felt too numb and frightened most of the time, never knowing when Daddy would explode with another burst of complaints. That was the year Daddy started to criticize my weight, too. He looked at me with such displeasure in his eyes that I felt my insides twist, turn, and shrivel. I tried to turn away, but then came his words which were like tiny knives poking at my heart.

"Your face looks like a balloon about to explode. Maybe we'll have to have your mouth sewn shut for a month and feed you through a straw like someone with a broken jaw," he said, bringing the blood so quickly into my cheeks, I'm sure I looked like I had a high fever.

It got to where I was afraid to put my fork into anything on my plate. My hand actually shook and my stomach tightened until I could barely breathe. A few times I actually threw up everything I had eaten. Mama got very angry at him then. She widened her eyes and stretched her lips so thin, they turned white, but even that didn't stop him. Brenda protested on my behalf, and when she did, Daddy turned his anger and criticism on her by saying, "What kind of a big sister are you? You should be on her back more than anyone, and especially more than me. You know what it means to be physically fit and how being overweight can cause so many health problems."

Brenda was an excellent athlete. At five feet eleven in her junior year, she was the star of the school's girls' varsity basketball team and the girls' volleyball team. She had already broken all the school's scoring records. Her picture was almost always in the weekend paper's sports pages. Scouts had come from colleges to watch her play. There was talk that she might have an opportunity to play for the United States volley ball team in the Olympics. Other fathers attended the games and sat watching with proud smiles on their faces. About the time Daddy became our own Mr. Hyde, he stopped going altogether and then started to ridicule Brenda by telling her things like, "You're not going to be a professional athlete, why waste your time?" He told her he thought her grades could be higher, even though she ran a good B+ average with all her extracurricular activities.

"If you didn't waste your time with all these games, you'd have A's instead," he said. "It's about time you got serious about your life and stopped all this childish nonsense."

He had never called it that before, and never tried to discourage her from participating.

When he spoke to Brenda like this, her eyes would become glassy with tears, but she would not cry or respond. Sometimes she could be harder than he was, and she would stand there as still and as cold as a petrified tree while he rained his lectures and complaints down on her. She looked like she had turned off her ears and turned her eyes completely around. I cowered in the corner or ran up to my room, crying as much for her as I did for myself and Mama.

Because of all this, our family dinners turned into silent movies. The tinkle of glasses, dishes, and silverware was like thunder. Brenda wouldn't talk about her games anymore, and Mama was afraid to bring up any subject because Daddy would either be sarcastic or complain. He would sit there scowling or rubbing his temples. If Mama asked him what was wrong, he would just grunt and say, "Nothing, nothing. Don't start nagging me."

I kept my eyes down. I was afraid to breathe too loudly.

After dinner, Daddy often retreated as quickly as he could to his law office, claiming he had work he had to finish, and on weekdays he was gone before any of us had gotten up for breakfast. He never used to do that. Mornings were a happy time for us once. We greeted each other as though we had been apart for weeks. Soon there were days when he didn't come home at night at all, claiming he had to make trips to service clients or deal with business matters. It seemed he would find any excuse he could to avoid being with us, and when he had to be with us, he was there only the minimum amount of time possible. Although Mama was ashamed to tell us, there were nights when he didn't come to bed. Instead, he claimed he had fallen asleep on the sofa in his office.

At first, Mama thought that he had found a lover and wanted to get rid of us. She theorized that in his eyes we had become a burden, dragging him down into waters that aged and weakened him. She was sure he blamed us for every gray hair, every wrinkle, every new ache.

"Men go through their own sort of change of life," she rationalized. "It actually terrifies them. He'll get over it," she said. It sounded more like a prayer she wasn't getting answered because neither Brenda nor I saw any signs of his getting over it. On the contrary, he was getting worse.

Mama spent hours and hours sitting in what we called her knitting chair because that was where she made our sweaters, gloves and hats, only now she wasn't knitting. She was just staring at the wall or through the television set no matter what we were all watching. She didn't laugh; she didn't cry. Her face, the face that people called "the porcelain face," began to show tiny cracks around the eyes and quivering lips.

The sadder she became, the angrier Brenda grew and the more frightened I was. Eventually, we found out why Daddy had turned into Mr. Hyde. The revelation was a bright flash that lit up all our dark confusion. It was like lightning piercing the walls of our home and making the air sizzle around us. All of our lives were caught in mid-sentence. Our hearts tightened like fists in our chests. Even our tears were caught unaware and too far down, buried under layers of anger and disappointment, to come quickly enough to the surface. I thought the whole world had stopped in surprise and shock. Everything I had thought real turned out to be illusion, and everything I thought was just an illusion turned out to be real.

The hardest thing for us to learn and accept was that Daddy had done all he had done, said all the nasty things he had said, avoided us as much as he had avoided us, because he loved us so much. To love someone so much that you would rather hurt them now than have them unhappy forever is a love so powerful it is beyond understanding.

Mama felt betrayed because he hadn't told her, Brenda hated herself for the things she had done and said to him, and I wondered what the difference really was between love and hate.

It took me a long time to find out, and I'm still not totally sure I know.

1

I used to feel like it was Christmas every day, all day long at our house. Mama's voice was so full of happiness whenever she spoke. Anyone who saw how we all woke and greeted each other in the morning would think we had expectations of gifts around a tree. Laughter and giggles rang like silver bells and Mama's smile beamed so bright that there were never dark days, even when the Tennessee sky was totally overcast and bruised, angry looking clouds threatened to drench us in a bone chilling rain.

I wasn't afraid to pretend, to dream, and to imagine anything. I'd blink and see sunlight glimmering off mounds of snow that looked like coconut, and Daddy seemed to know that those sort of days, days that threatened to depress us, were days when he should bring home surprises, whether it be a bouquet of Mama's favorite baby roses, a new doll for me, or some game for Brenda. Back then he bought her a

Ping Pong table and rackets, a wiffle ball and bat, a new tennis racket, and a set of golf clubs. She played every sport well, even though she eventually favored basketball and volleyball because of her height and speed. As soon as Daddy realized that, he built a basketball net and backboard in our driveway.

Mama said that back then his friends kidded him about his trying to turn his daughter into the son he didn't have. They had stopped having children after I was born. I never asked why. Brenda told me it was because Daddy wouldn't be able to stand having three girls. He was already outnumbered so much. However, we couldn't help believing it had something to do with Mama's health because I had been such a difficult birth, and in the end, she had to have a cesarean birthing. In the back of my mind, I couldn't prevent myself from thinking that if it weren't for me, Daddy might have had the son he wanted.

No one ever made me feel guilty about it. No one even so much as hinted at my birth being the problem. Despite it all, we were truly the perfect family in the eyes of all our neighbors and family friends.

I used to wish that we would be frozen in time. While most of my friends were hoping the hands would spin quickly over the faces of their clocks and watches so that they could drive their own cars, be able to stay out later and later on weekends, have dramatic heart-shattering romances, and collect boyfriends like butterflies, pinning their pictures on the walls, I tried to tread time like I would tread water. I wanted Mama and Daddy to be as young as they were forever, still passionate about each other, always holding hands or hugging and kissing.

At an early age, I noticed that the parents of my friends didn't stand as closely to each other, didn't touch or look at each other as much as my parents did.

I would hover close by, believing that just being in their shadow, bathing in their laughter and their smiles, was enough to protect me forever and ever.

Brenda wasn't as sensitive to all this as I was, and certainly wasn't interested in freezing time. She was anxious about trying out for college varsity teams and competing seriously in games where she could excel and win the appreciation and interest of people who could further her athletic career. Adolescence seemed to be more of a nuisance. She would get absolutely impossible when she had her period. On more than one occasion, she wondered aloud why boys' lives weren't equally interrupted. Why weren't their rhythms changed, their energy sapped, their moods depressed?

"If I could change my sex," she once whispered to me, "I'd do it in a heartbeat."

The very thought of such a thing made my own heart race. I had nightmares in which Brenda grew a mustache, but more frightening than anything, was the idea of her having a boy's sex organ. I dreamed of surprising her in the bathroom after she had taken a shower and seeing her cover herself just a second or two too late. That dream woke me and I sat up quickly, my heart pounding, my skin clammy. I was only twelve then. Brenda was nearly fifteen and close to five feet eleven inches tall. She took after Daddy's side of the family. He was six feet three and his father had been six feet five. Mama was five feet ten inches herself.

I had fears of being so short people would think I really wasn't a part of the family or I had been malformed. My body grew out more than it did up. I had bigger bones than Brenda and already had wider hips. My weight went first into my thighs and spread around to my rear. It crept up my back and thickened my waist. By the time I was twelve, I was one hundred and fifty pounds. Even though I was overweight from the age of seven on, Mama never made much of it. She used to say, "She'll grow out of it as she gets older and taller."

I grew older, only I wasn't growing all that much taller. I was still five feet three, and it began to look like when I had wished time would freeze, it had, but it had frozen only for me.

Another reason I felt out of place was because I was not half the athlete Brenda was. She didn't like to play any sport with me because I was so poor at it. I was no match for her in Ping Pong and I was pathetic when it came to basketball; half the time I didn't even reach the rim with a shot. And when I threw a baseball, or anything, for that matter, she would complain that I threw just like a girl.

What did that mean? I wondered. I was a girl.

Board games were my specialty. I could give Brenda a challenge at checkers or backgammon, but she never had the patience for sitting for hours playing board games. Through rain and snow, wind and gray skies, Brenda would be outside shooting baskets, practicing her putt for golf, or just running to stay in shape. She was driven. Daddy used to say that proudly. "That girl has drive. She loves competition."

Brenda did love competition, but she loved winning the most. She never played for the fun of it. When she and Daddy played basketball, she would work hard at defeating him. He was good, too, so it was always a battle. If he so much as seemed to let her win, she would rant at him and tell him she didn't need his charity. That would get him angry.

"Charity, huh?" he would puff, and they would play harder, play for keeps, and if she beat him, which she often did, her face would fill with a satisfactory glow that made him shake his head as if he didn't understand her at all, as if she wasn't his daughter but some stranger.

Daddy had been a very good athlete both in high school and college. He had his certificates and his trophies, and staying in good health was very important to him. He was always exercising, claiming the physical activity helped him to be a sharper thinker and gave him more energy when others were faltering. In that regard, he was far closer to Brenda than he was to me, but when I was younger, he did think I was cuter, more loveable. He called me his panda bear because I had Mama's coal-black hair and alabaster complexion, with ebony eyes he said were panda bear button eyes. One of the first stuffed toys he bought me was a panda bear. I kept it with me in bed, laying it against the pillows when the bed was made. I kept it under the blanket with me when I went to sleep. I called it Mr. Panda and often carried on long conversations with it, rattling away as if I really expected the stuffed toy would suddenly come to life like toys in the movies and reply.

Brenda made fun of that when she heard me. Mama thought it was cute and, at one time, so did Daddy, but when he became Mr. Hyde, he mocked it and told me I should put my panda bear in a carton in a closet or give it to a younger girl.

"Where are your real friends?" he would demand. "You don't get invited to parties or anyone's house, and do you know why, April? I'll tell you why. You're too overweight. You won't have any social life. Go on a diet," he ordered.

He wasn't wrong. I didn't have any social life. I had never had a boyfriend, and the only friends I had at school were other girls who had never had boyfriends and had none now. No one asked us to dances or parties, and what bothered me a little was the fact that I had never had a heart-throbbing crush on any boy either. It was a sensitive area for Brenda as well, and she was quick to come to my defense.

"People should be friends with her because of who she is, not because of what she looks like," Brenda told Daddy when he criticized me.

"Oh? And who is she?" he countered. "Mrs. Panda Bear?"

I could hardly breathe. My throat tightened and my chest constricted. Could a girl my age get a heart attack? I wondered.

I quickly retreated to my room and closed the door. I wanted to be like Brenda and never cry in front of him, but it was harder for me. Maybe I just had more tears inside me than she had. Thank goodness I had my own room, my own sanctuary. He had stopped barging in on me after I was about ten. Mama had told him I was a young lady and he had to recognize the fact. He wasn't upset about it.

In fact, his face lit up with happiness at the time and he nodded at the three of us around the dinner table, declaring he had three beautiful women in his home. How could he go so quickly from that sort of a daddy to Mr. Hyde?